'Tis the season to be naughty!

Wicked CHRISTMAS NIGHTS

Three sizzling Christmas stories from reader
favourites Leslie Kelly, Tawny Weber
and Cara Summers

Wicked
CHRISTMAS
NIGHTS

LESLIE
KELLY

TAWNY
WEBER

CARA
SUMMERS

Mills & Boon, an imprint of Harlequin (UK) Limited, Eton House, 18-24 Paradise Road, Richmond, Surrey TW9 1SR

WICKED CHRISTMAS NIGHTS
© Harlequin Enterprises II B.V./S.à.r.l 2013

The publisher acknowledges the copyright holders of the individual works as follows:

It Happened One Christmas © Leslie A. Kelly 2011
Sex, Lies and Mistletoe © Tawny Weber 2011
Sexy Silent Nights © Carolyn Hanlon 2011

ISBN: 978 0 263 91040 7

009-1113

Harlequin (UK) policy is to use papers that are natural, renewable and recyclable products and made from wood grown in sustainable forests. The logging and manufacturing processes conform to the legal environmental regulations of the country of origin.

Printed and bound in Spain
by Blackprint CPI, Barcelona

IT HAPPENED ONE CHRISTMAS
Leslie Kelly

Leslie Kelly has written dozens of novels for Mills & Boon. Known for her sparkling dialogue and humour, Leslie has been honoured with numerous awards, including a National Readers' Choice Award. In 2010, she received the Lifetime Achievement Award in Series Romance from *RT Book Reviews*. Leslie lives in Maryland with her husband and their three daughters. Visit her online at www.lesliekelly.com.

This one's dedicated to the Blaze Babes.
It's such a pleasure being one of you.
Merry Christmas!

1

WHEN LUCY FLEMING had been asked to photograph a corporate Christmas event, she'd envisioned tipsy assistants perched on the knees of grabby executives. Too much eggnog, naked backsides hitting the glass-topped copier, somebody throwing up in a desk drawer, hanky-panky in the janitor's closet—in short, a typical high-end work party where people forgot they were professionals and played teenager-at-the-frat-party, building memories and reputations that would take an entire year to live down.

She'd been wrong. Completely wrong.

Elite Construction, who'd hired her a few days ago when their previous photographer had bailed on them, had chosen to go a different, and much more wholesome, route. They were hosting an afternoon event, a family party for all of their employees as well as important clients, and whoever they cared to bring along—including small children. Catered food, from caviar to corn dogs, appealed to every palate. There were presents beneath a huge tree, pretty decorations, music filled with jingling bells and lots of smiles. It was almost enough to give a non-Christmas person like herself a little holiday tingle.

Oh. Except for the fact that she was working with a *very* cranky Kris Kringle.

"If they think I'm staying late, they can bite me. I got paid for three hours, not a minute more."

"We're almost done," she told the costumed man, whose bowl-full-of-jelly middle appeared homemade.

If only his nature were as true-to-character as his appearance. Though, she had to admit, right at this particular moment, his foul mood was understandable. He'd had to go dry his pants under a hand-dryer in the men's room after one boy had gotten so excited he'd peed himself. And Santa.

To be fair, Santa wasn't the only fraud around here this afternoon. Her own costume didn't exactly suit her personality, either. She felt like an idiot in the old elf getup, a leftover from her college days. But the kids loved it. And a happy, relaxed kid made for an easy-to-shoot kid…and great pictures.

All in all, she'd have to say this event had been a great success. Both for Elite Construction—whose employees had to be among the happiest in the city today—and for herself. Since moving back to Chicago from New York ten months ago, she'd been trying to build her business up to the level of success she'd had back east. Things were getting better—much—but a quick infusion of cash for an easy afternoon's work definitely helped.

Finally, after the last child in line had been seen to, Lucy eyed the chubby man in red. "I think that's about it." She glanced at a clock on the wall. "Five minutes to spare."

"Damn good thing," he said. "God, I hate kids."

Lucy's mouth fell open; she couldn't help gawking. "Then why on earth do you do this?"

He pointed toward himself—his white hair, full beard, big belly. "What else am I gonna do, play the Easter bunny?"

Not unless he wanted to terrify every child on earth into

swearing off candy. "Bet you can land a part in the stage version of *The Nightmare Before Christmas*," she mumbled. He sure looked like the Oogie Boogie man. And was about as friendly.

Lucy turned to the children lingering around the edges of the area that had been set up as "Santa's Workshop"—complete with fluffy fake snow, a throne and stuffed reindeer. Whoever had decorated for this party had really done a fantastic job. These kids had already had their turn on the big guy's lap, but were still crowded around the crotchety St. Nick. "It's time for Santa to get back to his workshop so he can finish getting ready for his big sleigh ride tomorrow night," she announced. "Santa, do you want to say anything before you leave?"

Father Friggin' Christmas grimaced and brushed cookie crumbs off his lap as he rose. "Be good or you won't get nothin'," he told them, adding a belly laugh to try to take the sting out of the words. His feigned heartiness fooled everyone under the age of ten, but certainly none of the adults. Waddling through the crowd toward the elevator, he didn't stop to pat one youngster on the head, or tickle a single chin.

Jerk.

For her part, Lucy found the little ones in their party clothes and patent leather shoes irresistible. Sweet, happy, so filled with life and laughter and excitement. There was one boy who was so photogenic he ought to be on the cover of a magazine, and she was dying to talk to his parents about a formal sitting.

You've come a long way, baby.

A very long way. To think she'd once vowed to never take a Santa photo, equating kid portraiture with one of Dante's circles of hell.

When she'd first set her sites on photography for her future, she'd argued with her brother over leaving Chicago to go to NYU to study. Then they'd argued when she'd decided to go from there to Europe, insisting she didn't want to take baby's-first-haircut pictures, dreaming instead of high fashion. Models and travel and exotic locations and *French Vogue* magazine covers.

She'd done all of that. Well, except for the magazine cover, though one of her shots had landed in a fashion week edition.

Yet, when all was said and done, she'd ended up finding her niche, her innermost talent and her satisfaction, back in the good old U.S. of A., working with children. It was, in this business, her claim to fame. Frankly, she was damn good at it. She'd made a name for herself in New York, her signature being the use of one color image in black and white shots. A toy, a piece of candy, a shirt or bandanna... something bright and sassy that demanded attention. Just like her photographs did.

Now she needed to drum up the same level of business in Chicago—which, despite her having been gone for so many years, was still her hometown. No, she'd never imagined moving back here, but when her brother, Sam, had gone through a messy divorce and seemed so lonely, she'd decided family came before anything else. She was all he had, and vice versa. So she'd returned.

Talk about changing your plans. Who'd have imagined it? Certainly not Lucy. And not her best friend from college, Kate, who still laughed about both her change in career path and in residence. Kate remembered Lucy's home-and-kids-are-boring stance in the old days.

Kate. She needed to give the other woman a call. Lucy hadn't seen her friend since she'd moved, though she and Kate kept in touch with frequent calls. Kate's two children were the ones who'd really opened her mind to the wondrous possibilities of tiny faces and hands and smiles, and she wanted to make sure their Christmas presents had arrived in time.

Those gifts—and working this party in the ridiculous

getup—were about the sum total of her Christmas activities this year. Her brother had to work the whole weekend, cops not getting every holiday off the way civilians did. And though she was now back near the Chicago suburb where she'd grown up, she no longer had any close friends here who might have invited her over.

Not that she would have gone. Lucy avoided Christmas like the plague, and had for years. She'd just as soon pretend the holiday wasn't happening.

Most people would probably think that pathetic; Lucy found it a relief. Especially since the weatherman was saying a storm to rival the one at the start of Rudolph the Red Nosed Reindeer was on the way. It was supposed to roll in tonight and shut down the city with a couple of feet of the white stuff by Christmas morning. Sounded like an excellent time to be locked in her warm apartment with her Kindle and a bunch of chocolate and wine. Or chocolate wine—her new addiction.

Eyeing the gray sky through the expansive wall of windows, she began to pack up her gear. The party was winding down, only a dozen or so people remaining on this floor, which had been transformed from cubicles and meeting rooms to a holiday funland. She smiled at those nearest to her, then, seeing the glances at her silly hat, reached up to tug it off her head.

Before she could do it, however, she heard a voice. A deep, male voice—smooth and sexy, and so not Santa's.

"I hear that you did a terrific job."

Lucy didn't respond, letting her brain process what she was hearing. Her whole body had stiffened, the hairs on the back of her neck standing up, her skin tightening into tiny goose bumps. Because that voice sounded familiar. *Impossibly* familiar.

It can't be.

"It sounds like the kids had a great time."

Unable to stop herself, she began to turn around, wondering if her ears—and all her other senses—were deceiving her. After all, six years was a long time, the mind could play tricks. What were the odds that she'd bump into *him* here? And today of all days. December 23. *Six years exactly.* Was that really possible?

One look—and the accompanying frantic thudding of her heart—and she knew her ears and brain were working just fine. Because it was *him.* Ross Marshall.

"Oh, my God," he whispered, shocked, frozen, staring as intently as she was. "Lucy?"

She nodded slowly, not taking her eyes off him, wondering why the years had made him even more attractive than ever. It didn't seem fair, or just. Not when she'd spent the past six years thinking he must have started losing that thick, golden-brown hair, or added a spare tire to that trim, muscular form or lost some of the sparkle from those green eyes.

Huh-uh.

The man was gorgeous. Truly, without-a-doubt, mouth-wateringly handsome, and every bit as hot as he'd been the first time she'd laid eyes on him. But he wasn't that young, lean, hungry-looking guy anymore. Now he was all fully realized, powerful, strong—and devastatingly attractive—man.

She'd been twenty-two when they met, he two years older. And during the brief time they'd spent together, Ross had blown away all her preconceived notions of who she was, what she wanted and what she would do when the right guy came along.

He'd been her first lover.

They'd shared an amazing holiday season. But after that one Christmas, they had never seen each other again. Until now.

Well, doesn't this just suck?

"Hello, Ross," she murmured, wondering when her life

had become a comedy movie. Because wasn't this always the way those things opened? The plucky, unlucky-in-love heroine coming face-to-face with the one guy she'd never been able to forget while dressed in a ridiculous costume? It was right out of central casting 101—what else could she be wearing other than a short green dress with bells and holly on the collar, red-and-white striped hose, pointy-toed shoes and the dippy green hat with the droopy feather? The only thing that could make the scene more perfect was if she'd been draped across the grouchy Santa's lap, trying to evade his gropey hands, when the handsome hero came up to rescue her.

He did rescue you once. Big time.

Her heart twisted, as it always did when she thought about that… The way Ross had been there for her in what could have been a horrible moment. Whatever had happened later—however much she resented him now—she would never forget that he'd been there to keep her from getting hurt.

But that had been a long time ago. She was no longer that girl and she no longer needed any man's rescue.

"It's really you," he murmured.

"In the flesh."

"I can't believe it."

"That makes two of us," she admitted.

Her brain scrambled to find more words, to form thoughts or sentences. But she just couldn't. If she'd woken up this morning to find her bed had floated up into the sky on a giant helium balloon, she couldn't have been more surprised than she was right now.

Or more disturbed.

Because she wasn't supposed to see him again. Wasn't supposed to care again. Wasn't supposed to even think of getting hurt by him again.

She'd played this scene once, and at exactly this time of year. No way was she ready for a repeat.

She knew all that, knew it down to her soul. So why, oh why, was her heart singing? Crazy expression that, but it was true. There was music in her head and brightness in her eyes and a smile fought to emerge on her lips.

Because it was Ross. The guy she'd met *exactly* six years ago today. The man she'd fallen crazy in love with.

At Christmastime.

2

Then
New York, December 23, 2005

HMM. DECISIONS, decisions.

Lucy honestly wasn't sure what would be the best tool for the job. After all, it wasn't every day she was faced with a project of this magnitude. As a photography student at NYU, she usually spent more time worrying about creating things rather than hacking them up.

Big knife? No, she might not get the right angle and could end up cutting herself.

Scissors? Probably not strong enough to cut through *that*.

Razor? She doubted her Venus was up to the task, and had no idea how to get one of those old-fashioned straight-edged ones short of robbing a barber.

A chainsaw or a hatchet?

Probably overkill. And killing wasn't the objective.

After all, she didn't really want to kill Jude Zacharias. She just wanted to separate him from his favorite part of his cheating anatomy. AKA: the part he'd cheated with.

Lucy didn't even realize she'd been mumbling aloud. Not until her best friend, Kate, who sat across from her in this trendy Manhattan coffee-and-book shop interjected,

"You're not going to cut off his dick, so stop fantasizing about it."

Nobody immediately gasped at Kate's words, so obviously they hadn't been overheard. Not surprising—they were tucked in a back corner of the café. Plus, Beans & Books was crowded with shoppers frenzied by the realization that they only had one and a half shopping days left before Christmas. Each was listening only to the holiday countdown clock in his or her head.

"Have *you* stopped fantasizing about having sex with Freddie Prinze Jr. and Jake Gyllenhaal at the same time?" she countered.

"Hey, *that* could actually happen," Kate said with a smirk. "It's at least possible. Unlike the chance that you, Miss Congeniality, would actually go all Bobbitt on a guy's ass, even if he does totally deserve it."

It wasn't Jude's ass she wanted to…Bobbitt. She knew, however, that Kate was right. Lucy wasn't the violent type, except in her fantasies. She might have fun playing a mental game of *why-I-oughta* but she knew nothing would come of it.

"Can't I at least wallow and scheme for an hour?"

"Sure. But we should've done it over beer or tequila in a dive bar. Coffee in a crowded shop just doesn't lend itself to wallowing and scheming."

True. Especially now that this place was no longer the same quiet, cozy hangout she'd loved since coming to New York three and a half years ago. It had once been her favorite place to meet up with friends, do some homework, or just enjoy the silence amid the scent of freshly ground arabica beans.

Since a recent renovation, though, it had turned from a cute, off-the-beaten-track coffee bar into a crazed, credit-card magnet, filled with overpriced gift books, calendars and stationery. Driven city dwellers who excelled at multitasking were flocking to the place to kill two birds with one stone. They could buy a last minute gift for Great-Aunt Susie—a ridiculously overpriced coffee table book titled *The Private Lives of Garden Gnomes,* perhaps—while they waited for their Lite Pomegranate Vanilla Oolang Tea Lattes with whip.

Christmas had been reduced to expedience, kitsch and trendy drinks. Fortunately for her, she'd dropped out of the holiday a few years ago and had no intention of dropping back in.

"Face it, girlfriend, revenge just ain't your style. You're as violent as a Smurf." Kate grinned. "Or one of Santa's elves."

"Not funny," Lucy said, rolling her eyes. "*So* not funny."

Her friend knew how much she disliked the silly costume she had to wear for her "internship" with a local photographer. Intern? Ha. She was a ridiculously dressed *unpaid* Christmas elf wiping the drool off kids' chins as they sat on Santa's lap. What could be more sad to someone who dreamed of being a serious photographer? Someone who was leaving to study abroad in Paris next month, and hoped to go back there to live after graduation? Someone who planned to spend the next several years shooting her way across Europe, one still image at a time?

That girl shouldn't care about Jude. That girl *didn't* care about Jude.

But at this moment, Lucy didn't feel like that girl. For all the violent fantasies, what *this* girl felt right now was hurt.

"You know, for the life of me, I still can't figure out why I ever went out with him in the first place." She swallowed, hard. "I should have known better."

Kate's smirk faded and she reached over to squeeze Lucy's hand. Kate had been witness to what had been Lucy's most humiliating moment ever. Said moment being when Lucy had let herself in to her boyfriend Jude's apartment, to set up his big surprise birthday party that was scheduled for tonight.

Surprise! Your boyfriend is a lying, cheating asshat!

Jude had already gotten started on his birthday celebration. Contrary to his claim that he was going to "pop in"
on his family for the day, Jude had apparently decided to
stay in town and pop in on his neighbor's vagina.

At least, that's who Lucy thought had been kneeling in
front of the sofa with Jude's johnson in her mouth when
she and Kate had walked into the apartment. She couldn't
be certain. They only saw the back of the bare-ass naked
woman's head—oh, plus her bare ass and, uh, the rest of
her nether regions. *Ew, ew, ew.* She was still fighting the
urge to thrust two coffee stirrers into her eyes to gouge out
the image burned onto her retinas. If she'd ever had any
doubt she was strictly hetero, her response to that sight
would have removed it.

"Maybe I should ask Teddy to beat him up."

Teddy, Kate's boyfriend, was as broad as a table, and
could snap Jude like a twig. There was just one problem.
"He's more of a pacifist than I am," Lucy said with a smile,
knowing Kate had intended to make her laugh. Teddy was
the sweetest guy on the planet. "Besides, we both know
Jude's not worth the trouble."

"No, he's not." Then Kate grinned. "I am glad you got
off a couple of good zingers, though. I still can't believe you
asked him if the store was out of birthday candles and that's
why he'd found something else that needed to be blown."

That, she had to admit, had been a pretty good line. It
was a rare occurrence; the kind of one-liner she usually
would have thought of hours later, when reliving the awful
experience in her mind. Though, in this instance, since she
was now feeling more sad than anything else, she might
have been picturing herself asking him why he'd felt the
need to be so deceitful.

If he'd told her it wasn't working out and he wanted to
see other people, would she have been devastated?

No. A little disappointed, probably, but not crushed.

But to be cheated on—and to walk in on it? *That* rankled.

"Of course, I wouldn't have been able to speak. I'da been busy ripping the extensions outta that ho's head," Kate added.

"She didn't cheat on me, Jude did." Then, curious, she asked, "How do you know they were extensions?"

"Honey, that carpet *so* didn't match those drapes."

Though a peal of laughter emerged from her mouth, Lucy also groaned and threw a hand over her eyes, wishing for a bleach eye-wash. "Don't remind me!"

Funny that she could actually manage to laugh. Maybe that said a lot about where her feelings for Jude had really been. This girlfriend-gripe session wasn't so much about Lucy's broken heart as it was her disappointed expectations.

She'd really wanted Jude to be a nice guy. A good guy.

Face it, you just wanted someone *in your life.*

Maybe that was true. Seeing the former man-eater Kate so happy was inspiring. But her brother Sam's recent engagement had also really affected her. Their tiny family unit—made even tinier when they'd been left alone in the world after the deaths of their parents—was going to change. Sam had found someone, he was forming a new family, one she'd always be welcome in but wasn't actually a major part of.

She'd wanted something like that, too. Or at least the possibility of something like that, someday. Heck, maybe deep down she also just hadn't wanted to haul her virginity along with her to Europe, and had been hoping she'd finally found the guy who would truly inspire her to shuck it.

Yes, that was probably why she'd let down her guard and gotten involved with Jude when she'd known he wasn't the right one in the long run. Being totally honest, she knew she was more sad at the idea of losing the boyfriend than at losing the actual guy. Not to mention continuing to carry the virgin mantle around her neck.

"Well, at least you didn't sleep with him!" said Kate, who'd had more lovers than Lucy had had birthdays.

"I'll drink to that," she said, sipping her coffee, meaning it. Because being stuck with a hymen was better than having let somebody so rotten remove it.

Something inside her must have recognized that about him, and held her back. Deep down she'd known there was something wrong about the relationship, even though he'd gone out of his way to make it seem so very right.

Maybe Lucy really was the oldest living virgin in New York—kept that way throughout high school by her bad-ass older brother's reputation, and throughout college out of her own deep-rooted romantic streak. Whatever the reason, she'd waited this long. So, as much as she wanted to know what all the fuss was about, she hadn't been about to leap into bed with Jude just because he'd said he liked her photography and opened the door for her when they went out, unlike most other college-aged dudes she knew.

Good thing. Because it had all been an act. The nice, patient, tender guy didn't exist. Jude had put on that persona the way somebody else might don a Halloween costume, sliding into it to be the man she wanted, then taking it off—along with the rest of his clothes—when she wasn't around. He shouldn't be studying to be an attorney, an actor would be much more appropriate. God, could she have been any more gullible?

Maybe Sam was right. Maybe she really had no business living on her own in New York or, worse, going off to Europe. Perhaps she was a lamb in the midst of wolves. She should've just stayed in the Chicago suburb where they'd grown up, gone to community college, done first-communion portraits at Sears, married a nice local guy and gotten to work on producing cousins for Sam's future kids.

At least then she wouldn't be sitting here all sad at being cheated on by someone she'd hoped was Prince Charming.

"More like King Creeper," she muttered.

"Huh?"

"Nothing. Just thinking about Jude."

Kate nodded, frowned and muttered, "Why are most men jerks? Other than Teddy, of course."

"Your guess is as good as mine."

"There have to be other decent men out there, right?"

"Sam's one," Lucy admitted. "And my Dad sure was."

"Mine is, too." Kate frowned in thought. "Your father managed a car dealership, didn't he?"

"Yes."

"And your brother, Sam, is a cop. My dad's in sales, and Teddy's a trucker. Hmm."

"Your point being?"

Kate tapped the tip of her finger on her mouth. "Most of the guys you've dated have been like Jude. Rich, future attorneys, politicians, doctors…and dickheads, one and all."

Lucy nodded, conceding the point.

"And that's the type I dated, before I met Teddy."

She started to get the picture. "Ahh."

"So maybe you need to look for an everyday guy, who works hard for a living, hasn't had everything handed to him."

That sounded ideal. Unfortunately Lucy couldn't remember the last time she'd met anyone like that. They sure didn't seem to be on the campus of NYU.

"A guy who's so hot he makes you stick to your chair when you watch his muscles bunch under his sweaty T-shirt as he works," Kate said, sounding lost in thought. She was staring past Lucy, as if visualizing this blue collar studmuffin. "Who knows what to do with his hands, and has enough self-confidence that he doesn't have to show off in front of a woman."

Not used to Kate being so descriptive—but definitely liking the description—Lucy could only nod.

"Somebody like *him*."

This time, Kate's stare was pointed and her gaze speculative. Surprised, Lucy quickly turned to look over her shoulder, toward the front corner of the shop, and saw the *him* in question.

And oh, wow, what a him.

He was young—in his early twenties, probably, like her. But he didn't look much like the guys she interacted with on a daily basis at school. He had on a pair of faded, worn jeans, that hung low on his very lean hips. They were tugged down even further by the work belt he wore over them, which was weighted with various tools. Powerful hammers, long screwdrivers, steely drills. All hard. Strong. Stiff.

Get your mind out of his toolbelt.

She did, shaking her head quickly to get her attention going in another direction. Of course, there wasn't any other direction to go…he was hot any way you looked at it.

So she looked at it. Er, him.

Lucy lifted her gaze, taking in the whole tall, lean, powerful package. Though he wore the tools of the trade, he was not built like a brawny construction-worker type. Strong, yes, but with a youthful leanness—Hugh Jackman as Leopold, not as Wolverine.

Yum.

His entire body told tales of hard work An impressive set of abs rippled visibly beneath the sweat-tinged T-shirt. His broad chest and thickly muscled arms moved with almost poetic precision as he finished installing a new bookcase in the back corner of the shop.

He lifted one arm and wiped a sheen of sweat off his forehead, which just emphasized the handsomeness of his face, seen only in profile. He had a strong, square jaw, a straight nose. High cheekbones emphasized the lightly stubbled hollows below, lending his lean face an air of youth and power.

His light brown hair was longish, a little shaggy, and he swept it back from his brow with an impatient hand. Seeing the strong hands in motion made Lucy let out a long, slow breath, and when he turned around and she beheld him from the back, she had to suck in another one. Oh, my, did the man know how to fill out a pair of jeans.

Apparently she wasn't the only woman who'd noticed. What she'd taken for shopper's distraction earlier she now realized had been female appreciation for the beautiful display of raw, powerful male in the corner. Every other woman in the place was either sneaking peeks or outright gaping.

She was a gaper. No peeking about it.

Finally realizing she was literally turned in her seat to stare, and probably had drool dripping down her chin, she swung back around to face Kate. Her friend wore a similar expression. "Wow," she admitted.

"Double wow. If I didn't love Teddy, I'd be over there offering to take care of his *tool* for him."

Lucy couldn't help being wicked when she was around Kate. "I bet it could use some lubrication."

"Atta girl!"

"But I think you'd have to stand in line."

"With you?" Kate asked, her eyes sparkling.

Lucy shook her head. "I don't think so. Cheated on and heartbroken an hour ago, remember?"

"Well, cheated on, anyway," said Kate, perceptive as always.

"Touché," Lucy admitted, not terribly surprised to realize she was already feeling better. What had felt like heartbreak ninety minutes ago had segued into a heart cramp. Now it was barely a heart twinge.

Kate glanced at her empty cup, and at Lucy's. "One more?"

"Sure."

"I got it," the other woman said, grabbing her bag. She stood up and walked toward the counter near the front of the shop.

Lucy sighed deeply, then forced herself to put Jude out of her mind. Time to forget about him. He hadn't been her lover, merely a boyfriend who'd gotten a hand down her pants just once in three months. Absolutely forgettable.

Besides which, she had other things to think about. Like Christmas, now just two days away. And the fact that she was spending it alone.

Your own fault. She'd made the choice. Kate was going away with Teddy tonight so the apartment would be empty. But Sam had begged her to come back to Chicago to celebrate Christmas with his fiancée's family. Lucy had refused, claiming she had too much work to do over the holidays.

Truth was, she couldn't handle a big family Christmas. The last traditional holiday season she'd experienced had been a week before her parents had been swept from her life by a stupid asshole who'd decided to celebrate a promotion by having a few bourbons, then getting behind the wheel of a car.

It had been just her and Sam for five years now, and each Christmas had been more nontraditional than the last. One year ago, they'd been in Mexico, lying on a beach, ignoring the merriment around them in favor of rum drinks and steel drums.

Though Sam was ready to dive back into the holiday spirit with his new fiancée, somehow, Lucy just couldn't face it yet. Honestly, she wasn't sure she'd ever be able to again. Christmas had once been her favorite holiday; it seemed almost sacrilege to enjoy it without the two people who had made it so special for the first seventeen years of her life.

Now she had another thing to add to her why-I-should-skip Christmas list: she'd been cheated on—right before the holiday. The angel on the top of Jude's tree had borne witness to the extension-wearing ho who went around sucking on dicks that belonged to other girls. Er, other girls' boyfriends.

"The whole holiday is just overrated," she told herself. "Better off just forgetting about it."

Not to mention a few other things. Like love. Romance. And men.

"EXCUSE ME, SIR, can I ask you a favor?"

Ross Marshall heard a young woman speaking, but since he knew she wasn't talking to him, he didn't bother turning around. He instead remained focused on putting the finishing touches on the custom-made bookcase he'd been asked to install today. Thankfully, despite his concerns about the off-kilter walls in this old New York building, every shelving unit he'd built for Beans & Books had fit beautifully. Including this last one.

"Sir?"

Though curious, since the voice sounded a little insistent, again he ignored her. He tried to avoid the customers and usually didn't work until later in the evening when the shop was closed. The owner really wanted the final unit installed today, however—gotta have more shelf space to grab those crazy day-before-Christmas-Eve shoppers who'd be filling the aisles tonight. So he'd agreed to come in right after the frenetic lunch hour but before the five o'clock rush.

He'd still arrived just in time to listen to modern-day robber barons having power coffees while making let's-take-over-the-world deals via Bluetooth. Oh, and their trophy wives stopping by between Junior League meetings and museum openings to grab a Fat-Free Cappuccino with Soy milk and carob drizzle.

Manhattan was like a different planet. He preferred Chicago, which he'd called home for the first twenty-three of his twenty-four years. It was almost as big and half as pretentious.

"Hellooooo?"

Finally realizing the woman might actually be speaking to him, which he hadn't imagined since in New York nobody called hammer jockeys "sir," he turned around. The young woman *had* been addressing him—she was staring at him, her eyes narrowed, her freckled cheeks flushed and her mouth tugged down into a frown.

"I'm sorry, I didn't realize you were talking to me." He offered her a smile. "I'm not used to being called sir."

The blonde relaxed. "Oh, yeah. Sorry. Hey, listen, could I ask you a big favor?"

He stiffened the tiniest bit. He might not be used to being called sir around here, but he'd received a lot of suggestive invitations lately. It seemed men with calluses were, for some reason, catnip to the rich Manhattan types. "Yes?"

"See my friend over there at the table in the far corner?"

Ross glanced over, seeing the back of a woman seated in the shadowy rear corner of the place. Then he looked again, interested despite himself in the stunning, thick brown hair that fell in loose, curly waves halfway down her back. She stood out from every other female in the place—most of whom sported a more typical, reserved, New York professional-woman's blow-out or bun. Ross's hands started to tingle, as if anticipating what it might be like to sink his fingers into those silky strands.

He shoved them into his pockets. "What about her?"

"She's my best friend—we're both students. Anyway, she needs some help for this project she's working on. We've been sitting over there talking about it and trying to figure out what tool would be best." She lifted her shoulders in a shrug. "But we're both pretty clueless about that kind of stuff. Do you think you could go over and offer her your expertise?"

It sounded screwy to him, and the young woman looked like she was about to break into a grin. But something—*that hair*—made him curious to see more of the girl with the tool problem.

He looked again. This time, the brunette had turned a little, as if looking around for her friend, and he caught a glimpse of her face. Creamy-skin. Cute nose. Long lashes. Full mouth.

His heart-rate kicked up a notch; he was interested in spite of himself. "What kind of job is it?" he asked as he began to pack up his portable toolbox.

"Well, uh...it might be best if she explains that herself." As if sensing he was skeptical, she added, "She's a photography student, you see, and I'm in journalism. Between the two of us, we barely know the difference between a hammer and a chainsaw."

He shouldn't. Really. Even though he was finished here, he had some things to do for another project scheduled to start the day after Christmas. He needed to phone in a few orders, go to the lumberyard, go over the design he'd sketched out.

Of course, all that would have to come after he risked life and limb at the most miserable place on earth to be today: the nearest shipping store. He had to get his family's Christmas gifts sent off, via overnight delivery, obviously. Seemed in the past week he had gone from busy self-employed carpenter to forgetful procrastinating shopper. Bad enough that he wasn't going home for Christmas; if he didn't get a gift in front of his youngest sister, he'd never hear the end of it.

Yet even with all that, he was tempted to take ten minutes to see if the brunette was really as attractive as she looked from here. Not to mention seeing what this mystery project was.

"Please? I'm sure it won't take long. Besides, helping someone else will put you in the holiday spirit," the girl said, managing to sound pious, despite the mischief in her expression.

He chuckled at her noble tone. Her smile and the twinkle in her eyes told him something else was going on. She was probably playing some kind of matchmaking game. Hell, for all he knew, the brunette had put her up to this, wanting to meet him but not wanting to come on too strong.

That was okay. Because he suddenly wanted to meet her, too.

And if the blonde was on the up-and-up, and the woman did need some help, well, that was okay, too. Maybe doing something nice for someone—someone super hot with soft-looking hair he wanted to rub all over his bare skin—was just what he needed. Certainly nothing else was putting him in the holiday spirit. He was too busy working—trying to prove to himself and to everyone else that he could make it on his own and didn't need to go to work in the family business—to care much about celebrating.

His mom suspected that was why he wasn't coming home for Christmas, because he didn't want to get another guilt trip or have another argument with his dad. She wasn't entirely wrong.

"Okay," he said, seeing the shop owner smiling broadly at him from behind the counter, obviously thrilled that even more expensive holiday junk could be shoveled in front of potential customers within the hour. "Just give me a few minutes."

"Oh, thank you!"

The freckled blonde turned and headed not for her friend in the back corner, but toward the door of the shop. Like she was making herself scarce so her friend could make her move. He grinned, wondering why girls went through these motions. He would probably have been even more interested if the brunette had just come up to him herself and said hello.

Finishing up with a customer, the owner came out from

around the counter. He offered Ross his exuberant thanks for having squeezed in this job so quickly. Ross accepted the check for final payment—which, he noted, included a nice holiday bonus—then shook the man's hand and picked up his tools. Then it was decision time. Head for the exit and get busy doing what he needed to do? Or take a few minutes out of his day to possibly be hit-on by a very pretty girl who'd gotten her friend to play matchmaker?

Hell. He might be hungry, might need work to pay his bills. But he was twenty-four, human and male. Pretty girl trumped food any day of the week.

Heading toward her table, he brushed some sawdust off his arms, nodding politely at the several women who smiled and murmured holiday greetings. The brunette hadn't moved from her seat, though he did see her look from side to side, as if she wanted to turn around to see if he was coming over, but didn't wish to be too obvious about it.

She so *set this up.*

Frankly, Ross couldn't bring himself to care.

He walked up behind her, about to clear his throat and introduce himself, when he heard her say something. She was alone, obviously, and had to be talking to herself. And what she said pierced a hole in the ego that had been telling him she'd sent a friend over to get his attention.

"You know you'd have been scared to even pick up a chainsaw," she muttered. "Or even an electric knife!"

Damn. She really was talking about tools? Some project that she needed to do?

Ross had to laugh at himself. Wouldn't his youngest sister—always his biggest critic—be laughing her ass off right now? He'd been all cocky and sure this sexy coed was about to come on to him…and she really was interested only in his toolbelt.

"Forget the electric knife," he said, intruding on her musings, the carpenter in him shuddering at the thought. "They're not made for cutting anything other than meat."

The girl swung her head up to look at him, her eyes rounding in shock and her mouth dropping open.

Big brown eyes. Full, pink-lipped mouth.

Then there was the perfect, heart-shaped face. And oh, that hair. Thick and shining, with soft brown waves that framed her face, and curls that tumbled well down her back. There wasn't a guy alive who wouldn't imagine all that hair being the only thing wrapped around her naked body; well, except for his *own* naked body.

He stared, unable to do anything else. She'd been pretty from across the room. Up close, she was beautiful enough to make his heart forget it was supposed to beat.

"Excuse me?" she said, shaking her head lightly as if she couldn't figure out what was happening. "What did you say?"

He cleared his throat. "I said, you need to use the right tool for the job. Electric knives are for cutting meat. Now what is it you were thinking about cutting through?"

"Meat," she replied, then quickly clamped her lips shut.

He laughed, admiring her quick wit. "Beef or pork?"

"I'd say pork loin," she replied, her mouth twisting a bit. "But I was joking. I definitely don't need to cut any meat."

"I figured," he said. Without waiting for an invitation, he walked around the table and sat in the vacant chair, facing her. He told himself it was because he'd promised her friend he'd offer her some construction advice. In truth, he just wanted to look at her a little more. Hear her voice. See whether she had a personality to go with the looks.

Most guys his age probably wouldn't care. Ross, though, did.

He might be young, but he wasn't inexperienced. And he'd learned very early on that a pretty face and smoking-hot body were enough before hitting the sheets. But after that, if there wasn't a great sense of humor, big heart and a brain to go along with the sexiness, he just couldn't stay interested. Some of his old college buddies used to joke about being happy with tits-on-a-stick. Ross preferred a real woman, from top to bottom.

She seemed like she had a brain. Right now, though, he was wondering about that whole personality thing. Because she just kept staring at him, her face turning pink, as if she didn't know what to say.

Or she was embarrassed.

Hmm. So maybe this wasn't about some mystery project. Because the way she was blushing made him suspect she'd had something wicked on her mind.

More interesting by the minute.

"So, what is this big project?"

"Project?"

"Yeah. Your friend came over, told me you needed some advice on tools for a project you're doing."

She sucked her bottom lip into her mouth and closed her eyes for a second, then whispered, "I'm going to kill her."

"Maybe that's why she left—she needed a running start."

"She *left?*"

"Yep. Right after she came to ask me to help you."

Groaning, she shook her head. "I can't believe this."

"So, she was trying to set us up?"

"I think so."

"What kind of friend does that?" he asked. "She doesn't know me—what if I'm some kind of serial killer or panty thief?"

Her brow went up. "Are you?"

"Am I what?"

"Either of those things?"

He grinned. "No on the first. I'll take the fifth on the second until we get to know each other." Certain he wanted that—to get to know her—he stuck out his hand. "I'm Ross."

She eyed it, then reached out and shook. Her hand was small, soft. Fragile against his own. Having worked only with his hands for months, he knew he had calluses on top of blisters, but she didn't seem to mind at all. In fact, she was the one who held on for a moment, as if not wanting to let go.

Finally, though, she pulled away, murmuring, "Lucy."

"Nice to meet you, Lucy."

"You, too. Especially now that I know you're not a serial killer." She flashed a grin. "As for the other, remind me not to walk into Victoria's Secret with you...wouldn't want to get arrested as an accomplice."

"What fun would there be in stealing brand-new panties?" Then, seeing her brow shoot up, he held up a hand. "Kidding. Believe me, stealing underwear isn't my thing."

"Helping mystery girls with mysterious projects is?"

"Uh-huh. Now, mysterious girl, back to the mysterious project."

"There isn't one."

"Your friend made it up?"

She shifted her gaze, those long lashes lowering. "Not exactly. I was, um, wondering which tool to use to, uh, remove something. And she obviously thought it would be fun to bring you into my fantasies." She gasped, staring him in the eye. "I mean, I wasn't...it's not that I was fantasizing about you!"

"Aww, I'm crushed."

"If you knew the fantasy, you wouldn't be," she said, her tone droll.

"So why don't you tell me?" he asked, only half-teasing. What *did* a beautiful young woman fantasize about? More importantly, *who?*

"Believe me, you don't want to know."

"Oh, trust me on this, I definitely do."

She studied him for a moment, eyeing him intently as if to see if he was serious. Then, apparently realizing he was, she came right out and told him.

3

Now
Chicago, December 23, 2011

JUST BECAUSE ROSS Marshall hadn't seen Lucy Fleming for six years did not mean he didn't instantly recognize her. It did, however, mean his heart literally thudded in his chest and his brain seemed to flatline. The huge, open reception area of his office—decorated with lights and greenery—seemed to darken. It also appeared to shrink, squeezing in tight, crushing his ribs, making his head throb, sending him off-kilter. He couldn't form a single coherent thought.

Well, maybe one. *You cut your hair?* He had the presence of mind to notice that the long, riotous curls that had once fallen well down her back had been tamed and shortened. Then everything just went blank.

She couldn't be here, right? Could not *possibly* be here. This had to be a dream—he was still sleeping and she was visiting his nighttime fantasies, as she so often had over the years.

He couldn't resist, needing to grab the moment before he woke up. He lifted a hand, put it on her shoulder, felt the solid, real person beneath the elf costume. She didn't immediately pull away, and he leaned a little bit closer, breathing deeply, recognizing the scent that was uniquely

Lucy. Not a perfume or a lotion or her shampoo. Just something distinctive and evocative that called to his memories, reminding him that she had been *the one*.

And he'd let her get away.

"You're not dreaming," she told him, her tone dry.

He dropped his hand and stepped back, needing to get his head back in the game. "Guess that means you're not, either."

"That thought did cross my mind," she said, her big brown eyes inquisitive. "I certainly never expected to run into you, today of all days."

He knew the day. Knew it well. Which just made the meeting all the more surreal. "Same here," he mumbled.

They both fell silent. Lucy appeared as stunned as he was.

Well, why wouldn't she be? They hadn't laid eyes on each other in years. Despite what had happened between them, what they'd shared over that one amazing holiday season, not one word had been exchanged between them since mid-January, nearly six years ago. Not a card, not a phone call. No chance of bumping into each other since, the last he'd known, she had been bound for Europe.

But here she was. Not just in Chicago, but in his office. *His freaking office!*

"What are you doing here?" he asked, his brain not catching up yet. It should be obvious. Lucy had been studying photography when they'd met. Besides which, she was carrying a camera bag. And was dressed as an elf.

A smile tried to tug at his lips. He remembered that elf costume. Remembered it so well.

Suddenly he was remembering everything so well.

Some things *too* well.

"I'm working," she said, her head going up, that pretty mouth tightening. "Did you happen to notice the picture-with-Santa session that's been going on for the past couple of hours?"

He'd barely noticed anything that was going on, being too busy working to socialize. The employee Christmas party had been a long-standing tradition with Elite Construction, the company his grandfather had founded, and he now ran. That didn't mean the boss ever had much time to participate in it. He'd made the rounds, thanked his employees, greeted their kids and wives, then retreated back into his office for the last two hours, only coming out to say goodbye now that things were winding down.

"I noticed," he finally replied.

"Well, that was me behind the camera."

"I know that, I heard you did a great job and was coming over to meet you," he said, still knocked off-kilter by her mere presence.

"Sorry, Santa's gone. No more pictures. Though, if you want to sit on the chair, I guess I could snap a shot of you holding a candy cane and a teddy bear."

Still sassy. God, he'd always liked that about her.

"I meant, I was coming to thank you for agreeing to do the party on such short notice."

"You didn't know *I* was the elf until just now?" she asked, sounding slightly suspicious. As if wondering if he'd set up this little reunion.

Huh. If he'd known she was nearby, he might have considered doing just that—even though Lucy probably wouldn't have been thrilled about it, judging by the look on her face.

"I swear, I had no idea." He was suddenly very interested in talking to his assistant, wondering how she'd found Lucy. He also wondered if the motherly, slightly nosy woman had been doing a little matchmaking. He wouldn't put it past her. She was nothing if not a closet romantic.

"My real question was," he continued, "what are you doing here in Chicago? You swore you'd never live here. Hell, I figured you'd be in Europe."

That had been her dream, living overseas, being a world-traveling photographer. So what had happened? She had seemed utterly determined that she would never stay near home and take…Santa pictures of little kids.

He glanced at the velvet-covered chair, the fluffy fake snow, the tripod, and her, back in that elf suit.

How on earth had her life gotten so derailed?

"I was for a while, did my semester abroad and went back right after graduation," she said.

Just as she'd planned. Which was one reason he'd stayed out of touch, knowing an entire ocean was going to separate them, so why bother trying to make something work when geography said it couldn't?

"And?"

"And I wasn't happy, so I ended up back in New York a few years ago."

Years. She'd been on the same continent for years. A short plane ride away. The thought made him slightly sick to his stomach, especially considering the number of times he'd thought about her during that same time span. The curiosity about whether she'd kept the same cell phone number and whether it would work in Paris.

Maybe not. But it probably would have in New York. Damn.

"How did Chicago enter the equation?"

"You remember, I grew up in this area?"

He remembered, but she'd seemed adamant about never coming back here, associating it with her tragic loss. "I remember."

"Well, I moved back here ten months ago to be closer my brother."

Even as another wave of shocked pleasure washed over him—she'd moved *here,* to the very same city—the brother's name immediately popped into his mind. "Sam?"

"Right. He went through a pretty bad divorce and I thought he could use some family nearby."

"That's a shame…about the divorce, I mean."

"Yes, it is. I really thought they'd make it."

"Does anybody anymore?" he mumbled before he could think better of it.

Her whole body stiffened, and he mentally kicked himself for going there. Because he and Lucy sure hadn't.

Then again, had they expected to? Hell, what had happened between them had been so sudden, so unexpected. Neither of them had been in the right place for any kind of relationship—mentally, emotionally, financially, or in any other way.

Except physically. Oh, yeah. There they'd been absolutely perfect together.

It had been so good during the incredibly brief time it lasted. Honestly, looking back, he could say it was the best Christmas Eve he'd ever had in his life.

Followed by the worst Christmas Day.

"How do you like being back in Chicago?" he asked, sensing she was trying to gracefully exit stage left.

"It's cold," she said with a shrug, not giving an inch, not softening up a bit. Hell, he supposed he couldn't blame her.

"You look like you've done well for yourself," she said, an almost grudging tone to her voice. She looked him over, head-to-toe, as if wondering where the jeans, T-shirt and tool belt had gone.

Some days—many days—he longed for them. Wearing a suit—even if he usually lost the tie and rolled-up his sleeves at some point every day—just didn't excite him the way working with his hands always had. "I guess. And you?"

She nodded. "I have my own studio."

"Still boycott Christmas?"

She glanced down at her costume. "As much as I possibly can, which isn't easy in my line of work. You still a sappy kid about it?"

He nodded, unashamed. "Absolutely." Even if, for the past five holiday seasons, he'd spent a lot more time wondering about Lucy—where she'd gone, if she'd stayed in Europe, become a famous photographer—than he had worrying about what present to get for which sister, niece or nephew.

As if they'd both run out of small talk for the moment, they returned to staring. Ross couldn't deny it, the years had been good to her; Lucy was beautiful. No perky little elf hat complete with feather could take away from that. Nor could the short dress, striped tights—oh, God, those tights, did they ever bring back memories—and pointy-tipped shoes.

She should look cute and adorable. Instead she looked hot and sexy, bringing wild, intense memories to his mind of the last time he'd seen her wearing that very same outfit.

He was suddenly—forcibly—reminded of how long it had been since he'd had sex.

Good sex? Even longer.

Fabulous, never-forget-it, once-in-a-lifetime sex?

Six years. No doubt about it.

He swallowed as memories flooded over him, having to shift a little. Lucy had always affected him physically. Damned if he wanted anyone to notice that now, though. The CEO wasn't supposed to sport wood at the corporate holiday party.

"I'm impressed that you can still fit into that," he admitted against his own better judgment. "But not too surprised. You haven't changed a bit."

She flushed. "Maybe not physically. But I'm not the same sweet, wide-eyed kid anymore."

He barked a laugh. "Sweet kid? Aren't you the same person who was planning to dismember her ex-boyfriend when we met?"

"I didn't actually *do* it."

No, she hadn't. As he recalled, Ross had enjoyed the pleasure of taking her ex apart. And it had felt damn good, too.

"That's good—I'd hate to think you've spent the last six years in jail."

"Maybe if you hadn't stopped calling, you'd know where I spent the last six years," she replied, ever-so-sweetly.

Direct hit. He winced. "Look, Lucy..."

She waved a hand, obviously angry at herself for having said anything. "Forget it. Water under the bridge."

"You know what I was going through—why I left New York." Of course she knew, she'd been there when he'd gotten the call that brought him back home.

"I know," she said. "I understood...I under*stand*."

Maybe. But that not-staying-in-touch thing obviously still rankled.

He'd probably asked himself a dozen times over the years why he hadn't at least tried to get back in touch with her once his life had returned to something resembling normal. Maybe a hundred times. It always came back to the same thing: he was stuck. His life was here. Hers was... anywhere she wanted it to be. And she'd wanted it to be in another country, and a completely different reality from his, which was filled with contracts and workers-comp issues and the cost of lumber.

She'd been off to capture the world one still image at a time. He'd been boxed in, chained to the past, owing too much to other people to just go and live his life the way he had wanted to.

Not that it had turned out badly. He actually loved running the business and had done a damn fine job of it. He was glad to live in Chicago. He liked the vibe of this city, the people and the culture. So no, he didn't regret coming back here. He had only one regret. Her.

"And now here you are," he murmured, though he hadn't intended to say it out loud.

"Don't make a big thing of it," she insisted. "I had no idea you worked here."

"And if you had known? Would you have taken the job today, risked bumping into me?"

She didn't reply. Which was answer enough.

Lucy really was mad at him. Well, that made two of them; he was mad at himself. Plenty of room for regrets, with six years of what-ifs under his belt. But at the time it had seemed like he was doing the right thing—the best thing—for both of them.

Of course, he'd questioned that just about every day since.

"Excuse me, Ross?"

He glanced away from Lucy, seeing Stella, his administrative assistant, who he'd inherited from *his* father. Who'd inherited her from his father. Older than dirt didn't describe her. She had dirt beat—you'd have to go back to the rocks that had been worn down into the dirt to describe her.

You wouldn't know it to look at her. From the bottled black dye job to the floral-print dress, she could pass for fifty. But Ross knew she'd passed that milestone at least two decades ago. He dreaded the day she was no longer around to keep him organized.

Or to matchmake? He was going to have to have a talk with Stella about that. He knew his assistant thought he was stressed and lonely and spent too much time in the office. Plus, Stella knew about Lucy—she was one of the few people who did, having gotten Ross to reveal the story after one long, stressful day. But would she have gone to that much trouble—tracking Lucy down and getting her here? It seemed crazy.

If it was true, he would have to decide whether to give her hell for meddling in his private affairs…or thank her.

The way Lucy wasn't bothering to hide her dislike made him suspect the former.

The thought that he might be able to get her to change her mind? Definitely the latter.

He didn't deny he was still interested. Still attracted.

Judging by the absence of a ring on her left hand, he suspected she was available—at least technically. So maybe it was time to take his shot. See if he could make up for six wasted years. See if there was any way she could forgive him for walking—no, running—away before they ever really had a chance to get started.

"Ross?" Stella prompted again. "Mr. Whitaker is about to leave, and he'd like to see you before he goes."

Whitaker—a client who'd sent a lot of work their way over the past several years. He wasn't somebody Ross could ignore.

"Okay," he said, before turning his attention back to Lucy. "Wait for me." It wasn't a request.

"No, I really have to go. It was nice to see you."

Said like she'd say it was nice to see an elementary school bully she'd loathed for decades. Damn. He'd screwed this up so badly. Six years ago, and today.

"Lucy, please…"

"Uh, Miss Fleming? If you'd step into the office, I can get you your payment right away," Stella interjected. "I'm sure you'd prefer not to have to wait until after the holidays."

Her lush bottom lip snagged between her teeth, Lucy looked torn. Ross glanced at Stella, wondering if she was intentionally using some stalling tactics to keep Lucy around. Then again, if she'd been trying to set them up, she probably wouldn't have interrupted about Whitaker, no matter how important a client he was. So maybe this whole thing had just been luck. Good luck. Incredibly good luck.

And maybe it meant he was going to have another chance with the woman he'd so foolishly let slip away.

HMM. MONEY OR DIGNITY? Go with the bossy assistant, or run like hell? *Decisions, decisions.*

Normally Lucy would have been heading toward the door the second Ross's back was turned. She had work to do, editing, photoshopping, cropping…plus all the stuff a small business owner was responsible for, but which often slipped through the cracks when the customers kept walking steadily through the door.

They wouldn't be walking through the door on Christmas weekend, though, so she should be able to catch up. And one thing she needed to catch up on was ordering. She had some equipment to buy, and paying for it by December 31 would make her tax bill a lot lighter come spring.

Which meant she should really stick around for the money. They'd offered her a *lot,* both for her time, and for the portrait packages the company had preordered for every family. It might even be enough money to get the new laptop *and* the new lens she needed.

Ross stared at her, not pleading, not ordering. Just asking her to wait, give them a chance to talk. To catch up on old times? Seriously, what was there to say except, *Hey, remember that time we had crazy wild sex in a pile of fluff in Santa's workshop?*

Good times.

Times that would never be repeated.

"I really should go," she said.

The administrator, who had a brusque manner that said she didn't like to take no for an answer, didn't take no for an answer. "Don't be silly, it won't take five minutes. It will save our accountants some trouble."

She eyed the woman doubtfully, suspecting this place did not keep their receipts and canceled checks in empty Amazon.com boxes the way she did.

"After the party, the offices shut down until New Year's. So I'd really like to get this taken care of today, clear the party off the books, if you will."

Huh. Sounded like every business had to deal with that pesky little IRS thing, even businesses as big as this one. Which, judging by the size of this brand-new six-story office building, and the fact that Elite Construction took up every floor of it, was very big, indeed. She wondered again what Ross did here. Obviously he no longer swung a hammer—he was dressed like a corporate guy.

She couldn't help wondering what had happened to his dream of someday buying a piece of property and building a house on it, every stone, every shutter, every plank of wood put there with his own hands. Had Ross given up his dreams? Or had they merely changed, like hers had?

As if realizing his presence was making her reluctant, Ross said, "I should go. It was great seeing you again, Lucy."

"You, too."

She forced a tight smile, wishing she could hit Rewind and go back a half hour to think of something else to say to this man. Something breezy and casual, something that wouldn't have revealed how she felt about not hearing from him after that one magical holiday. Something *other* than, "Well, if you'd called, you'd know where I'd been for the past six years."

Weak, girl. So weak. She could almost hear Kate's voice scolding her for making that snotty, hurt-sounding comment. Even though, now, there would be echoes of a baby and a toddler crying in the background as they had the conversation. Kate had married Teddy and started repopulating the planet.

Lucy, meanwhile, had managed only sexual affairs after Ross. But she hadn't come anywhere close to falling in love. Not after the one-two punch she'd taken at twenty-two. First Jude, then Ross—the latter being the one who'd truly taught her about love and loss. Her poor heart had formed an exoskeleton thicker than an insect's. Since then, she'd made love 'em and leave 'em a way of life, only substituting the *love* with *do*.

Even Kate had been impressed.

She watched him walk away, noting that he didn't look back. His departure should have made it easier to stick around for a few minutes to get paid. Instead it just pissed her off. Ross was always the one who got to walk away. One of these days she wanted to be the one to make the grand exit.

But grand exits didn't buy lenses and laptops. Money did. She'd spent a lot moving her studio from New York to Chicago. Yes, she was building a reputation and business was good. This one check, though, could do some nice things for her bottom line.

If she deposited the check tonight, then by this weekend, she could be happily shopping for laptops online while everybody else in the world unwrapped ugly sweaters and ate rock-hard fruitcake. She had bookings lined up all next week—a few of them big ones that could lead to some serious money. Plus, she was hoping to hear from a children's magazine in New York, to whom she'd submitted some work. She wanted to be ready if they called and said they wanted more.

"Okay, if you can pay me now, I'd really appreciate it," she finally told the administrator, who'd been waiting patiently, watching Lucy watch Ross.

"Excellent, come along."

Lucy put down her camera and lens bags, and followed the woman, who'd introduced herself as Stella when she'd called a week ago to hire her. They left the party behind, heading down a long corridor toward the executive offices. Lucy couldn't help noticing the opulence of this area, the thick carpet sinking beneath her feet, the beautiful artwork lining the walls. Somebody had spent a lot of time decorating this place and she suspected their clients ranked among Chicago's most wealthy.

At the back end of the executive wing was an enclosed suite, into which Stella led her. A broad receptionist's desk stood in the middle of a waiting area, blocking access to an imposing set of double doors. Stella breezed through them, into what looked like the head honcho's office. It was huge, a corner room with floor-to-ceiling windows on two walls. The building wasn't terribly high, but the location right on the water on the very outskirts of town meant nothing interrupted the beautiful view. The desk was as big as the kitchen in her tiny apartment, and in a partially blocked-off alcove, she saw an area for relaxation, complete with a refrigerator, TV and a fold-out couch...folded out. "Wow, is your boss a slave-driver? Do you have to be on call 24/7?"

The woman glanced around, then realized what Lucy was talking about. "That's just for him. Our CEO is only hard on himself."

"Does he live here or something?"

"It sometimes seems that way," Stella said. "When we moved into this new building, he was spending so many hours here, I ordered the couch and make it up for him when I suspect he'll pull an all-nighter."

"That's dedication." On Stella's part, and on her boss's.

"It's paid off. Elite is thriving when new construction is down nationwide."

"I could tell by the party," she admitted, knowing it must have set the company back a pretty penny. Few corporations bothered these days, and she suspected the happy atmosphere contributed to the company's success.

Stella stepped behind the desk and picked up a pile of sealed envelopes, shuffling through a half-dozen of them before she said, "Ah, here we are!"

Lucy accepted it, tucking the very welcome check into her purse. "Thanks very much."

"Thank *you*. Your photos were the hit of the party. I am actually glad the other company canceled. We've used them in the past and they've never had the response you did today. You're wonderful with children."

Lucy smiled, appreciating the praise. It was funny—six years ago, she probably would have been horrified at it.

Honestly, she wasn't sure herself how it had happened. She just knew that, after two years in Paris, photographing cold-faced fashion models had lost all appeal. Same with old, lifeless buildings and stagnant landscapes.

Then Kate had started having kids. Lucy had visited for summers and holidays, becoming a devoted godmother and falling head-over-heels for those babies. She had delighted in taking their portraits, finding in children's faces an energy and spontaneity she seldom found anywhere else.

So she'd gone back to New York. She'd set up a studio and begun exploring the amazingly creative world of little people. One thing had led to another, and then another. And soon she'd been getting calls from wealthy parents in other states, and had sold several shots to children's catalogs and magazines.

Who'd've ever thought it?

Not her, that's for sure. Nor would she ever have imagined that she'd really love what she was doing. But she did.

Life, it seemed, took some strange turns, led you in directions you'd never have imagined. It had taken her from the windy city, to the Big Apple, then to another continent. And now right back to where she'd started, in Chicago.

And back into Ross Marshall's life.

No, don't even go there, she reminded herself. She wasn't back in his life. She was in the same building with him for another five minutes, max. Then she could go back to forgetting about the guy. Forgetting how good he still looked to her. How his sexy voice thrilled her senses. How his touch had sent her out of her mind.

How he'd once seemed like the guy she could love forever.

4

LUCY HAD TO give this very handsome stranger—Ross—credit. He didn't stand up and walk out of the coffee shop when she admitted she'd been fantasizing about separating an ex-boyfriend from part of his anatomy. He didn't yelp, cringe, or reflexively drop a protective hand on his lap. None of the above. Instead he simply stared for a second, then let a loud burst of laughter erupt from his mouth.

She smiled, too, especially because she hadn't *really* been fantasizing about maiming Jude when this guy had walked up behind her. In fact, she'd been laughing at herself for having thought about it earlier. Somehow, her whole mood had shifted from the time she'd walked into the coffee shop until the moment this incredibly handsome man had approached her.

Incredibly. Handsome.

Around them, others in the café glanced over. Lucy wasn't blind to the stares that lingered on him. Heaven knew, any woman with a broken-in vagina would stare. Heck, hers wasn't broken-in and she could barely take her eyes off the guy!

He'd been super-hot from across the room. Up close,

now that she could see the tiny flecks in his stunning green eyes, the dazzling white smile, the slight stubble on his cheeks, well, he went from hot and sexy to smoking and irresistible. She'd actually shivered when their hands had met, unable to think a single thought except to wonder how those strong, rough fingers would feel sliding across her skin.

Gorgeous, sexy, strong. And a sense of humor.

Why couldn't she have met this guy on a day when she didn't loathe every creature with a penis?

You don't. Not every guy.

Truthfully? Not even one. She didn't loathe Jude. She would have had to care about him to hate him, and, honestly, having really thought about it, she knew she hadn't cared much at all.

"You're serious?" he asked once his laughter had died down.

"Not about doing it."

"But thinking it?"

"My turn to take the fifth."

"Why?"

"Probably because it's not very nice to admit you fantasize about dismembering someone."

"No, I meant why do you want to, um…dismember him?"

"I didn't, I was just indulging in a little mind-revenge. He wasn't the most faithful guy."

"I hate cheaters," he said, his voice both sympathetic and disgusted.

"Speaking from personal experience?"

"Well, not exactly," he admitted.

Yeah. Because any woman who cheated on him would have to have been recently lobotomized.

"Though, I did kinda get cheated on once…by a guy."

She didn't take the bait, knowing that there was no way Ross was gay. There wasn't one nonheterosexual gene in his body; you could practically smell the masculine phero-mones that surrounded him like a cloud, attracting every woman in the place.

"Let me guess…your best buddy in first grade decided he wanted to play dodgeball instead of tag and left you alone in the playground?"

"Almost," he said, his eyes gleaming with approval that she hadn't gone where most would have. "It was in high school. I wanted my best friend to stick with the wrestling team, he wanted to do the school musical." He shook his head sadly. "I just couldn't understand what he was think-ing. It wasn't until junior year that he finally told me the truth, and then I was so furious I didn't speak to him for a week."

Somehow disappointed in him, she stiffened slightly. "You were mad that he was gay?"

"Hell, no, he wasn't gay! He told me he left wrestling and went to drama because, let me see if I remember this exactly, 'Why would I want to roll around on the floor with a bunch of sweaty dudes, when I could be one of only a handful of guys surrounded by some of the prettiest girls in the school?' Man, some of those theater chicks were cute…and he never told me, he kept them all for himself!"

She laughed out loud, liking both the story, and that he had told it. He was obviously trying to distract her, to amuse her. It was a nice thing to do for a guy so young and good-looking.

"So, your first bro-mance ended up in a bad breakup."

"Yup. Now, back to yours…."

"Not a bro-mance, obviously. But also unpleasant. I only wish it were something as simple as him preferring *The Sound of Music* to pinning and undercupping."

His eyes widened. "Hey, you know wrestling!"

"Older brother."

"So is he going to kick this cheating dude's ass?"

"Sam? No. He doesn't live here, and even if he did, there's absolutely no way I would tell him about this."

"How come?"

"Because he's a cop. And he's extremely overprotective." Though she didn't usually discuss it, for some reason, she found this guy very easy to talk to, so she added, "He sort of became my father when our parents died."

Ross leaned forward in his chair, dropping his elbows onto the table. His fingers brushed against her hand, in a move that was as fleeting as it was sweet. A faint brush of *I'm Sorry* and *How Sad* and *Hey, I Understand*. All unsaid. All understood.

All appreciated.

She cleared her throat, feeling the lump start to rise, the way it always did when this particular subject came up. "Anyway, I don't need Sam to fight my battles. I can take care of myself."

"I don't doubt it," Ross said.

"Don't worry, I'm really not the violent type. This guy didn't crush my spirit, he merely dinged my ego."

He held her stare, as if assessing the truth of her words. Lucy stared right back, a tiny smile on her lips, relieved that she meant exactly what she'd said, hoping he realized that, too.

"I'm glad," he finally admitted, seeing the truth in her face.

"So am I."

"Still, if you change your mind and decide to get all sawcrazy on this boyfriend, remind me not to go with you. I wouldn't want to be arrested as an accomplice."

She chuckled as he turned her earlier words back on her, then clarified, "*Ex*-boyfriend." Shaking her head, she added, "Believe me, nothing could induce me to go back there." Then something occurred to her. "Oh, *no!*" Lucy put a hand over her forehead as she remembered something.

Because she was going to have to make a liar of herself. "I'm so stupid!"

"What?"

"My brother's Christmas present to me. It came in the mail today—he sent it to Jude's place because he knows mail sometimes gets stolen from the building where I live and Jude's has a doorman." She felt moisture in her eyes, furious at herself for forgetting the gift, but also worried about what Jude would do with it. "He's probably already thrown it down the trash chute."

"Jude?" he said doubtfully. "Lemme guess—spoiled, rich punk?"

It might have taken a little while for the blinders to come off, but Lucy had to admit, that pretty well described her ex. "How'd you know?"

"Having a doorman in NYC is a pretty big tip-off. So's having a name like Jude. Plus, he must've done something pretty bad if you're fantasizing about chopping the head off his trouser snake, yet he'd still throw out a Christmas gift from your brother…meaning he's an immature, petulant brat." He spread his hands. "Or a spoiled, rich asshole."

"All of the above would cover it."

"And you're with this guy…why?"

"I'm not with him."

"But you were as of…"

She sighed deeply. "About two hours ago."

He whistled, leaning back in his chair, extending his long legs, crossed at the ankle. "Was it serious? I mean, were you guys exclusive?"

"Not according to him, apparently."

His jaw tightened a tiny bit. "And according to you?"

"Well, I thought so, but maybe I just saw things differently than he did. We'd been dating three months, but we hadn't even…you know. So maybe he cheated since he'd never gotten anywhere with me."

Ross coughed into his fist, apparently surprised she'd

admitted that. Maybe he was turned-off; some guys would be at the thought that a girl would wait three months before getting down to business. If so, better to find out now if he was one of them.

Why that should be, she didn't know. After all, she might never even speak to this guy again once she left this shop. Somehow, the thought made her heart twist a lot harder than it had earlier when she'd thought about not seeing Jude anymore.

"Good for you," he said.

Okay, so he wasn't one of *those* guys, apparently. The realization warmed her a little on this very chilly day.

"Let him eat his heart out, wondering what he's thrown away."

She liked that idea. "I hope twenty years from now he's still wondering if he missed out on the best sex of his life."

Their stares locked as the heated words hung there between them. They were having a very intimate conversation for two strangers, and now, she suspected, they were both thinking a little too much about certain parts of that conversation

Like sex. Great sex. She might not have had it—great, or otherwise—but that didn't mean she was immune to desire. Looking at the man sitting across from her, feeling the heat sluice through her veins to settle with quiet, throbbing insistence between her thighs, she knew full well she had a basic understanding of want.

Or more than basic. Because it wasn't just her sex that was responding here. Every inch of her skin tingled as she thought of him touching her, pressing his mouth to all the more interesting parts of her body. Places that responded to the warm look in his eyes and how he opened his mouth to draw in a slow breath in a way they'd never responded to any guy's most passionate embrace.

His gaze dropped to her mouth and his voice was thick as he finally replied, "I almost feel sorry for the bastard."

She didn't. And she definitely didn't feel sorry for herself any longer. Not when, with one twenty-minute conversation, this complete stranger was introducing her to sensations her ex hadn't elicited in months of dating.

They remained silent for one more moment. Then, as if they both realized they were falling into something neither had anticipated—at the speed of light, no less—they shifted in their chairs and broke the stare.

Lucy forced a light laugh, trying to pretend she wasn't completely enraptured by the thought of pressing her mouth to the cord of muscle in his neck. "I'm not going to spare him any sympathy until I get my present back and make sure he didn't destroy it."

His gleaming eyes narrowed. "You really think he would?"

She considered it, remembered some of Jude's more spiteful moods. Not to mention his ridiculously misplaced indignation that she'd walked in on him today—as if it were all her fault because she'd caught him, not his that he'd cheated. "It's possible."

Ross's jaw clenched, a muscle flexing in his cheek. "Why don't you let me take care of this?"

"Why would you do that? You don't even know me."

"I know enough to know you shouldn't have to beg somebody who betrayed you to give you back something that's yours."

She heard the note of protectiveness in his voice, and found it strange. And very nice. Ross had just met her, yet he'd already been more thoughtful and considerate of her feelings than Jude had in the past three months.

"It's not that big a deal," she insisted, not wanting to drag somebody else into her troubles.

"It's from your only family member, Luce," he replied, shaking his head. "So of course it's a big deal. I want to make sure you get it back."

Lucy's breath caught. The soft way he'd said the nickname, Luce, seemed so tender. And the way he'd immediately understood why the gift from Sam was important to her, without her having to explain it…

Who are you? she couldn't help wondering. *Can you really be this nice a guy?*

"Do you think he'd really destroy your Christmas present?"

She didn't like to think so, but it was possible. "He was pretty mad when I left, mainly because I wouldn't stick around to listen to his explanation."

"Could there have been one?"

She snickered. "Sure." She tapped her finger on her cheek, as if thinking it over. "Hmm, okay, I have an idea how it could have, uh…*gone down.*"

A half smile lifted one corner of his oh-so-sexy mouth, as if he understood the reason for her inflection.

"So, his skanky neighbor was taking a bath, and she forgot she had no shampoo," Lucy explained. "Wrapped only in a towel, she came to his door to borrow some."

"Wait," he interrupted. "I bet I know what happened next. It just so happens, he was about to take a shower, too, so he was also only wearing a towel."

She giggled, wondering why she could already find this funny when it had brought tears to her eyes earlier today. More proof that her heart hadn't ever been involved in her relationship with Jude, she supposed.

"And then…hmm. Oh, I've got it," she said. "A pack of wild dogs somehow got into the building, rode up the elevator, burst into the apartment and ripped off both their towels. And in the ensuing struggle, slutty neighbor chick tripped and fell mouth first onto his sad, strange-looking little penis."

Ross winced. "Ouch."

"Ouch for her, or for him?"

"Well, mainly for you," he said, that gentle tone back in his voice. "For having to witness that." That sexy grin flashed. "But also ouch to him for having a sad, strange-looking little penis."

"Considering it was the first—and last—time I ever saw it, I can only say I'm glad I made the decision not to sleep with him."

"Me, too," he admitted, sounding as though he meant it. Which was odd, considering she didn't even know him and neither of them had any idea if they would ever share anything more than this one conversation at this one particular moment.

She hoped they would. It was fast, and utterly surprising and the timing was pretty bad. But she already had the feeling this sexy, hardworking guy was someone special. And even if the timing was all wrong, she might be the one with lifelong regrets if she didn't at least give this more time to play out.

"So, do you always go around telling strangers about your sex life?" he asked.

She played with her coffee cup, tracing her fingers on its rim, not meeting his eyes. "You're the first," she admitted. Hoping she wouldn't reveal too much, she shrugged and added, "You just don't seem like a stranger."

He didn't. She felt like she was already starting to know him, or at least know the essence of him. The physical attraction had been instant. But there was so much more. Earlier, when she'd mentioned her parents, there'd been that warmth, the smile, the tender looks, that ever-so-gentle brush of his fingers against her hand. Then there was his reaction to her having been cheated on. His indignance over her lost Christmas present.

All those things told a story. A nice one. A good one.

A story she wanted to explore a little more. Or a lot more.

"Okay then, if we're not strangers, I guess that means we're friends," he told her with a tender smile. Then, without explanation, he pushed the chair back and stood up. She

wasn't sure what he intended—to leave, to ask her out?—
until he extended a hand to her.

"So, come on, friend. Let's go reclaim your Christmas
present."

CONSIDERING HOW beautiful Lucy was, Ross didn't expect
her ex to be a total dog, even if he was a total dick. There
had to have been something she'd found attractive about
the guy. And even though he hadn't known her long, he
already felt pretty sure it hadn't been the money. She just
didn't seem the type. There wasn't a fake thing about her...
and he should know. He'd looked. Hard.

Hell, it had been impossible *not* to look, not to try to
get to know everything about her. Sitting across from each
other at that coffee shop, they'd fallen into an easy, laid-
back conversation that it had taken him a half-dozen meetings to achieve with other girls. Then things had gone from
warm and friendly to hot and expectant.

He shouldn't have started thinking about Lucy's sex life,
much less talking about it. Because it was damned hard to
get it out of his mind—or to stop wondering about that look
she'd had in her eye during the long silence they'd shared.

Walking outside to drop off his tools in his truck, then to
the subway so they could ride up to her dopey ex's neighborhood, he found himself more surprised by her with
every move she made.

She never stopped talking, but didn't jabber about stupid, inane stuff. He didn't once hear the word shoes. Or
makeup. Or shopping.

She talked about the city—how much she loved the energy of it, the pace, the excitement.

She stopped to take pictures—things that would never
occur to him to be interesting, like a pile of trash bags or
an old rusty bike against a fence.

She talked about her plans to go to Europe after she

graduated, to photograph anything that moved and lots of things that didn't.

She bought one of those disgusting hot dogs off a cart, and actually ate the thing.

She passed a five dollar bill to a homeless guy. She also dropped another five into a bell-ringer's bucket, even as she admitted she didn't really like Christmas, claiming her favorite response to anyone's "Merry Christmas," was "Bah, humbug!"

He had a hard time buying that one. She was too cute and sweet and generous to be a Scrooge. But he did see the shadow in her expression whenever she talked about the holiday and suspected she was serious about disliking it.

Other than that, though, she laughed a lot. She smiled at strangers. She turned her face up to meet the softly falling snow and licked its moisture off her lips. Sweet laugh, beautiful smile, sexy lips.

All in all, aside from totally attracting him, she charmed him. It was an old-fashioned description, but it fit. Lucy was, quite simply, charming. Plus adorable. And hot as hell. Every minute he spent with her made him like her even more…and made him more determined to ensure her cheating ex didn't get the chance to hurt her again.

She was, in short, fantastic. So, no, he definitely didn't see her hooking up with someone who had no redeeming qualities whatsoever. This Jude guy, who lived in a high-rise building with apartments that probably cost five times the rent in his own tiny place, had to have something to attract someone like Lucy.

Then he met the loser, face-to-face, and understood.

Jude Zacharias was spoiled, handsome and smooth—one of those old-money types whose family name probably hadn't been tainted by the stench of real work for a few generations. But the main thing about him, the thing that would suck in any girl, was the earnest charm.

He laid it on thick from the minute he answered the door

and saw Lucy. He even managed to work up a couple of tears in his eyes as he told her how sorry he was that he'd let some skank trick him into doing something bad—*ha*—how much he wished he could take it back and how glad he was that she'd returned.

Then he spotted Ross, who'd been hovering just out of sight, near the hallway wall.

"Who the fuck is *he?*"

Stepping forward, Ross said, "He the fuck is Lucy's friend, Ross. We're here to pick up the package she left behind. Now, would you get it, please? We're in a hurry."

Yeah. Not because he had errands to run, but because he was in a rush to get Lucy away from this prick who'd hurt her, even if it had been her pride, not her heart that had been dinged. Honestly, he'd wanted to rip the guy's hand off when he'd actually reached out and tried to touch her. Fortunately, Lucy had stepped aside, out of reach.

The guy's jaw hit his chest. He gaped, then sputtered, finally saying, "Who *are* you?"

Ross looked at Lucy and shrugged. "Is he brain damaged or something? Like I said, I'm Ross. I'm here to make sure you give Lucy her package, and that you don't try anything."

"Lucy, are you serious? Did you bring this guy to throw in my face, make me jealous or something?" He reached for her hand. "Babe, you don't have to do that, you know I'll take you back."

"Dude, get over it. You've been dumped," Ross said.

Jude's glare would have fried an egg. "Mind your own damn business. Why the hell are you here anyway?"

Lucy stepped between them. "Ross is a friend."

"Yeah, sure, right. How long has he been your…*friend?*"

She tapped a finger on her lips, as if thinking about it, then cast a quick, mischievous glance toward Ross. "Oh, about an hour now."

Jude sputtered. Lucy ignored him.

"He just wanted to come along in case you decided to be a jerk about my package."

The guy sneered. "Oh, yeah? And what's he gonna do if I say you can't have it?"

Ross's fingers curled into fists and his jaw tightened. He took a step toward the door. He couldn't remember if he'd ever felt this anxious to punch someone but he didn't think so. Something about hearing the way this little asshole talked to Lucy brought out the overprotective he-man in him.

She put up a hand, stopping him. "It's okay. Jude, please don't be a pain about this. Can I just have my package?" She reached into her purse and pulled out a key ring. "And here, you should have this back."

He snatched the key out of her hand, cast one more glare at Ross, then stepped back into the apartment. He returned a few seconds later, shoving a small, paper-wrapped carton toward her. It was mashed, dirty, slightly torn.

Lucy stared at it, her bottom lip trembling, then took it. A small shake elicited a tinkling sound from inside. The paper in which it was wrapped was damp.

Whatever had been inside had contained some kind of liquid. And it was broken.

"You didn't," she whispered, her voice thick. Her eyes were wet with unshed tears.

Jude shrugged. "Hey, just figured it must not have been important if you left it here, so I was gonna pitch it."

It looked as though the bastard already had. Against a wall.

Furious, Ross took another step toward him. "You petty little douchebag." This time, Lucy was too distracted by the ruined gift in her hands to stop him.

Good. That left Ross free to grab a fistful of her ex-boyfriend's top and shove him back into his apartment. The guy tripped over a table, stumbling backward a few steps before falling on his arrogant ass.

"Take another step and I'll call the cops!" he shrieked. Obviously pretty boy wasn't used to anybody threatening his perfect, spoiled little self.

"I could knock out your teeth before they get here," Ross growled.

The other guy scrambled backward as Ross stalked him, step by step.

"Look, I'm sorry, okay?" he said. "Lucy, come on, you know I wouldn't do anything to hurt you. It was an accident."

"Accident my ass," Ross said as he leaned down and hauled the guy up by the collar of his J. Crew sweater.

His right hand curled into a fist but before he could let it fly, Lucy grabbed his arm. "Let him go. Please, Ross, let's just get out of here." She cast her ex a withering look. "Hey, he did me a favor. If there was any doubt in my mind that he's a disgusting, hateful person, this eliminated it."

"Babe…"

"Bite me, Jude," she snapped.

Ross grinned, then, for good measure, pushed the dude backward until he hit the couch, sprawling out on it.

Ross glanced at Lucy, seeing she'd hugged the package to her chest, apparently not caring that it was wet. It was like seeing someone who'd lost their most prized possession. Nobody deserved to be cheated on, humiliated and then, to top it all off, have something important to them shattered. Remembering what she'd said about it being just the two of them after their parents had died, he felt his heart twist in his chest, knowing how much her brother's gift must have meant to her.

His own family drove him crazy sometimes—especially his overly controlling father—but he couldn't imagine life without them. She was so young to bear that kind of sadness. One thing he knew, Lucy Fleming had to be one hell of a strong young woman. And a forgiving one, if she was determined to stop him from kicking her ex's ass.

"Please, can we just go?" she asked.

Yeah. She seemed pretty determined. That was lucky for the ex, even though it didn't make Ross too happy.

"Fine," he told her.

He took her arm and led her to the door, glancing back over his shoulder before they walked through it. The ex still sat there on the couch, a sneer curling his lips. As if he were the injured party in this whole rotten mess.

The boiling well of anger inside him had rolled back to a slow simmer, and Ross knew he had to get out of here before it boiled back up. Mr. J. Crew dickhead had finally realized the merits of shutting the hell up, but that look on his face was seriously pissing Ross off. If he opened his mouth again, or if one single tear fell out of Lucy's eyes, he was gonna go postal on the squirmy punk.

Her hand tightened on his arm, as if she knew what he was thinking. So he wouldn't do it. But something wouldn't let him leave without one more parting shot. "Hey, dude, don't worry, I wouldn'ta hit you. Wouldn't risk damaging that pretty face of yours, 'cause it sounds to me like you really need it."

"What do you mean?" the other man snapped, starting to rise from his seat. Emboldened, perhaps, by the thought that Ross was admitting he wouldn't have hit him?

Just give me a reason, punk.

Ross shrugged as Lucy stepped into the hallway ahead of him. "I mean, it sounds like you need whatever help you can get. From what I hear, you not only have a scrawny neck, you have a scrawny dick as well." *Tsking,* he shook his head. "Even worse, a sad, strange-looking one."

The other guy's face erupted in scarlet, and he sputtered, but couldn't come up with anything to say. Which, in Ross's mind, confirmed what Lucy had said about him. A guy with an ounce of self-confidence would have laughed, or sneered. Jude just looked like he wanted to call Mommy and make the new kid stop saying mean things to him.

"Oh, by the way," he added. "Happy birthday."

Ross slammed the door, not waiting for Jude to come up with a crushing reply. Not that he could, really, because, man, any guy who couldn't defend himself against small-cock accusations didn't have much of a leg to stand on.

It wasn't until they were alone in the elevator, heading toward the bottom floor, that he looked down and saw Lucy's shoulders shaking. It was as if she'd held herself together, keeping her emotions in check until she got out of sight of her ex, but now that they were alone, her sadness over the day's events had come crashing down on her.

He turned her toward him. Ross fully intended to take her into his arms, awkwardly pat her back or whatever guys did to console crying women. But before he could do it, he realized he'd made a big mistake.

"Oh...my...God..." she said between gasps, which weren't caused by tears, but rather, by laughter. She looked up at him, her lips shaking, her eyes twinkling with merriment. "Did you see his face?"

"I saw," he said, smiling down at her, so pleased she wasn't brokenhearted over creepy Jude that he wanted to pick her up and swing her around in his arms.

"Thank you so much," she said. "You were my knight in shining armor."

He grinned and gestured toward his bomber jacket. "Carpenter in tarnished leather, at best."

Her pretty mouth widened in a smile. "Either way... my hero." Then, still looking playful, happy, appreciative, she rose on her tiptoes and reached up to brush her delicate fingers against his cheek. He had about a second to process what she was about to do before she pressed her soft lips against his.

It was a thank-you kiss, he had no doubt about that.

Sweet. Tender. Simple.

Incredibly good.

It should have been nothing but a three-second brush

of skin on skin, an expression of gratitude between two people who didn't really know each other yet but definitely wanted to.

But damned if Ross was willing to let it go down that way. Once he felt Lucy's mouth, shared her sweet breath, impulse took over. He lifted both hands, cupping one around her cheek. The other he tangled in her long, thick hair, taking pure pleasure in the softness of it, letting it glide through his fingers like water.

He deepened the kiss, sliding his tongue out to tease hers. Lucy groaned slightly, taking what he offered and upping the ante even more by tilting her head and widening her mouth. *Thank you* and *you're welcome* turned into *I-want-you* and *where's the nearest bed* in about ten seconds flat. Sweetness faded and heat erupted as their tongues thrust and twined.

"Ahem."

It took a second for the voice to intrude. But another throat-clearing and a titter finally invaded his Lucy-in-fused consciousness. It appeared they'd arrived at the bottom floor. The door had slid open and they were providing quite a show for the people waiting in the lobby.

Filled with regret, he pulled away, looking down into her pretty, flushed face, seeing the way her long lashes rested on her high cheekbones. She kept her eyes closed a moment longer, swaying a little toward him. But the box pressed against her chest prevented her from melting into his body.

And their sudden, unwelcome audience prevented him from moving the box.

"We're here," he whispered.

Her eyes flew open. Seeing the strangers watching them—two young men with their arms around each other's waists, both grinning widely, and an older, white-haired woman whose grin was, if possible, even wider—Lucy stammered an apology.

"No need to apologize," one of the men said, waving his hand as Lucy and Ross exited the elevator.

The other nodded in agreement. "Tell me this means you ditched 6C."

Lucy's jaw fell open. "Wha…?"

"He's a bad egg," the woman said, jumping into the conversation as if they had all known each other for years. In truth, Ross suspected they were complete strangers to Lucy. "A total fart-weasel."

Ross coughed into his fist at the description, but the two men were already nodding in agreement. "He sure is."

"Have we met?" Lucy asked, shaking her head in confusion, confirming Ross's suspicion.

"No," said the darker-haired man. "But we all live on six, too. And honey, 6C is just *nasty.* So not your type!"

"Thanks," she murmured, looking even more embarrassed than before. Considering complete strangers were dissecting her love life, he could see why.

The light-haired man eyed Ross. "Did you beat him up?"

"No."

Ms. Elderly Busybody sighed heavily. "That's too bad. I've been hoping somebody would. That boy could benefit from an ass-whupping."

"Well, given what I know of him so far, I have no doubt that someday your prayers will be answered," Ross said.

He and Lucy murmured goodbyes to their three new friends, then headed for the door. As they approached him, the doorman offered Lucy a conspiratorial wink, as if he agreed with the other residents' opinion of her ex. Which was nice, but probably had to be making Lucy feel even worse about ever having dated the fart-weasel in 6C.

He reached for her hand and squeezed it. "Don't beat yourself up about it."

She sucked in a surprised breath, and stopped halfway across the lobby. Looking up at him, she appeared shocked that he'd been able to figure out what she'd been thinking.

"He's a con artist, Luce," Ross said with a simple shrug. "He became what you wanted him to be."

"Yes, he did," she murmured. "But how did you know?"

"Guys do it all the time, especially with girls who won't, uh…." He didn't want to be crass enough to say *put out,* though that was what he meant.

"Gotcha," she said. "And thanks for not telling me I was a complete idiot for not seeing it sooner."

"You *did* see it," he told her, not liking that self-recrimination in her voice. "Which is probably why you wouldn't, uh…"

This time, during the pregnant pause while they both mentally filled in the blank, Lucy actually laughed. "You really are a nice guy, aren't you?"

"I have a few ex-girlfriends who would disagree, but my parents like to think so."

"I think I'll have to side with your folks on that one."

"I'll be sure to tell them that," he said with a grin.

She grinned back, then, without another word, slipped her hand into his and turned again toward the exit.

As her soft fingers entwined with his, Ross's heart jolted. He'd kissed her, touched her…but this was a little bit more. It wasn't just a simple touch. That clasped hand was so easy and relaxed, like she already trusted him, as if they'd known each other for weeks rather than hours.

He honestly wasn't sure what was going to happen when they walked out of this building. He'd done what he'd set out to do—escorted her to her ex's place to retrieve her present. But now what? They'd made no other plans. It was the day before Christmas Eve, the streets were a madhouse, he had a million things to do. But as they walked into the bracing December day, alive with the thrum of city life, laughter, and energy, all he could think was that the very last thing he wanted was to say goodbye to her.

5

Now
Chicago, December 23, 2011

THOUGH HE KNEW Stella had the checks for the subcontractors ready, Ross was hoping it would take a while for her to find Lucy's. While there were still people in the building, it would be far too easy for her to slip away. The longer it took, the better the chances were that she wouldn't be able to avoid him on her way out.

Yet somehow, she nearly pulled it off. He didn't even realize she was leaving until he spotted a thick head of dark hair—topped by a merry green, feathered elf cap—getting onto the elevator. "Damn it," he muttered.

"What?"

Seeing the surprised expression on the face of one of his project managers, who'd stopped to chat after Mr. Whitaker departed, Ross mumbled, "I'm sorry, I just remembered something I forgot to take care of."

Like getting Lucy's address, phone number and her promise to get together very soon so they could talk. Exactly what they'd talk about, he didn't know. Six years seemed like a long time for a how've-you-been type of conversation. So maybe they'd skip how've-you-beens in favor of what-happens-now?

Then he remembered that Stella had hired Lucy. She had to know how to get in touch with her. Plus, Lucy had mentioned she lived here, worked here—it shouldn't be hard to find her online.

So, yes, he could be reasonable and mature and patient about this. Could wait until after the holidays, then call her sometime in January to say hello and see if she'd like to meet.

But something—maybe the look in her eyes when she'd said he would know what she'd been up to if he'd called during the past six years—wouldn't let him wait. He couldn't have said it in front of anyone at the party; wasn't sure he'd have found the words even if they'd been left alone. Still, Lucy deserved an explanation from him. Even if she thought it a lame one and decided to keep hating him, he'd feel better if he offered it.

Then he'd get to work on making her not hate him anymore.

"Thanks for the party, Mr. Marshall," his employee said. "The kids really loved it."

"I'm glad. Hey, you and your family have a great holiday," Ross replied, already stepping toward the enclosed stairs that were intended for emergencies.

This was one. The elevator could have made a few stops on the way to the lobby—there were still employees on other floors, closing down for the holiday break. If he hustled, he might beat her to the bottom.

He might not be slinging a hammer and doing hard physical labor ten hours a day anymore, but Ross did keep himself busy in his off hours. So the dash down six flights of stairs didn't really wind him. By the time he burst through the doors into the tiled lobby of the building—surprising Chip, the elderly security guard—the elevator door was just sliding open, and several people exited, some carrying boxes, bags of gifts, plates of food, files to work on at home.

One carried nothing, but wore a silly hat.

Lucy saw him and her mouth dropped. "How did you...?"

"Staircase," he told her. "Were you really going to leave without saying goodbye?"

"Did you really stalk me down six flights of stairs?"

He rolled his eyes. "Stalking? That's a little dramatic."

"You're breathing hard and sweating," she accused him, stepping close and frowning. "Don't even try to tell me you didn't run every step of the way."

He couldn't contain a small grin. "Busted."

"The question is, why?"

"Here's a better one. Why'd you leave without saying goodbye?"

"We said our goodbyes a long time ago," she retorted.

He whistled.

"What?"

"You're still really mad at me."

Those slim shoulders straightened and her chin went up. "That's ridiculous."

Lucy was obviously trying for a withering look, but with that silly hat and the droopy feather hanging by her cheek, she only managed freaking adorable. He couldn't resist lifting a hand and nudging the feather back into place, his fingertips brushing against the soft skin of her cheek.

She flinched as if touched with a hot iron. "Don't."

"Jesus, Lucy, do you hate me?" he whispered, realizing for the first time that this might not be mere bravado. Was it possible that over the past six years, while he'd been feeling miserable even as he congratulated himself on doing the right—the mature—thing, she'd been hating his guts?

"Of course I don't hate you," she said, sounding huffy. As if she was telling the truth, but wasn't exactly happy about that fact.

So she *wanted* to hate him?

"Can we please go sit down somewhere and have a cup of coffee?"

A wistful expression crossed her face, as if she, too, were remembering their first meeting in that New York coffee shop.

"I can't," she murmured. "I need to get to the bank before it closes, and before the snow starts."

"I'll walk with you."

"I'm driving."

"I'll ride with you."

She huffed. "You're still persistent, aren't you?"

"Only when it's important."

"And when did I become important to you?"

The day we met. He didn't say the words, but he suspected she saw them in his face.

"Look, Ross, I swear, I am not holding a grudge," she said. "So you don't have to go out of your way to try to make up with me."

"That's not what I'm doing. I just…I've missed you. A lot."

"How can you miss someone you knew for only a weekend, years ago?"

"Are you telling me you don't feel the same way?"

If she said she didn't, he'd make himself believe her. He'd let her go. Chalk this up to one of those life lessons where a memory of a time you'd considered perfect turned out to be something less than that to the one you'd shared it with.

Lucy didn't respond at first. Not wanting her to breeze over this, to reply without thought, Ross lifted a hand. A few strands of her silky, dark hair had fallen against her face. He slid his fingers through it, sending heat all the way up his arm. Her eyes drifted closed, the long lashes stark against her pale skin. And he'd swear she curled her face into his hand for an instant.

Ross groaned, as helpless to resist her now as he'd been

that first day, in the elevator. Ignoring the surprised stare of the guard, who was the only other person in the lobby, he bent to Lucy and brushed his lips against hers, softly, demanding nothing more than a chance.

She hesitated for the briefest moment, then melted against him. This time there was no crumpled box separating their bodies; he was thrilled to discover she still fit against him as perfectly as ever. Her soft curves welcomed his harder angles, her feet parting a little as she brushed her legs against his and arched into him.

Sweetness flared into desire, just like it had the first time they'd kissed. Ross dropped his hands to her hips and held her close. Sweeping his tongue into her mouth, he dared her to go further. She, of course, took the dare, accepting what he offered and upping the ante by lifting her arms to encircle his neck. Their tongues thrust together, hot and languorous and deep, leaving Ross to wonder how he'd ever even imagined kissing any other woman had been as good as kissing this one. Everything about her was as intoxicating to him as it had been then. Maybe more so— because Lucy was no longer the sweet-faced co-ed. She was now every inch a woman. And he'd had the intense privilege of making her that woman.

Maybe that's what made this kiss different from their first one. Then, there'd been curiosity and wonder, riding on a wave of pure attraction.

Now they knew what they could be to each other. Knew the pleasure they were capable of creating together. Knew what it was like to be naked and hot and joined together as sanity retreated and hunger took over every waking thought. And many sleeping ones.

She lifted her leg slightly, twining it around his, and Ross echoed the tiny groan she made when she arched harder against him. There was no way she couldn't feel his rock-hard erection, any more than he could miss the heat between the thighs that instinctively cradled him.

Six years fell away, along with time, place and any concerns about an audience. There was just this, just the two of them, exploring something that had been missing from their lives for far too long.

Though he felt lost to everything else in the world except Lucy, Ross did finally become aware of a throat-clearing—Chip?—followed by a dinging sound that indicated the arrival of the elevator. A *swoosh* of the door was followed by a dull roar of laughing voices; the last few partiers…i.e., his employers, were about to make their way home.

He and Lucy quickly ended the kiss and stepped apart. "Déjà vu all over again," he muttered. Only this time, they'd been caught on the *outside* of the elevator.

She actually laughed a little, that sweet, warm laugh that was so distinctly hers. Over the past several years, he'd listened for that sound, always expecting to somehow hear it again, even though he'd never really let himself believe he would.

"Hopefully we're not going to hear some old lady say the guy on six is a fart-weasel."

"Hey, my office is on six," he said with a chuckle, pleased to realize Lucy remembered as much about that day as he did.

A group exited the elevator. "Have a happy holiday!" said one of his workers, who walked with his pregnant wife.

Ross nodded at the couple, and at the three others who'd come down with them. "Same to you. Be careful out there—it's supposed to be a bad one."

Murmuring their goodbyes, the group headed for the exit. They were escorted by Chip, who turned a key to operate the intricate, electronic locks that turned this place into a fortress. With the offices closed to the public today, Chip had been kept on his toes playing doorman, letting employees in for the party, and, now that it was over, back out.

Fortunately the guard never complained. Not even about

the fact that he had to work all night, during an impending blizzard, right before Christmas Eve. They might not have state secrets to be stolen, but some of their competitors would risk a lot for the chance to get at prebid documents. With millions of dollars in high-end construction projects at stake, corporate espionage had never been more of a danger. Plus, Elite had invested a hell of a lot of money in computers and equipment. Keeping security on-site 24/7 was one place where Ross had stood firm against his penny-pinching father, who loved to keep a hand in the business even though he was technically retired.

"Wait, I'm leaving, too," Lucy said as Chip began to relock the doors.

"Lucy..."

She held up a hand and brushed past him. "Please, Ross, I really need to go."

Hell, she sounded more determined to leave than she had before he'd kissed her. Not that he regretted it. Not one bit.

Chip glanced toward Ross, as if asking what Ross wanted him to do. He nodded once. He couldn't keep Lucy here against her will. Nothing had changed; he'd taken his shot, and he'd lost.

But just for now.

Definitely. They'd been caught off guard, taken completely by surprise when they'd bumped into one another today. Now, though, he knew Lucy was living in Chicago. There was no longer any geographic reason for him to bow out. Nor was he young enough—angry and resentful enough—to let outside situations and demands make him walk away from her for a second time.

It was as if she'd been delivered back into his life, like the best kind of Christmas gift. The one you never expected, didn't realize you needed, but, when you tore off the paper, suddenly understood that it was exactly what you'd been waiting for.

No, he wasn't about to let her get away again, but he

knew the old saying about picking your battles. Lucy had her guard up, she was uncomfortable here on his turf and hadn't had a moment to evaluate what all this meant to her. So he'd give her a few days to figure things out, then try again. And the next time he asked her to hear him out, he would not take no for an answer.

"Goodbye, Ross," she said, not even turning around to face him. Her voice was soft, low, and he suspected she was trying desperately not to reveal her emotions.

He had to let her go. Had to trust that was the right thing to do in order to get her back.

"Goodbye," he replied. "And Lucy?"

She hesitated, then glanced back at him over her shoulder.

"Merry Christmas."

A brief hesitation, then a tiny smile widened her perfect lips. "Bah humbug."

And then she disappeared out into the gray twilight.

IT USUALLY TOOK twenty minutes to get to the nearest branch of her bank. But today, Lucy was dealing with Friday evening, holiday weekend, impending-blizzard traffic. So she didn't reach the drive-thru until right before they closed at seven.

Thick flecks of white started to appear on the windshield of her Jeep as she waited in the long line of cars. New York got the white stuff by the foot, but here, the Snow Miser seemed to delight in sending wicked, bone-chilling winds along with his icy droppings. The flakes weren't the sweet, delicate ones that gently kissed your bare face. These were big, sloppy and wet, landing like punches, instead.

Once she'd made her deposit, Lucy headed right home. Luckily she had believed the weatherman's warnings and gone shopping yesterday. Having stocked up on chocolate, Diet Coke, and DVDs, she looked forward to a weekend inside, chomping on junk food, watching disaster movies, and shopping online.

Her trip home was difficult, even though the Jeep had 4-wheel drive. Her main concern was seeing through the swirling blanket of white in front of the windshield. Chicago was usually a bright city, even at night; yet this kind of snowstorm didn't reflect the light the way some did. It instead sucked it in, making streetlights hard to see.

It took almost two hours. By the time she arrived at her apartment building, she was not only cold and tired, she was actually jumpy from having been so on-alert.

Once inside her place, she wrenched off her coat and headed for the bathroom. A hot bath sounded like the perfect way to de-stress. She promised herself that, once in that bath, she would not spend one minute thinking about Ross. Or about that kiss.

Why did you have to go and kiss him back?

Probably because she'd been curious, wondering if her memories had been faulty. Could their brief relationship really have been as intense as she'd told herself it was? Had every other man she'd been with really paled in comparison, or was it wishful imaginings of the one that got away?

That kiss had answered all her questions: she hadn't imagined a damn thing.

"Stop thinking about it," she ordered herself as she got into the tub. The hot water stung her skin at first, but she welcomed the sensation, welcomed anything that would take her mind off the man she'd been kissing just a couple of hours ago.

It didn't work. Ross became more prominent in her thoughts. Not just the Ross of today, but the one she'd known before. The guy with whom she'd been so incredibly intimate.

The warmth, the fragrance of the bubble bath, the darkness of the room, lit only with candlelight—all seduced her. The sensation of water hitting every inch of her—between her thighs, caressing the tips of her breasts—made all her nerve endings leap up to attention.

But when it came to really turning her on, her brain did the heavy lifting. It was too easy to remember the magical feel of his hands on her body, the sweet, sexy way he kissed, the groans of pleasure he made when he came.

Her hand slid down, scraping across her slick skin, teasing the puckered tip of one breast. The contact sent warmth spiraling downward, until her sex throbbed. Her eyes closed, her head back, it was easy to think *his* hands were on her, *his* fingers delicately stroking her clit until she began to sigh.

She gave herself over to desire, and let her mind float free. Memories gave way to imagination and her body, starved of physical connection for many months—since she'd left New York—reacted appropriately. Before too long, a slow, warm orgasm slid through her. She sighed a little, quivering and savoring it. But the deliciousness went away far too quickly.

It just couldn't compare to the real thing. To Lucy, getting off had never been the point; it had been sharing the experience that she loved. And she couldn't deny it, even after all these years, after the silence and the regret, she wanted to share that experience with him.

She quickly finished her bath, replaying the day's events as she washed her hair. As she thought everything over, including the way she'd tried to skulk out of the building when his back was turned, something started to nag at the back of her brain. She couldn't put her finger on it at first, just feeling like there was something she had forgotten. Something important.

It wasn't until she was dressed in a comfortable pair of sweats, with her hair wrapped in a towel, that she realized what it was. "Oh, no!" she yelped.

Lucy ran to the living room of her apartment, seeing her purse on the table. Alone. "You *idiot!*"

Because, though she hoped and prayed she'd just forgotten to bring it in from her Jeep, she seriously feared she'd left her most precious possessions at the Elite Construction office: her camera bag and her very expensive specialty lenses.

She perched on a chair, trying to picture every moment. She remembered putting her equipment down on Santa's seat before leaving with Stella. When she'd returned, she'd seen Ross. Desperate to get away without being seen, she'd hurried onto the elevator. Without stopping to grab her camera bag and lens case.

"Damn it," she snapped, trying to decide if this was just bad or catastrophic. She had some big jobs lined up next week. Monday's was with a very wealthy family, who wanted to sit for a holiday portrait at their home. They were the kind of people who could really give her a leg up with the Magnificent Mile set.

Unfortunately Lucy remembered what Stella had said about the Elite office: after tonight, they'd be shutting down until January.

She glanced at the clock—almost ten. Then out the window. The snow still fell steadily, but it appeared the wind had died down some. She could actually see down to the parking lot, could make out cars slowly driving by on the main street, which had been plowed, though the lot itself hadn't been.

If the office was downtown, or as far away as the bank, she probably wouldn't risk it. But it was close, maybe two miles. And the security guard could still be working. There was no guarantee that would be the case on Monday, especially if the whole city was snowed in until then.

Of course, if that happened, her own portrait appointment could be canceled as well. But if it weren't—if the weatherman had overestimated this time, and everything was fine Monday—did she really want to risk not having the equipment she needed to do the job?

Convinced, Lucy raced to her room and changed into jeans and a thick sweater. Adding boots and her warmest coat, she headed outside. The snow on her car was heavy and wet, and every minute she spent clearing it reminded her she was crazy to go chasing after a camera at the start of a blizzard.

Fortunately, as soon as she exited the parking lot and got onto the slushy road, she could tell things were better than when she'd come home an hour ago. The snow was heavier, yes, but she didn't have to crane forward and press her nose against the windshield to see out. It appeared old man winter was giving her a break—a short, wind-free window. She only hoped it didn't slam shut until after she got back home.

The drive that had taken her a few minutes this morning took her fifteen tonight. But when she reached the parking lot for Elite Construction and saw the security vehicle parked there, plus the warm, welcoming lights on the first floor, she was glad she'd taken the chance.

Parking, she hurried to the entrance and pounded on the door. The man inside was so startled, he nearly fell off his stool. He came closer, calling, "We're closed!"

"I know," she said, then pulled her hood back so he could see her face. Hopefully he'd remember her, if for no other reason than that she'd been making out with one of his coworkers a few hours ago. "Remember me? I was here earlier."

He nodded and smiled. Pulling out a large key ring, he unlocked the door, and ushered her in. "Goodness, miss, what are you doing out on a night like this?"

"I wouldn't be if I weren't desperate." She stomped her feet on a large mat. "I need to get upstairs to where the party was held. I forgot something and I have to get it to-night."

"Must be pretty important," he said, his gray eyebrows coming together. "It's not a fit night out for man nor beast."

She chuckled, recognizing the quote from a show she'd loved as a kid. "Do you think you could let me go look for my things?"

"I'll take you up. Gotta make my rounds, anyway."

He escorted her to the bank of elevators, and punched in a number on a keypad by the nearest one. The light above it came on, and the door slid open. Pretty high-tech stuff. Of course, she'd noticed earlier today that the new building had all the latest bells and whistles.

Arriving on the sixth floor, Lucy hurried to the area where the photo booth had been set up. It had been dismantled. Santa's chair was gone, and so were her bag and case. "Oh, hell."

"Some stuff was left in the break room," he told her. "If it's valuable, it's possible somebody locked it up for you."

"Could be. Stella saw me leave my camera and lenses here."

"Let's check her office first, then," he said, leading her down the hallway to the executive suite. He preceded her inside, but before she even had a chance to follow, she heard him exclaim, "Oh, no, watch it, mister!"

Following his stare, she looked out the window to the street below, and saw a car spinning out of control. It skidded off the street, hydroplaning across the parking lot where the Elite Construction security truck was parked. She winced, doubting the driver could regain control.

He didn't.

"Dang it all," said the guard. He cast her a quick look. "Do you mind looking by yourself? I should run down and make sure that driver's all right. If your stuff's not here, check the break room, back down the hall, fourth door on the left."

"Of course," she said, then watched the elderly man hurry away. She quickly scanned the office area. No luck. She wasn't going to go snooping through Stella's desk drawers or file cabinet, even if they weren't locked. Her things wouldn't fit, anyway.

She next spent several minutes searching the break room. It was piled with boxes of decorations, and containers of unopened food. Lucy looked through every bag and box, to be sure nobody had tucked her things in there for safekeeping.

Growing frustrated—and worrying somebody might have picked up the camera and lenses and given themselves an early Christmas present—she opened a free-standing cabinet and at last, struck pay dirt. "Yes!" she exclaimed, spying the familiar bag and case.

So relieved she felt like crying, she scooped them up, hurried toward the elevator and pushed the call button. She waited. And waited. And waited. Nothing.

Apparently the guard needed to again enter the code on the keypad so she could get down. Wondering if he could still be outside after all this time, she went to the front window and looked down toward the parking lot.

What she saw surprised her. An ambulance, its lights flashing, was parked beside the two vehicles involved in the fender-bender. She hadn't realized the crash had been so serious, but apparently the driver had been hurt. They were putting him on a gurney and wheeling him over to the ambulance.

Suddenly that gurney was pushed under a streetlight, and she had a better view of the person on it. Even through the snow and the darkness she could make out the grizzled gray hair, not to mention the uniform.

It wasn't the driver of the other car. It was the guard.

"Oh, God!" she muttered, wondering what had happened.

He'd gone out to help the accident victim—had he slipped and fallen? Or, maybe he'd been trying to help dig the vehicle out of a snowbank. Considering his age, and knowing even the healthiest of men could be affected when they tried to shovel too-heavy snow, she prayed he hadn't had a heart attack.

Then she began to wonder something else.

What if she was trapped in this building?

Her heart started thudding as she replayed everything in her mind. The conscientious way the man had carefully locked the door this afternoon, even though people were still leaving. And the way he'd obviously kept the elevator turned off tonight, despite knowing she was up here.

Would he really... "No," she muttered, certain he wouldn't have locked her in when he went to help the other driver.

There was only one way to be sure. Remembering how Ross had beat her to the lobby today, she found a door marked Stairs and headed through it. Six flights down was not fun, but it was better than sitting in somebody's office all night.

Reaching the entrance, she held her breath and pushed the nearest door. It didn't budge. Neither did the one beside it, or the next. She really was locked in here.

"Every building has an emergency exit," she reminded herself. She just had to find it. How difficult could that be?

Not difficult at all.

At least, she didn't think so...until the power went out.

6

As THEY WALKED the busy streets of the city, Ross glanced at his watch and saw it was almost four o'clock. He began to do some mental calculations. What time did the shipping place close? How many people were lined up there already? How long would it take to get back to his place and pick up the wrapped presents?

Eventually he just started to wonder how much money he had in his checking account. He needZed to know that, since he suspected he wasn't going to make it to the mailing store today to send off gifts to his family. He had lost track of time with Lucy; plus, he hadn't even picked up something for his nephew yet. So it looked like he'd be paying a king's ransom to send it tomorrow and arrange for a Christmas Day delivery. If there was such a thing.

For some reason, though, that didn't bother him as much as he'd have expected. It seemed worth the price since it had let him spend more time with Lucy Fleming. After the unpleasant scene with her ex, followed by that amazing kiss in the elevator, he hadn't been about to say *nice meeting you* and walk away. Errands could wait. Plus, if worse came to worst, he could always send the family e-gift cards tomorrow. Having twenty-five bucks to spend at Amazon would make even his bratty youngest sister squeal; she was really into those teen romance books.

With a fallback plan in place, he let himself forget about everything else—missing the holidays with his family for the first time in his life. The job he was starting next week. The tense phone call he'd had with his father last week. It was sure to be repeated on Christmas Day, when talk would shift from turkey and Mom's great stuffing to the same-old question: *When are you going to give up that vagabond lifestyle and come back home to work for the company where you belong?*

Gee. He could hardly wait. *Not.*

So an afternoon spent with a beautiful young woman whose gold-tinted brown eyes actually sparkled as she looked in delight at the softly falling snow sounded like a great idea to him. The best one he'd had in ages—the last being when, after graduating from Illinois State, he'd decided to come to New York for a while rather than going home to work for Elite Construction. He didn't regret that decision. Especially today. Today, he was very happy to be right where he was.

"Do you want me to carry that?" he asked as they snaked up the street, weaving around street vendors and harried shoppers.

Lucy glanced down at the rumpled box containing her broken gift from her brother. She was still clutching it against her chest. Every once in a while, a distinctive tinkle of broken glass came from within. Each one made her wince.

His hands reflexively curled every time he saw her pain. He so should've laid-out her jerk of an ex. "Are you okay?" he asked, stopping in the middle of a sidewalk, earning glares from a dozen people who streamed past them.

She nodded. "I'm fine, really. Thanks for the offer, but I'd rather hold onto this for a while."

She'd probably like to find a quiet place where she could open her gift, but that wasn't going to happen here.

Taking her arm as they were nearly barreled into by a power broker yammering into his cell phone, he led her down Broadway. Manhattan at Christmastime was a world of mad colors, sounds, and crowds, and this area felt like the pulsing center of everything. It might not have all the high-end shop windows up on Park or Fifth, with their fancy displays that dripped jewels and overpriced designer clothes. But it had a million little electronics stores with huge Sale signs in their windows, kitschy tourist shops, street performers, barkers, camera crews and vendors selling everything from scarves to hot dogs.

It also had so much life. Walking one block up Broadway brought words from a half-dozen languages to his ears. While the city often got a bad rap for being unfriendly, Ross had never heard so many Merry Christmases. Even Lucy, who'd sworn she was a Scrooge about the holidays, seemed caught up in it.

"This is the worst place in the world to be today, you do realize that, right?" she said, laughing as they wove through a crowd of Japanese tourists loaded for bear with shopping bags.

They'd just headed down into a subway station, Ross having suddenly realized exactly where he wanted to go. "Nah. Maybe the second worst. Just wait till we get to our destination—that's number one."

"Uh-oh. Dare I ask?"

Grinning, he remained silent as they crammed into the subway car. Despite her pleas for clues, he didn't say anything, not until they were actually across the street from the store he most wanted to visit. Then he pointed. "We're here."

Her jaw unhinged. "You've got to be kidding! You seriously want to go into the biggest toy store in the universe *today?*"

"Come on, it'll be fun."

She took a step back. "It'll be insane. There will be a gazillion kids in there."

"Nah. Just their frenzied parents."

"Who are worse than the kids!"

"You'll like this, I promise. Come on, Miss Cranky Ass."

She gaped.

"Look, I need to get a present for my nephew. I know he'd love this walking, roaring dinosaur toy I've seen commercials for. My sister told me he's spent the last month with his arms hidden inside his shirt, waving his little hands and roaring at all his preschool classmates."

"Velociraptor?"

"Yup."

"Okay, at least he's got good taste in dinosaurs. They're my favorite, too."

"I always preferred the T-rex, myself."

"Not bad," she said with a shrug. "So I guess that means we're a couple of carnivores."

He nodded, liking the banter, especially liking that the bad mood her ex had caused appeared to have completely disappeared. "I guess so. Though, I don't suspect it would take a whole pack of you to bring me to my knees." No, he suspected Lucy would be quite capable of that all on her own.

He didn't elaborate, letting her figure out what he meant. When she lowered her lashes and looked away, he figured she had.

What could he say? He was affected by her, had been at first sight. The feelings had grown every minute they'd spent together. Not that she was probably ready to hear that from a guy she'd met a few hours ago. Nor, honestly, was he ready to say it. Knowing she was amazing, fantastic—and that he wanted her, badly—was one thing. Admitting it this soon was another.

So he went back to safer ground. "Anyway, that store's probably the only place I'm going to find the dino-toy I'm looking for today. It walks, it roars, he'll love it!"

"Preschool-age appropriate?" she asked, sounding dubious.

"Hell, no." He grinned. "But that's for his parents to deal with. I'm just the cool uncle who buys it."

Considering the present might be late, he wanted to make it a good one. No internet gift card could ever satisfy a four-year-old, and since Ross was the boy's godfather, and his only uncle, he had to do right by him.

"So, what do you say?"

"I dunno…"

"We're talking about going into FAO Schwarz, not Mount Doom and the fires of Mordor."

She rolled her eyes. "At least there are no screaming little ones on Mount Doom, unless you count the Hobbits."

He liked that she got the reference. He wasn't a total geek but couldn't deny being a LOTR fan. "None in there, either. They're all home being extra-good, hoping Santa will notice."

"How about I wait outside?" she offered, looking horrified by the idea of going in, but also a bit saddened by it.

Lucy was obviously serious about that not-liking-Christmas thing. Though, he wondered if it was the holiday she didn't like, or the memories that were attached to it. Given the few things she'd said about her parents, and the happy childhood she'd had before she'd lost them, he suspected that might be it.

Well, bad memories never truly went away, but they could certainly be smacked into the background by good ones.

"Your call," he replied, tsking. "But remember, you don't have to shop. Don't you think you'd have fun watching the crazed parents fighting over the last Suzy Pees Herself doll, or the My Kid Ain't Gonna Be Gay Monster Truck playset?"

Lucy laughed out loud, as he'd hoped she would. "When you put it that way, how could I possibly refuse?"

"You can't. Anyone with an ounce of schadenfreude in their soul—which I suspect you have, at least when it comes to Christmas and oddly-penised exes—would race me to the door."

Mischief danced on her face and a dimple appeared in her cheek as she offered a self-deprecating grin. She didn't deny it. That was something else he liked about her. Most other women he knew kept up that I-love-puppies-and-kitties-and-everyone front, at least at the beginning of a relationship. Lucy hadn't bothered. Hell, she freely admitted she hated Christmas, and had been fantasizing about cutting off a guy's dick when they'd met. Talk about not putting on some kind of nice-girl act. Was it any wonder he already liked her so much?

"Okay, Mount Doom, here we come," she said, taking his hand.

It was cold out—very cold—yet neither of them wore gloves. His were tucked in his pocket, and he knew she had some, too, since she'd worn them when they'd first left the coffee shop. But neither of them had put them on once they'd left her ex's place…once she'd taken his hand. Her fingers were icy cold, and he suspected his were too. But it was worth it.

Slowly making their way through the crowds outside, they ventured into the hell that was called a toy store the day before Christmas Eve. The moment they entered, they were assaulted with heat and noise and color. Any kid would have thought they'd entered wonderland—the whole place was set up to inspire thoughts of childhood fantasy. Well, if your fantasy included being pressed jaw-to-jaw with strangers. Oh, and getting into the spirit of the season by elbowing each other to get closer to the front of the long lines at the cashier stations.

"You've got to be kidding me!" she said when she realized it was worse than she'd predicted. Not a square foot of floor space seemed to be unoccupied. The merriment from outside hadn't worked its way in here. These people were shopping like they were on a mission: *Nobody gets between me and my Bratz dolls.*

"I think we've just entered shark-infested waters," she said, raising her voice to be heard over the loud music and the general thrum of too many people packed in too small a space.

"Stick close to me, minnow."

"Gotcha, big white. But please tell me this dinosaur you're looking for isn't the hottest toy of the season."

"Nah, that's the Suzy Pees Herself *and* Drives a Monster Truck doll."

"My kind of girl. Uh, other than the peeing herself part."

"Whew!"

Finally, after one too many stomps on her foot, Lucy reminded him she wasn't the one shopping. She ducked into a corner and waved him off. Every time he caught sight of her, watching the hysteria that surrounded her, he noted the expression on her face—amusement, yes. But also, he suspected, relief that she didn't have to actually be a part of this.

Maybe one day she'd want to. One day when she didn't have just her brother, and a single broken gift to look forward to for the upcoming holiday weekend.

And me.

Ross was reaching around a glowering man—who was arguing with a sharp-tongued woman over what was apparently the last Barbie doll in Manhattan—when that realization struck him. He was here, alone, with plans to do nothing more than eat Chinese food and watch *National*

Lampoon's Christmas Vacation this weekend. And Lucy was going to be here alone, too.

His mind didn't go where it might have gone a year or two ago, when he'd been more focused on what happened at the end of a date with a girl than during it. He didn't immediately picture the two of them naked under the mistletoe.

Well, it wasn't the *only* thing he pictured when he thought about spending Christmas with her. But mainly, he thought about seeing her smile, hearing her laugh, touching her soft skin and that amazing hair. Even if they spent the weekend pretending Christmas didn't exist, he really wanted to spend it with her.

After some hunting, Ross found the Robo-Raptor toy he'd been seeking. The thing was expensive, but, considering it would likely be late, he wasn't going to quibble over the cost.

Grabbing it, he made his way back to Lucy, finding her not too far from where he'd left her. She stood by herself, having found another quiet corner, and was gazing at a display in the games area. A huge Candyland display, with nearly life-size gingerbread men game pieces and tons of pink fluff that looked like cotton candy.

Lucy's expression was definitely wistful. As he watched from several feet away, she reached out and touched a large fairy-type doll—he couldn't remember the name, it had been a long time since his board game days. Her hand shook slightly, but the touch on the pale blue hair was tender. Sweet. As if she were reaching out and stroking the gossamer wings of a beautiful memory that flitted in her subconscious. Having noticed the hint of moisture in her eyes, he suspected she was.

As he approached, he noticed her reach up and swipe at her face with her fingertips, confirming that moisture had begun to drip. Ross dropped a hand on her shoulder. "You okay?"

She nodded. Her voice low, she explained, "This is so pretty. I loved this game as a kid."

"I was more of a Chutes and Ladders fan, myself."

She barely smiled, and he regretted making light of it when something was on her mind.

As if knowing he was curious, she admitted, "I used to beg my mother to play with me all the time. She ran the business with my Dad, and had more time at home than a lot of moms, so I assumed that meant she was mine 24/7."

"I think every kid feels that about their mom."

"Well, I was pretty relentless, and eventually we had to start negotiating. 'Just let me finish this paperwork, and I promise we'll play *one* game of Candyland.'"

"Kinda like how my parents negotiated with me—eat one more green bean and you can have ice cream after dinner."

She nodded. "Exactly. I outgrew the game, of course, but one day when I was older, it occurred to me that every time we had played, I would *always* get the Queen Frostine card within the first couple of hands. So I always won."

He glanced at the board on display, seeing how close that particular character was to the winning space, and smiled slightly. "Quickly."

She laughed. "Exactly. I was a world champion Candylander. My mom was a world champion cheater for fixing the deck so I'd get that card and win the game super-fast every time."

"Did you confront her about it?"

"Uh-huh. When I was eleven or twelve." Her laughter deepened. "She totally confessed, saying she'd never break a promise to me, and always played when she said she would. But that didn't mean she couldn't speed up the process a little."

Her eyes, which had been sparkling with tears a few minutes ago, now gleamed with amusement. The warmth of the good memory had washed away, at least temporarily, whatever sadness she'd been feeling.

"I miss her a lot," she admitted simply. "My dad, too. It'll be five years Tuesday."

He sucked in a surprised breath. She'd lost both parents, together, which could only mean some kind of tragedy. And just two days after Christmas... No wonder she'd just rather skip over the whole holiday season. Talk about mixing up happy thoughts with sad ones. "I'm so sorry, Lucy."

"Me, too." She glanced around the crowded store. "I guess you've figured out that's why I'm not a big fan of the season."

"Yeah."

"That's why my brother and I have unconventional holidays."

But this year, she'd already told him, she wouldn't be seeing her brother. And her roommate was going away. She would be entirely alone, surrounded by a merry world while she sunk deeper into memories of the past.

Not if he could help it. She wanted unconventional? Fine. One good way to start—how about Christmas with a near-stranger?

He lifted a hand to her face and brushed his fingertips across her cheek. "Well then, how about we make a deal? I promise not to sing any carols or serve you any eggnog... if you promise to spend this holiday weekend with me."

A FEW HOURS later, after having shopped a little more and laughed a lot more, they grabbed some dinner, then headed back toward Lucy's place. The tiny apartment she shared with Kate wasn't too far away from Beans & Books, where Ross had left his truck. She told herself he was just escorting her home and would then leave. But in the back of her mind, she couldn't help wondering just how *much* of the weekend he'd meant when he talked about them spending this holiday together.

And how much she wanted him to mean.

It was crazy, considering she'd dated Jude for three months and had barely let him onto second base, with one unsatisfying attempt to steal third. But she already knew she wanted Ross to hit the grand slam. What she felt when she was with him—savoring the warmth of his hand in hers, quivering when his arm accidentally brushed against her body, thrilling to the sound of his voice—was undiluted want. She'd heard it described, but now, for the first time, she *felt* it.

She knew she should slow it down. But something—not just the instant physical attraction, but also his warm sense of humor, his generosity, the sexy laugh—made him someone she didn't want to let get away. So, when they got back to her building, she intended to invite him up for a drink. And then see what happened. Or make something happen.

She and Kate shared a small efficiency, whose rent was probably as much as a mortgage payment for places outside the city. Right now, the apartment was empty. Kate had left for the holidays—she'd called two hours ago, right before Teddy was picking her up. So the place was all Lucy's for the weekend.

Hmm. Was it possible she was within hours of getting *it* at last? She didn't mean getting laid, she meant finally understanding. Finally grasping what it was like to be so overcome by pleasure that you lost track of the rest of the world.

Her steps quickened. She was so anxious to get home, to start finding out if the weekend included nights or only daytime hours, she didn't notice when Ross stopped walking. She finally realized it and looked over her shoulder, seeing him a half-dozen steps back. He stood in the middle of a crowded Sixth Avenue sidewalk, and was gazing up toward the sky.

No. Not the sky. Those twinkling lights weren't stars. Instead, thousands of tiny bulbs set the night aglow, their gleam picked up by a sea of sparkling ornaments gently held in the arms of an enormous evergreen.

"Can you believe this is the first time I've seen it?" Ross asked, staring raptly at the Rockefeller Center Christmas tree.

"Seriously?"

He nodded. "It's my first Christmas in the Big Apple, and I haven't happened to be over this way for the past few weeks."

Lucy might be Ebenezer's long-lost twin sister, but she couldn't be a scrooge when it came to seeing Ross with that delighted expression on his face. He looked like a kid. A big, muscular, incredibly handsome, sexy-as-sin kid.

She returned to his side, looking up at the tree. It was beautiful against the night sky, ablaze with light and color. Even her hardened-to-Christmas heart softened at the sight.

Saying nothing, Ross led her toward an empty bench ahead. It was night and the crowds had thinned to near-reasonable levels.

She sat beside him on the bench, giving him time to stare at the decor. But to her surprise, he instead looked at her. "Since this is probably as close to a tree as you're going to get this year, do you want to open your present now?"

She glanced at the tattered box, which she'd lugged around all day. She could wait and open it when she got home, but somehow, this moment seemed right. "I already know what it is."

"Really?"

"Well, not specifically." She began plucking the still-damp packaging paper from the box. "Sam and I have this tradition."

"I suspect it's a nontraditional one."

"You could say that." She actually smiled as she tore off the last of the paper and lifted the lid. Jude might have broken her gift, but it was the joy of seeing what Sam had found that delighted her. No broken glass could take that away from her.

"Oh, my God," Ross said, staring into the mound of tissue paper inside the box. "That is…is…"

"It's the ugliest thing I've ever seen," Lucy said. She lifted her hand to her mouth, giggling. Jude's petty destruction hadn't done much to make this thing less appealing, because it had already been pretty damned hideous. "Isn't it perfect?"

His jaw dropped open and he stared at her. "Seriously?"

"Oh, yeah," she said with a nod. Then she lifted the broken snow globe, now missing glass, water and snow, and eyed the pièce de résistance that had once been the center of it. Sitting on a throne was the ugliest Santa Claus in existence. His eyes were wide and spacey, his face misshapen, his coloring off. His supposedly red suit was more 1970's disco-era orange, and was trimmed with tiny peace signs. Beside him stood two terrifyingly emaciated, grayish children who looked like they'd risen from their graves and were about to zombiefy old St. Nick.

Hideous. Awful.

She loved it.

"Oh, this is so much better than what I got him—a dumb outhouse Santa complete with gassy sound effects."

"Do you always give each other terrible presents?"

"Just for Christmas. He gives me snow globes, I give him some obnoxious Santa, often one that makes obscene noises."

He chuckled. "My sisters would kill me if I did that."

"It started as a joke—a distraction so we wouldn't have to think too much about the way it used to be. And it stuck."

She couldn't be more pleased with her gift—unless, of course, it weren't broken. But she wouldn't let Sam know about that part. The center scene was the key.

Smiling, Lucy tucked the base of the globe back in the

box, trying to avoid any bits of glass. But when she felt a sharp stab on her index finger, she knew she hadn't been successful. "Ow," she muttered, popping her fingertip into her mouth.

"Let me see," he ordered.

She let him take her hand, seeing a bright drop of red blood oozing on her skin.

"We should go get something to clean this."

"It's okay, we're not too far from my place…as long as you're ready to leave?"

He rose, reaching for the now-open box, and extending his other hand to her. She gave him her noninjured one, and once she was standing beside him, he dropped an arm across her shoulders. Ross took one last look at the famous tree. Then, without a word, he turned to face her.

"I know this is cheesy and right out of a holiday movie," he said, "but I'm going to do it anyway."

She wasn't sure what the *it* was, but suddenly understood when he bent to kiss her. People continued to walk all around them, street musicians played in the background, skaters called from the icy rink below. But all that seemed to disappear as Lucy opened her mouth to him, tasting his tongue in slow, lazy thrusts that soon deepened. It got hotter, hungrier. Both of them seemed to have lost any hint of the restraint that had kept them from getting this intense during their previous kiss.

Ross dropped his arm until his hand brushed her hip, his fingertips resting right above her rear, and Lucy quivered, wanting more. A whole lot more.

"Get a room!" someone yelled.

The jeer and accompanying laughter intruded on the moment. Sighing against each other's lips, they slowly drew apart.

"Thank you," he said after a long moment, during

which he kept his hand on her hip. "I can check that off my bucket list."

"Kissing in front of the Rockefeller Center Christmas tree?"

"No. Kissing *you* in front of the Rockefeller Center Christmas tree."

She couldn't keep the smile off her face as they began walking the several blocks to her apartment building. Ross carried not only the bag with his robotic dinosaur, but also her snow globe. He had insisted on wrapping a crumpled napkin around her fingertip, but she didn't even feel the sting of the cut anymore. Because the closer they got to home, the more she wondered what was going to happen when they arrived. That kiss had been so good, but also frustrating since she wanted more.

Much more.

Unfortunately once they reached her building, and she looked up and saw what looked like every light in her apartment blazing, she realized she wasn't going to get it. Damn. "I guess Kate didn't leave, after all," she said, wondering why her friend had stuck around. It was nearly 10:00 p.m.; Kate and Teddy were supposed to get on the road hours ago.

"Your roommate's still here?"

"Sure looks like it. No way would she leave all the lights on—she's a total nag about our electric bill."

Ross nodded, though he averted his gaze. She wondered if it was so he could disguise his own disappointment.

It wasn't that she hadn't had dates up to her place before; Jude had been over numerous times. It was just, she'd wanted to be alone with Ross. *Really* alone. And there was no privacy to be had in her apartment. She slept in one corner on a Murphy bed, with just a clothesline curtain for a wall, and Kate used the daybed that doubled as a couch the rest of the time.

Being with him in a confined space, under the amused, knowing eyes of her roommate, would be beyond torturous.

He seemed to agree. "What time should I come tomorrow?"

She raised a brow.

"You promised me the holiday weekend, remember?"

"You really meant that?"

He lifted both hands and cupped her face, tilting it up so she met his stare. "I absolutely meant that."

Then he bent down and kissed her again. He kept this one light, sweet, soft. Still, Lucy moaned with pleasure, turning her head, reaching up to tangle her fingers in his hair. Once again, the damned box was between them, and now, a dinosaur was, too. But maybe that was for the best. Kissing him—feeling the warm stroke of his tongue in her mouth—was too exciting. If his hot, hard body were pressed against her, she'd be tempted to drag him up the stairs and see just how much privacy a clothesline curtain offered.

Ross ended the kiss and stepped back. "Good night, Lucy Fleming. I'm really glad I met you."

"Ditto," she whispered.

"See you tomorrow."

"Tomorrow."

Then, knowing she needed to get away now, while she had a brain cell in her head, she edged up the outside steps. She offered him one last smile before jabbing her finger on the keypad to unlock the exterior door, then slipped inside.

Her heart light as she almost skipped up the stairs, she felt like whistling a holiday tune. For the first time in several years, Lucy was actually looking forward to Christmas Eve. Because she had someone so special to share it with.

As she opened the apartment door, she looked around the tiny space for her roommate. "I thought you'd be long gone by now," she called.

Kate didn't respond. Lucy walked across the living room

to the galley kitchen, peering around the corner, seeing no one. Then she noticed the thin curtain that shielded her bed from the rest of the apartment shimmy. *Strange.* "Katie?"

The curtain moved again, this time fully drawning back. Lucy's mouth fell open as she saw not her pretty roommate but someone she'd truly hoped to never see again. "Jude?"

"Where have you been? I've been waiting for hours."

"What do you think you're doing here? How did you get in?"

"Had a key made a couple of weeks ago." He smiled thinly, stepping closer, a slight wobble in his steps. *Drunk.* "It's my birthday. You never gave me my present. I've been waiting for it a long time and expected to get it tonight."

He stepped again. This time, Lucy saw a gleam in his eye that she didn't like. Jude suddenly didn't look like a drunk boy. More like a determined, vengeful man. One who might like her to think he was a little more intoxicated than he truly was.

She edged backward.

"Where you going? C'mon, you're not *really* mad, are you? You know I don't care anything about that skank. I was just frustrated, waiting for you. Guys have needs, you know." He stepped again, moving slightly sideways, and she suddenly realized he was trying to edge between her and the door.

This was serious. Kate was gone, her next door neighbor was practically deaf and few people were out on the street in this area this late. And Jude knew all of those things.

"I still can't believe you got some dude to come with you to my apartment," he said, his eyes narrowing and his mouth twisting. "That was wrong, to bring some stranger into this."

Ross. Oh, God, did she wish she'd invited him up!

Lucy's thoughts churned and she went over her options, none of which included intervention by a knight in shining armor, *or* a carpenter in brown leather. Her brother had drilled college rape statistics into her head before she'd ever left home. He'd also taught her a few defensive moves. But better than trying to physically fight Jude would be to get him to leave.

She began thinking, mentally assessing everything in the apartment, knowing the knives in the kitchen were none too sharp. He now stood between her and the door. Her cell phone was in her purse and they didn't have a land line— not that anybody she called, including the police, would get here for a good ten or fifteen minutes. In that time, he could do a lot. And, she suspected, that's exactly what he intended to do.

"What's the matter?" he asked, a sly smile widening that petulant mouth. "Don't you want to give me something for my birthday? After making me wait all this time, you owe me."

"I don't owe you anything," she snapped, curling her hands into fists, deciding to go for the Adam's apple.

"Yeah, bitch, you do," he snarled, the mask coming off, the pretense cast aside. Any hint of the sloppy drunk disappeared as he rushed her, the rage in his expression telling her he was fully aware and cognizant of what he was doing.

But so was Lucy. She sidestepped him, kicking at his kneecaps with the thick heels of her hard leather boots. He stumbled, fell against the daybed and knocked over a lamp.

Not wasting a second, she headed for the door, hearing his roar of rage as he lunged after her. His fingers tangled in her hair and she was jerked backward. Ignoring the pain, she spun around and slashed at his face with her nails.

"Little cock-tease," he yelled.

Then there was another roar of rage. Only this one didn't come from Jude. It came from behind her, from the door to the apartment, which she'd neglected to lock when she came in.

Ross. He was here. Against all odds, for who knew what reason, he'd come up and gotten here just in time.

Stunned, Lucy watched as he thundered past her, tackling Jude around the waist and taking him down. A handful of her hair went with them, but she was so relieved, she barely noticed.

"You slimy sack of shit!"

The two guys rolled across the floor, knocking over furniture. Jude squirmed away and tried to stagger to his feet. Ross leaped up faster, his fists curled, and let one fly at Jude's face. There was a satisfying crunching sound, then blood spurted from that perfect, surgically enhanced nose.

Jude staggered back. "Dude, you broke my nose!"

Ross ignored him, striking again, this time landing a powerful fist on her would-be rapist's stomach. Jude doubled over, then collapsed onto the day bed, wailing.

Ross gave him a disgusted sneer before turning his attention to Lucy. "Are you all right? Did he…"

"No, I'm okay," she said, shaking as it sunk in just how bad this could have been. "Thank you."

"I was a block away, when I realized I was still holding your present from your brother." He gestured toward the floor, where the package lay. "I heard yelling from outside. Fortunately I remembered the numbers you hit on the keypad."

Thank God.

"I'm gonna have you arrested for assault!" Jude raged as he staggered back to his feet.

"Okay, sure. We'll share the back of the police car as you're hauled in for attempted rape," Ross replied, fury sparking off him as he took a threatening step toward Jude.

The other man dropped his shaking hand, eyeing Lucy, his mouth quivering. "Wait, I didn't mean…I wouldn't have…"

"Yes, you would have," she replied, knowing it was true. "And I am pressing charges."

"Don't—my parents…I could lose my internship! I'm sorry, I guess I just went a little crazy."

She didn't feel any sympathy for him. But she was worried about Ross. He was a carpenter, a flat-broke out-of-towner, and Jude was the only son of a rich corporate shark. Lucy only had her word to convince anyone that Jude had attacked her.

Well, that and a probable bald spot.

She needed to think about this. "Just go," she said, suddenly feeling overwhelmed.

"Thank you!"

"I'm not promising you *anything*. At the very least, I'm reporting you to campus security and to the dean's office."

Jude's bottom lip pushed out in an angry pout. But Ross cut him off before he could say a word. "Get the fuck out, before I hurt you some more."

Shutting his mouth, Jude beelined for the door, giving Ross a wide berth, as if not trusting him not to lash out. Probably a good call, considering Ross was visibly shaking with anger.

Just before he left, Jude cast Lucy one more pleading glance. She ignored him, focused only on Ross. Her knight in shining armor, whether he saw it that way or not.

Lucy had never been the kind of girl who wanted to be rescued. Nor had she ever thought she'd need to be. But tonight, that Galahad riding in on the proverbial white horse thing had come in incredibly handy.

Once they were alone, Ross strode to the door, flipping the lock. When he returned, he didn't hesitate, walking right to her with open arms. Lucy melted against his hard body, letting go of the anxiety of the past ten minutes and just holding on, soaking up his warmth and his concern. He kept stroking her, running his fingers through her hair, tenderly rubbing tiny circles on the small of her back. Murmuring soft words into her ear.

It was, quite honestly, the most protected and cherished she'd felt in years.

"It's okay, Luce, he's gone. He's gone."

Finally, after several long moments, he pulled back a few inches and looked down at her. "You shouldn't stay here alone."

No, she probably shouldn't. "He said he made a key..."

"You're *definitely* not staying then." He mumbled a curse and stiffened, and she knew he was mad at himself for not getting the key back before Jude had left.

"I guess I could go to a hotel..."

"Screw that," he muttered, looking at her with an incredulous expression, as if she'd said something absolutely ridiculous. "Pack a bag, you're coming home with me."

7

ROSS WAS AT his parents' house outside of the city when the call came in about Chip being taken to the hospital. The caller told him the elderly man had gone outside to deal with an accident, and the exertion of helping to push a car out of the snow had apparently caused a heart attack.

The police officer who called didn't have any more information, but that was enough to send Ross back into town. He didn't have the phone numbers of the other guards with him, nor could he be sure they'd be able to go in to the office. He had no idea whether Chip had even locked the main doors when he'd gone out to help the driver, so somebody had to get in there. And the buck always stopped at the boss's desk.

The drive would be bad, and he already knew he'd have to spend the night at the office. Fortunately Stella had made up the fold-out sofa in his office. Besides, while everyone was disappointed—especially his older sister, who'd just arrived with her family for the holidays—he couldn't deny he wouldn't mind getting away from all the holiday cheer. He hadn't been able to take his mind off Lucy, and the longer he stayed, the more likely it was somebody would notice. He just didn't feel like explaining his mood to a nosy sibling or parent.

It was nearly 2:00 a.m. by the time he arrived—the trip had taken three exhausting, stress-filled hours. The plows were barely managing to keep up with the thick snow—he'd earned a few scolding stares from their drivers as he followed them down newly plowed stretches of highway.

The private parking lot wasn't plowed, of course, and he was glad he drove a monster SUV that could clear the already foot-high drift. Parking, he bundled up, then stepped outside, his body immediately battered by the wild wind. It howled eerily in the night and the snow seemed to be moving in all directions—up, down, sideways. Not that he could see much of it in front of his face, and he suddenly realized why.

There were no lights on. Not anywhere.

Blackout. Wonderful.

Fortunately the building was well-insulated and plenty warm. He had a couple of extra blankets for the fold-out; he'd be fine overnight, and hopefully the power would be back on in the morning.

Hunching against the wind that tried to knock him back with every step, he made his way through the wet snow to the entrance, finding the doors locked. He had a master key, and used it to get in. Emergency reflective lights cast a little illumination in the lobby, and he cautiously made his way to the security desk, knowing a few industrial-strength flashlights were stored back there. Grabbing one, he headed for the stairs, trudging back up six flights, mere hours after he'd raced down them. Going up definitely took longer.

By the time he got to his floor, he was ready for sleep. It looked like he might be snowed in for a couple of days, so he'd have plenty of time to work. Right now, he was weary—physically and emotionally—and just wanted to call it a night.

Once inside his office, in familiar territory, he turned off the flashlight. Hopefully the power would be on tomorrow, but if not, he wanted to conserve the battery. Stretching, he stripped off his wet coat and kicked off his shoes, then walked across the office to the small, private sitting area.

Ross moved cautiously; it was even darker in this corner, since there were no windows. He still managed to bump into the edge of the fold-out, and muttered a curse. Then, glad the day was over, and that it couldn't get any crazier, he lifted the covers and climbed into the bed.

A noise split the silence. A low sigh.

What the hell?

The sound surprised him into utter wakefulness. Carefully reaching out, he patted the other side of the bed… and felt a body under the covers.

"Ross?" asked a soft, sleep-filled woman's voice.

A familiar woman's voice.

"Lucy?" he whispered, shocked.

Could it really be her? He knew that voice, and could now smell the sweet cinnamon-tinged scent she always wore.

She mumbled something and shifted, scooting closer as if drawn to his warmth. His eyes had adjusted a little, and he was able to make out her beautiful face. The creamy skin, the strand of dark hair lying across her cheek, the perfect mouth drawn into a tiny frown.

And she'd said his name in her sleep.

His heart pounded as he realized it was real. Lucy Fleming was asleep in his bed, in his office, in a building that was supposed to be deserted. It made absolutely no sense, was probably the last thing he'd ever have expected to happen. Considering how determined she'd been to get away without even talking to him earlier, climbing into this bed and finding the real live Santa Claus seemed more likely.

He frantically thought of the scenarios that might have landed her here. She had to have come back sometime after the building closed—when he'd left at seven-thirty, everybody had been gone except the guard. Why she'd returned, he had no idea. Maybe she'd forgotten something? Whatever the reason, Chip had to have let her in, probably recognizing her from this afternoon.

Beyond that…what? Had she offered to stay in the building when he was taken away by ambulance? That sounded incredibly far-fetched, and the officer who'd called hadn't mentioned it.

The doors. Shit. When the locking mechanism was engaged, they couldn't be opened, even from the inside, without a key. If Chip had gone out to help the motorist, he must have locked up behind him.

"You got locked in," he murmured, suddenly understanding.

And she had no way to call for help. The building was notorious for its poor cell phone reception even in the best weather, and the phone system fed off the power, so regular phones wouldn't have worked. The internet would be out, of course, plus all the computers in the building were password protected.

He could almost picture Lucy banging on the doors, trying to get someone's attention. But with the dark night, the swirling snow and the lack of people venturing out, it must have seemed like a hopeless proposition. She'd have known she was stuck here until at least morning.

So, like Goldilocks, she'd found a bed and crawled into it.

He was glad he hadn't followed his first instinct, leaped to his feet and bellowed, "Who's that sleeping in my bed?"

Lucy Fleming is who's sleeping in my bed.

A smile tugged at his mouth. What were the odds? Six years ago tonight she'd slept in his bed, too.

Remembering everything about that night—seeing the parallels—he had to laugh softly. If he were a more new age kind of guy, he might see fate having a hand in this.

But being a realist, he knew the fault lay with a blizzard, a blackout and a strong security system.

That didn't, however, mean he wasn't thankful as hell for it, as long as Chip was going to be okay. Because, trapped as she was with him in this building, it wasn't going to be easy for Lucy to walk out of his life again.

He could hardly wait until morning to see just how much snow had fallen. How long they were going to be stuck here.

And what Lucy would have to say about it.

LUCY WAS HAVING the nicest dream. In that state between asleep and awake, she somehow knew it was a dream, but didn't want to give it up.

She was lying on a beach, cradled by soft, sugar-white sand. The turquoise waters of the Caribbean lapped in gentle waves, caressing her bare feet, the crash of the surf steady and hypnotic. Above, the sun shone bright in a robin's egg blue sky. Occasionally a puffy white cloud would drift across it, providing a hint of shade, but mostly she just felt warm and content.

Except her nose. That was really cold.

Actually, so were her cheeks. She lifted a hand, pressing her fingers against her face, wondering how her skin could be so cold when she was lying in such deliciously warm sunshine.

Beside her, a man groaned, as if he, too, was loving the feel of the sun, and the island breeze blowing across his skin. The sound was intriguing, and she moved closer. He was hot against her, big and powerful, with sweat-slickened muscles that she traced with her fingertips. She kept her eyes closed, not needing to see his face, somehow sensing she already knew who it was.

Or, maybe a little afraid she wouldn't see the face she wanted to see.

"Mmm," she moaned as she pressed her cheek against

his chest. Languorous heat slid over her; she was lulled by his rhythmic exhalations, and by the sound of his steadily thudding heart.

Wait. Too scratchy. He should be bare-chested.

She waited for the dream to change, waited for the feel of slick, male skin against her face. Instead her cheeks just got colder, and the texture against her jaw scratchier. Not smooth, slick skin. Something like…wool?

Though she desperately wanted to grab the dream and sink into it again, she'd passed the tipping point into consciousness and knew it was no use. The dream was over. She was awake. Her face was cold because she was trapped in a building with no power and no heat. It was scratchy because…because….

She opened her eyes. Waited to let them adjust to the darkness. Saw a shape. A body. A scratchy sweater on which her cheek had been resting. A neck. A face. *Oh. My. God. Ross. Ross?*

She froze, unable to move a muscle as she tried to understand. She'd gone to sleep alone, worried, angry, wondering what would happen tomorrow if nobody came to check the building.

And had woken up in bed with Ross Marshall.

It was him, no doubt about it. The guy who'd broken her heart, the one she'd sworn would never get close enough to hurt her again, was sleeping beside her in the fold-out bed! Not just beside her, but practically underneath her. Apparently, in her sleep, she had curled up against him, raising one leg and sliding it over his groin, her arm draped across his flat stomach, her face nestled in the crook of his neck.

She was practically humping the guy.

And he was sound asleep.

Lucy's first instinct was to leap up and run. Her second, to grab a pillow and beat him over the head with it, demanding to know what the hell he was up to.

But then her brain took over.

Because, as far as she could tell, Ross hadn't been *up* to anything except sleeping. She'd been the one getting all creepy-crawly, sucking up his warmth while she'd dreamed of exotic beaches and blazing sunshine. Probably not too surprising, considering Ross was still just about the hottest man she had ever laid eyes on. Even in the nearly pitch-black room, it was impossible to miss the sensual fullness of his mouth, the slashing cheekbones, that angular, masculine face. His lashes were sinfully long for a guy, hiding those jewel-green eyes.

All the coldness she'd been feeling, at least on those parts, which weren't covered by Ross, dissipated. There was only warmth now. In fact, certain places of her anatomy throbbed with it.

She was suddenly very aware of the position of her arm across his waist, how it dipped low on his hip. Her leg had slipped so comfortably between his, she was almost afraid to move, lest she wake him. But staying like this was torturous.

Because it was simply impossible to have her legs wrapped around him, to feel him pressed against her, without remembering the past; all the ways he'd delighted her, pleasured her, thrilled her. The man had taught her things about her body she hadn't even known were possible.

While one day ago she would have sworn she was not the least bit susceptible to him anymore, the woman who'd had to get herself off in the bathtub a few hours ago would say otherwise. As would the one who now felt totally at the mercy of her girl parts.

Her nipples were tight and incredibly sensitive against his chest. The barest movement sent the fabric of her soft sweater sliding across them, and since she'd been in a hurry and hadn't grabbed a bra, the sensation was definitely noticeable.

That wasn't all. Her thighs were quivering, and between them, her sex was damp and swollen. The urge to thrust her hips nearly overwhelmed her, and she had to forcibly remind herself it was not polite to rub up against a sleeping man just to get a little satisfaction.

Though, to be totally honest, she suspected—no she knew—he could give her a *lot* of satisfaction.

She closed her eyes, took a deep steadying breath, willed her body into standby, then tried to extricate herself. Bad enough to have to wake him up and ask him what the hell he was doing here—or explain the silly story about why she was. But to do it when he knew she'd been using him as both a heating blanket and a potential sex toy was more than she could stand right now.

Holding her breath, she lifted her bent leg, drawing it back off his groin. Slowly, oh, so carefully. But when she shifted a little too low, and her jean-clad thigh brushed against the money-spot on the front of his trousers, she stopped with a gasp. Because those trousers were not flat anymore. Definitely not.

He was hard, erect, aroused.

And, she greatly feared, awake.

He confirmed it by dropping a big hand onto her arm, holding her right where she was—right against him.

"Stop."

"Uh…how long have you been awake?"

Please don't say long enough to know I've been climbing all over you in your sleep. Though, judging by the ridge in his pants—the big, mouthwatering ridge—that seemed pretty certain.

"I just woke up a few seconds ago," he claimed.

He could have been telling the truth, the gravelly note in his voice hinted at sleep. So maybe his body had just been doing its nocturnal thing. Perhaps the fact that her thighs were spread and practically begging to be parted further didn't factor into the big erection pressing against the seam of his pants.

Stop thinking about his pants. And what's in them.

Yeah, fat chance of that. Every cell she had was on high alert, and her blood roared through her veins. She might have told herself a thousand times that she never wanted to see Ross again. But being here, in his arms, knowing his body was reacting to her even if his mind didn't know it, was the most exciting thing she'd experienced in ages.

There was no sense denying it, at least to herself. She wanted him. Against all reason and all common sense.

Or maybe not. What if it *was* reasonable? Maybe it made *perfect* sense to take this unexpected moment and wring whatever she could from it.

She and Ross had been a perfect sexual match once. Lucy had spent six years learning that was a pretty rare thing. Other men had given her orgasms…nobody else had made the earth shake. Plus, she was no longer the inexperienced twenty-two year old who confused sex with love. She and Ross didn't need to love each other to experience pure, undiluted pleasure in each other's arms.

At least…as long as he *wanted* to. His body apparently did, but his mind had to be engaged in the decision-making process. Ross had walked away without a backward glance once before, so maybe this tension she was feeling didn't mean as much to him as it did to her. If not, she needed to know that before deciding whether to slide onto him and kiss his lips off, or roll over, get out of the bed and demand that he let her out of the building. Facing a blizzard sounded more appealing than admitting she wanted him and finding out he didn't really feel the same.

"You could have woken me up when you realized I was here. Why didn't you?"

"Maybe because I just wanted to sleep with you one more time," he admitted.

Nice.

Then, with a sigh, he added, "Plus I knew if I woke you up you'd put all those defenses back into place and insist on leaving in the middle of a blizzard."

She ignored the comment, since she'd pretty much just decided to do exactly that.

"So you just crawled in and curled up next to me?"

"As I recall, you were the one doing the curling," he said, his tone lazy and amused. Which confirmed he'd been awake a little longer than he'd let on. Hell.

"So," he continued, "what'd you forget?"

"Excuse me?"

"I think I put everything together—you must have forgotten something this afternoon, come back to retrieve it, then gotten stuck in the building when Chip went outside and had a heart attack."

"Oh, no! Is he okay?"

"The cop who called me said he thought he would be."

"I hope so. He was very nice, letting me come back in because, yes, I did forget something." Embarrassed to admit it, since every photographer considered their camera an extension of their own body, she explained, "I left my camera bag and my specialty lens case."

He chuckled softly, obviously reading between the lines, knowing he'd flustered her enough to make her forget her equipment. The man had always been a little too perceptive. Damn it.

This conversation wasn't going the way it was supposed to. She'd broached the topic, hoping to hear him say he'd climbed into bed with her because he wanted her so desperately.

Now they were talking about cameras and cops. Ugh.

The wind howled, and though the temperature hadn't fallen too much inside, she instinctively curled closer to Ross. They both fell silent, as if totally comfortable with the fact that they'd ended up in bed together by accident— which she still wanted to discuss, by the way.

But later. Not now. Not when he was so warm and strong, when his breath teased her hair, and his hard thigh fit so nicely between hers. Not when she was trying to breathe ever deeper, intoxicated by the warm, spicy scent of his skin.

Not when she needed to know if he really wanted her—Lucy Fleming—and not just the female body that happened to be beside him in the bed.

If he did, Lucy intended to let herself *have* him. Ross would be the ultimate Christmas present. Just this once, just for tonight.

As if he knew she had no intention of putting some distance between them, Ross lowered his hand to her wrist, lazily tracing circles on the pulse point. Like he had every right to touch her. Lucy sighed, shocked at how evocative that touch felt. Her already moist sex grew hotter, wetter, as she remembered how those strong but gentle fingers used to slide across her clit, making her come with a few deliberate strokes.

Stretching, he shifted a little, and she felt the flex of the powerful muscles in his shoulder. She'd noted earlier that his body had changed—he was bigger, broader across the chest and shoulders, though his lean hips would still be easily encircled by her thighs.

It was far too easy to visualize that. To visualize everything. In fact, she was having difficulty focusing on anything else.

Without warning, Ross moved his hand, dropping it to her hip, tugging her more tightly against his body. For warmth? For old time's sake? Because he had nothing better to do?

Oh, God, he was driving her crazy!

He continued with that steady, even breathing, remaining silent, and didn't reveal by word or deed whether he was just killing time or trying to start something.

Finally, unable to take it anymore, she sat straight up in the bed and glared down at him. "Well, are you going to do something about this?"

She was asking a lot more than that. *Are you interested? Do you feel this? Do you want me?*

He didn't respond for a second, didn't reply with a confused, *Like what?* But then, just when Lucy was about to launch herself out of the bed and call him an idiot, he moved, quickly and deliberately.

Between one breath and the next, Ross sat up, pushed her onto her back and slid over her, his powerful body pressed hard against hers. His face lowered toward her, and Lucy's heart thudded with excitement as she saw the hunger in his expression.

Then he said two words…the only two she wanted to hear.

"Hell, yes."

After that, no words were needed. Her heart flying, all thoughts disappearing, she rose to meet his lips with her own. Their tongues plunged together, frantic, hungry for a connection.

There was nothing slow and quiet about it. Only driving need and demand. Their hands raced to touch each other, and Lucy hissed when he moved his mouth to her neck and sucked her nape. He nipped lightly and she quivered, wanting that mouth, that tongue, those nibbling teeth, on every inch of her body.

The Ross she'd made love with all those years ago had been slow, tender and deliberate. This Ross was wild. Desperate. She felt his driving need, and answered it with her own. Emotion had been chased away by lust, and she realized, suddenly, that she'd been waiting for this since long before the moments they'd just spent in his bed.

She'd longed for years to feel like this, through other affairs and other men. She'd wanted to experience the intense, nearly animalistic passion she felt right now. Deep down, Lucy knew she'd been waiting for him. Ross. Waiting until they met again—as if knowing someday they would—to truly let go of every inhibition, every doubt, every question about her own desirability. To know she was someone's sexual obsession, if only for one night, one moment in time.

And she was. He wanted her with every fiber of his being. His desperate touch proclaimed it and her own body was already screaming a silent *Yes* to every little thing he might ask of her.

They separated only far enough to remove their clothes. His sweater came off, revealing the golden-skinned chest beneath, and she had to reach out and run the tips of her fingers across his impressive abs. He was built perfectly— broad chest, lean at the waist and hips. Like he'd been the model used to create the prime example of man.

When his hands touched her waist and began yanking her sweater up, Lucy arched toward him. She heard his low groan when he realized she wasn't wearing a bra, and even in the near-darkness, could see the look of pure appreciation as he visually devoured her.

Lucy had been built a little differently six years ago. She'd been more girlish, more lean. Now she was curvier, carrying an extra ten pounds in all the right places...places he obviously liked. A lot.

"God, you're gorgeous," he muttered. Then he bent to her breast, no warning, no hint, his mouth landing on her nipple and sucking hard. As if he couldn't help himself, had to quench his ravenous thirst with the taste of her.

"Oh, yes, please," she groaned.

She sunk her fingers into his hair, pressing him even harder, needing to feel it, deep down. And with every deep pull of his mouth, she did feel it. All the way down to the throbbing center of sensation between her thighs.

He leaned over to give her other breast the same attention. Plumping it with his hand, he rolled her nipple between his fingertips before he blew lightly, then suckled her. Lucy cried out at how good it felt. Savoring his attention, she kissed his neck, his shoulder, raking her nails down his bare back, wondering how he could possibly be so strong when he appeared to now be a suit-and-tie kind of guy.

She wanted to cry when he moved his mouth away again. But she got with the program when he kissed his way down her midriff to the waistband of her jeans, which he quickly unfastened. He backed away, kneeling on the edge of the bed and straightening her legs. Lucy lifted her hips, arching up toward him, helping as he tugged the denim away.

Thank God she'd been in too much of a hurry to put on long johns or something equally as hideous before she'd left home. Her pink panties weren't Frederick's of Hollywood worthy, but they were cute and sexy. And Ross seemed to like them. A lot.

Or maybe not. Because without a word, he ripped them off her, tearing the fabric. She didn't give a damn. The hunger in his every movement excited her beyond anything.

"Gotta taste you, Luce."

She had a second to prepare, then his mouth was on her, licking at her core. She actually shrieked, shocked by the raw intimacy. He didn't carefully sample her, he dove deep, thrusting his tongue into her opening, then up to her clit, then back again. She was whimpering, her hips bucking freely, helpless to do anything but take what he wanted to give. Her first orgasm smashed into her like an earthquake, making her whole body quiver. He didn't stop, merely holding her hips in his big hands, continuing to lick at her as if he couldn't get enough.

Then came the aftershocks—the tsunami—wave after wave of hot, electric delight, popping in little explosions that made her head spin. Colors, instruments, spinning lights—a whole freaking carnival seemed to be taking place all around her, all calliope music and the thrill of spinning and riding until you were breathless and just couldn't take anymore.

She couldn't take anymore.

"Stop," she ordered dazedly, knowing she'd reached that point. Pleasure overload. She could barely breathe, her heart was pounding hard enough to burst out of her chest, and she was almost hyperventilating from all the gasping.

Mostly she was stunned. Shocked.

Awakened.

They hadn't had a lot of time together six years ago, and oral sex was one intimacy they hadn't shared. She'd been young, a virgin, and he'd been tender and incredibly patient. She suspected that if Ross had ever used his mouth on her like that, she would have stalked him to Chicago.

Now, she wanted him to feel that same unadulterated freedom. Wanted to give him what she'd never given him before. Not just to please him, but also to make him as absolutely crazy as he had made her.

More, though, she wanted that intimacy for her own sake. She'd never viewed oral sex as anything more than foreplay, a tit for tat return on a guy's earlier tongue investment. This time, though, she wanted to take that thick ridge of male heat into her mouth and explore the flavors of his body. Wanted to taste him, explore him, suck his cock until his willpower gave out, or his legs did.

She scooted away, grabbing his hair and pushing him up. He eyed her from between her legs, his eyes glittering, his mouth moist. "You taste good," he growled.

Licking her lips, she murmured, "I bet you do, too."

Sitting up, she became the aggressor, stalking him to the end of the bed, until he hopped off it. Eyeing her hungrily, he said nothing as she scooted to the edge, parting her thighs around his legs.

She was eye level with that wonderful, thick ridge straining against his zipper. Though she felt just as desperate to tear his clothes away, she hesitated, holding her breath. For that moment, she felt like she was about to open a Christmas present—just one, on Christmas Eve, the way she always had as a kid. The excitement of choosing the right one, and the certainty that there would be so many more good things to come all washed over her.

Catching her lip between her teeth, she unbuttoned his jeans, then eased the zipper down. He hissed as her hands brushed against the cotton of his boxer-briefs. Burying his hands in her hair, he held her tightly, not painfully, yet more forceful than she'd ever expect from him. It felt possessive. Demanding. Unlike the tender Ross she'd known, but perfect for the hungry man who'd eaten her like he'd been served his last meal.

Pushing the jeans and briefs down, she took a second to admire his cock—strong, erect and powerful. Lucy moistened her lips, then leaned forward and kissed the tip of it, hearing him groan as skin met skin.

That groan egged her on. She parted her lips, taking him into her mouth, swirling her tongue over and over. She swallowed the hint of moisture his body released, liking the salty taste, wanting a mouthful of it. She didn't worry that taking him to the edge would cut into what she wanted from him later. Ross was young and vital, and right now he looked like he could easily do her all night long, take a coffee break, then get right back in there and bang her brains out another half-dozen times.

Her thighs clenched, moisture dripping from her sex, still swollen, maybe even a little sore, from the thorough attention of his mouth.

She gave him the same attention, sucking hard. He swayed a little, which she took as a good sign. So she took more of him, deeper into her mouth, until she could take no more. Reaching between his legs, she carefully cupped the taut sacs, timing each stroke of her hand with one of her mouth, pulling away, then sucking him deep, over and over.

His groans deepened. The pace quickened. She knew by the tenseness of those powerful muscles that he was close.

He stopped. "Uh-uh. I've waited six years. No way am I coming in your mouth."

Pulling back, he reached into his pocket and grabbed a condom. As he hurriedly donned it, she considered telling him she had the birth control covered. But she figured they should err on the safe side when they were being so impulsive, so crazy.

Ross shoved his pants completely off, then reached for her. Lucy let him lift her, wrapping her legs around his waist. He held her easily, her bottom cupped in his hands, then backed her against the wall, bracing her between it and his chest.

She sunk her fingers into his hair, tugging his mouth to hers for a deep kiss. He plunged his tongue deep…then did the same thing with his cock.

Oh, yes.

He didn't move at first, just stood holding her there, impaled on him. She felt her body soften and adjust, taking him completely. Savoring the fullness, she rocked against him, signaling him that he didn't need to go slow.

She didn't want him to go slow.

"Next time," he promised.

"Whatever," she panted

Then there were no words. Just hard thrusts of his body into hers. Deeper and deeper, he reached heights no one ever had before. Or maybe she was reaching those heights. It certainly felt like she was flying, almost out-of-body with sensation.

Moisture fell on her cheeks. Lucy realized she was crying. But not sad tears, God-it-feels-so-good-and-I've-waited-so-long tears.

She closed her eyes, dropped her head back and just took and took and took. The rocking of his groin against hers brought just the right friction and she felt all that familiar pressure boiling up again. Her clit throbbed and swelled. Then the dam burst and she came again.

"Oh, yes, God, yes."

Her words? His? Both?

She didn't know. She just knew they were both crying out, both sweating and twisting and thrusting. And finally, both coming.

He groaned, suddenly growing very still. Lucy kissed him. She could feel his pulse thundering, both against her chest, and where he was inside her, and she found herself wishing she had told him not to bother with the condom. She wanted all that heat bursting into her.

Fortunately, however, they were just getting started.

They had time. Plenty of it. Because, judging by the wind battering the building, and the dark snow swirling around the windows, they weren't going anywhere anytime soon.

8

Then
New York, December 24, 2005

THOUGH ROSS HAD wanted Lucy to call the police right after Jude had slithered out, he had sensed her desperation to get out of her apartment. She didn't just *want* to leave, she *needed* to. He suspected the place suddenly felt tainted to her, and had to wonder how long it would take before she ever felt safe there again.

That definitely wouldn't happen until he got her locks changed. And no way in hell was she staying there alone until then.

So, after she'd thrown a few things in a bag, they'd headed for his place. After a short walk to his truck, and a long drive out of the city, they arrived in Brooklyn. Every mile put the ugly scene further into the past, and Ross was finally able to begin clearing his mind of the mental images of what might have happened had he not shown up when he did.

The very idea made him sick. And violence surged up within him when he so much as thought Jude's name.

But now it was time to think about something else. Making sure she was okay and felt safe, for one. Wondering what the hell had happened with his life in the past twelve hours for another.

Nah, he'd think about that tomorrow.

"Here we are," he said when he pulled up outside the tiny rental house where he lived. It wasn't much to look at, but it was a place of his own—a place nobody had helped him get. He didn't love the location, but he loved not feeling like he owed anything to anybody. Especially his father.

"I can't tell you how much I…"

"Forget it," he said, waving off her thank you. Probably her twentieth since they'd left her place.

Reaching into the tiny back compartment of the truck, he grabbed her small suitcase and her camera bag, then got out, going around to open her door. She didn't wait, hopping out before he had made it around the bumper. "What a cute house!"

He raised a brow. "Seriously?"

"Sure. You have a yard and everything. I can't tell you how much I miss backyard barbecues in the summer."

"The last tenant left a grill. Maybe I'll cook up some burgers tomorrow."

She laughed. "In the snow?"

"You call this snow? Yeesh. Until you've experienced a lake effects winter, you don't know the meaning of snow."

"I have," she told him. "I grew up in Chicago."

Shocked, he almost tripped. "Seriously?" The woman he had begun to suspect was the girl of his dreams had grown up in the same city, and he'd never even been aware of her? That seemed wrong on some cosmic level.

"Uh huh. And even the thought of that windy winter reminds me why I'll never go back."

His heart twisted a little at that admission, but he pushed aside the disappointment. "Yeah, I can't say I'm missing it right now, either."

"Do you think you'll ever go back?"

"Yeah, I think so."

Actually he didn't just think it, he knew it. One of these days, he was going to have to return and face up to his responsibilities. His father wasn't getting any younger, or any healthier, and not one of his sisters showed any interest in construction.

Ross, on the other hand, genuinely loved it. He'd had a toy tool set as a kid, had built his first birdhouse at four. By the time he was ten, he had constructed a four-story Barbie house for his kid sister. He just had a real affinity for building things, and had never wanted to do anything else. Some even called it a gift.

Going away to college, then to grad school, and learning drafting and architecture had just made him better at his craft. More than that, he truly *wanted* to run the company one day, as his grandfather and now his father always said he would.

He just didn't want to be forced to work there under his father's watchful eye *now*. Having spent every summer and school holiday building things for Elite Construction, and knowing he'd end up doing that for much of his life, he just wanted some time to himself. To be free, to go somewhere new, to be totally on his own. That wasn't too much to ask, was it?

Well, it was according to his father.

"Ross?"

Realizing he'd fallen into a morose silence, he shook his head, hard. "Hold on a sec," he told her, going to the back of his covered truck to retrieve the robotic dinosaur and the bags of presents he'd been supposed to mail today. He'd told Lucy about them on the way home, and she'd promised to help him package them up tonight, then find a UPS store tomorrow.

Once inside, he flipped on the lights, and zoned-in on the thermostat. No, this wasn't a Chicago winter, but it was still pretty damn cold. Plus the house was old and drafty.

He jacked up the heat, then turned back to Lucy, who

looked a lot less shell-shocked than she had when they'd left the city. He didn't try to hide his relief, glad for that strong, resilient streak he'd sensed in her from the moment they'd met.

Right now, she acted as though she didn't have a care in the world. In fact, she was wandering around, comfortable enough to be nosy and check out the house. "Oh, my God, is that really a lava lamp?"

"Like the grill, also left by a former tenant. As was the couch and the ugly kitchen table."

Lucky for him. After laying out cash for a security deposit, plus first and last month's rent, he hadn't had much money for furnishings.

Kinda funny, really, how he was living now. He'd been raised in a house with ten bedrooms on twenty acres. His sisters had each had a horse in the stable, and he'd had his choice of car when he'd turned sixteen. He hadn't necessarily been born with a solid silver spoon in his mouth, but it would have to be called silver-plated.

And now he lived in a drafty, tiny old house with hand-me-down furniture and an old analog TV that got only one station, and that only if there wasn't a cloud in the sky. He drove a five-year-old truck whose payments were still enough to make him wince once a month. Ate boxed mac-and-cheese and Ramen noodles, the way a lot of the scholarship kids in college had.

Most shocking of all? He liked it.

You do this and you're on your own, totally cut off! Don't expect a penny from me!

His father's angry voice echoed in his head. But so did an answering whisper: *But I did it anyway, didn't I? And I'm doing just fine.*

"What about the bean bag chair?" Lucy asked, interrupting his thoughts of the angry scene last summer, right after graduation, when he'd decided not to move back home.

He admitted, "What can I say? I bought that one. It seemed to go with the decor."

"Lemme guess…thrift store shopping spree?"

"Bingo." Shrugging, he added, "I was on a budget."

"I think my groovy, peace-sign Santa would fit in very well here."

"Don't even think about pawning that thing off on me. Even if it weren't broken, I wouldn't let that drugged-out St. Nick and those zombie-kids anywhere near my Christmas tree. It might lose all its needles in pure fear."

She finally noticed the small tree, standing in the front corner near the window. Her smile faded a little, as if she'd suddenly remembered it was Christmas Eve, albeit very early on Christmas Eve—only about 1:00 a.m.

It was a sad-looking thing. He'd bought it on impulse— it had been the last one on a lot up the block, scrawny and short, with half its needles already gone. It had reminded him of Charlie Brown's tree…in need of a home. So he'd shelled out the ten bucks and brought it here, sticking it in a bucket since he didn't have a tree stand.

Nor had he had any real ornaments to put on it. Right now, an empty aluminum pot-pie tin served as a star on the top, and a bunch of picture hangers and odds-and-ends hung from the few branches.

As she stared at the pathetic thing, Lucy's sadness appeared to fade. She shook her head, a slow, reluctant smile widening her pretty mouth. "Are those beer can tabs?"

"Just a few," he admitted. "I was experimenting. I'm not a big drinker, so I only had a few cans in the fridge. I finally raided my toolbox."

Putting a hand on her hip and tilting her head, she said, "And you had the nerve to criticize my Christmas decorations?"

"Hey, mine's pathetic, not terrifying."

"My snow globe from last year wasn't terrifying."

"Oh, no? Let me guess. A tiny female elf wearing pasties and a G-string?"

Her eyes rounded. "Ooh, that sounds fabulous! But, no, it was just a North Pole scene."

He crossed his arms, waiting.

"With a clown that popped out of Santa's chimney like a Jack-in-the-Box."

Shuddering, he said, "Clowns are terrifying. What's wrong with Jack?"

"Why would a Jack-in-the-Box be in Santa's chimney?"

"Why would a clown?"

"Well, that's the point," she said, laughing at the ridiculous conversation. "None of it makes any sense!"

"Which makes it perfect to you and your brother. Merry Christmas to the Scrooge siblings."

"Exactly!"

Liking that her good mood was back, he asked, "Hey, are you hungry? I've got frozen pizza, frozen bagels, frozen burgers...."

"Typical single guy menu, huh?"

"Yep. Oh, if you want some wine, I think I have a box in the back of the fridge."

She snickered.

"It was a housewarming gift from a neighbor."

One pretty brow went up. "Oh? Not a basket of muffins?"

"Let's just say my neighbor's of the cat persuasion."

Her brow furrowed in confusion.

"The cougar variety." Frankly whenever his neighbor came over, he felt like putting on another layer of clothes.

"Never mind," he said, waving his hand. "So, why don't you help yourself while I go get cleaned up."

"You look clean to me."

"Under these clothes is a layer of sawdust—I'm itchy all over. I need to take a shower."

"Help yourself," she said, waving a hand as she headed

to the kitchen, already making herself at home. "Want me to make you something?"

"Whatever you're having."

"Filet mignon it is."

He snorted. "Hungry Man Salisbury steak frozen dinner, if you're lucky."

Still smiling, glad her good mood had returned and thoughts of her vicious ex—who still had a lot of bad stuff coming to him—were gone, he headed for his room. The bed was unmade, clothes draped across it, the dresser drawers open. It looked like a single guy's room. Considering he intended to offer Lucy the bed, and take the couch for himself, he took a few minutes to straighten up.

As he did so, he couldn't help thinking about how much different his life seemed now than when he'd left this morning. He'd figured he'd be coming home to a quiet house, a solitary holiday, maybe a turkey sub from Subway. And he'd been okay with that. Not happy, but okay.

But he had to admit, in recent days, as the holiday season zoomed in like a rocket ship, he had really begun to think about his family back in Chicago. He had a few friends here, but not the type you'd share Christmas with. Being from a big family—which got bigger with every sister's marriage and the births of new nieces and nephews—he began to realize there were times living alone wasn't so great. As December marched on, he'd resigned himself to a lonely, kinda pathetic holiday weekend.

Wow, did things ever change on a dime.

Still thinking about those changes, he headed into the bathroom—spent another few minutes cleaning it—then got in the shower. He hadn't been kidding about that sawdust; the stuff had filtered into his clothes as he'd maneuvered the custom-made bookcase into place at Beans & Books.

Finally, his hair damp from a quick towel-dry, he pulled on a clean pair of jeans and a T-shirt and headed back out to the living room. Smelling something—popcorn?—his gaze immediately went to the kitchen, but didn't see Lucy there.

After a second, he spotted her in the one place he had not expected her to be, doing something he had *never* expected her to do. "Lucy?"

She looked up and smiled at him, a little self-conscious. "I couldn't take it anymore, it was just sad."

Ross could only stare. It appeared she had gone all Linus on his Charlie Brown Christmas tree, and had decided to give it a little love—how appropriate for a *Lucy*. What had been just sticks, needles, picture-hangers and beer can tabs an hour ago now at least resembled a bedecked evergreen.

"Where did you…"

"I just used stuff that was lying around. Hope you don't mind, but I cut up a couple of mac-and-cheese boxes…the packets are still in the cupboard. I assume you've made it often enough that you didn't need the directions?"

"Not a problem," he mumbled, still a little shocked at how much she'd done, how quickly she'd done it, and how good it looked.

"I'm glad you're the healthy type and your microwave popcorn wasn't buttered. That would have been sticky," she said as she plucked another piece out of a bowl and stuck it on the edge of a needle. A whole thread full of them dangled on her lap. "Oh, and I hope you don't mind me digging through your kitchen drawers. I was pleasantly surprised to find that sewing kit."

"Old tenant," he murmured, still a little stunned.

"Well, thanks to the former tenant then. Unfortunately he didn't happen to leave any twinkle lights or pretty red bows behind. But luckily, I hadn't cleaned out my camera bag," she added. "I had picked up some construction paper, glitter and glue to make decorations for the studio where I'm interning."

She'd used all those things to full advantage. Right now, glittery snowmen and Santa shapes dangled from several branches, apparently with directions for making mac-and-cheese on the other side. She had also managed a long strand of construction paper garland, like the kind he'd made as a kid. Red, green and white loops encircled each other, making a colorful chain that draped around the tree.

But that wasn't all. His pot-pie pan-topper had actually been cut into a star shape. And there was some kind of red-and-white fabric tucked around the bucket, creating a tree skirt. Having no clue where she could have gotten that, he quirked a questioning brow.

She chuckled. "My elf tights. I had two pair in my bag."

Good God. Tight, shimmery fabric, usually used to encase what he suspected were a pair of beautiful legs, was now hugging a dirty bucket at the base of an old, dead tree?

"I didn't have any lights, obviously, but I think this'll work. Hold on."

He watched as she crawled around the baseboard and fiddled with something on the floor. Suddenly the tree was bathed in a soft, reddish light from below. "Glad I had the red gel on me!"

Not knowing what she meant, he bent to peer at the light, which he realized was a camera flash with a sheet of red plastic over it.

"Voilà!"

He reached for her hand, pulling her to her feet and together they stared at her masterpiece. She'd taken a pretty pathetic stick, added a bunch of random objects and Mac-Gyvered the whole thing into a work of art.

"Wow," he whispered, genuinely impressed. "It's amazing."

She shrugged. "But it's still not exactly traditional."

He heard the tremor in her voice and knew where her thoughts had gone—to that dirty word, *traditional*. For four years, she'd tried hard to distance herself from happy holiday traditions, keeping those sweet memories at bay for fear they'd be accompanied by sad ones. Yet now, she'd stepped out of her comfort zone, doing things she probably remembered doing with the parents she'd lost, even though it was painful for her.

And she'd done it for him.

He turned to her, dropping his hands to her waist, pulling her close to him. Lucy looked up at him, her eyes bright, shining in the holiday light, and he'd swear he had never seen a more beautiful face in his life.

"Thank you," he whispered. Then he punctuated the thanks by dropping his mouth to hers, kissing her softly.

She reached up and wrapped her arms around his neck, pressing her soft body against him. He'd kissed her earlier, but they'd both been wearing coats, and layers of clothes. Now, with just his T-shirt and her blouse, he was able to feel the fullness of her breasts against his chest. She moaned lightly, moving one leg so their thighs tangled.

As if needing to feel his skin, Lucy moved her hands under the bottom of his shirt, stroking his stomach. He pulled away enough for her to push it up and over his head, liking the way her eyes widened in appreciation as she began to explore his chest. She scraped the back of her finger over his nipple, and Ross hissed in response. This time, when he pulled her close to kiss her again, he could feel the rigid tips of her breasts, separated from his bare skin by only by that silky blouse.

Saying nothing, Lucy began to pull him with her, toward the couch. Rather than follow, he bent and picked her up. Cradling her in his arms, he crossed the room and sat down, keeping her on his lap. They never broke the kiss. It just went on and on, slow and deep and wet.

Unable to resist, Ross reached for her stomach, trailing his fingertips over the blouse, hearing her purr in response. She arched up to meet his touch, telling him she wanted more. He tugged the material free of her pants, almost shaking in anticipation, knowing he'd been dying to touch her since they'd met.

As he'd expected, Lucy's body was silkier than her clothes. He took pure, visceral pleasure in the sensation, delighting in the textures against his callused hand.

"Oh, yes, more," she whispered against his mouth.

Glad for the invitation, he began to slide the buttons open, exposing more of her warm, supple skin. Lucy shifted a little, helping him tug the blouse free of her pants, so that by the time he unfastened the last button, the shirt fell open completely.

Ross stopped kissing her long enough to look at her, soaking in the breathtaking sight. Her breasts were high and round, every inch of her creamy smooth. Her lacy bra did nothing to conceal the tight, puckered nipples. And the way she arched up toward him told him what she needed.

He happily complied, covering one taut peak with his mouth, before tasting her with his tongue through the fabric.

She jerked, tangling her hands in his hair, pressing his head harder to her breast. Ross heard her tiny, raspy breaths, the little whimpers she couldn't contain, and knew she was loving every bit of this.

So was he.

With care, he lowered one of her bra-straps, releasing her breast and catching it in his hand. Her tight nipples demanded more attention, and he licked and kissed her there, sucking deep until she was squirming on his lap.

That squirming drove him a little crazy. His cock was rock-hard beneath her sexy butt, and the way she slid up and down on him told him she knew it. It also told him she wanted to keep going.

Needing to feel her heat, to see if she was as tight and wet as he suspected she was, he unsnapped her pants and slid the zipper down. He was careful in his movements, intentionally scraping his hand against the skimpy yellow panties she wore beneath. *Satin over silk.*

She didn't pull away, instead pushing against his hand,

practically demanding that he touch her more thoroughly. *As though he needed to be asked?*

His mouth still on her breast, he could feel the raging beat of her heart and knew she was almost out of her mind with excitement. Breathing deeply to inhale that musky, feminine scent that practically drugged him into incoherence, he tugged the elastic away and moved his hand to the curls covering her sex. She whimpered, digging her nails lightly into his bare back. She was begging for more, though she didn't say a word.

Needing more, too, he slipped his finger between the warm, soft lips of her sex, almost groaning at how slick and wet she was.

"Oh, God," she cried, her eyes flying open. "Please, don't stop."

As if.

"Okay, time for the clothes to go," he growled.

He helped her push the pants all the way down and off, and once she was naked in his lap, he had to just pause and visually drink her in. She was perfect, from head to foot, laid out in front of him like a feast. He didn't know where to start, he just knew he already didn't want it to end.

He reached down to the front of his jeans, unfastening them, wanting to get naked and pull her leg across his lap to straddle him. Sitting there, looking up at her while she rode him sounded like the perfect way to start this night.

"Ross?" she whispered.

"Hmm?"

"Um…there's something you probably should know."

"Unless the house is on fire, there's nothing I really need to hear right now," he said as he unzipped and pushed the jeans down his hips. His body was already on fire, and as he pushed his shorts away, too, and his cock came into contact with her bare hip, he groaned.

She gasped. "Oh, my goodness."

"Give me another five minutes and it will be both *yours,*

and *good,*" he told her as he stopped to kiss her breast, and stroke that sweet, quivering spot between her thighs.

"Ross, uh, really, I need to tell you something."

Hearing the quaver in her voice, and feeling the slight stiffness of her body, he finally shook off the haze of lust in his head. He lifted his mouth from her perfect breast and slid his hand into safer territory down on her thigh.

"What's wrong?"

She lowered her head, eyeing him through a long strand of hair. Lucy's cheeks were pink, like she was embarrassed. Well, hell, they'd known each other less than a day and now she was lying naked on his lap. But she wouldn't be embarrassed for long, not once he showed her how much he wanted her.

"Um…I just wanted to say…"

She bit her lip, shook her head slightly. Which was when a thought—a shocking, crazy one—burst into his head. His whole body went stiff and he leaned back into the couch.

"Lucy, are you trying to tell me you've never done this before?"

A hesitation, then she slowly nodded. "That's what I'm trying to tell you."

Holy shit. She was naked in his arms, thrusting into his hand like she needed to come or die and she was a virgin?

Well, honestly, the needing to come or die made sense. Seriously, how many twenty-two-year-old virgins were out there? He'd certainly never met one. The beautiful, sexy woman had to be a seething mass of sexual frustration.

Something he could well appreciate right now.

"I mean, you said you and Jude had never…but, seriously, nobody else, either?"

"No. Never."

"That's incredible."

"I guess right around the time most girls were giving it away in the backseats of their boyfriends' cars, I was grieving and helping my brother figure out what to do about our parents' business, their house, their lives. And ours. It just sort of...never happened."

He nodded, understanding. She hadn't been thrust into the role of sexual grown-up while in high school. She'd landed in the adult world through one brutal tragedy.

That, as much as the fact that he was not a ruthless bastard like Jude, was enough to make Ross find the strength to do what had to be done. Knowing he'd have blue balls tonight, he still cleared his throat and carefully pushed her off his lap.

"Okay. It's all right, Lucy, I understand."

She grabbed his arm before he could get off the couch and head toward the bathroom for an icy cold shower.

"No, I don't think you do." Reaching for his face, she cupped his cheeks in her hands and leaned close, her soft hair falling onto his bare shoulders. "I want you, Ross. I want you to be my first. Now. Tonight."

LUCY HAD THOUGHT a lot about the moment when she'd finally have sex. She'd pictured it being with someone she knew, someone she'd dated for a long time, someone she trusted.

Well, one out of three wasn't bad, right?

She didn't know Ross that well. She'd never dated him. But she trusted him. Oh, did she trust him.

Telling him the truth about herself hadn't been easy, but she certainly wasn't going to try to fake her way through her first time having sex. Not only was that unfair to herself, it was unfair to him. He deserved the chance to say, "Thanks but no thanks." After all, some guys just didn't seem to want to deal with the drama of it.

She would have predicted Ross wouldn't be one of those guys.

She wouldn't have predicted the incredibly tender, loving way he kissed her, then stood and took her by the hand to lead her to his bedroom. As if now that he knew the truth, the responsibility of it was weighing on him, and he didn't want a quick lay on a couch. Like she deserved the whole package, big bed and all.

The walk to the bedroom seemed incredibly long. And while her whole body was still burning from the incredible way he'd touched her, she couldn't deny a faint trepidation, the tiniest bit of self-consciousness.

After all, she was naked. He still wore jeans. And she'd just told him she was a virgin.

"It's okay," he told her when they'd reached his room, standing by his bed. He brushed her hair off her face, then touched her cheek. "It's gonna be fine."

She smiled. "Do you think I'm afraid?"

He eyed her, visibly unsure.

"I'm not scared, Ross. Maybe a little embarrassed about being so...exposed."

He stepped back and looked at her naked body, shaking his head slowly and rubbing his jaw, as if he just didn't know what to say. Then he said exactly the right thing. "If there's any such thing as a perfect woman, Lucy Fleming, you're her."

She went soft and gooey inside, everywhere she wasn't already soft and gooey. As she'd already suspected, she'd most definitely chosen well.

"Thank you."

"So don't be nervous, Luce, I won't do anything to hurt you," he added, tenderly cupping her cheek.

"I won't. I swear to you, my only fear is that it won't be as good as I've made it out to be in my head."

A slow smile curled those handsome lips upward. He shook his head, then sunk his hands in her hair and dragged her close.

"It'll be better. I guaran-damn-tee it."

He pushed her down onto the bed, and set about proving it.

Lucy honestly hadn't known sex could be both incredibly hot and amazingly tender. He kissed her deeply, slowly, like he wanted to memorize the taste of her mouth. And his hands did magical things to her, gliding across her breasts, offering her barely there caresses that left her a quivering pile of sensation.

But then, his control would slip a little. He'd groan as he nipped her breast, or shake when she reached out and brushed her fingertips against the soft head of his erection. Lucy wanted to do more, longed to explore his body, but he seemed determined to make this all totally and completely about her.

Which was wonderful…and incredibly arousing.

"Please," she said on a sob when he again teased her clit with his fingers, giving her light touches that made her long for firmer ones. Her hips thrusting, Lucy was on the verge of going over the top, she knew that from her own explorations of her body. And she was dying for it.

As if knowing he'd teased her as much as he could before she smacked him, Ross murmured something sweet and unintelligible, then slid a finger inside her. She practically cooed; the unfamiliar invasion felt *so* good. He moved his thumb back to her clit and this time, there was no teasing. Just slow, deliberate caresses, with just the pressure she needed.

Her breaths grew choppy. Sighs turned into gasps when he slid another finger into her channel, using both to stretch and fill her, even while he continued stroking her clit.

Then it came, sweet, warm relief. She quivered as the orgasm rolled over her, amazed at how much stronger it was when shared. She cried out, let her body shake and stretch, then sagged back into the pillows.

"You're gorgeous," he whispered.

"So are you," she said, absolutely meaning it. Ross's body was delicious—so hard and muscular, all power and steel. When combined with the thoughtfulness, the boyish smile, the twinkle in his green eyes, he was an absolutely irresistible male package.

She smiled at him, wrapping her arms around his neck. "I want you now."

He didn't ask if she was sure, as if knowing they were way past that. Reaching for a drawer in the bedside table, he took out a condom. Lucy caught her lip between her teeth, watching as he maneuvered the tight sheath over his thick, powerful erection. Seeing the rubber stretch to accommodate him, she felt the first thrills of nervousness. But they were immediately drowned out by utter excitement.

Just watching him sent even more heat to her sex and she had to drop her legs apart, the skin there was so engorged and sensitive. Ross looked down at her, masculine appreciation written all over his face, then moved between her thighs.

"Tell me if…"

"I will," she said, cutting him off. Then she lifted her hips, wrapping her arms around his shoulders and staring up at him.

They didn't kiss. They didn't blink. They barely breathed.

Lucy's heart skipped a beat when she felt his rigid warmth probing into her, nuzzling between her folds and into the slick opening of her body. He moved slowly, so carefully, so tenderly. Each bit of himself he gave her just made her hungry for more.

She arched her hips toward him, silently telling him to continue. Seeing the clenched muscles in his neck, the sweat on his brow, she knew he was hanging on tightly to his control.

"I'm fine," she insisted. "Please, Ross, please fill me up."

He bent to her, covered her lips with his and kissed her

deeply. And with each stroke of his tongue, he pushed into her, filling her, inch by inch, until he was buried inside her.

There had been only the tiniest hint of pain; now there was just fullness. Thickness. A sense that she'd finally been made whole and didn't ever want to go back to feeling empty again. Like he was exactly where he was meant to be.

"Okay?" he asked.

"Definitely."

She slid her legs tighter around his, holding him close. Ross began to pull out, then slowly thrust back in, setting an easy pace. She caught it, matched it, giving when he took, taking when he pulled back. It was, she realized, like dancing…one step he led, then she did. Only no dance move had ever felt so good, so sinfully delicious.

"You're so tight," he groaned, picking up the pace.

She knew his control was slipping. Frankly she marveled that he'd been able to maintain it this long. Every molecule in her body was urging her to thrust and writhe, to just take in so much pleasure that she'd never remember what it was like to not feel it. She knew he had to be feeling the same.

The rhythm sped up a little, his thrusts deepening. Lucy met him stroke for stroke, clinging to his broad shoulders, sharing kiss after kiss. Reality had faded, there was nothing else except this feeling, this rightness. This perfect guy on this perfect night.

And then, the perfect moment. Warm delight spilled through her as she climaxed again, differently than she ever had before. It started deep inside and radiated out, a ripple widening into a wave.

Even as she savored the long, deep sensations, she heard Ross's shallow breaths grow louder and felt him tense against her.

"Beautiful, you're so beautiful," he muttered as he strained toward his own release.

His low cry and the deepest thrust of all signaled that he'd found it. He buried his face in her hair and continued to pump into her, as if every bit of him had been wrung dry.

Though she knew he had to be totally spent, he didn't collapse on top of her. Instead, Ross rolled onto his side and tugged her with him. They were still joined, and she slid her thigh over his hip, liking the connection.

His eyes were closed, his lips parted as he drew in deep breaths. When he finally opened them, she didn't even try to hide her smile.

"What?"

"I liked it."

He chuckled. "I'm glad."

"When can we do it again?"

His chuckle turned into a deep, masculine laugh. "Give me a half hour."

She stuck out her lower lip in a pretend pout.

"Okay, okay," he said, reaching down and stroking her hip. "Twenty minutes."

"I guess I can live with that," she said, with a teasing smile. She rubbed against him, stealing his warmth. The bedroom was cool, but she definitely hadn't noticed it before. Ross gave off a lot of heat…whether he was right beside her or across the room.

She much preferred him right beside her.

They fell silent for a few moments, just touching each other, exchanging lazy kisses. She loved the way he kept a possessive hand on her, as if making sure she didn't disappear on him.

That wasn't going to happen. Definitely not. In fact, she was already wracking her brain, wondering how on earth they could make this work for a lot longer than this one weekend. He hadn't said he wanted to, neither had she. But she definitely felt it.

Yet, she was leaving for Europe in three weeks. She'd

be gone for months, then had intended to come home only long enough to graduate, then go back again.

None of that had mattered when she'd been with Jude. Not even when she'd been thinking about sleeping with him.

Now, though? With Ross? The very thought was devastating. How could she possibly walk away when, for the first time in her life, she'd met someone she wanted desperately to hold on to?

"Is there anything you need?" he whispered, his voice breaking the silence in the shadowy room.

"Like what?"

He shrugged and looked away, as if not wanting to embarrass her. "I mean, you know, are you hurting?"

"Definitely not. Honestly, I don't know that I have ever felt better." Unable to help it, she yawned. "Okay, maybe I do need something—a catnap. A twenty-minute one."

He laughed softly and tugged her even closer, until she was actually lying on his chest. He kissed her brow, stroked her hair, whispered sweet things about how good she'd felt to him.

Lucy's cheek was right above his heart and she not only heard its beat, she also felt its steady, solid thrum. His words lulled her, his touch soothed her. Quite honestly, she couldn't recall a more perfect moment in her life.

Not ever.

She only hoped there would be many more to come, and could hardly wait to see what tomorrow would bring.

9

Now
Chicago, December 24, 2011

THEY WERE SNOWED IN. Totally trapped in a world turned white.

Standing at his office window and assessing the situation Saturday morning, Ross could only shake his head in wonder. He hadn't seen a storm like this in a lot of years, probably not since he was a kid. He tried to estimate how much of the white stuff had fallen; judging by the way it climbed up the side of his SUV, he'd say at least three feet so far. And still it came down, swirling, spinning, blowing up and down and sideways.

This might be one for the record books.

"You left and took your body heat with you," Lucy grumbled from the fold-out.

"Sorry."

She'd been asleep when he'd slipped out of bed a few minutes ago. Now she was curled on the side he'd vacated, the blankets pulled up to her nose, like she was trying to suck up any residual warmth.

She looked both adorable and sexy as hell.

And a little chilly.

Though it wasn't freezing, by any means, the temperature had definitely dropped below what it normally was in the building. Not that they'd really noticed during the night. God, had they *not* noticed. In fact, Ross would have sworn there was an inferno blazing in this little corner of Chicago. Because he and Lucy had redefined hot throughout the long, erotic hours after she'd awakened to find him in bed with her.

"How does it look out there?"

Shaking off the sultry images in his mind of the ways they'd explored and pleasured each other in the darkness, he smiled. "Like Santa decided to move here and brought the North Pole with him."

"Oh, that's just perfect," she said, sounding sarcastic.

"What's the matter, did you have big plans for the day?" He somehow doubted it. Lucy didn't seem any more of a Christmas fan now than she had been six years ago.

She thought about it, then shook her head. "Actually, no. Sam's working all weekend. I was figuring on staying in, being lazy, going online and spending that money your company paid me yesterday."

Well, she couldn't do any shopping, but staying in and being lazy sounded ideal. Especially if they were lazy between bouts of being as energetic as they'd been last night.

Damn. Lucy had become a wild woman.

Seeing her shiver, he clarified that—a *cold* wild woman.

"Here," he said, walking over to the bed, carrying two cups of coffee, which he'd just brewed.

"So the power's back on?" she asked, appearing both relieved and disappointed.

"'Fraid not," he said, shaking his head. "Fortunately, we get a lot of vendors coming in here. One of them makes a battery-operated coffeemaker and suggested we get them for sites that aren't wired yet. We did—and they gave us a few for the office as a thank-you for the contract."

"Thank goodness for free samples," she said, sitting up and letting the covers drop to her lap. Ross managed to not slosh hot coffee all over her. Seeing her in the daylight—as murky as it was—was enough to make the earth jolt. Not to mention his dick.

He hadn't realized it was possible to be so insatiable about another person. They'd had sex three or four times during the night, and he was ready to have her again. It had been dark—now he wanted to watch her face pinken as she came, see the perfect body as he licked every inch of it.

"Wonderful," she murmured as she sipped, then blew on the steaming rising from the mug. "Cream, no sugar—you remembered."

"Of course I did," he murmured. He remembered everything.

It was funny, considering he'd tried so hard to put Lucy out of his mind over the years. But she'd refused to leave, haunting his memories through other women—two of them serious—and so many other changes.

Lucy glanced at him and their stares held. She didn't try to lift the blanket, didn't blush or feign embarrassment at sitting right in front of him so beautifully naked. He'd worried she would feel some kind of doubts or uncertainty in the cold light of day. But he'd been wrong. She looked confident—serene even. Like she didn't regret a damn thing.

He smiled at the realization.

"What?"

"I half expected you to leap up, wrap the sheets around your body and accuse me of molesting you during the night."

She snickered. "I think I was the one who molested you. Although, you did creep into my bed while I was sleeping."

"*My* bed, Goldilocks. Speaking of which, I don't have any porridge to offer you for breakfast, but there's a ton of leftover party food in the break room."

She didn't seem to care about the food, instead focusing on the first part of his statement. "*Your* bed? Are you serious?"

"As a heart attack."

She looked around the office, taking note of its size and furnishings. It was, he knew, probably bigger square-footage wise, and better furnished than his entire rental house had been back in Brooklyn.

"So if the bed is yours, I guess that means this office is yours as well? I mean, I don't suppose you were just sneaking into your boss's bed since you got stuck here, too?"

"It's mine," he said with a laugh. "I'm assuming you didn't notice the nameplate on the desk."

She glanced over. Even from here it was easy to make out the "CEO" before his name. Her eyes wide, she turned her attention back to him. "You really run this place?"

"I really do."

"Wow," she said, sagging back against the pillow. "I mean, I knew you were talented, but going from handyman to CEO in six years? That's pretty remarkable."

Ross put his cup down and sat in a chair opposite her. Lifting his jean-clad legs, he used the end of the foldout as a footrest, crossing his bare feet there. "Not that remarkable, really. I inherited the position. It's my family's company."

Lucy's mouth rounded into an O. "Your father…"

"Yeah."

"How is he?" she asked. "Did he…"

"Pull through? Yes, he did. It took a long time, a lot of rehab and he still doesn't have full use of his right side, but he made it." Chuckling but only half-joking, he added, "He's still the same demanding tyrant he always was."

It would take more than a massive stroke to get his old man to stop being bossy, pushy and opinionated. And Ross should know; he dealt with that bossy, pushy opinion every damn day.

His name might be on the letterhead of Elite Construction, but his dad still held a lot of shares. They'd had a few major battles once the elder Marshall had started feeling like his old self again. It had only been lately, in the past year or so, that he'd conceded Ross was doing an excellent job, and stopped questioning every little decision.

Not that Ross wasn't very grateful his dad had lived, of course. Though they hadn't been getting along at the time, he'd been shocked and devastated by his father's massive stroke six years ago. Though he'd only been fifty-five, nobody had thought he would make it, not the doctors or the industry. Nobody except his family, who knew Ross Marshall, Sr. was too stubborn to do what everyone predicted he would.

"I'm so glad he survived," Lucy murmured.

"Thanks."

He didn't doubt she meant it. But he also didn't doubt Lucy's mind had gone right where his had—to the timing of his father's stroke. She'd been there when he'd received the frantic phone call from his sister at the crack of dawn on Christmas morning. After a weekend of pure excitement and happiness with Lucy, his world had come crashing down with one conversation.

His entire life had changed on a dime. Before that, he'd known he would someday go back to Chicago and take his place beside his father in the business. But he'd thought he had time—a couple of years, at least—to live the life he wanted. Hell at that particular moment, he'd even been considering asking Lucy if she thought he might be able to pick up some carpentry work in France for a year or two. They'd gotten *that* serious *that* quickly.

Then the phone had rung. His sister's sobs had finally made sense, and he'd left for the airport right away. As much as he'd hated bailing out on Lucy on Christmas Day, she'd been completely understanding. Hell, if anyone would understand, it would be her—she'd received her own horrifying phone call one holiday season.

He'd wasted no time packing, not even a single bag. He'd been desperate to get back to Chicago, convinced his father was on the verge of death. And horrified, realizing that the last words they'd exchanged had been angry ones.

The vigil at the hospital had been long and difficult. He'd dealt not only with the worry, and with his family, but also with stepping right in to look after the company. That, in itself, had been a battle, considering he was so young. But he hadn't been about to let the whole thing founder while his father fought for his life.

Despite being so busy, he'd found time to call Lucy every day that first week—especially knowing she had a tough anniversary of her own to contend with. During each call, she'd expressed concern about his father, but inevitably the conversation would turn to her preparations for her upcoming trip. Her plans for her future. Her great life.

Then a couple of days went between his calls.

Then a week.

Then it was almost time for her to leave for her semester abroad.

And he'd stopped calling.

"I never stopped thinking about you. I swear, you were on my mind constantly." He got to the point, the main thing he wanted to say. "I'm sorry, Lucy."

"For?"

"You know what for. I couldn't stop thinking about you…but I couldn't bring myself to call you, either."

She stiffened, didn't reply for a second, then tossed off a casual, "Hey, don't sweat it. The phone lines were notoriously unreliable that year."

He saw through the feigned humor. She'd been plenty hurt yesterday; no way had she gotten over it in one single night.

But, maybe last night had at least opened her to the possibility that he wasn't a user who'd taken her for the ride of a lifetime then dropped her flat.

"You know, I never went back to New York."

Her brow went up. "What about your house? Your things?"

"I hired somebody to take care of it that winter, once it became obvious that not only was my dad going to have a long recovery ahead of him, he would almost certainly never be able to work again."

"That must have been really tough."

"Tough doesn't begin to describe it." He swiped a hand through his hair and sighed. "Anyway, I didn't mean to get into all that. I just brought it up so I could finally tell you what I meant to tell you then and never got the chance to say."

She eyed him warily. "And that would be?"

He held her gaze, daring her not to believe him. "That I fell in love with you that weekend in New York."

She sucked in an audible breath, and slowly shook her head.

Ross nodded, not worrying about looking like a fool or fearing any kind of rejection. Maybe something great would happen between him and Lucy now. Maybe it wouldn't, and last night would be his final memory of a relationship he'd once thought would define his whole life. But no matter what, he owed her the truth about the past.

"It's true. I was crazy in love with you."

"You might have told me…"

"To what purpose?"

Rolling her eyes and looking at him like he was an idiot, she said, "Maybe just because the words would have been nice to hear once in my life?"

He couldn't imagine no man had ever fallen in love with the beautiful woman in front of him. But he didn't particularly want to think about her with anyone else. The very idea made his stomach heave.

"Maybe I should have," he said with a simple shrug. "But I was trapped."

She tilted her head in confusion.

"Lucy, you were about to leave to go grab the world by the balls."

She didn't try to deny it, but a wistful expression crossed her face, as if she were remembering the feisty, passionate girl she'd been. One of these days, hopefully, he'd find out what had brought her back here, why she was photographing children when she'd sworn she would do anything but.

Right now, though, he had his own story to tell.

"But me? Dad was on his deathbed, my family was falling apart, and I was the one who had to hold them—not to mention this business—together." He rose from his chair and walked to the fold-out, sitting beside her and reaching out to stroke a silky strand of her hair. "My life was here. It *is* here. Yours was—" he waved a hand "—out there. We were going to be living in two different worlds and as much as I wanted you in mine, I knew that wasn't going to happen. Just because my dreams fell apart didn't mean I could ask you to give up yours."

"So...you let me go?"

A simple nod. "I let you go."

Moisture appeared in her eyes, though no tears spilled from them. Sniffing, she curled her face into his hand, rubbing her soft skin against his.

They remained silent for a long time. The room was quiet enough that he could hear the plink of tiny, icy snowflakes striking the window. Then, with a low sigh, Lucy looked up at him and smiled.

"Thank you for telling me," she whispered.

"You're welcome."

Nothing else. No promises. No requests. It was as if they'd just wiped clean the slate and could now start again, fresh. And see where the road took them.

"I'VE GOT TO admit it, Papa Bear, this beats porridge any day."

Lucy licked a few cookie crumbs off her fingers, sighing

in satisfaction at the strange Christmas Eve brunch they'd just shared. Cookies, eggnog, cheese and crackers, chips, chocolate and fruit.

The food at the party had been plentiful and delicious. It had also kept very well in the large refrigerator, which was doing a pretty good job holding its temperature despite the power outage. Though, if they were going to be stuck here much longer, they were going to have to ditch the eggnog in favor of unopened bottles of soda or fruit juice.

"I think there's even some leftover sliced turkey for Christmas dinner," he replied. "If it comes to that."

Judging by the way it continued to snow, it could definitely come to that.

She should be bothered by it. Should be worried about being trapped, should at least be freaked out about not having a spare pair of underwear—not that she expected to wear them for long.

But the truth was, she didn't care. She had no obligations to anyone else, didn't have holiday plans, other than shopping. Her brother had already been scheduled to work all weekend, and with the weather, she doubted he'd have time to even drop by before Monday or Tuesday.

So why not spend a few days trapped in a secure building with plenty of food and water, and someone to provide plenty of entertainment. If, that was, she could survive that much…entertainment.

"I guess this meets your requirements for a nontraditional Christmas, huh?"

"Hey, I ate a bell-shaped cookie, didn't I?" Then she chuckled. "Though, believe it or not, I've gotten a little less stringent about that."

"Seriously?"

"Kate has kids now, and I actually went and spent Christmas with them a couple of years ago. It was…nice."

More than nice. It had been lovely. Sweet and wholesome and fun. And yes, a bit painful. But after many years,

Lucy had been able to let down her guard and let some of the magic of the season back into her heart. She wasn't ready to go out and chop down a tree or download a copy of *Now That's What I Call Christmas #948* to her MP3 player. But she could at least hum Silent Night—her mother's favorite Christmas carol—and not want to break into tears.

"You must know I'm curious…"

"About?"

"Paris. Europe. Photographing Fashion Week, landing the cover of *Vogue?*"

She sighed, remembering that girl, those dreams. How important they'd once seemed, when she was running away from anything resembling the life she'd once had and so painfully lost. Changing her plans completely had helped her evade the memories for a little while, but not forever. Eventually she'd had to face them.

She explained that to him, as best she could, wondering if the explanation would make any sense to anybody else.

When she was finished, Ross nodded slowly. "And now that you know you don't have to go halfway across the world to keep from caring too much about anyone or anything…are you happy?"

Wow. He'd obviously read between the lines. She hadn't mentioned anything about not wanting to care about anyone. But she couldn't deny it was true.

"I'm happy," she admitted. "I love what I do—you remember how I swore I'd never work with kids?"

"Even though you were great at it."

"Exactly. I guess I was the last one to see it. But I love it, and I'm good. I've had more success with my kid portraiture than I ever did with adults. I actually had a photo in *Time* magazine last year."

He whistled. "Seriously?"

"Yep. I've had shots picked up by the AP, and magazines and catalogs. I actually just submitted a photo essay for Parents Place Magazine as well, and I'm hoping they'll take me on for more freelance work."

"Sounds wonderful," he told her, sounding like he meant it. "I'm really happy for you."

"Thanks." Suddenly remembering something, and knowing he'd be interested, she said, "Oh, guess who I ran into a year or so ago in New York?"

He raised a curious brow.

"Remember Jude the jackass?"

His sneer said he did. "Please tell me he ended up in prison being some Bubba's bitch."

"No, but his daddy did."

Ross's jaw dropped.

"His family ran one of those businesses that was 'too big to fail.' Only, it failed during the financial meltdown. Daddy went to jail, the family lost everything. Jude was very humbled—and very poor—when I ran into him."

"Couldn't have happened to a nicer guy."

Almost unable to remember the girl she'd been when she'd thought Jude could be "the one," she said, "I guess that catches you up with what's been going on with me."

And he'd already caught her up on what his life had been like. It had been full of family and work and duty. Not much downtime, from the sound of it, although he had apparently had time to start building that dream house of his—oh, she would love to see it.

As for his personal life, though she hadn't pried, not wanting to be nosy, she had sort of rejoiced when he admitted he hadn't had any romantic relationship that had lasted longer than six months. That made two of them.

"Wait, what about your brother?" Ross asked. "Does he still give you ugly snow globes every Christmas?"

She chuckled, thinking about the collection that she set out every single year. With the exception of the broken groovy Santa, she still had each and every one.

"I put out my entire collection every holiday season."

"*All* of them?" he asked, his voice soft and serious.

She knew what he was asking. Knew he wondered if she'd kept the one and only Christmas present he'd ever given her. Considering she'd been heartbroken shortly after he'd given it to her, the answer probably should have been no. But in truth, she'd never been able to part with that special gift, even though, every time she took it out of its box, she'd wondered about Ross. Where he was, what had happened to him.

Now she knew. He'd been living his life as best he could...after having freed her to follow her dreams.

"Yes, Ross," she murmured. "Every one."

"I'm glad."

"Me, too." Then, wanting to keep the mood light, she added, "The one my brother got me last year had to take the prize for kookiest ever."

"Do tell."

"Sam found one from some weird cult that believes the three wise men came from another planet. Balthazar had green skin and claws. Melchior had a spiked tail. And the other one was furry all over."

Tossing his head back, Ross laughed. "Please don't tell me the baby Jesus was an alien, too."

"No, but he looked terrified."

"Is it any wonder? I mean, with the cast of a bad episode of *Star Trek* standing over him?"

Snorting as she realized that's exactly what the three kings had looked like, she got up and began clearing away the plastic dishes they'd used for their late-morning feast. They'd eaten in the break room, since it was closest to not only all the food, but all the supplies, too.

"So, you ready to go down and check things out?" Ross asked.

They'd agreed that, after eating, they would head downstairs to the lobby and try to get a better idea of what was going on outside. From up here on the sixth floor, it looked like they were trapped in a spaceship that had landed on a marshmallow planet.

"Ready when you are."

Though they didn't expect to get anywhere, the two of them dressed warmly. They had raided a coat closet to add layers to their own clothes. There were a few jackets, scarves and hats that had been left behind over the years—enough so that they shouldn't freeze if they dared to step outside.

Once they trudged down the six floors to the lobby, and saw that the snow had drifted almost all the way up the glass doors, though, Lucy realized they needn't have bothered.

"This is crazy!" she said, standing up on tiptoe to try to see over the white mountain. "Can you see the parking lot?"

Ross cupped his hand around a spot of glass that wasn't obscured by snow. "There are three lumps out there—I assume your car, mine and the security truck. It would take a sled and a team of dogs to get us to them, though."

Meaning, even if the power came on and the streets were cleared, they weren't going anywhere until Ross's private snow removal contractor showed up to clear the walks and the parking lot. And who knew when that would be?

"We're not going anywhere, are we?"

"Nuh-uh." He turned to face her. "Is that okay? I mean... you're not scared about being trapped here, are you?"

She scrunched her brow. "Have you turned into a cannibal sometime in the last six years?"

He wagged his eyebrows. "You complaining about what I like to eat?"

Good Lord, she was never going to complain about that for the rest of her life.

"Never mind," she said, knowing she sounded off balance.

The man was good at distracting her, putting wild thoughts in her head. He was good at a lot of things. Making her laugh, making her sigh, making her crazy. Giving her incredible pleasure.

At twenty-two, she'd found Ross Marshall to be the sexiest guy she'd ever met. Now, six years later, she knew he was more than that. Still sexy, oh, without a doubt. Probably even more so, actually, because he had a ton of confidence and a man's mature personality to go along with the looks and charm.

But she now saw him as a whole lot more than a broke carpenter with a bean bag chair and a lava lamp. He was successful, very smart, and incredibly likable. She'd seen the way he talked to all those people at the party yesterday; now, knowing he was their employer, she was even more impressed.

"Seriously, you're not too worried, are you?" he asked. "We have plenty of food, the building's secure. And I don't think it's going to get unbearably cold. If it does, we can move to an interior room with no windows."

She shook her head. "Honestly, I'm not worried. The only question is, what on earth are we going to do to occupy ourselves?"

She accompanied that question with a bat of her eyelashes.

Ross stepped closer, dropping his hands onto her hips. Even through the padding of her pants, sweater, somebody's hoodie, somebody else's jacket and her heavy coat, she felt the possessive weight of it.

"I'm sure we'll think of something."

She gazed up at him, licking her lips and smiling. "I already have thought of something."

"Oh?"

She leaned up on tiptoes, brushing her lips against his jawline and whispered, "Close your eyes."

He did. Immediately.

"Count to twenty."

"Uh…why?" One eye opened and she immediately frowned. He closed it again. "Sorry. Counting. One."

She stepped away. "No peeking. Keep counting."

"Two."

A smile crossed his face, as if he were picturing her stripping out of her clothes, laying herself out naked on the security desk. Hmm. That could be kind of interesting. Though they couldn't possibly be seen through the drifts or the still-falling snow, it sounded extremely daring.

"Three."

She shook her head and tiptoed backward toward the closed stairwell door. He was saying four as she carefully pulled it open and five as it swung closed behind her. Hopefully, by the time he reached twenty, she'd be back up on the sixth floor.

Hide-and-seek in a six-story office building. Sounded like a good way to kill some time.

Especially if she made sure she was naked by the time he found her.

10
―――

As much as Lucy would have liked to stay in Ross's little house and learn everything there was to know about making love, she had to work on Christmas Eve. The photographer for whom she was interning had families coming in for holiday portraits and she needed to be there with bells on.

Literally. Jingle bells. They were attached to the curled-up toes of her silly elf shoes and she tinkled with every step.

One day, when she was a world-famous photographer, she'd laugh about this. But not now. It was just too ridiculous and embarrassing. So much for wanting to seem like a cool, collected, mature woman during her first-ever "morning after." Ross was going to look at her and think he'd spent the night with a teenager.

"Please tell me you'll wear that outfit tonight," Ross said, not attempting to hide his amusement when she emerged from the bathroom early Saturday morning.

"Ha ha."

"I mean it. You're totally hot. Hermie would never have left the North Pole to become a dentist if you were around."

"Dork."

"Elf." He grabbed her by the hips and pulled her close,

laughing as her bobbing red feather poked him in the eye. He was still laughing when he pressed his mouth against hers for a deep, good morning kiss.

Lucy wobbled on her feet a little. Somehow, she suspected Ross's kiss—or even just the memory of his kiss—would *always* make her wobble.

"Are you ready?"

"Don't I look ready?" she said with a disgusted sigh. Then she added, "You're sure you don't mind driving me all the way back up to the city?"

"I told you, I have errands to run."

They'd spent time this morning wrapping and packing up his holiday gifts to his family. But she suspected there had to be shipping stores somewhere closer than Manhattan.

"I could take the train."

"Forget it," he said, ending the discussion.

The traffic heading into the city wasn't as bad as it would have been on a weekday. Most cars were heading out—obviously people who'd been stuck working right up until the twenty-third leaving for holiday weekends with family.

They reached the studio about a half hour early, and Lucy, who had a key, led him inside. "You really don't have to stay," she told him as she turned on the lights.

"I'm staying," he insisted, immediately stepping to a front window to glance back out at the street.

She knew why. Ross didn't trust Jude not to come here and harass her. Not that either of them really thought he'd try anything violent in broad daylight, while she was at work. But she wouldn't put it past him to come in and try to talk to her about why she should let last night's ugly incident go.

She wouldn't. In fact, this morning, with Ross's encouragement, she'd already called and spoken to someone at the police precinct near her apartment.

"Are you usually here alone in the mornings?" Ross asked, when, after ten minutes, nobody else had arrived.

"My boss is always late." Rolling her eyes, she added, "He's the irresponsible, creative genius type."

"So I see," he said as he followed her into the studio, where a holiday scene had been laid out. A large sleigh with velvet cushions stood in a corner, in front of a snowy backdrop. Surrounding it were mounds of white fluff that looked like snow. Woodland creatures, decorated trees, candy canes and icicles finished the scenario. "This is cute."

"Thanks," she said, pleased at the compliment, since she was the one who'd designed the whimsical scene. Her employer had never done more than drop a snowy screen behind a stool before she'd come onboard, and he'd already complimented her on the increased amount of traffic, telling her she had a knack for this kind of thing.

Funny, really, since she never intended to do it again. Surprisingly, though, as she stood looking at the results of her creativity, she felt a pang of sadness at the thought. She'd put a lot of effort into this and had actually enjoyed doing it.

Forget it. Paris fashion beats North Pole kiddieland any day.

Right. Definitely. Even if she did love hearing the squeals of delight of some of the littlest children who came in for holiday sittings, she would almost certainly love the squeals of millionaires as they eyed the latest fashions on the catwalk.

Hearing her cell phone ring, Lucy retrieved it, recognizing the studio owner's name. "Uh-oh," she mumbled, hoping this didn't mean the man would be later than usual.

A few seconds into the conversation, she realized it was worse than that. "You're not coming in today at *all?*"

"I'm sorry, it can't be helped! I fell last night and hurt my knee. I can't walk."

Huh. Considering the older man liked to dig into the spiked eggnog by noon, she had to wonder how he'd fallen.

"We only have a few appointments—you can handle them."

Lucy sputtered. She was an intern—an unpaid one at that. And he seriously wanted her to do his job, on Christmas Eve?

"I know this is going above and beyond," he said. "But I'd be so grateful. I will absolutely compensate you for your time."

She could just imagine what he'd consider fair compensation. Considering she had worked like a slave for three months without earning a penny, she'd be lucky to make a hundred bucks.

But hell, she was here. She was a photographer. And even if she didn't ever want to take the kinds of photographs he took, it was her chance to work professionally. So she agreed.

After she disconnected, and explained the situation, Ross offered to stay and help her. Lucy appreciated it, but knew he had things to do. Insisting that he go mail his packages, she added, "I'll check the book, but I think there are only appointments between ten and one. If you can get back by then and greet people as they come in, I'd really appreciate it."

Then she'd be finished for the day, and they could go do…whatever two lovers, who were strangers a day ago, one of whom didn't do Christmas, did on Christmas.

She could hardly wait.

"You're on," he promised as he headed toward the door. Before exiting, he said, "Keep this locked until ten, okay?"

She nodded. "I swear. Don't worry."

He gave her one of those devastating smiles that lit up his green eyes. "Can't help it, Lucy."

The way he said it, the warmth in his expression, made

her smile for several minutes after he'd gone. But eventually, she had to set up for work.

Given the freedom to experiment, she decided to try out a few ideas, as long as the paying customers were willing. So by the time the first was scheduled to arrive, she'd already played around with some lighting effects, as well as a couple of her boss's specialty lenses.

Ross arrived back right on time, and with his help, she spent the next couple of hours enjoying the heck out of her job. For the first time, she wasn't just signing people in, collecting checks, selling overpriced packages, and trying to make cranky, wet little kids laugh, while nodding at every single idea her boss had. She was creating, trying new positions and lighting and special effects. She could feel the energy as she worked, and suspected these images would turn out to be something special.

By the time she'd finished with the last customer, it was after two. Ross had been a huge help, and once they were alone in the front office, she threw her arms around his neck and kissed him. "Thank you so much—what a fun day!"

"It was," he told her, laughing as he dropped his hands to her hips and squeezed her tighter. "You were fantastic. I don't know that I've ever seen anyone as great with kids as you are."

She rolled her eyes. "I wouldn't go that far."

"I would," he insisted. "You were really amazing. You should specialize in this."

"Fat chance," she snorted. "I have other plans. Big plans."

"Like?"

They began to clean up, getting ready to shut the studio down for the next few days. And while they did, Lucy told him about her upcoming study abroad trip. About her plans to photograph her way around the world. About the bright, exotic future she envisioned for herself, which had nothing to do with Santas or reindeer or chubby-cheeked infants.

He broke in with a few questions, but for the most part, just nodded, agreeing that her future sounded wonderful. But when all was said and done, he still murmured, "I still say you'd be great doing this, too."

"Not happening," she told him, knowing he didn't truly understand. How could he? She hadn't come right out and told him that her need to escape to somewhere far away had a lot in common with her need to avoid Christmas and all the happy family trappings that came with it.

Lucy had loved photography from the time she was twelve and her parents had given her a "real" camera. She'd been the family photojournalist from that moment on, recording every event and capturing every wonderful smile.

But then the family and the smiles had disappeared. Their loss had been almost more than she could bear. So going out into the world and seeing exotic places and people through the lens of her camera sounded ideal to her, now that she could no longer see the people she'd always loved. Exciting, of course…but more, it sounded a lot less painful. Her heart wasn't going to be broken if a shot didn't land on the pages of a magazine. Not caring as much about her subjects was the smart choice, the right choice. The perfect way to live her life.

Ross's voice suddenly jolted her out of the moment of melancholy. "So, little girl, have you been good all year?"

Spinning around, she saw him sitting on the sleigh, patting his lap suggestively, like the world's sexiest Santa.

"Hmm," she said, sauntering over. "That depends on your definition of good."

He pulled her down on top of him. "After last night, you are my definition of good," he told her. "They should just put your picture on the G page in Webster's."

"Are you sure I'm not a little bit bad?"

He nuzzled her neck. "Only in the very best way."

Feeling soft and warm all over, she dropped her head back, inviting him further, loving the feel of his unshaven cheek against her skin. When he pressed his mouth to the hollow of her throat, she sighed. And when he moved lower, to tease the V-neck of her blouse, she leaned back even further. So far, she fell off his lap, onto a mountain of white, fluffy fake snow.

"Ow," she said, even as she laughed at herself.

He leaped off the seat and knelt beside her. "Are you okay?"

"I'm fine."

"You'd better let me check you all over and make sure you're not hurt."

Hearing the naughty tone, she feigned a deep sigh and sagged back into the fluff, which cushioned her like a giant feather bed. "Maybe you should. I do feel a little weak."

His eyes gleaming, Ross did as he'd threatened. Slowly, gently, he caressed her neck, brushed his thumbs over her collarbones, cupped her shoulders. As if he couldn't be certain using just his hands, he began kissing his way down her body as well. Every time she sighed, or flinched, he'd look up at her and ask, "Did that hurt?"

"Definitely not," she mumbled, rising up to meet his mouth.

He didn't tease her for long. Neither of them could stand that. As if he couldn't wait to be with her again—though it had only been hours since they'd left his bed—Ross unbuttoned her blouse, pulling it free of her flouncy skirt. He kissed his way to her breasts, bathing the sensitive tips through her bra.

"Mmm," she groaned, wrapping her fingers in his thick hair.

She loved that he was so into her breasts, loved the way he slipped the bra strap down and plumped each one with his hand before sucking deeply on her nipples. Each strong pull of his mouth sent a jolt of want through her body, and her tights felt even more restrictive than usual.

"Luce?" he mumbled as he pulled her skirt up around her waist and cupped her thigh.

"Hmm?"

"Since tomorrow's Christmas, does that mean you don't need this costume anymore?"

"I guess so," she murmured.

"Good."

He didn't explain what that meant, he simply showed her. Rising onto his knees, Ross reached for the crotch of her tights and carefully yanked. They tore open, exposing her sex completely, since she'd been wearing nothing underneath.

"Good God," he muttered, sitting back on his heels to look at her.

Seeing that shocked delight in his face gave her such a feeling of feminine power. She deliberately spread her legs, revealing more of herself, loving the way his hand shook as he lifted it to rub his jaw.

It wasn't shaking when he reached out to touch her, though. She hissed as his long, warm fingers stroked her, delving into the slick crevice between her thighs. She was wet and ready, wanting him desperately.

Fortunately, Ross had brought a condom, and she laid back in the fluff, watching him push his jeans out of the way and don the protection. She lifted a leg invitingly, knowing he'd like the feel of the silky fabric of the tights against his bare hip.

She imagined he'd like it in other places, too. But his hips and that amazingly tight male butt were a good start. Without a word, she pulled him down to her, inviting him into her warmth.

She was still new enough at this to gasp when he entered her, but Ross kissed away the sound. His warm tongue made love to her mouth as he pressed further into her body, until they were fully joined. Lucy wrapped her legs around him and rolled her hips up in welcome.

He lengthened his strokes, filling and stretching and pleasing her so much she cried out at how good it felt. He was so thick and hard inside her, and she was used to this enough to want him harder, faster. Deeper.

"More," she demanded. "You're being so careful...you can stop. I want it all, Ross. Give it to me."

He groaned. Then, as if he'd just been awaiting the invitation, pulled out and slammed back into her. Hard, deep. Unbelievably good.

"Oh, yeah. More."

"You're sure."

"Absolutely," she insisted. "Give me everything you've got."

He didn't reply with words. Instead, to her surprise, Ross pulled out of her and reached for her hips. His face a study in need and hunger, he rolled her over onto her tummy, then wrapped an arm around her waist and pulled her up onto her knees. Lucy shivered, more excited than she'd ever been in her life.

She was wet and hot and ready, and when he thrust into her from behind, she threw her head back and screamed a little.

Still buried deep inside her, he grabbed her tights again. It took just one more tug and he'd ripped them completely in half from waist to thigh, baring her bottom entirely. Filling his hands with her hips, he drove into her again. Heat to heat, skin to skin.

Lucy just about lost her mind. She loved it sweet and slow and tender. But oh, did she ever love it hot and wild and *wicked*. In fact, she realized, she loved each and every thing Ross Marshall did to her.

Especially that. And, oh, *that.*

They strained and writhed, gave and took, and soon, a stunning orgasm tore through her. As if he'd just been waiting for her to reach that point, Ross immediately buried his face in her hair, kept his arms wrapped tightly around her waist and let himself go over the edge, too.

They collapsed together on the fluff. He rolled onto his side, tugging her with him, spooning her from behind. Lucy had a hard time catching her breath, but oh, God, was it worth it.

Finally, when their breathing had calmed down a bit, Ross said, "So, since you're finished with work, was that the official start of the holiday?"

"If so," she said, sounding vehement, "then merry Christmas to us!"

He hugged her closer. "And to us a good night."

THEY HAD A hell of a good night. An amazing night, as far as Ross was concerned.

After he and Lucy had cleaned up the studio and left, they hadn't headed right back for Brooklyn. Instead they'd tooled around the city a little bit. He'd even managed to convince her to go up to Rockefeller Center and go ice skating. Sure, they'd been blade-to-blade with a thousand other people who had the same idea, but it was worth it.

They'd walked past every decorated window on Park and Fifth Avenues, had gone down as far as Macy's and jostled a place in line to see those, too. Lucy grumbled a lot, but beneath the complaints he'd heard something that tugged at his heart. A sweetness, an excitement, a longing she hadn't verbalized, but was there all the same.

Underneath it all—the vibrant, gonna-go-see-the-world, and I-don't-care-about-Christmas veneer—was a pretty innocent twenty-two-year-old. One who had lost her anchor at a young age and didn't trust the world not to slam her again. Hard.

He wouldn't have admitted it, but Ross really liked trying to get Lucy to enjoy the holiday season, despite her own best efforts to dislike it. And while he wasn't totally certain she'd like the gift he'd bought her before going back to help at the studio this morning, he hoped she at least understood the intentions behind it.

"That was great," he said as he set his fork onto his empty plate. They'd just finished dinner at his tiny kitchen table.

Lucy had insisted on cooking for him, though she'd warned him she wasn't up to anything fancy. Still, it had been the first real "home-cooked" meal he'd had in ages, and he didn't think meatloaf had ever tasted so good.

He stood to clear the table and clean up the kitchen.

"Let me help you," she said, starting to rise.

"You cooked," he told her. "Go sit down and relax for a while. I've got this."

"You're sure?"

"Of course." It struck him, suddenly, how domestic the whole thing was. Which was pretty bizarre, considering they'd known each other for a day and a half.

The best day and a half ever.

That was a crazy realization, but it was true nonetheless. He couldn't remember a better time than he'd had since meeting Lucy Fleming. Honestly, wondering what was going to happen next had him more excited than anything in a very long time.

Cleaning the kitchen quickly, he went into the other room, and found Lucy sitting on the sofa, with her head back and her eyes closed. She'd turned on the stereo and Christmas music played softly in the background. He was about to open his mouth to tease her about breaking her own rule when he saw the teardrop on her cheek.

Saying nothing, he joined her on the couch, tugging her against him so that her head rested on his shoulder. They sat there for a long time in silence, listening to the music, watching the way the silly camera flash—now covered with a green sheet of plastic—cast glimmers of light on the Christmas tree.

Finally, she shifted in his arms and looked up at him. "This is the nicest Christmas Eve I've had in a very long time."

"I'm glad. Not *too* traditional for you?"

"No. It's perfect." She licked her lips. "I know you're very close to your family, and this is all probably hard for you to understand..."

"I can understand it with my brain," he told her, meaning it. "But my heart doesn't even want to try to understand. I just can't imagine what it must be like."

His father drove him crazy, but Ross still loved him, and his mother. He couldn't even fathom having his world yanked out from under him like Lucy had, couldn't comprehend getting a phone call telling you the people you'd always assumed would be there were suddenly gone.

People expected to outlive their parents, that was natural. But not until they reached at least middle age. Not until their own kids had gotten a chance to meet their grandparents. His own parents were pretty young, only in their early mid-fifties, and Ross fully expected another twenty to thirty years of arguing with his Dad and being fussed over by his Mom. He wouldn't have it any other way.

"I can tell you what it's like," she said. "It's like waking up one day and realizing someone's torn half your heart out of your chest. Your life is no longer about the number of years you've lived, or the ones you have in front of you. It becomes measured by before and after that one moment."

He understood. It broke his heart, but he definitely understood. He hugged her close, smoothing her hair, kissing her temple.

"But then," she whispered, "the hole starts to fill in. You remember the good times from before that moment, and also start to acknowledge the good ones that come after." She shifted on the couch, looking up at him. Her beautiful brown eyes were luminous, but no more tears marred her cheeks. As if she wanted him to see that she was melancholy, but not heartbroken. "This weekend, you've given me good moments, Ross. And I'll never forget them."

He bent to her, brushing his mouth across hers in a tender kiss. She kissed him back, sweetly, gently, then smiled up at him.

"So," he said, knowing the time was right, "is it okay if I give you your Christmas present now?"

She eyed him warily.

"It's not much," he told her as he got up and went to the tree. He'd hidden the wrapped package behind it when they'd arrived home earlier this evening.

"You shouldn't have gotten me anything," she insisted. "I don't have anything for you."

He winked and raised a flirtatious brow. "I'm sure I'll think of something you can give me later."

"Hmm...why don't we see what's in here, then I'll decide just what you deserve to get in return." She took the present, and though a shadow of trepidation crossed her face, and she nibbled her lip lightly, he would also swear he saw a glimmer of a smile.

He sat on the opposite end of the couch, watching her unwrap the box. As she opened the lid, and stared down in silence at the gift inside, he couldn't help wondering if he'd made a mistake.

Maybe it was too soon. Maybe she wasn't ready. Maybe she'd think he didn't understand, after all.

She reached in and pulled out the snow globe, shaking it gently, watching the white glitter swirl around the scene inside.

It wasn't anything funny, like her brother would give her, and certainly wasn't intended to replace the peace sign Santa that had been broken. Instead it was simple, pretty—traditional. A house with a snowy roof and a wreath on the door. Warm, yellow light coming from the windows, where a family could be imagined to have gathered. A car parked outside. A tree-studded landscape. It portrayed a quiet Christmas night, when all was calm and bright.

"I just thought, since your other one was broken…"

"It's beautiful," she whispered. "Absolutely beautiful."

She twisted the knob on the bottom, and Deck The Halls began to play. Smiling, Lucy carefully set the globe down on the table. "Thank you."

"You're welcome, Lucy."

The song on the radio ended, and an announcer came on to mention the time—midnight on the nose.

They looked at the tree, then at each other. With no more sign of those tears, Lucy whispered, "Merry Christmas, Ross."

She rose from the couch and extended her hand. Ross took it and together they walked to his bedroom. They exchanged langorous, intimate kisses as they slowly undressed. Throughout the long night hours, they didn't have sex, they made love. He had never been sure of the distinction before, but now, he finally got it.

He fell asleep with a smile on his face, and was pretty sure it stayed there all night long. Because he was still smiling hours later, on Christmas morning, when he woke up to a naked Lucy wrapped in his arms…and a ringing phone.

"What time is it?" she asked in a sleep-filled voice.

He glanced at the clock. "Only six-thirty."

There would only be one person calling this early. His kid sister was always the first one up on Christmas, and she'd probably already checked her email and seen the cyber gift card he'd ordered for her.

Checking the caller ID on his phone, and seeing his parents' phone number, he chuckled and opened it, fully expecting to hear his sister's joy-filled, chattery voice.

"Hello?"

A pause. A sob.

Then the bottom fell out of his entire world.

11

LUCY WOKE UP Christmas morning feeling nice, warm and toasty. That wasn't just because of the incredibly hot, sexy, naked man against whom she was lying, but also because the heating vent right above the foldout was blowing out a steady stream of warm air.

The power was on. *Hallelujah.*

She lay there for a few minutes, relieved, but also a tiny bit sad. Power was good. Great, in fact. But it signaled something: a return to normalcy. The real world was knocking at the doors of their romantic little love nest, reminding them it was really a six story office building in Chicago.

For thirty-six hours, they'd been able to pretend the rest of the world didn't exist. Now that they were wired again, however, they were just a phone call away from everyone.

She should make use of that and call Sam, who might be worried. Hopefully he had been too busy to try to reach her. But at the very least she needed to call and wish him a merry Christmas…or at least a *bah, humbug*.

She wondered if it would be merry for her. Before yesterday, she would have laughed at the idea. Now, though, she honestly wasn't sure.

It would probably be smart to cut her losses, grab the memory of the gift she'd already received this holiday season, and get out while the getting was good. She and Ross had shared a magical Christmas Eve—for the second time in her life. But they'd already proved once that they couldn't last much beyond that. So what kind of fool would she be to let him back into her heart again, the way she'd let him back into her arms?

Anybody could make a lovely, romantic memory out of the holiday season and some snow. They'd never had to try to exist out in the real world.

And maybe they shouldn't. Maybe they weren't meant to.

Saddened by that thought, she slowly sat up and stretched. She peered over Ross's shoulder toward the wall of windows and realized that not only had the snow stopped, but the sky was trying to be all blue and sunny. There was also a distinct sound of some kind of motor nearby.

Curious, she climbed out of bed and went to the window, which overlooked the parking lot. To her surprise, it was already half-cleared. A truck with a plow was working on the lot, and a small skid loader was taking care of the mounds of snow on the walkways.

"Damn," she whispered. Not only were they now connected electronically with the world, it looked like their "snowed-in" status was about to change, too. Their private holiday adventure had come to an end.

"Merry Christmas," he said from the bed, his voice thick with sleep.

Though she wanted to respond in kind, the words stuck a little in her throat, which had thickened with every second since she'd awoken. "Good morning."

"Does it feel warmer in here, or is it just because I'm staring at you and you're naked?"

She laughed softly and returned to the bed, bending to kiss him as she crawled in beside him. "Power's on. And the parking lot's almost cleared."

He frowned. "Remind me to fire that snow clearing company."

Ross didn't sound any happier about being "rescued" than she felt. Maybe because, like her, he wasn't sure what was going to happen when they returned to reality.

Did they have what it took to go beyond this weekend? To actually work in a day-to-day relationship? With his ties to his family and this business and this city…and her sometimes whimsical need to change direction and explore new opportunities, were they really cut out to be together?

She had no idea. Nor did she really want to talk to him about it yet. She had some thinking to do. And it would probably be best to do it alone.

"I guess you ought to call your family and let them know you're okay," she said. "They've probably been very worried."

He nodded. "Listen, why don't you come with…"

She knew what he was going to ask and held a hand up, palm out. "Thanks, but no thanks."

"I'm sure they'd love to meet you."

"Bah humbug, remember?"

"Lucy…"

"Please don't," she said as she got up and reached for her clothes and began pulling them on. As much as she'd like to stay naked in bed with Ross, she knew things had changed. She felt a lot less free and a lot more worried than she had last night. The presence of the rest of the world in their strange relationship had thrown her off-kilter. Where a few hours ago she had been filled with nothing but contentment and satisfaction, now the only things that filled her head were questions and concerns.

"I need some time," she told him. "I'd really just like to go home and take a shower."

"What about Christmas dinner?"

Turkey subs out of the break room had sounded just about perfect. Going with him to his parents' estate for a grand meal with a big family? Not so much.

"Please don't push it," she said, hearing the edge in her voice and getting mad at herself. He was trying to share something special—his family's holiday.

"Okay," he said. "I understand."

Since she didn't understand herself, she doubted that, but didn't want to argue with him. Not after the wonderful day they'd had yesterday and the beautiful, amazing, incredible nights in that narrow foldout bed.

"You can use the phone on my desk if you want to call Sam," he told her. "If the power's on, the lines should be working. Just dial 9 first."

Thanking him, she finished dressing and went to the desk. She got Sam's voice mail and left him a message. She checked her cell phone—still no reception—and decided to call her home phone and see if there were any messages.

She dialed home, then entered the security code. When she heard she had two messages from Friday, she winced, realizing she'd never even listened to them when she got home the other night. She'd been too busy masturbating in the bathtub while thinking of Ross.

A voice she didn't recognize came on the line. "Ms. Fleming, this is Janet Sturgeon, I'm with *Parents Place* magazine. I'm sorry for calling right before the holidays, but we really wanted to reach you. Everyone in the office just loved your photo essay."

She sent up a mental cheer. But the voice wasn't finished.

"And of course we all remember the great work you've done for us in the past. Anyway, we're making some changes here at headquarters and were wondering if you might be interested in coming to New York to discuss a more permanent working position with us? We're looking for an artistic director. We all really like what you do and think you would be a great fit with our staff."

Lucy's jaw had slowly become unhinged while she listened. She'd been hoping for a *Yes, we'll take your work and pay you X dollars*. But a job offer? At least, the offer of an interview for a job? She'd never imagined it.

Well, that was a lie, of course she'd imagined it. She'd thought many times about getting out of the self-employment wading pool and into the bigger publishing ocean. And *Parents Place* was a huge part of that ocean. The chance to work for them, to be an artistic director for a major national publication…honestly, it was like someone had just handed her the winning prize for a lottery, when she'd never bought a ticket.

Her mind had drifted off, and she'd missed the phone number the caller had left at the end. Lucy saved the message to listen to again when she got home and thought about what to say when she called the woman back tomorrow.

"Lucy? Are you okay?"

Ross was watching her from the alcove. He'd finished dressing, and swept a hand through his thick, sleep-tousled hair, looking perfect and sexy and gorgeous. Her heart somersaulted in her chest, as it always did when she looked at the man in broad daylight. Or, hell, in pitch darkness.

Only now, there was a faint squeezing sensation in her heart as well.

Don't be silly, you don't even know if you'd actually get the job yet. Or if you'd take it.

True. She couldn't let herself get upset about what could possibly happen in the future, and what it meant for her and Ross. For all she knew, there was no her and Ross. This weekend had been amazing and wonderful…but she had already acknowledged there might not be more than that.

There won't be if you're in New York.

Which made her wonder—would he care if she left?
Would he ask her not to go?

"Lucy? Is everything okay? Was it Sam?"

She shook her head slowly and lowered the receiver
back onto the cradle. Trying to keep her voice steady, so
she wouldn't reveal either her excitement, or her incredible turmoil over what this could mean for them, she told
him about the phone call.

Ross didn't react right away. He didn't immediately
smile and congratulate her. Neither did he frown and insist that she couldn't possibly think about leaving now,
when so much between them was up in the air.

*So maybe it's not. Maybe everything was settled in that
bed in the past thirty-six hours, and it's all over and we are
both supposed to just go merrily on with our lives.*

God, did she not want to believe that. But it was possible. To Ross, this may have just been a one-time thing.
Maybe he couldn't care less if she went. She just didn't
know. And honestly, she wasn't sure how to ask.

"I see. Well, that's exciting," he finally said.

"It could be," she replied carefully.

"When would you go back to New York?"

Yell, damn it. Show some kind of emotion.

"She said they wanted to interview me immediately,
this week if possible."

"I don't imagine the airports are going to be open for a
day or two. Maybe by late Tuesday, or Wednesday."

"Maybe," she said, wondering how he could be so calm,
why he wouldn't reveal a thing about what he was thinking.

Why he wasn't telling her he didn't want her to go.

But he didn't. Instead, still calm and reasonable, as if
they'd just finished a dinner date rather than a thirty-six
hour, emotionally-charged sexual marathon, he helped her
straighten up the office and the break room, hiding evidence of the wild weekend idyll that had taken place there.
Everything went back in its spot, the borrowed coats re-

turned, the food neatly put away. Even the foldout was made and folded up. No evidence that they'd been here at all.

The realization made her incredibly sad. But there was nothing she could do about it.

Finally, with nothing left to do, they dressed in warm clothes, and headed downstairs. They had no problem getting out to the parking lot, and Ross paid his contractor a little extra to dig out their cars. So, by twelve noon, they were ready to go, neither too concerned about their drive, considering the plows and salt trucks had been out in force most of the night.

Chicago was a city that was used to dealing with snow. Despite the wicked Christmas Eve blizzard, things would likely get back to normal pretty easily. If anything was ever normal again. Right now, Lucy wasn't sure about the definition of that word.

"You sure you're okay to drive home?" he asked.

She nodded. "I'll be fine, it's only a couple of miles."

He opened her car door for her. It was warm inside; she'd let it idle for a few minutes while they stood outside saying goodbye. Or, not saying goodbye. So far, they'd said anything but.

She wasn't sure what she was waiting for him to say. Or if he was waiting, too. Or what either of them could say that would make this all right, make them both understand where they'd been and where they were going.

In the end, they didn't say much of anything. Ross simply leaned down and brushed his mouth across hers, their breath mingling in the icy air. Then he whispered, "Merry Christmas, Lucy."

She managed a tremulous smile and nodded.

"Bye, Ross."

Her heart was screaming at her to say something else. Her brain was, too. But she couldn't find the words, didn't know what he wanted to hear.

So she simply got in her car, watched him get into his, and then they both drove away.

AFTER GOING HOME to change and shower, and call the hospital to check on Chip—who was going to be all right— Ross headed out to his parents' place. His family had been holding their celebration until he got there. So he tried to pretend he gave a damn about the holiday and wasn't utterly miserable.

He didn't think he succeeded. His smile was tight, his laughter fake and the strain had to be visible. He couldn't keep his mind on the games, got lost in the middle of conversations and generally walked around in a daze for most of the afternoon.

All he could think about was Lucy. The time they'd spent together...and the way they'd parted.

He just couldn't understand it, couldn't begin to comprehend how she could have spent the weekend with him, doing everything they'd done, saying everything they'd said, then casually talk about moving back to New York. It made no sense.

He would have bet his last dollar that she loved him, that she'd always loved him, as he'd always loved her. But the words had never come out of her mouth, not even when he'd told her how he'd felt about her all those years ago.

You're the one who left her. You did the heartbreaking, a voice in his head reminded him. So maybe it wasn't so surprising that she wasn't going to just rush right back into this.

But to rush to the east coast instead? What sense did that make?

"So, are you going to tell us who she is?"

Ross jerked his head up when his kid sister Annie—who was no longer a little kid, but instead a college junior—entered the room. "Excuse me?"

"Come on, everybody can tell you've got woman troubles. We haven't seen you this mopey about a girl since you moved back home from New York after losing that girl…Linda?"

"Lucy. Her name is Lucy," he muttered, looking away and frowning.

Hearing Annie's surprised gasp, he wished he hadn't said a word. "Wait, are we talking about Lucy now?"

"What makes you ask that?"

"Well, you said her name *is* Lucy. Plus, the way you say her name, bro. It's like going back in time six years. I remember exactly how you were when you first got back after Dad got sick. I've never seen you so hung up on anyone."

There was a good reason for that. He'd never *been* so hung up on anyone else.

"So what's the story? Why didn't you invite her over for Christmas dinner?"

"I did. She…doesn't really like Christmas." He didn't want to share any details of Lucy's private life, but did explain, "She has some pretty bad memories of this time of year."

"So where is she? Is she here in Chicago?"

"Yes, she moved here. She's home at her apartment now."

"Dude! Harsh!"

He rolled his eyes, still not used to hearing his sister talk like an eighteen-year-old guy, which seemed to be how all young women talked now.

"You left her sitting at home, alone in her apartment, on Christmas?"

"Like I said, I asked her to come here. She wanted to go home. Alone."

Annie's eyebrows wagged, which was when he realized he'd slipped up. Again. "*Go* home, huh? As in, she was with you for the past couple of days during your big trapped-in-the-snow emergency?"

"Shut up," he muttered.

She laughed. "Look, all I gotta say is, if I was seeing someone, and he left me sitting at home all alone on Christmas, I'd feel absolutely sure he didn't give a damn about me."

"You're not Lucy," he muttered.

"Good thing for you," she said, getting up and sauntering toward the door. "Because if I were, I'd have said later, dude, and made you think I didn't care any more about you than you did about me."

She left the room, leaving Ross sitting there alone. But his sibling's words remained. In fact, they somehow seemed to get louder…and louder.

He knew Lucy wasn't the type to play games. But he also knew she had to be feeling very unsure about them—about him—right now. Considering he'd walked out on her Christmas Day six years ago and had stopped calling her shortly thereafter, why wouldn't she have doubts? Why wouldn't she have questions?

Why wouldn't she expect that he wouldn't give a damn if she decided to move back to New York?

In trying to be calm and rational and fair, had he made her think he didn't care? Had hiding his fear of losing her again made it that much more likely to happen?

No. That just wouldn't do. No way was he going to let her think he didn't want her. Lucy might want to leave, she might view this great career move as the next logical step in her life. But he wasn't going to let her make that decision without making sure she knew how he felt.

Which meant he needed to go talk to her. And this time, there would be nothing left unsaid.

OF ALL THE sucky Christmases Lucy had ever experienced in her life, this one had to rank right up there among the suckiest.

Oh, it had started off great. Magically, in fact. She'd

awakened this morning in the arms of an amazing man, sure she'd never been happier in her life.

But since she'd arrived home—alone—and moped around her apartment—alone—and eaten a frozen dinner—alone—Lucy couldn't find a single positive thing about it.

She'd tried doing her online shopping—boring. She'd cleaned her apartment—more boring. She'd answered a few emails, checked her appointment book, looked into flights to New York.

Boring. Boring.

And heartbreaking.

Heartbreaking, because she didn't want to fly to New York. Not under these circumstances, anyway. Not without knowing how Ross felt about it—whether he gave a damn.

This morning, when she'd first heard the message about the potential job offer, oh, it had been exciting, a great validation. Thinking that a major magazine was seeking her out for her talent was a huge ego boost and a true reinforcement that she'd made the right choice when switching gears in her career.

But she didn't particularly want to move back to New York. She liked Chicago. She liked living near her brother again. She liked the people she'd met and the studio she'd rented and the life she was living.

Most of all, she liked being near the man she loved.

"Hell," she whispered that evening as she sat on her couch, listening to Christmas music on an internet radio station.

She loved him. She loved Ross Marshall. She always had. He'd entered her heart six years ago and had never left it, despite time and distance and other relationships.

Some people could fall in and out of love. Some loved only once in a lifetime. She suspected she was one of those people. Which would be wonderful, if only she didn't love a guy who didn't seem to care if she moved a thousand miles away.

Feeling truly sorry for herself, she almost didn't hear the knock. At first, she assumed her neighbors' kids were banging around with all their new Christmas toys. They'd been filled with joy and laughter all day, and she'd smiled at the sounds coming through the thin walls. But the sound came again, and she realized someone was at her door.

She glanced at the clock, seeing it was after eight. She'd finally reached Sam this afternoon, and he'd told her he was working all night again. But perhaps he'd managed to swing by on a break or something.

She went to the door and opened it with a smile. The smile faded when she saw not her brother, but someone she'd never expected to see at her doorstep tonight.

"Ross?"

"Can I come in?"

Stunned, not only because he'd told her he was going out to his family's, but also because, as far as she knew, he'd had no idea where she lived, she stepped aside and beckoned him in. "How did you…"

"Stella. She had both your work and your home addresses in her BlackBerry."

"Is everything all right? Your family?"

"Fine. By now they're probably engaged in the annual Trivial Pursuit Christmas marathon."

Still unsure why he'd come, and not knowing what to say, she quickly asked, "And your security guard?"

"He's going to pull through," he said.

"I'm so glad." Twisting her hands together, she finally remembered her manners. "Can I take your coat? Would you like to sit down?"

He took off his coat, but didn't sit in the chair to which she gestured. Instead, sounding and looking somber, he stared into her eyes and said, "If I ask you a question, will you answer me truthfully?"

"Of course."

"Okay." Stepping closer, close enough that she smelled his spicy cologne and felt his body's warmth, he asked, "Do you want to move back to New York?"

Talk about putting her on the spot. She crossed her arms over her chest, rubbing her hands up and down them and thought about her answer. Her first instinct was to answer his question with a question—*do you want me to stay?*

But they'd played enough games, lost enough time dancing around the truth or making decisions for each other without benefit of a real, genuine conversation. So she would be nothing but honest, both with him, and with herself.

"No. I don't."

He closed his eyes and sighed, so visibly relieved, she almost smiled.

"My turn to ask you a question," she countered.

"Okay."

Drawing a deep breath, and hoping her voice wouldn't quiver, she asked, "Do you want me to stay?"

He didn't hesitate, not even for an instant. "Oh, *hell* yes."

Though pleased by his vehemence, she tilted her head in confusion. "Then why did you act like you didn't care earlier?"

"Why did you let me think you wanted to go?"

Neither answered for a second…then they both replied in unison. "Because we're idiots."

Laughter bubbled between them, then Ross stepped closer, dropping his hands to her hips and tugging her to him. She lifted hers to his shoulders and looked up at him, seeing the warmth and the tenderness in his green eyes. Even without the words being said, she knew what he was thinking, what he was feeling. What his heart was telling him.

Because her heart was telling her the same thing.

They were meant to be together. They always had been.

Time and circumstance had separated them, yes. But, maybe that was how it had to be. They'd been young and impulsive. And she hadn't truly been ready to accept love and happiness, to offer the kind of trusting, loving relationship Ross deserved.

Now she was ready. And they'd found their way back to each other. It had taken years, and moving to another city, but their lives had come full circle and this week, they'd recreated the past.

Only, this time, it would end differently. They weren't going to let anything come between them.

This time, they would make it work.

"I love you," he said, and her heart sang.

He lifted a hand to cup her face. "I let you go once. I wasn't about to make the same mistake again."

"What if I had said I wanted to go to New York?"

"I would have said fine, when do we leave?"

She started to smile, at least until she saw he meant it. Then she could only stare at him in shock. "Are you serious?"

"Very serious."

"But how—"

"I talked to my father when I was out at the house today. I told him I had let you get away once, but it wasn't going to happen again. And that while I'd like to stay at Elite, if it came down to it, I was going to do what was right for *me* for a change. Live my life for myself, since I've been living it for everyone else for the past six years."

"How did he react?"

He looked away. "I think that's the closest I've ever seen my father to tears."

She sucked in a breath.

"Not because he was upset, but because he finally had the chance to tell me how damned grateful he is for everything I've done, and how much he wants me to be happy."

Ross shook his head slowly. "To tell you the truth, I couldn't believe it. He's never said anything like that to me before."

Knowing how much that had to have meant to him, Lucy rose on tiptoe and brushed her mouth against his. "I'm so glad."

"Me, too."

"But your father doesn't have anything to worry about, and neither do your shareholders."

"We can go if you want to," he insisted.

"I don't," she insisted back, being completely honest. "I'm finished running off to do new things, in new places, just to avoid having to ever expose myself to pain and hurt again. There's no love without risk…but there's no life without love."

Then, realizing she had never actually said it, she gave him the most honest, genuine present she could think to give him. "I love you, Ross. I always have, I always will."

He smiled tenderly, then bent to kiss her, slowly, lovingly. And having those words on their lips made it taste that much sweeter, made it mean that much more.

When they finally ended the kiss, they remained locked in each other's arms, swaying slowly to the holiday music playing softly in the background. "Joy to the World."

How fitting. For the first time in what seemed like forever, her life felt filled to the brim with joy. Because Ross was in it. And she knew, deep down to her very soul, that he always would be.

"Merry Christmas, Lucy," he whispered against her cheek.

"Merry Christmas, Ross."

She tightened her arms around him, wanting to capture this feeling and imprint it in her mind forever, like a beautiful photograph. The first moment of the rest of their lives.

There would be many more, she knew. Some beautiful, probably some sad.

But no matter what, they would all be filled with love.

Epilogue

Two Years Later

CURLED UP TOGETHER on the sofa, Lucy and Ross watched out their front window as the first flakes of Christmas snow began to fall. The weatherman wasn't predicting a major storm—nothing like the one that had trapped them in Ross's office building two years earlier—aka the best blizzard of all time. No, this was quiet and sweet, a night-time snow as gentle and peaceful as the carols playing softly on the stereo behind them.

Wrapped in the arms of the man she loved, here inside the beautiful home they'd finished building together and had moved into last spring, Lucy didn't mind if it snowed all night. She had everything—and everyone—she needed, right here within these walls.

"Here it comes," he murmured, tightening his arms around her.

"Mmm-hmm."

They remained silent for a moment, watching the white flakes drift down, slowly at first, then more steadily. Lucy suddenly realized, looking out that huge front window that overlooked the water, that this must be what it was like to be inside a snow globe. Perhaps the very one Ross had given her all those years ago, which now had a place of honor on the center of the mantelpiece. She was tucked inside that happy home, with the warm yellow light in the window and the cars in the driveway and the snowy ever-greens all around.

She smiled, loving the image, thinking back to that Christmas Eve. What, she wondered, would that girl, that twenty-two-year-old Lucy, have thought if she could have foreseen this future? She probably wouldn't have believed it, and it would have scared her to death. But, deep down she knew she would have been very hopeful—because that day had opened her eyes to a world of possibilities.

All because of the man holding her so tenderly, hum-ming Silent Night as he kissed her temple.

She looked up at him, so handsome in the glow from the fire, and whispered, "Merry Christmas, Ross."

He smiled back and brushed his lips against hers. "Merry Christmas, wife."

No more *bah humbug* for Lucy. No more building walls against things like memories, and holidays…and love. That part of her life was over.

Ross stretched a little and chuckled. "Am I rotten for being glad my parents and your brother decided to stay home and come over tomorrow, after they see how much snow falls?"

She laughed softly, understanding him so well. "Not un-less I'm rotten, too, because I feel the same way."

It wasn't that either of them begrudged the visit—she actually adored his family, and her brother's new girl-friend. They certainly had plenty of room for everyone in the huge house. But she couldn't deny being happy things had worked out this way. Now they would have tonight and tomorrow morning for themselves, getting a start on creat-ing holiday memories and traditions of their own.

She was ready for that. Ready to incorporate the ghosts of her Christmases past into her present and her future.

Ready to open her heart to the magical season of giving that she'd once loved so very much...and move forward, molding it, changing it, shaping it into something that was just hers, and Ross's, and their family's.

"It's not that I don't love them..."

"It's just because tomorrow's so special," she replied.

Very special. Not just because it was their first holiday season in their new home. Not just because it was the first Christmas since they'd gotten married last year, on Christmas Day. Not just because they were still wildly in love and so incredibly happy. Not even because Lucy had become a fan of Christmas again.

No, they were glad to be alone because they both wanted to savor and rejoice in the early present they'd received ten days ago. Well, two presents.

They were sleeping upstairs in matching cribs, one with a blue baby blanket, the other pink. Scott and Jennifer—Jenny—named after the grandparents they would never know.

When Ross had suggested the names, she'd thought her heart would break. Not with sadness, but because of how happy her parents would be to see her so deeply loved by such an amazing man.

That, she knew, was the greatest Christmas gift she would ever receive. And she'd be getting that gift every day for the rest of her life.

* * * * *

SEX, LIES
AND MISTLETOE
Tawny Weber

Tawny Weber is usually found dreaming up stories in her California home, surrounded by dogs, cats and kids. When she's not writing hot, spicy stories for Mills & Boon® Blaze®, she's shopping for the perfect pair of shoes or scrapbooking happy memories. Come by and visit her on the web at www.tawnyweber.com or on Facebook at www.facebook.com/TawnyWeber. RomanceAuthor.

To all the wonderful people who read my books.
You bring untold joy to my life.
Thank you!

Prologue

"I'VE MADE THE ARRANGEMENTS. Everything is in place."

As the assurance echoed through his speakerphone, Tobias Black leaned back in his Barcalounger, shifted an unlit
cigar between his teeth and grinned.

"That was fast. I didn't think you'd pull it off."

A lie, of course.

He'd known once the challenge was issued, it'd be impossible to resist. Just as he'd known that the person he'd
challenged had the power to make it happen. Tobias Black
only worked with the best. Even when the best's main goal
in life had once been to arrest him.

Tobias looked at the pictures framed and fading on his
study wall. A gap-toothed trio of schoolkids with wicked
looks in their golden eyes and hair as black as night.

Damn, he missed them. All three had turned their backs
on him eight years ago. Caleb because he rejected what his
father stood for. Maya out of disappointment. And Gabriel?
Tobias gave the photo of his middle child, his youngest son,
a worried frown. Gabriel in fury, determined to prove that
he was twice as good and twice as clever as his old man.

They'd all felt justified in leaving.

And Tobias felt justified in bringing them back. A man
spent his life building a legacy, he needed his children to
hand it down to.

"You're sure you can handle your part?"

Tobias laughed so hard the cigar fell from his lips. Him? Handle a part? That was like asking if the sun was gonna rise in the morning.

"I'll play my part like Stevie Ray Vaughan played guitar."

Silence. Tobias rolled his eyes. Maybe it wasn't so farfetched to ask if he could handle the part if he could so easily forget who he was talking to. "Let me rephrase that. I'll play my part like Babe Ruth hit the ball."

"If you're not careful, cockiness could be your downfall."

Tobias almost brushed that away like an irritating bug. Then he sighed. Only a stupid man ignored a fair warning.

"There's a fine line between confidence and cockiness. I'll watch my step." He glanced at his eldest son's photo. "Caleb will take the bait. He won't want to come home, but he will. Loyalty is practically his middle name."

"You think he's loyal to you after all these years?"

"To me? Absolutely not." And that hurt like hell, but it was the price Tobias paid for ignoring his kids to feed his own ego. "But he's loyal to Black Oak."

Tobias was gambling everything on Caleb caring about Black Oak. A small town in the foothills of the Santa Cruz Mountains, Black Oak was in many ways the same as when it'd been founded a hundred years ago. A quaint and friendly community.

And now it had a drug problem. Tobias might have no problem skirting the law—or hell, laughing in its face— but he was a man who had zero tolerance for drugs. Especially when those drugs were being dealt in a way that conveniently pointed the finger his way.

It would be smarter to let the locals deal with the drug problem. If the evidence kept pointing at Tobias, they could be more easily…influenced. Because the sad truth was, there were still a few outstanding crimes that Tobias could be arrested for, with the right evidence. And there were hints that whoever was pulling off this drug ring had access to the right evidence. So bringing the feds in was a huge risk.

Someone was framing him. And they had enough dirt to do the job well. And it looked as if they were planning it all here in Black Oak.

That little bit of info he wouldn't share with the feebies.

Because he knew he had to offer up a big enough lure to get the FBI's attention, but not so big that they'd insist on coming in and playing it their way.

He wanted control of this venture.

"This is a huge undertaking, Black. All indications are that the drugs moving into Black Oak are yours. And now you're planning to play your family, who know you well enough to see the game. You're talking about playing a townful of people, many of whom depend on you. And more important, you're going to have to play the FBI, who, as a general rule, want nothing more than to arrest you."

He wanted to point out that he'd played them all, quite successfully, many times before. But bragging was rude. More important, ego was the first nail in the coffin of a good con.

"And your point is?" he asked instead.

"My point is, you're not as young as you once were. And you've been out of the game for a while." There was a pause, then a soft sigh that made Tobias's smile drop away. "You've got a lot on the line. Are you sure you're willing to risk it all? Because if this goes bad, the FBI is going to reel you in and toss your ass in jail for a good long time."

Tobias rolled the cigar between his fingers, staring at the unlit cylinder.

He considered what he'd built here in Black Oak. After a lifetime of running cons, he'd settled down and gone legit five years ago. He'd been quietly making reparations over the years, but paying back a few hundred grand wasn't going to stop the FBI from nabbing him if they had a chance. He could opt out, let someone else take point. The risks were huge.

But then, so were the stakes. And every good con knew, it was the high-stakes games that were worth playing.

"I can handle it."

"And your kids?"

Tobias sighed, pushing to his feet and pretending his bones didn't protest at stretching quickly in the damp winter chill. He tossed the cigar on his desk and strode over to stand before the pictures.

Caleb, Maya and Gabriel.

Smart kids. Good-looking, shrewd and nimble-fingered, even as little punks. Once, they'd thought he'd spun the sun on the tips of his fingers and carried the moon in his back pocket. Once, they'd believed in him. Once, they'd been in his life.

Now? Now he'd settle for one out of three.

"I can handle it," he repeated.

And before this game was through, he'd know who was behind the drugs, who was trying to set him up. Whatever fledgling crime ring was forming would be busted.

If he won, his kids would be a part of his life again.

And if he lost? At long last, his ass would be locked up in the federal pen.

But Tobias Black didn't lose.

1

DAMN SEX. IT RUINED everything.

"I can't believe I'm back in Black Oak." Pandora Easton's murmur was somewhere between a sigh and a groan as she dropped a dusty, musty-smelling box on the floor behind the sales counter.

"No guy, no matter how good in bed, is worth losing your job, your reputation or self-respect for," she muttered to herself as she looked around Moonspun Dreams. The morning light played through the dance of the dust motes, adding a slightly dingy air to the struggling New Age store.

Sometimes a girl just needed to come home. Especially when she didn't have a choice.

Even if that home was falling apart.

Two months ago, she'd been on top of the world. An up-and-coming pastry chef for a well-known bakery in San Francisco, a gorgeous boyfriend and a strong belief that her life was—*finally*—pretty freaking awesome.

Then, *poof,* everything she'd worked so hard for the last several years was gone. Destroyed. Because she'd fallen for a pretty face, been conned by a smooth line, and worst of all, ruined by a good lay.

Nope. Never again.

Pandora was home now.

Which was *really* just freaking awesome.

With a heavy sigh, she poked one finger at the box she'd rescued from next to a leaking pipe in the back room. It was unlabeled, so she'd have to see what was inside before she could figure out where to put it.

To disguise the musty scent, she lit a stick of prosperity incense. Then Pandora rubbed a speck of dust off a leaf on the braided money tree she'd brought in this morning to decorate the sales counter, and tidied a row of silken soy wax candles with embedded rose petals.

"Not a bad display from a recently fired bakery manager," she commented to Bonnie.

Bonnie just cocked her head to one side, but didn't comment. Since she was one of the two store cats, Pandora hadn't expected much response. Probably a good thing, since the last thing Pandora's ego needed was anyone, human or feline, to point out all the crazy reasons for her thinking returning home to start her life over was going to work.

The cats, like the rest of Moonspun Dreams, were now Pandora's responsibility. She was excited about the felines. But the jury was still out on the quirky New Age store that'd been in Pandora's family for decades. The very store Pandora had wanted to get away from so badly, she'd left town the day after she'd graduated high school.

Before she could settle into a good pout, the bells rang over the front door. Bringing a bright smile and a burst of fresh air, Kathy Andrews hurried in. One hand held a bakery bag, the other a vat-size cup of coffee.

"I'm here to celebrate," Kathy sang out. She stepped over the black puddle of fur that was Paulie the cat sunning himself on the braided carpet, and waltzed across the scarred wooden floor.

"What are we celebrating?"

"That you're back in Black Oak. That you're taking over the family store. Not just for the month your mom is in Sedona for that psychic convention, but for good. And, more important, we need to celebrate the news that your best friend had some really great sex last night."

Pandora exchanged looks with Bonnie. There it was, sex again. But this was Kathy's sex. It wasn't as if that could mess Pandora's life up.

"I'm not so sure having to come home because I failed out there in the big bad world is an excuse to party," Pandora said with a rueful laugh as she took the bakery bag and peeked inside. "Ooh, my favorite. Mrs. Rae's éclairs. I thought she'd retired."

"Mr. Rae's off competing in some pumpkin-carving contest until next Saturday, leaving Mrs. Rae home alone for their anniversary week. Cecilia said her mom dropped off four dozen éclairs this morning with notice that she'd be making pies, too."

One of the joys and irritations about living in a small town was knowing everyone, and everyone knowing your business. In this case, both women knew Mrs. Rae's irritation meant cherry pie by dinner.

"Cecilia seemed surprised when I mentioned I was coming here," Kathy said, not meeting Pandora's eyes as she took back the bag and selected an éclair. "She said she thought Moonspun Dreams was doing so bad, your mom had given up keeping it open on weekends. I know I should have given her a smackdown, but the éclairs smelled too good."

While Kathy dived into her éclair with an enthusiastic moan, Pandora sighed, looking around the store. When she'd been little, her grandmother had stood behind this counter. The store had been filled with herbs and tinctures, all handmade by Grammy Leda. She'd sold clothes woven by locals with wool from their own sheep, she'd taught classes on composting and lunar gardening, led women's circles and poured her own candles. Grammy had been, Pandora admitted, a total hippie.

Then, when Pandora had been thirteen, Granny Leda had retired to a little cabin up in Humboldt County to raise chinchillas. And it'd been Cassiopeia's turn.

Her mother's intuitive talents, the surge of interest in all things New Age, and her savvy use of the internet had turned a quirky small-town store into a major player in the New Age market. Moonspun Dreams had thrived.

But now that the economy had tanked and New Age had lost its luster, it was almost imploding. Leaving Pandora with the choice of trying to save it. Or letting it fade into oblivion.

"Cecilia was right. Things are really bad," Pandora said. "No point in risking the best éclairs in the Santa Cruz Mountains over the truth."

"And now Moonspun Dreams is yours. Are you going to give up?" Kathy asked quietly, holding out a fingerful of the rich cream for the cat. They both watched Bonnie take a delicate taste while Pandora mulled over the slim choices available.

Her mother had said that she'd run out of ideas. She'd told Pandora before she left to be the keynote speaker at the annual Scenic Psychics conference that the store was hers now. And it was up to her to decide what to do with it.

After sixty years in the family, close up shop and sell the property.

Or fight to keep it going.

Her stomach pitched, but of the two, she knew there was only one she could live with.

"I can't give up. This is all I have, Kath. Not just my heritage, given that Moonspun Dreams has been in the family for four generations. But it's all *I've* got now."

"What are you going to do? And what can I do to help?" Both questions were typical of Kathy. And both warmed Pandora to the soul, shoving the fears and stress of trying to save a failing business back a bit.

"I don't know. I've been racking my brain, trying to

figure something out." Her smile quirked as she gestured to the small table in the corner. Rich rosewood inset with stars and moons, part of the table was covered by a brocade cloth and a handful of vividly painted cards. "I've finally reached the point of desperation."

Kathy's eyes widened. Pandora had sworn off all things metaphysical back in high school, claiming that she didn't have the talent or skill. The reality was that Cassiopeia was so good at it, nothing Pandora did could measure up. And she'd hated knowing she'd never, ever be good enough.

"What'd the reading say?"

"Tarot really isn't my forte," she excused, filling her mouth with the sweet decadence of her éclair.

"Quit stalling. Even if you don't have that psychic edge like your mom, you still know how to read."

That psychic edge. The family gift. Her heritage.

Her failure.

"The cards weren't any help," she dismissed. "The Lovers, Three of Swords, the Tower, Four of Wands and the Seven of Swords."

The éclair halfway to her lips, Kathy scrunched her nose and shrugged. "I don't understand any of that."

"I don't, either." Pandora's shoulders drooped. "I mean, I know what each card means—I was memorizing tarot definitions before I was conjugating verbs. But I don't have a clue how it applies to Moonspun Dreams. It doesn't help me figure out how to save the business."

Yet more proof that she was a failure when it came to the family gift. Handed down from mother to daughter, that little something extra manifested differently in each generation. Leda, Pandora's grandmother, had prophetic dreams. Cassiopeia's gift was psychic intuition.

And Pandora's? Somewhere around her seventeenth birthday, her mother had decided Pandora's gift was reading people. Sensing their energy, for good or bad. In other words, she'd glommed desperately onto her daughter's skill

at reading body language and tried to convince everyone
that it was some sort of gift.

Despite popular belief, it hadn't been her mother's over-
dramatic lifestyle that had sent Pandora scurrying out of
Black Oak as soon as she was legally able. It'd been her
disappointment that she was just an average person with no
special talent. All she'd wanted was to get away. To build a
nice normal life for herself. One where she wasn't always
judged, always found lacking.

Then she'd had to scurry right back when that nice normal life idea had blown up in her face.

"You're going to figure it out," Kathy said, her words
ringing with loyal assurance. "Your mom wouldn't have
trusted you with the store if she didn't have faith, too."

"The store is failing. We'll be closing the doors by the
end of the year. I don't think it's as much a matter of trusting me as it is figuring I can't make things any worse."

Pandora eyed the last three cream-filled pastries, debating calories versus comfort.

Comfort, and the lure of sugary goodness, won.

"These are so good," she murmured as she bit into the
chocolate-drenched creamy goodness.

"They are. Too bad Mrs. Rae only bakes when she's
pissed at her husband. Black Oak has a severe sugar short-
age now that she's retired." Kathy gave her a long, considering look. "You worked in a bakery for the last few years,
right? Maybe you can take over the task of keeping Black
Oak supplied with sweet treats. You know, open a bakery
or something."

"Wouldn't that be fun," Pandora said with a laugh. Then,
because she was starting to feel a little sick after all that
sugary goodness, she set the barely eaten éclair on a napkin and slid to her feet. "But I can't. I have to try to make
things work. Try to save Moonspun Dreams. Mom was
hoping, since I'd managed the bakery the last two years,

that maybe I'd see some idea, have some brilliant business input, that might help."

"And you have nothing at all? No ideas?"

Failure weighing down her shoulders, Pandora looked away so Kathy didn't see the tears burning in her eyes. Her gaze fell on the dusty box she'd hauled in earlier.

"We've got a leak in the storeroom," she said, not caring that the subject change was so blatant as to be pathetic. "Most of the stuff stored in that back corner was in plastic bins, so it's probably seasonal decorations or something. But this box was there, too. It's my great-grandma's writing, and from the dust coating the box, it's been there since she moved away."

"Oh, like a treasure chest," Kathy said, stuffing the éclairs back in the bag and clearing a spot on the counter. "Let's see what's in it."

Pandora set the box on the counter and dug her fingernail under one corner of the packing tape. Pulling it loose, she and Kathy both winced at the dust kicking them in the face.

She lifted the flaps. Kathy gave a disappointed murmur even as Pandora herself grinned, barely resisting clapping her dirty hands together.

"It's just books," Kathy said, poking her finger at one.

"My great-grandma Danae's books," Pandora corrected, pulling out one of the fragile-looking journals. She reverently opened the pages of the velvet-covered book, the handmade paper thick and soft beneath her fingers. "This is better than a treasure chest."

"Oh, sure. Piles of gold coins, glistening jewels and priceless gems is exactly the same thing as a box of moldy old books." Still, Kathy reached in and pulled a leatherbound journal out for herself, flipping through the fragile pages. Quickly at first, then slower, as the words caught her attention.

"These are spells. Like, magic," she exclaimed, her voice squeaking with excitement. "Oh, man, this is so cool."

A little giddy herself, Pandora looked over at the book Kathy was flipping through. "Grammy Danae collected them. I remember when I was little, before she died, people used to call her a wisewoman. Grammy Leda said that meant she was a witch. Mom said she was just a very special lady."

"Do you think she really was a witch?" Kathy asked, glee and skepticism both shining in her eyes.

"I'm more inclined to believe she was one of the old wives all those tales were made from." Pandora laughed. "Despite the rumors, there's nothing weird or freaky about my family."

She wanted—desperately needed—to believe that.

"But wouldn't it be cool if these spells worked? Say, the love ones. You could sell them, save the store."

"It's not the recipe that makes a great cook, it's the power," Pandora recited automatically. At her friend's baffled look, she shrugged. "That's what Grammy always said. That words, spells, a bunch of information…that wasn't what made things happen. Just like the tarot cards don't tell the future, crystals don't do the healing. It's the intuition, the power, that make things happen."

"I'll bet people would still pay money for a handful of spells," Kathy muttered.

"They'd pay money for colored water and talcum powder, too." Pandora shrugged. "That doesn't make it right."

"Maybe you can offer matchmaking or something," Kathy said, studying the beautifully detailed book. "People would flock to the store for that kind of thing."

For one brief second, the idea of people believing in her enough to flock anywhere filled Pandora with a warm glow. She wanted so badly to offer what the other women in her family had. Comfort, advice, guidance. And a little magic.

Then her shoulders drooped. Because she had no magic

to share. Even the one little thing her mother had tried to claim for her had been a failure.

"I'd let people down," she said with a shake of her head. "Hell, when it comes to love stuff, I even let myself down."

"You can't let that asshole ruin your confidence," Kathy growled, lowering the book long enough to glare. "It wasn't your fault your boyfriend was a using, lying criminal."

"Well, it was my fault I let him dupe me, wasn't it? If I was so good at reading people, I'd have seen what was going on. I wouldn't have let the glow of great sex cloud my vision."

Just thinking about it made her stomach hurt.

She'd thought she was in love. She'd fallen for Sean Rafferty hard and fast. The bakery owner's son was everything she'd wanted. Gorgeous. Funny. Sensitive. Her dream guy. She'd thought the fall was mutual, too. Great sex with an up-and-coming pharmacist who seemed crazy about her. He didn't care that she didn't have any special gift. And she hadn't cared that she couldn't seem to get a solid read on his body language. He'd said plenty. Words of love, of admiration.

Then Sean had been busted in an internet prescription scam. And, as if her shock of misreading him that much hadn't been enough, they'd informed her that she was under arrest for collusion. Apparently, her own true love had run his scam using her computer IP address, and then told the police it was all her idea. It'd taken a month, a pile of lawyers' fees and the word of one of Sean's colleagues shooting for a plea deal to convince the cops that she'd been innocent. Clueless, gullible and stupid, but innocent.

His mother firing her had been the final straw. Whether she fit in or not didn't matter, Pandora had needed to come home.

"What's that book?" Kathy asked, clearly trying to distract her from a confidence-busting trip down memory lane.

Pandora gave an absent glance at the book in her lap. Faded ink covered pages that were brittle with age. Some of the writing she recognized as Grammy's. Some she'd never seen before. Then, a tiny flame of excitement kindling in the back of her mind, she flipped the pages. "It's a recipe book."

"Oh."

"Make that *Oh!*" Pandora angled the book to show her friend the handwritten notes above the ingredient list. "These are recipes for aphrodisiacs. Better than love spells, these don't rely on a gift. They just require a talent for cooking."

"Oh, I like that. Maybe you can whip up a tasty aphrodisiac or two for me?" Kathy said with a wicked smile. "I'd be willing to pay a pretty penny for guaranteed good sex."

"Hot and fresh orgasms, delivered to your door in thirty minutes or less?" Pandora joked.

"Sure, why not? Maybe your éclairs aren't quite as amazing as Mrs. Rae's, but you're still a damn good cook. So why not use that? Use those recipes? Put the word out, see what happens. If nothing else, it'll stir up a little curiosity, right?"

It was a crazy idea. Aphrodisiacs? What the hell did Pandora know about sex, let alone sexual aids? The last time she'd seen Sean, he'd been behind bars and, probably for the first time in their relationship, honest when he'd told her that she'd been easy to use because she was naive about sex.

So unless it was a how-to-survive-and-thrive-alone, a do-it-yourself guide to pleasure on a budget, Pandora had very little to offer.

But could she afford to turn away from such a perfect idea? Her mother would say she'd found this box, this idea, for a reason. Could she take the chance and ignore fate?

Pandora puffed out a breath and looked around the store. This was her heritage. Maybe she didn't have a gift like the rest of the women in her family, but couldn't this be her gift? To save the store?

While her brain was frantically spinning around for an answer, she paced the length of the counter and back. On her third round, Paulie lifted his black head off the carpet to give her the look of patience that only cats have.

"I guess we should do some research," she finally said.

"Don't you have all the recipes you need in that book?"

"I'm sure I do. But I need to find out what kind of food is going to lure in the most customers. Then I can use the recipes to add a special dash of aphrodisiac delight."

As she reached under the counter to get a notepad and pen so she and Kathy could brainstorm, she had to shake her head.

Wasn't it ironic? It was because of sex that she'd had to run home and now sex was going to be the thing that saved that home.

Two months later

"I NEED A FAVOR… A sexual favor, you might say."

The words were so low, they almost faded into the dull cacophony of the bar's noise. Pool cues smacking balls and the occasional fist smacking a face were typical in this low-end dive. Sexual favors were plentiful, too, but usually they involved the back room and cash in advance.

Caleb Black arched a brow and took a slow sip of his beer before saying, "That's not the way I roll, but Christmas is coming. Want me to slap a bow on the ass of one of those fancy blow-up dolls and call it your present?"

Hunter's dead-eyed look didn't intimidate, but it did make Caleb hide his smirk in his beer. Caleb was known far and wide as a hard-ass dude with a bad attitude. But when he was around Hunter, he came off as sweetness and light on a sugar high.

The man was a highly trained FBI special agent swiftly

rising in the ranks thanks to his brilliant mind, killer instincts and vicious right hook.

He was also Caleb's college roommate and oldest, most trusted friend. Which meant poking at that steely resolve was mandatory.

"Okay, crossing blow-up doll off my shopping list," Caleb decided. "But you should know that my sexual favors don't come cheap."

"From what I've heard, dirt cheap is more like it."

Caleb's smirk didn't change. When a man was as good as he was with women, he didn't need to defend his record. Knowing Hunter would get to the point in his own good time, Caleb leaned back, the chair creaking as he crossed his ankle over his knee and waited.

Always quick on the uptake, Hunter pushed his barely touched beer aside and leaned forward, his hands loose on the scarred table between them. Even in the dim bar light, his eyes shone with an intensity that told Caleb the guy was gonna try to sucker him in.

But Caleb had learned suckering at his daddy's knee.

"You're coming off a big case, right?" Hunter confirmed.

Not quite the tact he'd expected. But it wasn't his game, so Caleb just nodded. And waited.

"Word is you've hit burnout. That you're taking some time off to consider your options."

The smirk didn't shift on Caleb's face. But his entire body tensed. He wasn't a sharing kind of guy. He hadn't told anyone he was burning out except his direct superior, who'd sworn to keep it to himself.

"Word sounds like a gossipy, giggling teenager," was all Caleb said, though. "Who's the gossip and when did you start listening to that kind of crap?"

"It's amazing how much information you can pick up through speculation." Hunter sidestepped. "So while you're considering those options, maybe you might be interested in doing a friend a favor?"

"I'm more interested in lying on a beach in Cabo with half-naked women licking coconut-flavored oil off my body," Caleb mused, taking another swig of beer.

"What if I used the owe-me card?" Hunter asked quietly, his gaze steady on Caleb's. Intimidation 101.

Last week, Caleb had faced down a Colombian drug lord who'd preferred to blow up the building he stood in than be arrested when he found out his newest right-hand man was actually DEA.

It would take a lot more than 101 to make Caleb squirm.

Then again, he did owe Hunter. Back in their first year of college, Caleb had been a better con than a student. Overwhelmed by the realities of college life, he'd cheated on his midterm psych project. Hunter had caught him. He didn't threaten to turn him in. He didn't lecture. He simply threw Caleb's own dreams back in his face until he'd cracked, then helped him pull together a new project. He hadn't snagged the A he'd hoped for, but Caleb had found a new sense of pride he'd never known.

Shit.

Caleb hated unpaid debts. Especially sappy emotional ones.

"Cut the bullshit and get to the point," he suggested.

Realizing he'd won, Hunter didn't gloat. He just leaned back in his chair and took a sip of his own beer. "You're from a small town in the Santa Cruz Mountains, right? Black Oak, California."

It wasn't a question, but Caleb inclined his head.

"You still have family there."

"Maybe." Probably. He knew his sister was living just outside of San Francisco, playing the good girl. And who the hell knew where his brother was. A chip off the ole block, Gabriel was probably fleecing some rich widow of her wedding ring. But their father's family had founded Black Oak, and while Tobias Black hadn't ever gone for the political game, he'd always kept his fingers on the strings of his hometown.

But Caleb hadn't lived there since he'd left for college twelve years before. And he hadn't been back at all since he'd graduated and joined the DEA.

Eight years before, two months before Caleb had graduated, they'd had one helluva family brawl. Ugly accusations, bitter recriminations and vicious ultimatums.

Tobias Black had raised his three kids alone when his wife had died, keeping the family tighter than peas in one very conniving pod. But with that explosion, they'd all gone their separate ways. Caleb had grown up with an almost smothering sense of family. These days he was more like an orphan.

Just as well. Spending time with Tobias was an emotional pain in the ass at best, a conflict of interest at worst.

"It's an interesting little town. Quaint even. Your maternal aunt is the mayor, but word is that it's actually your father who runs the town. Tobias Black, a known con artist with a huge FBI file and no convictions. Estimates of his take over the years is in the millions. And even knowing he was behind some of the major scams of the century, they've never gathered enough evidence to convict him."

Arching his brow, Hunter paused. Caleb just shrugged. So his dad was damn good at what he did. Maybe it was wrong to feel pride in the old man, given Caleb's dedication to the law. But you had to admire the guy for his skills.

"Five years ago, for no apparent reason, Tobias Black pulled out of the con games. He reputedly went straight, focusing his attention on his motorcycle shop and the small town he calls his own."

"You're saying a whole bunch of stuff we both know. Why don't you get to the part where you fill me in on the stuff I don't."

"For the last few months, we've been getting reports of a new drug. Some new form of MOMA."

"Ecstasy?" Caleb pushed his beer away since they appeared to be getting down to business. "What's new about it?"

"It's been refined. Higher-grade ingredients, some obscure herbs that counteract a few of the side effects."

"Herbs? Like, what? Holistic shit?"

"Right. Not a major change, really. Enough to give sellers the 'healthier choice' pitch, but that's about it. The problem stems from the addition of pheromones."

Eight years in the DEA had told Caleb that just when he'd thought he'd seen and heard everything, some clever asshole would come up with a new twist to screw with the human body. He sighed and shook his head. "So not only does it give the user a cheap sexual zing, but they can drag unsuspecting suckers down with them?"

"Pretty much. As far as the labs can tell, it's not a high enough grade to classify as a date-rape drug, but the potential is there."

The potential to make things worse was always there. Once upon a time, Caleb had figured he could make a difference. But he'd been wrong. After years of fighting drugs in the ugly underbelly of society, Caleb was pretty much done waging the useless battle. He'd turned in his resignation two days ago, but his boss had refused to accept it. Instead, he'd told Caleb to take some time off. To go home, visit family, come out of deep cover for a few months and reconnect with himself before he made any major decisions.

The only piece of that advice Caleb had planned to take was the time off.

He noted the rigid set of Hunter's jaw, then met the man's steady gaze and gave an inward sigh. Looked as if he was wrong on that count, too.

"Can't you feebs get in there on your own?" he asked. The bureau didn't have the same mandate as the DEA, but still, they should have the resources to go in themselves.

"Let's just say I'd rather use my own resources first."

Caleb nodded. He'd figured it was something like that. Second-generation FBI, Hunter had a rep for playing outside the tangled strings of bureaucracy more often than not. His close rate was so high, though, that the higher-ups tended to ignore his unorthodox habits.

"You're looking at Black Oak as the supply center. Have you narrowed down any suspects?"

Caleb wasn't a fool. He knew where Hunter was going with this. But he wasn't biting. He'd pony up whatever info he had on the town that might help the case, but that was it. He wasn't going back to Black Oak.

Which Hunter damn well knew. One drunken college night, Caleb had opened up enough to share how much he hated his father, how glad he'd been to get the hell out of Black Oak. And how he'd vowed, once he'd left, to never return.

"Black Oak appears to be the supply center, yes. But that's not the big issue for me." For the first time since he'd strode into the bar and sat across from Caleb, Hunter's eyes slid away. Just for a second. That's all it took, though, to let Caleb know he wasn't going to like whatever came next.

No matter. Wasn't much about life these days he did like.

Still, he took a swig of the beer. Never hurt to be prepared.

"We've tracked the source. As far as we can tell, there's only one suspect."

Caleb waited silently. Most people, when faced with six feet two inches of brooding intimidation blurted out secrets faster than a gumball machine spewed candy. But Hunter wasn't most people.

"A reliable source tipped me to the suspect."

Caleb dropped the chair back on all four legs, bracing himself.

"Tobias Black."

Caleb mentally reared back as if he'd taken a fist to the

face. He managed to keep his actual reaction contained to a wince, though. So much for bracing himself.

"He's out of the game," Caleb said, throwing Hunter's own words back at him. He didn't know if it was true, though. Sure, his father might claim he'd quit the con, gone straight. But the only thing Tobias was better at than playing the game was lying. Still, while cons were one thing, drugs were an ugly place Tobias wouldn't go.

"He's been making noises lately." Hunter's dark gaze was steady as he watched Caleb.

"Noises don't equal manufacturing drugs."

Hunter just stared.

Fuck.

"It's not his style," Caleb said, none of his frustration coming through in his tone. "I'm not defending him—without a doubt, he's a crook, a con and a shill. The man's spent his life pulling swindle after scam. But he operates on his own. Drugs come with partners. Unreliable, unpredictable partners."

Which had been the crux of his family's explosion. Tobias had found himself a lady friend. A lonely widower, he'd become a cliché, falling hard for a nice rack and promises made between the sheets. She must have been damn good, because she'd blinded the king of cons into letting her into his game. Fifty-fifty split.

His little sister, Maya, had screamed betrayal, claiming her father cared more about his bimbo than his own kids, the memory of his late wife and the legacy they'd built together.

His younger brother, Gabriel, had been pissed over losing half the take.

Caleb had just seen it as a sign to get the hell out.

He ignored Hunter's arched brow. For the first time since sitting down, Caleb looked away. His gaze rested on the mirrored wall behind Hunter. In it, he could see the tattoo on his own biceps. The sharp, snarling teeth of the lone wolf was clearly visible beneath the black sleeve of his T-shirt.

A teenager's ode to the father he'd worshipped before the idol had fallen. An adult's acceptance of the simple fact of life—that he could depend on no one.

"What do you want me to do?" Caleb asked, swinging his eyes back to Hunter.

"Just nose around. You can get into town, get close to the right people, without arousing suspicion. Nobody there, other than your father, knows you're DEA, right?"

Caleb shrugged. "Most think I'm the lowlife I use as a cover. The rest probably figure I was shivved in prison years ago."

"That'll work."

Caleb sighed. He could walk away. It wasn't his gig and nobody was pulling his strings. But Hunter's accusation was a game changer. Whatever went down, Caleb would be the one uncovering the truth. How or what he'd do with it, he had no clue.

"I'm not making any promises," Caleb said. "Dear ole dad isn't much for welcoming the prodigal back into the fold, you know."

"I have faith in your powers of persuasion."

Caleb smirked, tilting his beer bottle in thanks. "You're buying."

"One last question," Hunter said as Caleb pushed back from the table.

"Yeah?"

"Do you really do Christmas shopping?" For the first time that night, emotion showed on Hunter's face. Skepticism with a dash of amusement.

"Yeah. But now you can consider this little favor your gift, instead of the blow-up doll." Caleb stood, shrugging into his worn denim jacket. "She was a nice one, too. Vibrated and everything."

2

A LUNCH-LADEN TRAY held high over her head, Pandora
nodded at Fifi's frantic signal to let her know she'd make
her way into the store as soon as she could.

Rehiring Fifi, a young blonde as cute as her name, was
the second smartest thing Pandora had done since she'd
taken over the store. The first, of course, was to serve up
the promise of hot sex.

She wound her way through the throng of customers
packing the solarium attached to the back of the store. It
was amazing how a few tables, some chairs and minimal
investment had transformed what two months ago had been
storage into Pandora's brainchild, the Moonspun Café.

All it'd taken was a list of her skills, a couple bottles
of wine with Kathy and a huge hunk of Pandora's favorite
seven-layer chocolate cake to nail down the details. She'd
spent years off and on working in restaurants. She was a
really good pastry chef, but sandwiches and salads had
been an easy enough thing to add to the menu.

Between Great-Grammy's cookbooks, a list of foods
reputed to be aphrodisiacs and the judicious start of a few
rumors, and she'd launched the lunch-only venture last
month.

And it was a hit. If this kept up, Pandora was thinking
about starting a little mail-order business. Sexy sweets,

aphrodisiac-laced treats for lovers. A great idea, if she did say so herself. And—*ha!*—one that didn't require any special family talent.

She grinned and shifted the heavy tray off her shoulder.

"Here you go, the Hot-Cha-Cha Chicken on toasted sourdough for two, a side of French-kissing fries and ginseng-over-ice tea," she recited as she set the aphrodisiac-laced lunch order on the small iron table between a couple of octogenarians giving each other googly eyes.

Pandora carefully kept her gaze above the table as she smiled into the couple's wrinkled faces. Yesterday, she'd bent down to pick up a dropped fork and saw more than she'd bargained for. She'd never be able to look librarian Loretta and the office-supply delivery guy in the eye again after seeing Loretta fondle his dewy decimals.

"This looks lovely, dear," said the elderly woman, who's granddaughter had babysat Pandora back in the day. The woman giggled and shot the age-freckled man across from her a naughty look before adding, "You'll bring us up a slice of the molten hot-chocolate cake, won't you?"

"Wrap that cake up to go," the gentleman said, his voice huge in his frail body. "We've got a little siesta loving planned."

Pandora tried not to wince. She loved how well this little venture was taking off, but holy cow! She sure wished people wouldn't equate her making their sexy treats with wanting to hear the resulting deets.

Proving that wishes rarely came true, Mrs. Sellers leaned closer and whispered, "Since you started serving up these yummy lunches, I haven't had to fake it once. This stuff is better than Viagra. Now my sweet Merv, here, is a sex maniac."

Ack, there were so many kinds of wrong in that sentence, Pandora couldn't even wrap her mind around it. Trying to block the images the words inspired, she winced and shook her head so fast her hair got stuck in her eyelashes. "No. Oh, no, Mrs. Sellers. Don't thank me."

"Don't be modest, young lady. You've done so much for the sex drive of Black Oak as a whole. Not just us seniors, either. I heard Lola, my daughter's hairdresser who can't be much older than you, telling the gals at the salon how you've saved her marriage with your mead- and sexy-spiced chocolate-dipped strawberries."

What was she supposed to say to that? All she could come up with was a weak smile and a murmured thanks. She caught Fifi's wave again and held up one finger to let the girl know she was on her way.

"My favorites are those sweet-nothings ginger cookies, Pandora. I'd ask for your recipe, but I know you put a little something special in there. You have your gramma's magic touch, don't you?" Mrs. Sellers joked, poking a bony elbow into Pandora's thigh. "Your mom must have been so happy to have you come back to Black Oak. Are you running the store on your own now?"

"Mom's thrilled," Pandora said, the memory of Cassiopeia's excitement at her daughter's plans to save the store filling her with joy. "But if you'll excuse me, I need to check in with Fifi. Don't forget to look over the fabulous specials for the holiday season. We're offering a Christmas discount in the store for our diners, if you wanted to do a little shopping."

With another smile for her favorite elderly couple, Pandora gratefully excused herself and hurried over to the wide, bead-draped doorway that separated Moonspun Dreams' retail side from the café.

"What's wrong?" Pandora asked.

Two months ago, whenever she'd asked that question it was because the store seemed to be spiraling into failure. She'd been freaked about vendors demanding payment, customers complaining about a lack of variety in the tarot card stock or, on one horrific occasion, a mouse so big it had scared the cats.

In the past five weeks, Moonspun Dreams had done a one-eighty. Now she had vendors begging her to take two-for-one discounts, customers complaining about waiting in too long a line and the health department stopping in for lunch.

And yet, her trepidation of that question hadn't lessened one iota. Funny how that worked.

"Nothing's wrong," Fifi said, her smile huge as she bounced on the balls of her feet like a kid about to sit on Santa's lap. "Sheriff Hottie's here again. Lucky girl, this is the third time he's been in this week. He's the best catch in Black Oak. And he's here to see you."

Pandora's smile was just a little stiff. It wasn't that she had anything against Sheriff Hottie, otherwise known as Jeff Kendall. He was a nice guy. A former class president, Jeff had an affable sort of charm that half the women in town were crazy about. She glanced over to where he was chatting with a shaggy-haired guy who kept coming in to moon over Fifi and winced.

She had no idea why he rubbed her wrong. Her mother would claim it was intuition or her gift for reading people. But Pandora knew she had neither.

Christmas carols crooned softly through the speakers, singing messages of hope as she crossed the room. It took a minute, since the space was filled with shoppers, quite a few with questions.

"Sheriff," she greeted as she stepped behind the counter. She offered him a friendly smile, then folded her hands together before he could offer to shake one. "What can I do for you today?"

He gave her an appreciative glance and a friendly smile that made it easy to see why the town called him Sheriff Hottie. Blue eyes sparkled and a manly dimple winked. Still, a part of her wished she could be back in the café, listening to Mrs. Sellers share the details of her last passionate excursion with Merv the sex maniac.

"Pandora, looks like business is booming nicely for a weekday," he observed, his eyes on her rather than the store. He was tall, easily six feet, and still carried the same nice build that'd made him a star quarterback in school. "Cassiopeia must be thrilled. Is she coming home soon?"

Having combined her yearly spiritual sabbatical with the psychics' conference, Cassiopeia was still in Sedona, Arizona. Pandora's mother was, hopefully, too busy balancing her chi to be worrying about the store.

"She's due home by Yule," Pandora answered. At his puzzled glance, she amended it to, "The week before Christmas."

"Ah, gotcha. Your mom is really into that New Agey stuff, isn't she?"

Pandora just shrugged. She wanted to hide away from that friendly look. There was no innuendo, no rudeness, but she still felt dirty. Instead, she made a show of lifting Bonnie, cuddling her close so that the cat was a furry curtain between Pandora's body and the sheriff's gaze.

"My mother's interests are many-faceted. Right now, I'm sure if she were here, she'd be asking if you'd finished your holiday shopping, Sheriff. We're running a few specials in the café and have a stocking-stuffer sale on tumbled stones and crystals today. Maybe you'd like to check it out?"

"Maybe. But I'm thinking if I did all my shopping now, I wouldn't have an excuse to come back and visit you every day," he said, putting a heavy dose of flirt in his tone. Leaning one elbow on the counter, he gave her a smoldering look before he glanced at the shoppers milling around, many with wicker baskets filled with merchandise swinging on their arms.

"I really am blown away by how you've increased business here," he said. "That whole aphrodisiac angle is really drawing them in, isn't it? How'd you come up with that?

Don't tell me it's from personal experience or I might have a heart attack."

His flirty grin was easy, the look in his eyes friendly and fun. Pandora still inwardly cringed.

"Actually," she corrected meticulously, her fingers defiantly combing through the soft, fluffy fur of the cat, "the recipes have been handed down from my great-grandmother. Do you remember her? She's the one with all the experience."

Pandora tried not to smirk when his smile dimmed a little. Nothing like offering up the image of a white-haired old lady to diffuse a guy's sexy talk.

"How about dinner Friday night?" he said. "I'll pick you up at seven and you can tell me all about your great-grandma and her recipes."

What a stubborn man. But she was just as stubborn. She knew she had no reason to refuse—that she was getting a weird vibe wasn't good enough—but still, Pandora shook her head.

"I'm sorry, but no," she told him. Then, seeing the disappointment in his gaze, she tried to soften her words with a smile.

"I really wish you'd change your mind," Sheriff Kendall said, reaching over Bonnie to give Pandora's cheek a teasing sort of pinch. She gasped, her fingers clenching the cat's fur. Whether it was in protest, or because the sheriff was just too close, Bonnie hissed and leaped from Pandora's arms.

"I'm sorry," she said again, stepping back so she and her cheek were out of reach. "I'm trying to focus on the store right now. I need to get us back on our feet before I start thinking about dating."

"Okay. I understand." He offered that friendly smile again and turned to go. Then he looked back. "Just so you know, though, I plan to keep coming back until I change your mind."

Crap.

She waited until he stepped over Paulie, who carpeted the welcome mat like a boneless blanket of fur, and watched him slide behind the wheel of the police cruiser he'd parked to blocking the door. Then she almost wilted as the tension she hadn't realized was tying her in knots seeped from her shoulders.

"No offense, boss, but you're crazy," Fifi declared, stepping next to Pandora and offering a sad shake of her head. "I'd do anything to date the sexy sheriff. I can't believe you turned him down."

What was she supposed to say? That her internal warning system was screaming out against the guy? That same system had hummed like a happy kitten over Sean.

So obviously, the system sucked.

She gave Fifi a tiny grimace and said, "I guess I might have been a little hasty turning him down."

"A little? More like a lot crazy. Dude's a serious heart-throb."

Pandora grinned as the blonde gave her heart a thump-thumping pat.

"Okay," she decided, squaring her shoulders against the sick feeling in her stomach. Just nerves about dipping back into the dating pond, she was sure. "I'll tell you what. The next time he asks, I'll say yes."

Fifi's cheer garnered a few stares and a lot of smiles, especially from the young man with shaggy brown hair who was watching her like an adoring puppy.

Well, there you have it, Pandora decided with a grin of her own. The town obviously approved.

Ten minutes later, Pandora was ringing up a customer and still worrying over whether Sean had ruined her for all men, when a sugary-sweet voice grated down her spine.

"My mother said there was a blown-glass piece in here she thought I'd like as a Christmas gift. She probably mixed up the store names again, though, poor dear. I don't see anything in here I need."

Crap. Pandora took a deep breath, gesturing with her chin for Fifi to close up the café for her. This would probably take a while. She'd gone to high school with Lilah Gomez, and eight years later the other woman still held the privilege of being Pandora's least favorite person—which, given the events of this last year, was really saying something.

Knowing the importance of not showing weakness to her sworn enemy, she cleared her face of all expression and turned to the brunette.

"Your mother has excellent taste. Too bad she didn't pass it, and the ability to dress appropriately, on to her only daughter," Pandora said sweetly. She made a show of looking the other woman up and down, taking in her red pleather tunic with its low-cut, white fur-trimmed neckline that showed off her impressively expensive breasts. She raised a brow at the shimmery black leggings and a pair of do-me heeled boots that would make any dominatrix proud. "What do you call this look? Holiday hussy?"

"I'm the customer here. Why don't you put on your cute-little-clerk hat and show me whatever overpriced joke my mother saw so I can reject it and go shop in a real store."

"From where I'm standing, which is right next to the cash register, in the handful of times you've been in Moonspun Dreams you've never bought a single thing. So you're not a customer. You're a loiterer."

Lilah responded with a haughty look. She'd never bothered with her frenemy act before. Probably because she knew that Pandora would see right through it. Instead, the brunette leaned both elbows on the counter and bent forward to say under her breath, "You'd know crime, now, wouldn't you? What was it you were busted for? Something to do with drugs? Or was it lying?"

The only thing that persuaded Pandora to unclench her teeth was the fact that she couldn't afford to get them fixed if one broke. Instead, she turned on the heel of her own unslutty boots and retrieved a blown-glass peacock, each feather shimmering delicately in the light.

Before she'd even set the piece on the counter, she could see the covetous spark in Lilah's eyes. But instead of saying she liked it, the other woman turned her nose to the air and gave a sniff.

"It's okay. Just the kind of thing I'd expect to find in this dingy little store."

"The artist is one of my mother's clients," Pandora said, surreptitiously scraping the sale sticker off the price tag. She'd be damned if Lilah was getting thirty percent off. "Her work is currently in the White House and was recently featured in a George Clooney movie."

Drool formed in the corner of Lilah's heavily painted mouth. Her hand was halfway to her purse before she thought to ask, "How much is it?"

The desire to make a sale warred with the desire to kick the bitchy woman out of the store. But responsibility always trumped personal satisfaction for Pandora. Which was probably why women like Lilah, and Cassiopeia, Fifi and even old Mrs. Sellers, had a lot more fun that she did.

With one unvarnished fingernail, she pushed the price tag across the counter. Lilah's eyes rounded and her lips drooped.

"Will you hold it? My mother hinted that she'd get it for me as a Christmas gift."

"You want me to hold an overpriced joke?"

The woman's glare was vicious, but she jerked her chin in affirmation.

Hey, that was fun. Maybe all Cassiopeia's lectures about karma were true.

Before Pandora could decide whether to go for gracious or gloating, a loud roaring rumbled through the air.

She and Lilah both stared as a huge Harley slowed down, the helmeted rider turning his head to stare into the store. A shiver skittered between Pandora's shoulder blades. Another out-of-towner? Usually tourism went dry in Black Oak between Thanksgiving and Valentine's. It was probably someone visiting Custom Rides, the motorcycle shop that backed up to Moonspun.

"Company?" Fifi speculated, coming in from the café to stare, too.

"Must have heard about the yippee-skippy you're offering up," Mrs. Sellers predicted, heading out the door hand in hand with her tottering hunk of afternoon delight.

As one, Pandora sighed and Lilah sneered.

"That's disgusting," Lilah muttered.

"What is? The idea of two people enjoying each other's company?"

"You know they're sneaking off to have sex," the woman said, hissing the last word as if it were pure evil. The overblown brunette averted her eyes from the elderly couple as though she was worried that they wouldn't hold out until they toddled all the way to their love nest, instead giving in and doing the nasty right there in the doorway.

"And sex is bad… Why?" Pandora put on her most obnoxious, innocently sweet smile. "From what I heard, you were having it a couple nights ago. Wasn't it in the backseat of an old Nova parked behind Lander's Market?"

Fifi giggled, forcing Lilah to split her glare between the two women.

Before she could spill her ire, though, the chimes over the door sang. And in walked Pandora's worst nightmare. The sexiest man she'd ever seen, wearing black leather and a dangerous attitude. The kind of guy who could make her forget her own name, right along with her convictions, her vow of chastity and where she'd left her underpants.

Black hair swept back from a face worthy of a *GQ* cover. Sharp cheekbones, a chiseled, hair-roughened chin and vivid gold eyes topped broad shoulders and long, denim-clad legs that seemed to go on forever.

Pandora's hormones sighed in appreciation as desire flared, smoking hot, in her belly. She wanted to leap over the counter and slide that leather jacket off those wide shoulders and see up close and personal if his chest and arms lived up to the promise of the rest of his body.

"Oh, my," Fifi breathed.

"Hubba hubba," Lilah moaned.

"Go away," Pandora muttered.

The guy paused just inside the door, then knelt down to give Paulie's head a quick rub before straightening and looking around. His narrowed gaze seemed to take in everything in one quick glance. Then his eyes locked on Pandora's. Nerves battled with lust as she felt something deep inside click. A recognition. And that soul-deep terror that this was a man who spelled trouble in every way possible.

"LADIES," CALEB GREETED, barely aware of the two women on his side of the counter. His eyes were glued on the sweet little dish on the other side.

Her hair, a dark auburn so deep it looked like mahogany, tumbled over her shoulders in a silken slide, the tips waving over the sweet curve of her breasts. She wore a simple white shirt that draped gently over her curves instead of hugging them, and tiny silver earrings that made her look like a sweet-faced innocent. From the fresh-faced look, she didn't have any makeup on, either. Or maybe it just seemed that way because she was standing next to a gal who troweled it on like spackle.

"Well, hello there," Spackle Gal said. The brunette, dressed as if she moonlighted on the stroll, minced her way across the floor to lay a red-taloned hand on his arm. "It's a pleasure to have you here in Black Oak. I'm the welcome wagon, and I'd be happy to show you a good time while you're visiting our little town."

His brow arched, Caleb glanced at her hand, then back at her face. It only took her a second to get a clue and move her fingers back where they belonged.

"I know the town just fine, thanks," he dismissed. His gaze went back to the sweetie behind the counter. "Apparently I don't know everyone in town as well as I'd like, though."

The brunette gave a little hiss. Caleb ignored her. Despite her clear message of a free-and-easy good time, he wasn't interested.

He'd only come in to check the place out. Not because he was interested in... He looked around, wondering what the hell they sold here. This store shared the alley with what was apparently his father's motorcycle shop. His dad had still been on the take when Caleb had lived in Black Oak, so his shop was new, and Caleb's familiarity with this side of town sketchy.

So this weird store was going to be his new home away from home. By hanging here he could scope things out. Get the lay of the land, keep low for a few days and see how much intel he could scout. Then he'd decide if he wanted to let Tobias know he was in town or not.

"Some people aren't as important to know as others," the brunette said, trying her luck again by nudging close enough to press one impressive breast against his arm. Caleb was grateful for the extra protection of his leather jacket. "Why don't you and I go to Mick's for a drink and I'll introduce you around."

Caleb wanted to sigh. God, he was tired. Undercover standard operating procedure said take her offer. She was the perfect cover. A resident who probably liked her gossip, she could fill him in on all the townspeople. As blatantly sexual as she was, she might even have an in with the ecstasy crowd.

She'd obviously be happy to offer up any manner of information, favors and probably kinky acts, and walk away with a smile and no regrets the next morning. But he was tired of using himself, losing himself, like that.

And, dammit, he was supposed to be on vacation. A man shouldn't feel guilty about turning down cheap sex while he was on vacation.

"I'm good," he said, stepping away to make his rejection clear. From her glare, she got the message loud and clear. Color high on her cheeks, she shot an ugly look at the girls standing at the counter before heading for the door.

"You might want to slow down on testing your wares from the café, Pandora," the vamp warned over her shoulder as she teetered out of the store. "Not only is that aphrodisiac crap in danger of making you sound like a slut, but you're gaining weight."

Caleb's eyes cut to the women behind the counter, noting the shocked horror in the blonde's eyes and the sneer on the redhead's face. He grinned, liking her screw-you attitude.

"What's she so bitchy about?" he asked, keeping his smile friendly. Nothing connected with a mark—or suspect—faster than sympathy. Besides, facts were facts…the woman had been a bitch. He wandered the store ostensibly looking at merchandise while eyeing the back wall and its bead-covered doorway.

"That's her default personality," the redhead said.

"Pandora, is it?"

He wondered why she was looking at him as if he was a wolf about to pounce. Sure, he'd been a troublemaker as a teen, but he'd been gone almost twelve years. Was his rep still that bad in Black Oak? He didn't recognize her. Younger than him, she was closer to his sister's age.

"Hello?" he said, giving her a verbal nudge as he picked up a clear rock shaped like a pyramid, pretending to inspect it. Her worried stare was starting to bug him.

"I'll go make sure everyone's out of the café since it's closed now," the blonde murmured.

"Yes, I'm Pandora," the other woman said, grabbing the arm of the blonde before she could move away. "I'm the, um, owner. Can I help you?"

"Owner? You don't sound so sure."

"I'm still getting used to the idea." Pandora's smile was as stiff and fake as the blow-up doll Caleb had shipped off to Hunter the previous day. "What can I do for you?"

God, so many things. Let him taste those lips to see if they were as soft and delicious as they looked. Slide that silky-looking hair over his naked body. Tell him about all her favorite sexual positions and give him a chance to teach her his.

"I'm just looking around. You've got a nice place here."

"Thanks. Was there anything specific you were shopping for?"

His grin said it all. A sweet pink flush colored her cheeks, but he saw the flash of reciprocated interest in her eyes. Then, for some bizarre reason, she slammed that door shut with an impersonal arch of her brow.

What the hell? Unlike his brother, Gabriel, he didn't expect women to fall at his feet. And the hard-to-get game did have appeal sometimes. But to totally deny the attraction? What was up with that?

Focus, Black, he reminded himself. He'd come to town for a crappy reason and wanted to leave as fast as he could. So her denial was a good thing.

And maybe if he told himself that a few hundred more times, he'd believe it.

"So you have a café here, too?" he asked, poking through a basket of glossy rocks and trying to take his own advice to focus. Now that he was closer, he noted the noise and tasty scents coming through that beaded curtain. Was the back door to the alley through there?

Before he could poke his head through to see, a group of

people strode out with a clatter of beads and a lot of laughter. They'd obviously been having a happy holiday lunch.

There, in the center of the group like a king surrounded by his royal court, was Tobias Black. His lion's mane of black hair had gone gray at the temples. His face sported a few more wrinkles, adding to its austere authority. Still tall and lean, he wore jeans and biker boots, a denim work shirt and a mellow smile.

Caleb froze. Control broke for a brief second as he closed his eyes against the crashing waves of memories as they pounded through his head—and his heart. Holidays and hugs, lectures and encouraging winks. Watching his dad pull a con, then pulling his first con while his dad watched. The trip to Baskin-Robbins afterward, where Tobias let Caleb treat to hot-fudge sundaes with his ill-gotten gains, cementing the lesson that winning was sweet, but the money had to be kept in circulation.

And then his last day of college. The day when Caleb had told dear ole dad that he was bucking family tradition and basically becoming the enemy. A cop. And when he'd threatened, in cocky righteousness, that if his dad didn't dump his new partner and go straight, Caleb was leaving the family. That'd been the point his dad had told him to get his ass out.

Good times.

Caleb took a deep breath, his eyes meeting the wide hazel gaze of the pretty redhead behind the counter. He frowned at the sympathy and concern on her face. In the past eight years, he'd faced down whacked-out drug addicts and homicidal drug lords for a living with a blank face. Why did this pretty little thing think there was anything to be sympathetic over? Something to mull over later. Right now he had to pay the piper.

Caleb slowly turned around, automatically shoving his hands into the front pockets of his jeans and rocking back on his heels. He'd known this moment would come, but now that it had, he wasn't ready. He'd walked away from his family and used that lack of emotional ties in building his career. But now he was back, face-to-face with his father.

And he had no idea how he felt about it.

Like a bull who'd suddenly hit a steel wall, Tobias slammed to a halt. His midnight-blue eyes went huge. But only for a second. Then he grinned. A charming grin that Caleb knew was hiding that shock he hadn't meant to show.

"Well, well," Tobias said, slowly walking forward. "What have we here? If it isn't the prodigal son."

3

OH, MY. MR. TALL, HOT and Dangerous was one of the wild and mysterious Black clan? Along with the rest of the gawpers standing around the store, Pandora stared, rapt, as the two men faced off.

"Wow," Fifi breathed.

Pandora nodded. Wow, indeed.

The Black clan was legend. History said a Black had founded the small town a hundred years back. But for all their standing in the town, people still passed rumors and innuendo in whispers, wondering where the Black fortune came from. Everything from inheriting from an eccentric relative to robbing banks to wise investments. All anyone knew for sure was that they were the wealthiest family in Black Oak, that Tobias's wife had died of leukemia before his youngest child could walk, and until five years ago when Tobias had opened a custom motorcycle shop, they hadn't appeared to work for a living.

"I'm surprised to see you here," Tobias was saying. Pandora frowned, though. The older man didn't look so much surprised as... What? She studied his body language, the way he rocked back on his heels, the set of his shoulders. If she had to guess, she'd say he looked satisfied.

"I didn't realize I had to check in with you as soon as I crossed the city limits," Caleb returned.

"Check in?" Tobias's hearty laugh filled the store, making half the customers smile in response. "Son, you know I don't make rules like that. But if I'd known you were gonna be in town for the holidays, I'd have had Mrs. Long get your room ready."

Caleb's only response was an arched brow.

Pandora tensed. They seemed amiable enough, but she still felt as if she was watching a boxing match. The two men circled each other without even moving. The gorgeously sexy biker looked even more dangerous than he had when he'd walked in. On the surface, he was relaxed, leaning against the wall. She could see the bored look on his narrow face and the general sense of *screw-you* surrounding him. But his feet gave him away. Instead of crossed at the ankle, or rocked back on the heels, his boots were planted as if he were ready to run.

This reunion was a family thing. Private. Especially if one of them decided to throw a punch.

"Maybe the two of you would like some privacy," she offered. The customers turned as one, a few shooting her guilty looks while the rest glared. Black Oak loved its gossip.

"No." Caleb shook his head before stepping forward to lay a warm, strong hand on Pandora's arm. The only thing that kept her from gasping and scurrying away was a desperate need to not add more fuel to the already out-of-control whisperfest brewing.

"We need to talk, son," Tobias insisted. His words were quiet, they were friendly and they were offered with a smile. They were also hard as steel.

"Maybe later," Caleb dismissed them. "Right now Pandora's promised me lunch."

"What?" she yelped. Caleb's fingers tightened on her arm.

"Really?" Tobias said at the same time, drawing the word out and giving them both a toothy smile.

Rock, meet hard place. Pandora's eyes swept the store, noting the slew of avid townspeople staring, waiting to see what she did. A few even mouthed the words *stay here*. Even the cats were watching her, Bonnie with her head tilted in curiosity, Paulie peering at her through slitted eyes, as if she was disturbing his nap. Then her gaze met Caleb's.

His eyes didn't beg. His face was passive. He simply returned her stare, his eyes steady. She could only hold his look for a few seconds, the intensity of those gold eyes sending crazy swirls of sexual heat spiraling down through her belly.

"Um, yes. Lunch," she murmured, finally pulling her arm out from under his hand. Needing to move, she headed toward the café.

Caleb sauntered beside her, his long legs easily keeping up with her rushed steps.

Everyone in the store moved, too. Apparently, customers were positioning themselves for the best view into the café.

Tobias, however, followed them right through the beads.

"I'm so glad to see so many holiday shoppers," Pandora called back through the beaded doorway of the café. "I know Cassiopeia will be thrilled when I tell her who was in buying merchandise today."

That got them going. Customers scurried to shelves, displays and tables in search of something to keep the town woo-woo queen from cursing them. Or worse, not giving them a peek into their future the next time they asked.

"I'm sure Pandora won't mind if we have a little chat before lunch," Tobias said.

She shook her head no, and was about to offer to wait in the kitchen, when Caleb laid his hand on her arm again.

She froze. Her breath caught and her legs went weak at his touch. The guy wasn't even looking at her and she was about to melt into a puddle at his feet. While his only use for her was to avoid talking to his daddy.

Yep, he was bad news.

Needing to unfog her brain, and unlust her body, she stepped away.

"I'm just passing through," Caleb said, leaning casually against the wall. But the smirk he shot Pandora was amused, as if he knew exactly what kind of effect he had on her.

"How long until you passed through my front door?" Tobias challenged. "You were going to let me know you were in town, weren't you?"

Silence. The hottie had that intense, brooding rebellious thing down pat. Without him saying a word, Pandora knew he hadn't planned to see his father, would have preferred that dear ole dad didn't even know he was in town and was thoroughly pissed to be put in the position of defending himself.

The air in the café was heavy with tension. So out of her element she wanted to turn heel and run all the way back to San Francisco, Pandora shifted from one foot to the other, forcing herself to stay in place.

"Today's special is a hot and spicy double meatball sandwich and four-layer Foreplay Chocolate Cake for dessert," she blurted out in her perkiest waitress voice.

It wasn't until both men shot her identical looks of shocked amusement that she realized what she'd offered. Oh, hell. She wanted to smack her hand over her mouth in horror. Her lust for Caleb was bad enough, but for it to sneak out in front of his father?

"I mean, um, that's the menu. Not an offer, you know? I wouldn't do that. Hit on a customer, I mean. That'd be rude."

Holy crap, Pandora thought. It was like taking her foot out of her mouth and shoving her ass in instead.

Thankfully, Caleb was sticking with his brooding silence. Wincing, she glanced at Tobias, who still looked amused. With an actual reason this time.

"I'll let the two of you do lunch, then," the older man

decided. He glanced through the beaded doorway. Pandora followed his gaze and cringed. How'd the crowd get even bigger?

She couldn't make Tobias go out there. They'd be on him like a pack of rabid dogs. And yes, she eyed the older man, noting the freakishly calm stance and lack of anger emanating off him, he could probably handle himself fine. Better than she could, that was for sure.

Still…

"Tobias, did you want to—"

Before she could finish the sentence, Caleb snapped to attention, straightening from the wall like a stiff board. Nice to know he could get stiff that fast; she almost smirked. Then she saw the intense anger in his eyes and swallowed.

What? Did he think she was going to invite his dad to stay?

"It's a little crowded with shoppers in the store now," she finished slowly, choosing her words as if they would guide her through a live minefield. "So, um, would you like to go out the back and cut across the alley to your own shop?"

Tobias rocked back on his heels, mimicking his son's stance and considered the two of them. He glanced through the beads again and then arched a brow at Caleb.

Clueless, Pandora looked at the younger man, too, trying to figure out what the silent question was that had just been asked. But she couldn't read a thing on either man's face.

She wanted to scream. Even if it wasn't a talent, she'd at least had a decent grasp of reading body language—bs, that was. Before Sean. Now? She might as well be blind.

She eyed the two men and their stoic faces and apparently relaxed stance. They came across as totally mellow strangers. And the hair on the back of her neck was standing up due to all the antagonism flying through the room.

It was frustrating the hell out of her.

"Thanks, Pandora," Tobias accepted. Then he flashed

her a charming smile. "And is there any chance I could get a piece of that cake to go? I was too full after lunch, but it'd be a nice snack later."

Pandora bit her lip, not sure why she felt as if she needed to stick around and protect Caleb. The man obviously didn't need little ole her standing in front of him.

But still…

"I'd appreciate it," Tobias prodded.

Unable to do otherwise, Pandora nodded and hurried into the tiny kitchen at the far end of the sunroom. She cut a fat slab of cake and scooped it into a cardboard box, not bothering to lick the decadent ganache off her knuckle as she pressed the lid down and rushed back out.

Neither man had moved. From what she could tell, neither had said a word, either.

"Here you go," she said, staying by the kitchen and its door to the alley, instead of taking the cake over to Tobias. "I hope you enjoy it. It's my favorite recipe."

Tobias gave his son a nod, then strode toward Pandora. A goodbye? Or acknowledgment that Caleb had won this round? Pandora wasn't sure which.

Caleb, of course, just stood there. Did nothing rile the guy?

"I do appreciate your hospitality," Tobias said as he reached her. "For the cake, and for making my son feel welcome. I'm sure one bite of your delicious offerings and he'll be ready to stay in Black Oak and enjoy himself for a while."

"Um, you're welcome?" Pandora murmured. She wanted to point out that as delicious as chocolate was, it wasn't magic cake. He was asking for an awful lot from a lunch that she wasn't even sure Caleb would eat.

Without another word to her, or to his son, Tobias gave a jaunty wave and headed out the back door. Pandora plaited her fingers together, staring in the direction Tobias had gone until she heard the door close. She shifted her gaze to the café tables then, noting that half needed tidying.

Her gaze landed everywhere but on Caleb.

Murmurs rose from the store. She turned, grateful that something might demand her attention.

Then she winced. She could almost feel the barbs of fury shooting at her from the disappointed crowd. They'd obviously thought the show would move into the store, where they could get a better view. They'd probably positioned themselves to best greet, and grill, Tobias as he left the café. And she'd ruined it.

But she didn't hear the chimes over the front door ring at all, which meant they were still circling, waiting for fresh meat. Or in this case, a hunk named Caleb.

They could just keep waiting. And, hopefully, purchasing. After all, she was apparently giving away cake back here.

Speaking of…

"Would you like something to eat?" she asked, finally looking directly at Caleb.

Under his slash of black brows, his eyes were intense as he inspected her. His expression didn't change as his gaze traveled from her face, then skimmed down her body in a way that made her wish she was wearing one of those loose, New Agey dresses Fifi and Cassiopeia wore.

Or that she was naked.

Either one would be better than this feeling that there wasn't a chance in hell she could measure up to the sexual challenge Caleb presented.

A sexual challenge she wasn't even positive he was issuing. For all she knew, the guy gave that same hot but unreadable look to his mail lady when she asked him to sign for delivery.

Her body on fire, her mind a mess of tangled thoughts, she gave in to the desire to run.

"I'll be right back," she muttered as she hurried back

to the small kitchen again. This time, instead of hacking through the cake and throwing it in a container, she carefully selected a plate, cut a precise slice and centered it on the cobalt glass plate. She retrieved a can of whipped cream and sprayed a sweet little rosette of white on top of the chocolate.

This was crazy. It wasn't as though the guy was going to ask her on a date. He was here to… What? Shop for Christmas gifts? Score an aphrodisiac-laced lunch?

Pandora groaned. Oh, wouldn't that be sweet? Insane, impossible and inconceivable—but so sweet to have sex with a man like Caleb Black. A man who, with just one look, could make her body go lax, her legs quiver and her nipples beg in pouty supplication.

But Caleb Black was the kind of guy who went for powerful women. A woman who could hold her own, who would demand he fulfill her every fantasy and in doing so, would show him things he hadn't even dreamed of yet.

In other words, totally not Pandora.

Except…she wanted him for herself.

She grabbed two forks, setting one neatly on the plate. With the other she stabbed a huge chunk from the cake still on the serving dish. Shoving it in her mouth, she closed her eyes and, with a sigh, let the chocolate work its way through her system. Calming, centering, soothing.

God, she loved chocolate.

More than sex, she insisted to herself. Which was a lie, of course, but with a little work she might start believing it. After all, chocolate's only threat was to her hips.

Swallowing hard as she imagined what kind of threat Caleb might pose to her body, she scooped up the plate and forced herself to return to the café.

"You look like that visit barely registered on your stress meter, but mine is off the charts. Nothing pulls me out of the dumps like chocolate, so I figured you might want some," she said with a sheepish smile as she set the cake on a nearby table. Glancing through the beads at the nosy crowd, she sighed, then sat opposite the plate and waited.

"Why's it empty in here?" he asked, his voice as surly as his scowl. But hey, words were words. Who was she to quibble over tone?

"The café closes at two. We still have shoppers in the store, but Fifi is helping them. People know we're closed. They won't come back here," she assured him. "It's not much, but at least it's a tiny semblance of privacy."

He gave her a look, those gold eyes dark. She could see the anger in them now, as clearly as she could see it in the set of his chin and his clenched fists. But now she could see hurt, too, in the way he hunched his shoulders, the droop of his lips.

"I guess this isn't a surprise visit for the holidays," she said with a tentative smile, wishing he'd smile again.

"Prodigal son, didn't Tobias say?"

"You call your father by his name?" Why was she so shocked? It wasn't as if he was the kind of guy to call his old man daddy.

He shrugged, staring at the door to the alley. Finally, he came over and sat across from her. She didn't know if it was because she'd worn him down with her inane chatter or if he was emotionally exhausted from the confrontation. It definitely wasn't because he was suddenly in the mood to be friendly. Not the way he was glowering. The frown didn't detract from his mouth.

A deliciously sensual mouth, she noticed. She licked her own lips, wondering what he tasted like. How he kissed. Whether he was slow and sensual or if he liked it wild and intense.

"You interested in providing a little prodigal entertainment?"

"Hmm?"

She'd bet he was a wild kind of guy. One who'd take her

mouth in a hard, mind-blowing kiss and leave her begging for a taste of his promised sexual nirvana.

"Yeah, you're interested."

Pandora ripped her gaze off his mouth to meet his eyes in horror. Was she that obvious? Was she so unskilled that she couldn't even hide her should-be-secret lusty thoughts?

What the hell was she doing? The man was off-limits. He was bad news, with a capital H heartbreak. And while she was intrigued enough to risk her heart, she still had the bruises from risking her reputation and ego.

"No, sorry. I'm not interested, I'm just curious."

"Curious?" His smile was pure temptation. Wicked and knowing. He didn't push, though. Instead, he cocked a brow at the slice of cake she'd set on the table between them, then pulled it toward him. He pressed his finger on a crumb and lifted it to his mouth.

Pandora swore her thighs melted. Heat, intense and needy, clawed through her good intentions.

PUZZLED, CALEB STUDIED the woman in front of him.

He'd got what he wanted out of this visit—to see the back room and access to the bike shop. Her interest would be easy to use to get back in, anytime he wanted.

But could he do it?

Seated at the table like a dainty lady about to serve some fancy-ass tea, Pandora looked as calm as a placid lake. Except for those occasional flashes of hunger he saw in her pretty eyes. With her smooth, dark red hair and porcelain complexion, she looked like the special china doll his sister had as a kid. If he remembered correctly, he'd broken that doll at one point or another.

Something to keep in mind.

He noted the lush fullness of her lips and the sweet curve of her breasts beneath the white silky fabric of her conservatively cut blouse. His body stirred in reluctant interest.

Good girls weren't his thing, but his body wasn't paying much attention to that detail.

"Were you going to try the cake?" Pandora prodded, looking a little put out at his inspection. She sounded as if she wanted to say something—probably something rude—but good girls didn't do things like that.

He grinned. Yet another reason not to be good.

He had questions, so more to pacify her than because he wanted any, he swiped his finger over the frosted cake and sucked the sweet confection while holding her gaze.

Her eyes narrowed. He imagined she was trying to look stern, but came off as cute instead. Her store location was handy, she probably had an inside track to the town and townspeople, and she looked as if she was one of those crazy trust-until-proved-untrustworthy kind of people.

A much better cover than the loosey-goosey vamp who'd hit on him before. She was going to be easier to, well, manipulate.

"I remember this store now," he mused as he looked, noting the deep purple walls with garlands of flowers, stars, suns and moons painted along the ceiling. "I broke in here one night on a dare, hoping to see a rumored séance. It wasn't a restaurant then, though."

"Broke in? I always heard that you were wild, but I thought those rumors were exaggerated."

He just shrugged. It wasn't as though it was a secret that he'd been well on his way to a life of crime in his teen years. Hell, he considered it early training for his undercover assignments.

The frosting was good. Ready for more, he took the fork and scooped up a big bite.

"This room used to be set up for classes and readings," she explained, still frowning at him in a chiding sort of way. "My mother started using it for storage when the mayor changed the permit requirements to demand a twenty percent kickback."

Caleb snorted. He'd grown up the son of an infamous con artist and spent his adult years dealing with criminal dregs. But he was pretty sure politics were the biggest scam around.

"Gotta hand it to her. The mayor's big on clever ways to line the town coffers."

She gave him a narrow-eyed look at odds with his sweet, goody-goody image of her. "Isn't Mayor Parker your aunt?"

Realizing he was starving, he forked up more of the rich cake and grinned. "Yep."

"So this is like old home week. Will you be staying with your aunt instead of your father?"

"Nope. I'm at the Black Oak Inn. Room seventeen, if you're out wandering later," he said with a wink.

Her eyes rounded. She caught her breath as if grabbing back a response that scared her. The move made her cotton top slide temptingly over rounded breasts. He watched as her nipples beaded against the fabric. Suddenly starving, he wanted nothing more than to lean across the table and taste her.

Her reaction was gratifying. His own irritated him, though. She wasn't his type, and given the situation, she was off-limits. He just had to remember that.

"I'm sure I'll see her, though. Want me to talk her into dropping those fees for you?" he offered with another wink.

"I don't do readings."

That sounded bitter. His chewing slowed; he gave her a searching look.

She gave a tiny shrug and looked away.

Off-limits? A part of him wanted to push. To ask questions and get to know her better. The rest of him, the burned-out, disenchanted, cynical DEA-trained part of him, said that unless it pertained to the case, it didn't matter.

Since he wasn't sticking around longer than it took to clear his old man, the cynic got to call the shots.

"So what's the deal?" Caleb asked instead. "You seem to know Tobias pretty well, right?"

"I wouldn't say I know your father well," she mused, her eyes skimming toward the alley. "No more so than anyone else in town. I mean, he's the patriarch, isn't he? From what I understand, he's got more power than the mayor and the sheriff combined. People look up to him, turn to him for advice. I've been hearing accolades since the day I arrived."

"You're not a native of Black Oak?" Why had he thought she was?

"I am native," she said, drawing the words out. "I think I was even in a few classes with your sister, Maya. But I left for college and haven't been back much since."

"So why'd you get a job here? You're interested in this New Age stuff?"

She looked toward the dangling beaded doorway with shelves of crystal balls lining either side and rolled her eyes.

"Interested? I don't know about that. More like indoc-trinated." At his arched brow, she shrugged and admitted, "Cassiopeia is my mother."

He might only have a vague recollection of the store, but he definitely remembered Cassiopeia. Third-genera-tion woo-woo queen, all the guys in high school had had crushes on her. Bodacious, outrageous and eccentric, the outgoing redhead had a scary handle on that psychic stuff she sold to her customers.

"I remember your mom. She did readings at my senior carnival."

"Mine, too." Pandora didn't sound nearly as intrigued as he'd been. The son of a colorful character, Caleb could sympathize.

Talk about the apple falling so far from the tree it could make orange juice. Now that he knew what to look for, he could see the resemblance in the curve of her cheeks, the rounded eyes more hazel than her mother's emerald. And, of course, the red hair, again, more muted in Pandora's case. It was as if she'd stepped into a shadow instead of embracing the full wattage her mother liked to wave around.

Interesting.

Even more interesting was that Caleb was finding muted about the sexiest thing he'd ever encountered. He just couldn't figure out why since he'd always been a Technicolor kind of guy.

"You know what I heard while we were still in the store, then again while you were in the back getting cake?"

"You mean while you were hiding back here?" she corrected.

Caleb grinned, glad to see she had claws. It was always more fun to tangle with a wildcat than a pussycat.

"I heard people saying you serve up something besides food back here."

This time the color wasn't subtle. Nope, she blushed a hot, brilliant red. Her eyes flew to the store, then to the cake before meeting his gaze. A stubborn line furrowed between her brows.

"I have no idea what you're talking about," she dismissed.

"You're a horrible liar."

"A gentleman would take the hint and change the subject."

"Sweetie, I've never worried about being a gentleman."

"Obviously."

Grinning, Caleb decided it was time to change gears. He stood, and with a glance at the still-milling crowd in the store, decided to take his cue from his father and head out the back way.

"Walk me out?" he said, making the demand sound like a request.

"The back? The door's right there," she pointed out. But she got to her feet anyway.

Caleb didn't know why he was pushing it. He'd already declared her off-limits, and while he was a guy who was all about pushing boundaries, he never crossed lines he, himself, drew.

But right now, he didn't care.

"So is it true?" he asked, heading toward the door, counting on her being trapped by good manners into following.

"Is what true?"

"Do you really serve aphrodisiacs?"

She ground to a halt so fast, she teetered in her flat-heeled boots. "Don't believe everything you hear," she said dismissively.

"So, it's a lie?"

"It's more of an...exaggeration," she decided. "After all, who's to say whether aphrodisiacs are real or whether they're a figment of the imagination?"

"I have a really good imagination." He reached out and took her hand, lifting it to his mouth.

"What are you doing?" she asked with a gasp, tugging. But he didn't let go.

"You have chocolate," he told her, "just...here."

He swiped his tongue over her knuckle. Her eyes went heated, her breath shuddered and she leaned against the wall with the cutest little mewling noise.

In an instant, Caleb went from amused to rock-hard. An overwhelming urge to touch her, to taste her, washed over him.

Never a man to ignore his gut, he went with the feeling. Stepping forward, the rich taste of chocolate still on his lips, Caleb pressed her body between his and the chilly glass. One hand on either side of her head, he leaned closer.

"This is crazy," she breathed, twisting her hands together at her waist. But she didn't pull away. Instead, she lifted her chin.

That's all the encouragement he needed.

Holding her gaze captive, he brushed his lips over her

soft, sweetly moist mouth. He slid his tongue along her lower lip, then gently nibbled at the cushioned flesh.

Passion throbbed, urging him to take it deeper, to go faster. But he resisted.

For the first time in forever, Caleb felt as if he'd come home. Even as the sexual heat zinged through his body like lightning, he relaxed. Need pounded through him, making him ache. But he was at peace.

It was that confusion more than any desire to stop that had him pulling back. He stared, waiting for Pandora to open her eyes. In them he saw confusion, hunger and a hint of fear.

The same as he was feeling.

"You might want to go easy on that cake," he suggested, brushing his knuckles over her cheek before forcing himself away. Stepping back from the warm, soft curves of her body was harder than it should have been. Way too freaking hard. Caleb frowned, not sure what the hell was going on here.

Hand on the doorknob, he looked back. She was still leaning against the wall, her breath ragged and her eyes huge.

"Like I said, I'm in room seventeen. Come on by if you want to do something about that interest. Or serve up something a little hotter than cake."

4

"I'LL HAVE THE PASTA SPECIAL, the house salad with rasp-
berry vinaigrette and the house white," Kathy ordered over
the melodic jingle of crystal and silver.

"And you, madam? What would you like?"

"I'd like what's in room seventeen," Pandora muttered,
staring blindly at the menu.

"Beg your pardon?"

"What's in room seventeen?" Kathy prodded with a
nudge of her toe under the white linen-covered table.

Playing back what she'd said, Pandora scrunched her
nose in a rueful grimace. God, she couldn't get Caleb Black
out of her head. His intense gold eyes, his sexy swagger
and oh, baby, those magic lips.

He'd tasted so good. So enticing. Like the most deliciously decadent chocolate éclair. Rich and tempting and
mouthwateringly hedonistic. All she had to do was close
her eyes and she could relive the sweet slide of his mouth
over hers, her body heating instantly at the memory.

"Dory?"

Pandora blinked. Damn, she'd done it again. Spaced off
into Caleb fantasyland. She'd been taking that trip over and
over and over for the past two days. She'd just bet his body
was a wild amusement park, too. One she was in desper-

ate danger of knocking on the door of room seventeen to beg to ride.

"Pandora!"

Pandora winced and gave the waiter an apologetic smile and said, "Sorry, I'll have the same thing."

Not that she had any idea what Kathy had ordered.

Clearly clued in to big news by Pandora's dinginess, Kathy leaned forward on both elbows and demanded with her usual rapid-fire pace, "What's going on? You've got news, don't you? How's the store doing? Have you put your stamp on it? Do you love the café angle? Are people doing the deed on the tables thanks to that menu we came up with?"

Pandora's fingers tapped a rhythm on the table as she pondered.

"Well?" Kathy used one perfectly manicured finger to poke Pandora in the arm.

"I was waiting to see if you had more questions," she replied with a wicked grin.

"Cute. Now spill."

She'd called Kathy to meet her for lunch for just this reason, to spill the dirty deets about Caleb Black and his hot lips. Her friend was the only person she could tell, because not only was Kathy a great sounding board, she was sane. She'd be the voice of reason and keep Pandora from doing something insanely stupid, like chasing a man who was totally wrong for her. But she'd also keep Pandora from chickening out if her idea—and Caleb—were actually doable.

But now that the moment of truth was here, she couldn't quite share. Wasn't sure she was ready for this kind of risk. So she sidestepped.

"The store is actually doing well. There's a ton of business. The new café is bringing in lots of customers. They're shopping in the store, heck, even the online storefront is getting a lot more traffic. Sales are up forty percent over this time last year and I've banked almost enough to cover the quarterly tax payment."

Pressing her lips tight to stop the bragging, Pandora waited for a reaction. She was a little embarrassed at how proud she was of the store. Even more embarrassed at how much she wanted people, any people—but especially people in Black Oak—to know she was kicking butt. To know that she wasn't a failure.

"Wow," Kathy said with a huge grin, clapping her hands together in delight. "I told you it would work. You're totally rocking the businesswoman gig. I'm excited for you."

"I wouldn't say rocking it," Pandora said, blushing a little. "But it is going so much better than I'd expected. I thought I was going to have to work a lot harder to convince people that oysters, strawberries and asparagus would make their love lives more exciting. But I barely had to advertise. Just opened the café, showed the menu and once word got out, it's been packed."

"Beats little blue pills, right?"

Pandora laughed, leaning back in her chair and letting the soothing elegance of the restaurant wash over her.

"Oh, yeah, I have it on good authority that I'm way ahead of the little blue pill," she agreed with a grin. "Do you know how much I now know about sexual aids for the elderly? I mean, yes, the customers are all ages, but it's the elderly that want to share."

Pandora paused while the waiter set a basket of sourdough bread and a dish of roasted garlic and olive tapenade on the table. As soon as he left, she continued.

"They are so grateful and excited about the aphrodisiacs—and to give them credit, about a place to get killer desserts—that they seem to have a need to fill me in on their newfound vigor, enthusiasm, length…. It's TMI run amok."

Kathy choked on her wine. "Length?"

Pandora's brow quirked, then as she realized what Kathy must be thinking, she giggled. "Eww, no. I meant how long their little trysts are lasting now. Apparently chocolate cake is accredited with an extra twenty minutes of good lovin'."

"And they never discovered the power of chocolate before?"

"Not naked."

This time it was Kathy who wrinkled her nose.

"It sounds like you've had plenty of entertainment. Leave it to Black Oak to stay lively."

"Yep, the town is chock-full of characters." Pandora hesitated, then took another fortifying sip of wine. "Including Tobias Black's kids. Do you remember them?"

"Ooooh, baby," Kathy said with a low-throated growl. "I had one memorable night with Gabriel right after graduation, remember? I still consider that my introduction to real pleasure, if you know what I mean."

Pandora winced. Maybe she really did have a sex-confessional sign floating over her head. Before Kathy could share details, she changed the subject. "Did you know the rest of his family?"

"Not so much. Maya is a little younger than we are, Caleb a few years older than Gabriel. Their mom died when they were really little and I think their aunt tried to get custody but Tobias wouldn't let them go. I remember my mom saying he might not have done them any favors since the boys ran pretty wild. He used to travel a lot, and sometimes he took the kids, but mostly they stayed home on their own." She frowned, sopping up oil with her bread before picking it apart in tiny little bites. "They had a few minor brushes with the law, teenage things, but nothing major. I remember they were scary smart in school, though. Like they didn't even have to study to ruin the curve, you know?"

Mulling this over, Pandora nodded.

"Why? Are you selling bed-y-bye snacks to old man Black? Now, *that's* a guy who's aged well. Talk about a hottie. I'd think he'd have little need for a chocolate-coated pick-me-up."

Mr. Black? A hottie? Pandora wasn't sure what to say to that. It wasn't that she didn't agree with Kathy, because Tobias Black was definitely a good-looking man. But it was kinda creepy thinking about him that way when she was nursing a serious case of the hots for his son.

"If he's as good a kisser as his son, I'm sure he doesn't," Pandora agreed, nibbling at her own piece of bread and nervously waiting for the reaction. Once upon a time, she'd have relied on her own ability to read a person, to gauge their body language, and had trusted her own judgment. But now? Now all she was sure of was that she couldn't be trusted.

The question was, did that mean she shouldn't trust her lust for Caleb? Or her fear of him?

Kathy gave a gratifying gasp, tossed what was left of her bread on her plate and leaned forward to grasp Pandora's arm. "Spill. All the details. Which brother, how was it, where'd you do it and were you naked?"

Pandora giggled.

"Caleb. It was amazing. In the café, and oh, my God, of course not."

"But you wanted to be?"

"Absolutely," she admitted with a sigh. Her smile softened as she remembered his lips again. The taste of him, male, hot and just a little chocolaty. Their bodies hadn't even touched, yet she'd been more turned on than the last time she'd had full-on, two-naked-bodies and real-live-orgasm sex.

More turned on than she'd ever been in her life, actually.

"In the café?" Kathy said, a naughty look dancing in her green eyes. "Had you shared one of those sexy treats?"

Pandora opened her mouth to say no, then closed it.

She hadn't put much thought into it, but he'd had a few

big bites of the Foreplay cake. So had she, for that matter. But their lust had been the real deal. At least, hers had.

Doubt, always lurking somewhere but now painfully close to the surface thanks to Sean, reared its ugly head.

"A couple bites is all," she admitted with a frown. "But a lot of the power of an aphrodisiac is in the mind, isn't it? My grammy always said that most magics require belief to work. The power of suggestion and all that."

"Kinda like a low-cut dress, huh?"

Pandora grinned, acknowledging Kathy's point with a wave of her fork. "A little."

Then her smile fell away. "Do you think that's why he kissed me? Of course it is," she answered herself. "I mean, he just got to town, he's so gorgeous he probably has women throwing themselves at him. Why else would he kiss a perfect stranger?"

Why had she thought he'd found her special? That was crazy. She wasn't the type to inspire uncontrollable lust. Heck, she rarely inspired a second look.

Seeing where her mind was going, Kathy shook her head and gave Pandora's forearm a chiding tap. "Stop that. You're counting yourself out before you even consider the situation."

"What's to consider?"

"The details, of course. Start at the beginning."

Pandora arched one brow. "When the dinosaurs roamed? Or back further than that?"

"Smart-ass. When did you first meet Caleb Black?"

Pandora picked at her slice of bread again, wishing she'd never brought the subject up. For just a while there she'd been riding high on the idea that a man so sexy he made her toes curl had been attracted enough for a kiss at first sight. But now? Now she figured she should raise the prices in the café, since her aphrodisiacs were that strong.

"Deets," Kathy prodded. "Has he been in town long? When was the kiss?"

"Two days ago," she finally confessed. "He came into the store. There was this big confrontation between him and his dad, then I gave him a piece of cake and he kissed me."

Just remembering gave her shivers. It'd been so incredible. For a guy who came across as a total hard-ass, his lips had been so, so soft.

She took a shaky breath and brushed the bread crumbs off her fingers.

Maybe the why didn't matter. She'd had an incredible kiss. Wasn't that what counted?

"Wow, talk about a lot going on. I'll want the details of all the rest later. But for now, how was the kiss?" Kathy asked, her eyes huge. "Was it amazing?"

"It was…special," she decided with a soft smile.

"Uh-oh."

"What uh-oh?" Pandora saw the concerned look in Kathy's eyes and shook her head. "No. No uh-oh. I'm not getting romantic ideas. That'd be crazy, considering he only kissed me because of the cake. I'm just saying, it was a hot kiss that didn't follow the standard moves, you know?"

"Standard moves?"

"Yeah. You know how usually the first kiss with a guy is more about the anticipation and, well, introduction to his style?"

Kathy nodded.

"There was no anticipation because, I mean, who the hell kisses a complete stranger in a café while sneaking out the back door?" Kathy's brows creased, but before she could ask, Pandora continued, "And he wasn't so much introducing his style as he was…"

"Was…what?"

"Making me melt?" Pandora admitted with a helpless little laugh. "Honestly, I have no idea why he kissed me. I just know that it was amazing."

"Once again, uh-oh," Kathy worried, apprehension clear in her eyes.

"What?"

"Be careful. Those Black men are heartbreakers. They went through girls like crazy. They always left them smiling, sure. But they never stuck around. Still, you don't need that," Kathy warned.

"I know he's off-limits," Pandora said with a bad-tempered shrug. "I didn't say I was crazy enough to think one flirty little kiss—especially one that didn't include tongue—means I'm in for some hot and wild bad-boy sex."

"He's not off-limits. He's just trouble. But if all you're thinking about is getting naked and doing the horizontal tango, then maybe you should. Just as long as you're clear from the start that it's just sex. Nothing more."

Caleb Black. Naked. Oh, man, she'd bet he was deliciously built. Those wide shoulders would have the kind of muscles she could cling to as he moved in her, his long torso and slender hips arched over her straining body. She knew he had a sweet little hiney, but it'd look even better bare than it had covered in denim. She'd bet it was firm, so hard she'd barely make a dent if her fingers gripped it. Heat washed over Pandora so fast she had to take a sip of her wine before she combusted.

"That is all you're thinking about, isn't it?" Kathy prodded.

"Well, now I'm thinking about Caleb naked and can't remember your question," Pandora said with a pout.

"You're only looking for sex, right? Not a relationship? Not a wild time that might turn into something special once he realizes how great you are?"

"No," she protested vehemently. This was a stupid conversation. All she'd wanted was to share her little bit of sexy news and suddenly she was defending a fling with a guy who probably kissed every woman he met. That didn't mean he had any interest in actually getting naked and slippery. "I'm not going to do anything stupid. I'd have to be crazy to fall for a guy like Caleb Black. I'm not his type and that kiss was probably the last contact we'll ever have."

Kathy leaned back in the booth and gave her a long, searching look. After a few seconds, Pandora squirmed. She didn't like people looking that close, or that deep.

"Okay, I've changed my mind. I think you should go for it."

"Go for what? It wasn't like an invitation to a relationship. It was more like a hit-and-run."

"Maybe. But maybe not. I'm just saying if he hits again, you should take him up on a little ride. I'll bet he's the kind of guy who'll make you see stars."

Stars. Pandora wasn't a virginal prude. She liked sex. Especially if it was good sex. She read the how-to articles in women's magazines and erotic books, she knew her body and wasn't shy about giving directions when necessary.

But, typically, the guys she'd been with weren't big on directions.

Which was probably why she'd never seen stars. With Sean, she'd seen a flicker or two but never full-oh-my-God stars.

"So?" Kathy prodded.

"So what?"

"So, are you going to shoot for the stars? Or are you going to take the route of avoidance?"

Avoidance. All the way.

After all, the last time she'd given in to a sexy fling, she'd paid. Big-time. And Sean hadn't been anywhere near as hot, gorgeous or tempting as Caleb. Getting involved with him was crazy.

The last thing she needed was to get herself all upside down over a guy. Even a just-sex-and-nothing-more kind of guy. A more confident woman might be able to handle a sweet fling with someone like that, but her? She wasn't that kind of woman.

For once, though, she wanted to be. She wanted to have a purely sexual fling based on nothing more than physical satisfaction and excitement. She wanted to be exciting and dynamic. Fun and maybe a little wild. No expectations of anything long-term or emotional.

And maybe, just maybe, to relax knowing that because she didn't expect anything, her inability to read him couldn't be termed a failure.

"He's not going to ask me out," she said again.

"So why don't you ask him out?"

Why didn't she jump up on the table and strip naked while singing Katy Perry's "Hot N Cold"? "I can't do that," she excused.

Kathy just gave her The Look.

Pandora pressed a hand to her stomach, feeling as if she was about to jump off a very high cliff.

It was scary.

But it was also exciting as hell.

"I'm not promising anything. But—and it's a teensy-tiny but—but…if I do, and if he says yes, then our next kiss *will* involve tongues," she vowed.

CALEB LEANED HIS LEATHER-CLAD shoulder against the black iron lamppost and stared across the street at the warm welcome of Moonspun Dreams.

He'd promised Hunter he'd give it two weeks. So in between watching the store, he'd spent the past four days nosing around. He'd hit what passed for the party scene in Black Oak. Bounced through a few bars, made himself known to the major partiers and netted a couple easy introductions to the town's lower-level drug dealers. The first step was to get the lay of the land, to gauge how challenging the bust would be and to establish his identity.

The ecstasy was definitely available and at discounts usually only seen in Black Friday sales ads. Marketing 101, make the product cheap and plentiful until you'd hooked enough suckers, then bleed them dry. As he would on any DEA job, he'd scored a little from each dealer, sending it all to Hunter for analysis. But experience and instinct told him it was all coming from the same source. A source nobody could—or would—pinpoint.

So far this visit was a bust. He hadn't found out much for Hunter. He hadn't cleared his father. Of course, he'd done his damnedest to avoid seeing his father at all after that first surprise visit, but that was neither here nor there.

And all he could think about was that one small kiss from the intriguingly reticent Pandora.

Unlike his usual M.O. in breaking a drug ring, this time he had no cover. Around here, everyone and their granny knew who he was. Many had pinched his cheeks at the same time they'd bemoaned his probable criminal career. That all worked in his favor, his lousy rep ensuring that nobody questioned his activities.

Still, that was then. He'd have liked to come home and be appreciated for who he really was now. An upright citizen who'd made a life outside of crime.

Except, he realized with a tired sigh, that he really didn't have any life outside of crime. Which was why he'd quit. To relax, to get a hobby and to figure out what he wanted from life.

Which brought his thoughts back, yet again, to Pandora. He couldn't figure out why the woman fascinated him, but she did. She was quiet, when he usually went for the flamboyant. She seemed sweet, which he was pretty sure he was allergic to. And she was friendly with his father, which meant she had questionable taste.

As he pondered, and yes, stared at Moonspun's window hoping to catch a glimpse of the sexy Ms. Easton, some-

thing on the corner across the street caught his eye. Two
guys in black hoodies, both hunched over as if they were
trying to blend in with the brick siding of Pandora's building. Caleb shook his head in disgust. He didn't need years
of DEA experience to recognize a drug deal going down.
Hell, the little old lady walking her Pomeranian was shooting the two guys the same disgusted look. When one of the
guys made a hulking gesture toward her, obviously trying
to intimidate, she flipped him the bird and kept mincing
along in her fluffy pink knitted hat. Caleb could see the
goon growl from across the street. He made as if to go after
her, when his buddy grabbed his arm, saying something
and showing him a bag of what Caleb assumed were the
drugs in question.

Hulk flexed a little, then followed the Baggie into the
alley. Caleb considered trailing them. He had no jurisdiction. Hell, he was on a pseudovacation with his resignation sitting on his boss's desk. It was the *pseudo* part of
that equation that made him hesitate, not the vacation or
the resignation.

But, really, how far did fake authority go? Favors for
buddies and an unexplained need to vindicate his father
didn't give him the jurisdiction to bust a deal going down.

Then again, when had he ever worried about rules?

Before he could step off the curb, though, Hulk slunk
out of the alley. His hoodie pulled low so his face was shad-
owed, he loped down the street.

No point following the doper. Caleb wanted the guy
hooked into whoever was running the game. He waited
for him to come out.

But the alley opening stayed empty.

Five minutes later, Caleb was mentally cussing and
ready to hit something. There were only two businesses
accessible through that alley. Moonspun Dreams and his
dad's bike shop.

Dammit.

Before he could decide how he wanted to handle it, a car pulled up next to him. Caleb's sigh was infinitesimal as he cut his gaze to the sheriff's cruiser. His eyes were the only thing he moved, though.

Because he knew damn well the lack of reaction would piss Jeff off.

"I heard you were back in town," Jeff Kendall, the bane of Caleb's high school years, said as he unfolded himself from his car, leaning his forearms on the open door and offering an assessing look.

"Looks like you heard right."

"C'mon, Black. Just because we didn't get along before doesn't mean you should be holding a grudge," Kendall said with his good-ole-boy smile. The one he'd perfected in grade school, usually used in tandem with tattling to the teacher about the bad Black kids.

It still made Caleb want to punch him.

Hunter had broached the possibility of bringing in local law enforcement, but Caleb had nixed the idea. If the locals knew about the drugs and hadn't shut them down, they might be dirty. And that'd been before he knew who he'd be dealing with. When he'd heard that this guy was in charge of the law in town, Caleb had sneered. No wonder they had problems.

"Look, I'm just offering a welcome home, okay. I hear you've seen your share of trouble after leaving town. I'm not here to add to it. But if you don't mind a friendly warning, keep it clean while you're enjoying Christmas with your dad."

Caleb didn't even blink. After all, that was his cover. Prodigal loser back for the holidays, nothing to his name except a bad attitude and a crappy reputation. And, of course, a whole lot of family baggage.

All in all, it was pretty damn close to the truth.

His silent stare seemed to bug Kendall, though. The guy shifted from foot to foot, then frowned.

"Are you standing here for a reason?" the sheriff prodded.

"Just biding my time."

Kendall glanced around, his gaze lighting on Moonspun Dreams, then flashing back to Caleb. "Looking for a little help in the sack, are you?"

Caleb didn't move. Didn't bat an eyelash. But his entire being snapped to attention.

"Thanks to Pandora and her little concoctions," the sheriff continued, "Black Oak is seeing more sex than a teenager with his daddy's credit card and a link to online porn."

"Geez, Kendall. Can't you score your own credit card yet?"

The sheriff glared, then jerked his head toward the store again. "You must be in the market for a little bedroom boost. There's nothing else in there for you."

It took a second before that sunk in. Caleb's grin was just this side of a smirk as he raised his brows to the other man. "You warning me off?"

"I'm just saying you need to watch your step." Kendall rested one hand on the gun at his hip and tilted his head. "This isn't your town. It's mine. Crime is low and trouble is rare. I'm not going to like it if you sweep in here, stir up a bunch of problems, then make me kick you out."

Low crime and rare trouble? Was the guy really that bad at his job? Caleb's eyes slashed to the corner where the drug deal had gone down. Good thing Hunter had sent him here, since Kendall clearly had no clue what was going on.

"Do you watch John Wayne movies on your nights off and practice that shit in front of the mirror?" was all he said, though.

Kendall's red face tightened, right along with his fist. "I'm a sworn officer of the law. That makes me in charge of this town, Black. So watch your ass."

The guy's delusional self-importance amused Caleb enough that he could easily ignore the jabs.

Besides, he was pretty sure he'd just seen the first break in this case. And he'd much rather follow that up than exchange insults with this dipwad.

"Tell you what. You've piqued my interest," Caleb said, straightening for the first time and stepping toward the curb. "I'll head on over and see if the lady's interested in fielding a hit or two."

"I warned you, Black—"

Caleb just grinned and offered a jaunty salute before crossing the street.

The only thing better than having an excuse to flirt with Pandora handed to him on a silver platter was knowing how much it pissed Jeff the jerk off.

He was still grinning when he walked through the heavy brass door of Moonspun Dreams. Not seeing Pandora among the dozen or so people milling about the store, he made his way toward the back.

"The café is closed," the airy blonde said, tearing herself away from a shaggy-haired guy by the counter.

"I'm here to see Pandora."

"Oh." Her look was speculative, but she just shrugged and went back to helping her client.

Caleb swept the beads aside and stepped through the door.

Then he almost tripped over his own size thirteens.

And grinned at the sight before him.

Holiday music playing loud enough to inspire a little swing of the hips as she arranged a bunch of green Christmas stuff, glittery bows and... Caleb squinted, were those blown-glass suns and moons...? Pandora stood at the top of a tall ladder before the wall by the door to the kitchen.

Her arms stretched high, her purple sweater pulled away from her jeans, showing off the pale silkiness of the small of her back. His gaze traced the tight fit of the denim, noting the hint, maybe, of a tattoo on her left hip.

Nah. She wasn't the tattoo type. She was the good-girl type.

Wasn't she?

Damned if he wasn't tempted to find out.

Whichever she was, she was one sweet sight.

Caleb's grin turned contemplative as he studied the curve of her butt, noting how perfectly those hips would fit in his hands.

A man who rarely tempered his impulses outside of work, Caleb figured why not find out. He glanced around, noting that there weren't any customers, or drug dealers, lurking about. Striding forward, he stepped behind the counter and planted a hand on either side of the ladder.

Just in time for Pandora's descent.

One step down, and her butt was level with his face. Right there within nibbling distance. Another step and he could push aside that nubby purple sweater and slide his lips along the small of her back. One more and, oh, yeah, baby…

Pandora gasped, her head swiveling to give him a wide-eyed look of shock.

"What the…?"

"Hi," he said, his voice low with more desire than he should be feeling for a woman he hadn't even groped yet.

A woman who was staring at him as if he was a combination of the Grinch and the Ghost of Christmas Future. The one who pushed poor Scrooge McDuck into his grave. In other words, she looked just as thrilled as dip-wad Kendall had.

He shouldn't tease her. She was obviously on the shy and quiet side. Caleb didn't bother to move, though.

"What are you…? I mean, why…?" She stopped, closed her eyes and took a deep breath, then opened those hazel eyes again and offered a stiff smile. "What are you doing?"

"Making sure you don't fall off the ladder."

She looked down at the five inches between her feet and the ground, then met his gaze again with an arched brow. She had a little more makeup on today than she had earlier in the week. Something was smudged around her eyes, darkening those lush lashes. Her lips, though, those soft, soft lips, were temptingly bare.

"Aren't you the hero."

Caleb barked out a laugh. So much for shy and quiet. He'd expected her to get a little huffy. But no, she was a lot more fun than that.

And then she blew his mind. She slowly turned on the ladder, her hip brushing against his chest as she did. Awareness spiked through his body, hot and needy.

She licked her lips, the sensual move at odds with the nerves shimmering in her golden-green eyes. And she stepped down. They were so close, the tips of her breasts skimmed, just barely, a path down his chest, leaving behind a fiery trail.

Caleb's smile slowly faded.

He'd pegged Pandora as a sweet, small-town girl, maybe a bit naive but with an open, curious mind. He'd figured on having a little fun flirting while he gathered info.

He definitely hadn't counted on a hard-on within the first three minutes of seeing her again.

Had he underestimated the sweet Pandora?

"Are you looking for a hero?" he asked, mentally rolling his eyes. At the question, because wasn't that what all women were looking for? A mythical guy to sweep them away and make all their dreams come true? And at the idea of *him* being hero material.

"Nah, I'd rather take care of things myself," she said with a smile and a tiny shrug. Her shoulder brushed against his wrist. "The term *hero* always makes me think of perfection. Since I can't live up to it, why would I want to have to deal with it?"

"So… What? You're looking for an antihero?" he joked, his gaze wandering over the soft, round curve of her face, noting the tiniest of dimples just there, to the left of her mouth.

"More like I'm not looking for anything," she said.

Yeah, right.

He looked closer, noting the stubborn set of her chin and the hint of anger in her eyes. Something, or someone, had burned her. Which meant she might be serious. A not-anything relationship, short and sweet, was right up his alley.

Besides, she had info he needed.

"You might not be looking for a hero, but from what I hear, you're exactly what I'm looking for," he told her.

"And what do you hear?" she asked, leaning back against the ladder, apparently not bothered at all that he was still holding her there, trapped by his arms. He didn't know if he liked that. He was used to making women nervous.

So he leaned in a little closer. Close enough that the scent of her perfume wrapped around him like a sensual fog. Close enough to see her heart beating a fast tattoo against the silky flesh at the base of her throat. Close enough to feel the tempting heat of her body.

His voice husky with need, his grin just a little strained, he said, "Rumor has it you're the lady to see if I'm looking for some really hot sex."

5

PANDORA'S MOUTH DROPPED, and with it all her bravado. Color washed, hot and wicked, over her cheeks as she blinked fast to try to clear her desire-blurred vision.

She stared at him, desperately trying to read him. Was this for real? Was he asking her for sex? Without even a bite of Foreplay cake or a nibble of an Orgasmic Oatmeal cookie? Did she say yes? Or ask him to wait until after her shift? The back room was empty, but still…

God, was she crazy? She gave herself a mental smack upside the head and tried to pull herself together. *Control, girl. Grab some control.*

But all she could think of was what he'd taste like naked and whether his chest was as tanned as his face under that tight black T-shirt.

Caleb's laughter washed over her, breaking the shocked spell. As soon as it did, color slid from her cheeks, leaving behind icy-cold humiliation.

"I guess that's what I get for listening to rumors," he said, still chortling. "Crazy, huh? That you'd be selling sex in here."

She frowned, his easy dismissal taking the edge off her embarrassment. What? He didn't think she could sell sex? He didn't think she was hot enough, wild enough, savvy enough? Was she so dismissible that he didn't think of sex after kissing her? Even now, when he had her trapped between his body and a ladder?

What the hell?

She'd put makeup on. She'd bought perfume, something sexy and inviting. She'd worn her tightest freaking jeans. And he dismissed her? Shoulders hunching, Pandora felt herself withdrawing. Pulling inside, where she could pretend it didn't hurt that, yet again, she didn't measure up. Or in this case, was so easily dismissible.

Here she'd spent the past three days in a state of horny anticipation, acting like a teenage girl wishing and wondering when her crush would reenter her sphere of existence. And what happened when he did?

He laughed at the idea of her and sex.

Before she could duck under his arm and scurry off, back to the obscurity of the kitchen or storage room, she caught sight of Bonnie the cat staring at her from the window seat with her pretty black-and-white head tilted to one side as if she was waiting for Pandora to find her spine.

The spine Sean had damaged with his lies, betrayal and oh-too-believable charm.

Then she thought of her vow to Kathy. Sure, it'd mostly been bravado, but still, she wanted to taste him. To feel his tongue on hers. To experience, at least one more time, hot and sexy Caleb kisses. She pressed her lips together, remembering. Then she squared her shoulders and gave him an arch look.

"Actually, most of Black Oak is thanking me daily for the effect I've had on their sex lives," she told him, lifting her chin.

His laughter trailed off, his smile slowly fading as a weird look came into his eyes. A chilly sort of calculation that made Pandora, for the first time since he'd swaggered into her store four days ago, want to pull away from him.

He looked dangerous. And just a little scary.

"You don't say? Half the town, hmm? And why's that?"

"Aphrodisiacs, of course."

His gaze didn't change.

She shivered, this time letting herself duck under his arm and move away from the ladder. She needed some distance so she could reengage her brain. She made a show of petting Paulie, who was draped over a chair like a black, silky blanket. With a couple of feet between them, she watched Caleb turn, his leather-clad arms crossed over his chest as he leaned casually against the ladder.

"Aphrodisiacs?" he asked, his words as drawn out as his frown. "Like drugs?"

"What?" She yelped so loudly the mellowest cat in the world gave her a kitty frown before leaping in disapproval to the floor. Seriously shocked, Pandora gaped for a second before shaking her head. "No. Of course not. We're holistic here at Moonspun Dreams. The store, and my family, believes in herbal remedies. We even sell charts on acupressure pain relief instead of aspirin."

He kept staring as if he was measuring each word carefully. He didn't look happy, though. Pandora frowned. What? Was he looking for some kind of drug? She took in his long, shaggy hair, the hard look on his face and the black hoop piercing his ear. Her gaze skimmed over his beat-up leather jacket and the faded black T-shirt, down to the frayed hem of his jeans and his scuffed biker boots.

Sexy as hell? Check.

Bad boy personified? Double check.

A drug user?

She'd heard myriad rumors about those bad Black boys. They were wild and untamed, they were trouble through and through. But she'd never heard even a whisper about drugs.

Her eyes skimmed that deliciously broad chest again, his muscles defined beneath the soft-looking fabric of his shirt. She looked into his vivid gold eyes, noting that they were shuttered but clear.

He looked as if he could and would beat anyone up, was hell on wheels and was way out of her league. But he didn't look like a druggie.

Of course, she had lousy man skills and was body-language illiterate, so what did she know? What she couldn't afford, though, was to be mixed up with a guy who played fast and loose with the law. Never again.

Suddenly as irritated with herself for wanting to cry as much as she was with Caleb for putting himself on the off-limits list, she scowled.

"If you're interested in drugs, you need to look some-where else," she said in a chilly tone, wrapping her arms around herself to ward off the disappointment. She wished she hadn't scared away the comfort of the cat.

Caleb didn't say a word. He just arched a brow and con-tinued to study her with those intense eyes of his. After a few seconds, she wanted to scream at him to say some-thing. Anything. Or better yet, to leave. She couldn't pout properly with him there, staring.

"I didn't say I was interested in drugs," he finally said, stepping closer, invading her thinking space yet again.

"You—"

"No," he interrupted. "I said I'd heard you were the lady to talk to about hotting up my sex life."

Pandora bit her lip, mentally replaying their discussion. Had she jumped to conclusions? Was she so awkward at this flirtation thing that she'd misinterpreted a gorgeous man hitting on her?

Caleb reached out, rubbing the pad of his thumb over her bottom lip. Pandora barely held back her whimper as her entire body melted into a puddle of goo.

"I hate to see you damage such a pretty mouth," he murmured.

Nope. No misinterpreting that move. She didn't need a dictionary to define his meaning. Nerves simmered low in her belly. She wanted nothing more than to reciprocate the move. But as she'd told Caleb, and despite her teasing with Kathy, she wasn't in the market for a relationship.

Then again, Caleb Black wasn't a relationship kind of guy.

He was, however, a hot, sexy, have-a-wild-time and give-thanks-afterward kind of guy.

She didn't know if it was the freedom she felt in accepting that her only goal in being with him was to enjoy the ride.

Or maybe it was the sphere of calcite she'd taken to carrying in her pocket, hoping it'd help with her self-esteem.

Whatever it was, it was giving her a sense of purpose, a sense of self-confidence, that she welcomed with open arms.

She was so ready to give herself the best Christmas present ever. A guilt-free pleasurefest that she'd enjoy in decadent delight for as long as it lasted.

As far as gifts went, it beat the hell out of a new pair of slippers.

So when he rubbed her lip a second time, Pandora forced herself to dive out of the safety zone. She took a deep breath, then touched, just barely, the tip of her tongue to his thumb.

His eyes narrowed like golden lasers, then he grinned. A slow, wicked curve of his lips that set off warning bells in Pandora's head.

She was playing with fire.

After one last brush of his thumb across her oversensitized lip, his fingers caressed a gentle trail over her cheek, along her jaw, then down her throat. It was like being touched by a cloud, his fingers were so soft, so barely there.

Pandora stopped herself from whimpering.

"Is that why you came in here?" she asked breathlessly as his fingers worked their magic along her throat. A slide up, then down, sending tingles through her body. "Because you wanted to ask about aphrodisiacs?"

"Yes," he said, stepping closer. So close she could feel the heat of his body wrapping around her like a warm blanket of lust. "And no."

"Which?"

"Both."

His hand curved behind her neck, fingers tangling in her hair as he pulled her closer. Her head rested in his huge palm as she stared up into his eyes. He looked amused, but his dilated pupils and the tension in his jaw told her he was just as turned on as she was.

At least, that's how she was reading him.

Nerves, huge and frantic, scrambled in her stomach. But she had to know. Finding out how he would respond to her was worth the risk of rejection.

Pandora took that last step, closing the distance between them. Pretending her fingers weren't trembling, she pressed her hands against the cool leather covering Caleb's biceps. Even through the thick fabric, she could feel his muscles bunch tight.

"I wish you weren't wearing this jacket," she said, her words so low even she could barely hear them. But he heard. He gave her a long look that made her nipples harden, shrugged off the leather and tossed it on the counter.

Paulie instantly padded over and curled himself into a puddle on the discarded jacket, his black fur blending perfectly with the leather. Caleb grinned before turning his gaze back to Pandora. "Anything else?"

The mouthwatering sight of his arms, the muscles round and hard beneath the long sleeves of his T-shirt, made her want to wish he'd take that off, too.

But it was his amused reaction to her pet that sent her over the edge.

"I want a kiss," she told him. "A real one."

"I only do real," he countered, curving his hands over her hips and pulling her close. Close enough to feel that his arms weren't the only impressive muscles Caleb was sporting.

She wanted him to keep going. To take control, to kiss her crazy. But he didn't. It was as though he'd looked deep into her soul and saw how scared she was of taking center stage and being in charge, and was forcing her to face that fear if she wanted a taste of him.

Her head was spinning so fast, she needed to steady herself, and desperately wanted something to hold on to. Pandora gripped those deliciously hard arms and let her body melt into his.

She stood on tiptoe, her thighs brushing that hard length of his. Her nipples pebbled against his chest as she breathed in his scent. Excitement and anticipation fought for control of her emotions and she sucked in a breath. Then she did it.

She kissed Caleb.

And when her lips pressed against the firm fullness of his, it was suddenly the easiest hard thing she'd ever done in her life.

She wanted to close her eyes and sink into the pleasure. To hide, deep in the intense delight of his mouth on hers. But his gaze held hers captive.

Needing more, she gave in to the desire and slipped her tongue out to trace his lips. As if that's all he'd been waiting for, he suddenly turned voracious. His mouth took control. His tongue swept over hers, dancing at a wild pace that made her whimper and give over fully to the power of his kiss.

His fingers shifted from her hips to press, palms flat, against her butt. She almost purred with pleasure when she felt his rigid length—and holy cow, was he long!—pressing hard against her stomach.

Just as quickly as he'd gone wild, Caleb shifted into low gear. The wild, untamed intensity left his kiss and cool control took its place.

His mouth softened, his lips brushing gently over hers.

His fingers unclenched, smoothing their way up to the small of her back as he pulled away, not completely, but enough that she couldn't revel in the power of his erection anymore.

Then, another brush of his lips, and he stepped away.

Oh, God. He was incredible. Eyes fluttering open, her knees wobbled as she settled her feet flat on the floor again.

Not caring if he saw how overwhelmed she was, Pandora closed her eyes and heaved a deep sigh. Then, meeting his gaze again, she bit her lip before forcing herself to step up to the plate.

All she wanted to do was strip that soft T-shirt off him so she could plaster herself against his hard chest before licking her way down his belly. His taste filled her senses, his scent wrapped around her and her butt still tingled from the pressure of his fingers.

He was like her every sexual fantasy come true.

But she'd been in trouble once already, with a guy who didn't even make the fantasy list. So she'd be an idiot not to make sure Caleb wasn't more trouble than she was willing to answer for.

"Can I ask you something?" she said softly. Needing every intuitive, people-reading skill she'd ever learned, and any that might be floating through her genes, she forced herself to relax and open her third eye. She scrunched her forehead, not feeling anything special there and settled for just relaxing. "And will you promise me you'll be honest?"

Her eyes locked with Caleb's. His gaze was intense, as if he was trying to read her mind before he committed. His shoulders were back, in honesty? Or braced for a hit?

She waited for him to tell her that she didn't have the right to ask for such a promise. She knew she didn't. Just because they were having a mind-blowingly sexual affair in her imagination didn't mean that in reality he owed her a damn thing.

But she couldn't risk her heart, her reputation or her

fragile self-esteem on a man who broke the law. And even though she didn't trust her intuitive skills enough to believe she'd know if he lied, she needed to ask the question anyhow.

Finally, just as she was about to start fidgeting again, he nodded. Then he qualified his nod with, "You can ask whatever you want."

Good enough.

"Do you, um, are you into…" She bit her lip, wishing her cheeks weren't burning, then blurted out, "Do you do drugs?"

CALEB HAD BEEN ASKED that question plenty of times. And he'd always answered yes. More often, he didn't even have to answer, his image spoke for itself.

But this time…? He stared at Pandora, her hazel eyes wide but wary. He could still taste her, sweet and tempting. He was here in Black Oak for a reason. He had a crime to solve. And he'd never, ever, broken cover before. Not for anything, and especially not for a woman.

But with those pretty eyes staring at him, he saw only one option available.

Tell the truth.

"No," he answered. "I'm clean."

He watched her face, waiting to see the doubt. He told himself it didn't matter if she didn't believe him. After all, he'd spent six years crafting his image as a badass with drug connections. An image that had held up to South American drug lords, to the FBI and to L.A. street-gang leaders. An image that was based on the reputation he'd had growing up here in Black Oak.

Her sigh was so deep, the tips of her breasts singed his chest. Talk about a sweet reward for copping to the truth.

A part of him wanted to pull her close, just to wrap his arms around her and revel in the closeness. There was a sense of peace in Pandora, like a calm lake of serenity, that he craved desperately. At the same time, she made him want to strip her naked and lick her body from head to toe, seeing how many times he could make her come before he got to her feet.

Baffled by the conflicting emotions, both in direct opposition to his training and his own reticent nature, Caleb took a step back. He immediately missed the warmth of her body, the heat of her breasts against him. But he needed room to think. And to make sure he didn't screw up. His life might not be on the line this time, but his father's reputation was.

For what that was worth.

Caleb's mind raced, wondering whether he'd just made a major mistake. Time to do damage control.

"Not that I believe in aphrodisiacs, either," he told Pandora, needing to get them back on track.

And he might as well keep up this honest trend and see where it went. It was like following an unfamiliar road. There might be a treasure at the end. A very delicious, very sexy treasure. More likely, though, he'd slide right off some damn cliff.

She just laughed, though.

"Believing in aphrodisiacs is like believing in evolution. Some buy into the idea, some don't."

"Sure, but the theory of evolution has been around for, well, ever. Sex food, though? Isn't that a by-product of the seventies?"

Amusement flared in her eyes as Pandora gave a shake of her head that indicated that he was a sad, misinformed man.

"Their history can be traced back centuries," she pointed out. "My great-great-great-grandmother was a wisewoman who created aphrodisiacs for royalty. Those were the kind of people who beheaded fakers, you know."

Caleb remembered Pandora's mother. Flowing dresses, fuzzy headpieces and huge jewelry glinting through mounds of long red hair. Her granny was a little fuzzier.

He wasn't sure what the woman had looked like. His only impression was granola.

But Pandora looked... Well, normal. Not that that was saying much coming from a guy who spent most of his life around women who thought a G-string was ample coverage. Her hair fell in a smooth curtain, warm and sedate. She wore makeup, but nothing like the showgirl look he remembered her mother sporting. She wore a crystal on a chain around her neck, but her jeans and thick purple sweater seemed ordinary enough.

He looked around the café, noting the display of candles, pretty statues and chunks of rocks on the bistro tables. Circling the perimeter were bookcases, decks of cards and yes, a few crystal orbs and glittering things. He didn't know what most of the stuff was, but it didn't look that weird to him.

It looked pretty. Inviting, interesting and unthreatening. Word on the street, and his own impressions, said that was Pandora's doing. From what he'd heard, the store had been sinking to its death before she'd come along. Which just proved that she was a smart businesswoman. Not that she was weird.

And yet, she believed in aphrodisiacs? Really?

"This is all an act, though, isn't it?" he asked with a tilt of his head to indicate the most obvious New Agey thing he saw, a statue of a half-naked woman riding on the back of a flying dragon. "You're not telling me you really buy into all that..." Crap? "...stuff? Psychics and aphrodisiacs and woo-woo? Isn't it just a part of the show? Something to help sell a few candles and rocks?"

"Woo-woo?" she echoed, sounding as if the magical effects of his kiss had pretty well worn off. "Did you know the art of divination dates back to Greeks and Romans? Tarot cards to the Renaissance? Cleopatra used aphrodisiacs. This isn't a New Agey sales scam to buy into or not.

And while these methodologies might have cultural stig-
mas, it's wrong to dismiss them as being part of a show."

Caleb mentally grimaced. He was usually better at gauging his quarry before he opened his mouth. But Pandora
had a way of short-circuiting his brain.

"I'm not saying it's all bullshit. But you have to admit
there're a lot of scams associated with this type of thing.
And you don't come across as naive," he prevaricated. "I
mean, your granny danced naked around the old oak at the
base of the mountain, and your mom… Didn't your mom
tell the future for dogs and cats?"

Her lips twitched, but she didn't let him off the hook.
"My grandmother only danced naked on the full moon,
and that was for religious reasons. And as for my mom…
What? You don't think cats and dogs have futures?"

"Do you?"

"I do." She nodded, her hazel eyes wide and sincere.
Caleb sighed, disappointment pouring through him as he
revised his seduction plan. Then Pandora grinned. "But
I doubt their thoughts and feelings can be scryed in their
water dishes."

So used to being tense, he barely noticed himself relaxing under her smile. He did pay attention to the stirring interest his body felt, though, when he shifted a little
closer so he could smell her sweet perfume again. It was a
warm scent, making him think of a dark, mystical forest.

"So? What's the real deal? Are you a believer? Or are
you just here to make a living?"

She narrowed her eyes, obviously sorting through his
words. He liked watching her think. He'd just bet she had
mental lists and a brain like one of those supercharged
computers that'd calculate, analyze and summarize in seconds flat.

He gave in to temptation and reached out to rub a lock of
her rich, thick hair between his fingers. It was as silky as it
looked. He'd bet it'd feel even better sliding over his thighs.

"There's bullshit out there, sure," she acknowledged with the tiniest of nods. "There's a group, the Psychic Scenery tour bus, that stops here twice a year. These people travel all over the West Coast, visiting metaphysical stores and psychics, readers and healers. You could say they are the experts on the subject. Believe me, they've seen it all. And they never visit anyone or anywhere more than once if they deem it bullshit."

"How many times have they visited Moonspun Dreams?" he asked, both amused and impressed at how strongly she defended her store and her beliefs.

"Every spring and autumn for the last ten years," she said with just a hint of triumph in her smile. "Our store is one of the highlights of their tour, a selling point they use in their brochure."

"Because of the aphrodisiacs?" Tension he'd thought was gone returned to poke steely fingers in Caleb's back at the idea of hordes of people swarming into town looking for a sex fix. It was the perfect cover for moving drugs, and it pissed him off that Pandora was ruining his comfortable assurance that she was innocent.

"Oh, no," she told him. "I just opened the café two months ago, after the last tour. But I'm sure the regulars at Psychic Scenery are going to be over-the-moon excited when they visit in April."

"Okay, so you're popular with these people and they're going to go crazy over your cookies when they visit. What does that have to do with whether or not you believe in all this?" he prodded.

He had no idea why he cared so much. Maybe it was the result of growing up the son of a clever con man. It'd taught him that people could sell a whole lot of things with a big fat smile on their face, even as they handed over a shopping bag filled with nothing but hot air.

That wasn't criminal. Not like selling drugs. But it'd sure as hell ruin the sweet image he had of Pandora to find out she was happily invested in selling lies.

"What that does is prove that we're time tested and cynic approved," she said. "I think there's a whole lot of stuff out there that we can't explain. I think some people tap into it more easily than others. And I think that believing has a power of its own."

"Isn't that the same thing as gullibility?" Caleb asked.

"Do you think that all this—" she waved her hand to indicate the store filled with the promise of magic "—is based on the power of suggestion?"

Caleb's brow shot up. She didn't sound offended. More like… Satisfied. Wasn't that interesting? Pandora was more intriguing by the second.

"Isn't most everything based on the power of suggestion?" he mused. "For instance, if I suggested that I'd like to kiss you again, you'd think about it, wouldn't you?"

Color washed from her cheeks, pouring down her slender throat and tinting the mouthwateringly showcased curves of her breasts with a pale pink glow. He wanted to touch and see if her skin was as warm as it looked.

"The brain is the most powerful erogenous zone," he told her, his tone low. "Half of seduction takes place in the mind, first. Before I ever touch you, I could have you crazy with wanting me."

She bit her lip, her eyes huge as they darted from him to the store filled with customers just a few beads away.

Caleb gave her a smug wink as he leaned against a table, his feet crossed at the ankles and hands tucked in the front pockets of his jeans.

He was having fun. It'd been so long, he hadn't realized how good it could feel. At least for him. He wasn't so sure Pandora was the teasing type.

"And one meal of my aphrodisiacs could make you so turned on, you'd almost forget your own name," Pandora countered with a wicked smile at odds with the nerves dancing in her eyes. "You'd have the most delicious meal and the most memorable dessert you've ever dreamed of."

Even though his expression was as smooth as glass,

Caleb was mentally reeling. What the hell? He blew out a breath, wanting to tug at the collar of his T-shirt. Yeah, she was pretty damn good at the teasing. Had she just propositioned him?

"What do you say?" Pandora prompted, her smile a soft curve of those luscious lips as she leaned against the counter so her hip bumped against his.

"You realize I'm attracted to you, regardless of what you serve for dinner," he said, trying to figure out what she thought a plate of oysters was going to do when he'd happily take her right then and there on the bistro table, in full view of her cats and anyone who walked by.

"Attraction is a necessary ingredient for an aphrodisiac to work," she explained quietly. "Unlike pharmaceuticals that change a person's will, aphrodisiacs are a natural enhancement. They make so-so sex fabulous. And great sex? Mind-blowing."

This time Caleb did run his finger around the collar of his shirt, needing to release a little of the heat. It was either that or grab her in front of her customers.

As if they knew he was about to pounce, a giggling pair of women walked through the beaded doorway. They both carried overflowing wicker shopping baskets. Looked as if Pandora was about to score.

In more ways than one.

"Fifi asked me to get more cookies," a guy said, sticking his shaggy head through the beaded curtain. "You have a few customers out here asking for them. You know the ones, the sexy cookies."

Pandora's gaze cut from him to Caleb, then back again. She looked torn, and just a little mischievous. He was afraid she'd drag the kid into this discussion to support her point.

"C'mon back, Russ," she said, her smile widening.

Time for him to get the hell out of there. Caleb grabbed his jacket, then leaned in close to whisper in Pandora's ear.

"Prove it to me."

6

THIS WAS THE PROBLEM with wanting something as desperately as she wanted Caleb, Pandora mused. Once you got it, you had to figure out how the hell you were going to handle it.

"So what's the plan?" Kathy asked from her perch in a chair by the glistening lights of the three-foot-high Christmas tree with its shimmering golden balls and little red bows. "Are you ready for tonight?"

Ready? Biting her lip, Pandora scanned the plethora of food spread over the counter of the tiny cottage she was renting. Walking distance from the store, she'd chosen it for its location. Asparagus and oysters, celery and ginseng and chocolate. A roast was marinating in red wine and mushroom caps were waiting to be stuffed. All the fixings for an aphrodisiac-rich dinner for two.

Completing the theme, she'd brought home a dozen red candles for passion and had frankincense incense waiting to light.

"Maybe I shouldn't have him here," she worried. "I mean, it's like saying, 'Hey, eat up fast. I'm horny and wanna do it.'"

"Well, it's not like you could have him to dinner in the café. After all, you have a point to prove. And since it's one of those naked kind of points, it's better done in private, don't you think?"

"Naked…" Pandora pressed her palm against her belly, trying to quiet the butterflies flinging themselves against the walls of her stomach as they attempted to escape. "What the hell was I thinking?"

"That Caleb Black would look mighty fine naked," Kathy said with a wicked grin. Then her smile faded and she gave Pandora a searching look. "Are you sure you want to do this? You don't have to go through with the evening if you don't feel comfortable, you know. You can call it off, or just call it quits after dinner."

A part of Pandora grabbed on to that exit option like a lifeline. It was one thing to challenge Caleb face-to-face, when she was in the throes of sexual overload. But the idea of following through, here and now, once she'd had plenty of time to worry? That was something else entirely.

"I don't want to call the evening off," she decided. "I want this. I really do."

Sorta. She wanted the fantasy of having mind-blowing sex with Caleb. The man was obviously a sexual god. He was gorgeous. He was mouthwateringly sexy. He had that bad-boy, done-it-all and gone-back-for-seconds vibe going on.

And her? The naughtiest thing on her sexual résumé was wearing a see-through Santa nightie with black stiletto do-me boots.

"If you want him, and he wants you, then you'd be crazy to let nerves stop you. I mean, how many chances does a girl have for incredible sex?" Kathy challenged.

"Easy for you to say. You've already done one of the Black brothers," Pandora retorted.

"Yes, I did," Kathy said with a wicked smile, running her hand through the smooth curve of her hair. "Which is why I feel qualified to say do it, do it, do it."

Pandora laughed. Living close to Kathy was her favorite benefit to being back in Black Oak. A girl needed her best friend when she was gathering up the nerve to get naked with a guy.

"Okay, let's just say the night is great," Pandora suggested, pacing over to the tree to rearrange the bows and balls on the crisp evergreen boughs. Can't have the two gold balls next to each other, after all. It might ruin the ambience. "Say the sex is incredible. The best in my life. Maybe even one of his top ten. Multiple-orgasm, headboard-banging, seeing-stars incredible. Say it's all that. What do I do then?"

After a long pause, Kathy got to her feet and headed for the tiny kitchen.

"What are you doing?" Pandora called after her.

"Getting a glass of ice water."

"Seriously!"

"Seriously?" Kathy filled a cup with water from the pitcher in the fridge and gulped it down. "Seriously, then you'll probably collapse in an exhausted, albeit very satisfied, heap."

"But…" Pandora dropped onto the overstuffed chair, picking at the deep blue fabric with her fingernails. "But what if it's so great I want more? How did you have the greatest sex of your life, then walk away?"

"It's all about expectations," Kathy said, setting her water aside and coming over to sit across from Pandora. She leaned forward, her pretty face serious. "You know going in that it's special, that it's just that once, and you ring every drop of pleasure from it possible. Like seeing Baryshnikov dance, or visiting Stonehenge or meeting Johnny Depp at Comic-Con last year. They were all amazing experiences, but you don't expect to do them repeatedly, right?"

"What are the chances that sex with Caleb Black will be as good as Baryshnikov, Stonehenge and the amazing Johnny Depp all rolled into one experience?"

"I think the chances are pretty damn good."

Pandora sank her head into the chair's pillowed back and sighed. She thought so, too.

"Look, you deserve this. Every woman deserves this. One night of absolute pleasure, with no strings or worries or stress. Just wild and mindless sex, with no rules or expectations."

"You think?"

"Don't you?"

Pandora looked at the array of food covering the two short countertops. Her grandmother's recipe book was there, too. Filled with recipes that had, so far, increased Moonspun Dreams' coffers beyond her wildest dreams.

Despite her run-don't-walk departure from all things associated with Black Oak and her mother, Pandora had been raised to believe certain things. And many of those tenets she still subscribed to wholeheartedly. Karma and the golden rule. Respecting nature and conserving resources. Prayer and faith. And as she'd told Caleb, she believed in what she did. In what the store offered.

Sure, she'd launched this aphrodisiac sideline as a desperate attempt to dig the store out of a financial pit. But obviously the aphrodisiacs worked. She saw proof five days a week between the hours of eleven and two, after all. All they required was a spark.

And even she had to admit, she'd definitely inspired a few sparks in Caleb.

"The bottom line is, do you want to do this?" Kathy prodded. "Or don't you?"

A thousand arguments still running through her head, Pandora sighed. Yes, she wanted it. It being this night with Caleb. And more important, a chance to step out of the shadows and have a little excitement in her life. The kind she'd enjoy, not the kind that made her cringe.

Pandora bit her lip again, then squared her shoulders and headed for the kitchen to wash her hands.

"What are you doing?" Kathy asked.

"Getting dinner started." She shot her friend a look of combined terror and excitement. "Who am I to deny myself the absolute pleasure I deserve?"

THREE HOURS LATER and that statement had become Pandora's mantra.

"I deserve absolute pleasure," she muttered to herself as she pulled a floaty black dress knitted of the softest cashmere over her shoulders and slipped the tiny mother-of-pearl buttons closed from cleavage to knee. The fabric molded gently over her breasts, showing just a hint of her red lace bra, and ended a few inches shy of her ankles, where she'd chosen to go barefoot except for a glistening ruby toe ring and gold anklet.

Not quite a see-through Santa nightie, she mused as she stared at her reflection, but it'd do. She fluffed her hair around her shoulders, added a smidge more mascara and took a deep breath.

"I do. I deserve absolute pleasure." The reminder had turned into an affirmation about an hour ago, but like most law-of-attraction-type things, she knew it was basically useless without real belief behind the words.

So she'd fake it. A quick glance at the clock told her that Caleb was due in five minutes. Which meant that as appealing as hiding under the bed was, she'd better get the appetizers ready.

Pandora hurried from the room, checking to see that the fire was burning bright in the fireplace and that all the red candles—for passion—were lit around the room. The cottage smelled delicious. The subtle waft of incense, the appealing scent of smoky apple wood. And the food.

That was the only thing she had complete confidence in tonight. Her food rocked. The roast was done and resting, tender and juicy in a gravy of rosemary, celery seed and just a pinch of ginseng. There wasn't really any aphrodisiac ingredients in the fresh rolls, but Pandora had filled in the menu with things that played to the theory that the way to a man's heart was through his stomach. If the rolls could open that door, she figured the aphrodisiacs should reroute things southward.

"Absolute pleasure," she murmured as she checked the chocolate-espresso mousse with whipped caramel crème in the fridge, then the wine that was breathing on the counter. Figuring it'd make her look less anxious, and might just help her chill out, she poured herself a glass.

"Yep, all ready for that pleasure. Absolutely."

The doorbell rang.

Pandora started, slopping wine all over her hand.

Right that second, if the cottage had a back door, she would have taken absolute pleasure in sneaking out through it.

Deep breath and a quick rinse of her fingers under the tap, she then wiped nervously down her dress before almost tripping over her own bare feet on the way to the door.

Another deep breath and she pulled it open.

"Hi," Caleb said.

Hubba da hubbada, her brain stuttered. Holy hunks, the man was pure eye candy. The moon at his back, his face was thrown into shadows. His black hair slicked down so it flowed like silk over his collar, he wore slacks, boots and a dark dress shirt. He smelled incredible. Male but with a hint of musk.

His smile was just this side of wicked as he gave her an appreciative look, those warm gold eyes tracing her curves, from collar to breast, down her waist and over her hips until he reached her naked toes.

One look from him and she was ready to strip the rest of herself bare and see how many kinds of pleasure they could offer each other. Whether it was because he looked sexy enough to slurp with a spoon, because she was wearing her do-me undies, or if it was the day spent creating a meal meant for seduction, all Pandora could think about was how long she'd have to wait for dessert.

"Pandora?" he prompted, his smile tipping into a grin as he leaned his shoulder against the door frame. "You gonna let me in?"

Doh. They couldn't do dessert until he was inside, could they?

"I'm sorry. It's just... Wow." She stepped aside for him to enter. "You look fabulous."

Realizing how that'd probably sounded, color warmed Pandora's cheeks. "Not that you didn't look great before," she said. She winced, then tried again. "I mean, I wouldn't have thought you'd have dress clothes tucked away in your motorcycle saddlebags."

"Always pays to be prepared," he said as he dried his feet on the mat before entering the cottage. She shut the door behind him, its click echoing the beat of her heart in her chest.

"Do you have to dress up often?" she asked, suddenly realizing that she had no idea what Caleb did for a living. Gossip had run wild since his return to town last week, speculating on everything from career criminal to mechanic to construction. One person had thought he might even be a lawyer.

"It's the holidays," he said absently, looking around. "I figured I'd get roped into some Christmas fluff or other."

He gave her a slow smile, making her tummy slide down to her toes. "But this is a much better option."

Heat poured through Pandora's body like molten lava, hungry and intense.

She had to say something before she wrapped herself around his body and begged him to let her lick him from head to toe.

"So what do you do for a living?" she blurted out.

His smile changed. It was a tiny change, one she doubted

most people would notice. It got a little hard, like his eyes.
"I'm in the middle of changing jobs right now," he said.

Trying to study his body language without being obvious, Pandora bit her lip. Other than the slightly scary look in his eyes, he seemed totally relaxed. Did that mean he was out of a job, or just looking for something else before he left? And did it matter? It wasn't as if she needed to see his résumé. This was a one-night, prove-the-aphrodisiacs-work and have-great-sex fling.

So change the subject.

"Are you going to the big party tomorrow night at your father's motorcycle shop?" she asked.

His smile fell away, his shoulders tensed up. His body language had gone from friendly to unfathomable in less than a heartbeat. Her fault. She knew there were issues with him and his father. So she should have known that bringing him up wouldn't be a great conversation starter.

Wasn't she the hostess with the mostest.

"No."

Awkward.

Crazy with curiosity but not wanting to ruin the evening by asking more uncomfortable questions, Pandora was grateful when the oven timer went off.

"Please, make yourself comfortable," she invited as she hurried toward the safety of the food.

"I thought you'd be staying at Cassiopeia's place," Caleb said as he followed her into the kitchen.

Payback? She gave him an arch look over her shoulder, trying not to grin. Gotta love a guy who knew how to get revenge without drawing blood.

"Oh, no," she said, laughing a little at the idea of staying in her mother's. It would be like staying on a movie set. Nobody who knew Cassiopeia ever had to ask if she believed in the woo-woo. She lived it, right down to the celestial designs on her carpet.

Pandora pulled the roasted asparagus from the oven and set it on the stove top, then turned back to Caleb.

"No. My mother's house is too crowded for me. She collects as much stuff there as she does in the store, plus there are always people in and out when she's home. Even now, with me just stopping by to collect her mail and water the plants, they pop in hoping for a reading or chat. I think it drives her nearest neighbor, the mayor, a little crazy."

Caleb flashed a quick grin as he handed her a bottle of wine. She glanced at the label and raised her brows. Pricey.

"I forgot my aunt had moved."

"Haven't you been to see her yet? I hear she throws a huge holiday open house. Is that next weekend? Someone was saying that your dad never goes, but you probably will, right?" Busy setting the mushroom caps and oysters Rockefeller on a serving plate, it took her a few seconds to pick up on the sudden tension in Caleb.

She'd done it again.

"I'm sorry. I don't mean to make you uncomfortable by bringing up your father." She met his eyes. He didn't look uncomfortable anymore, though. More like…intrigued.

"Don't worry about it. If I had a problem talking about Tobias, I'd say so."

"Okay," she said slowly. Except that he didn't talk about his father. Or his family at all. Despite the tension and hurt she saw in his face, she had to know more. Was desperate to understand more about Caleb Black. So she quirked a brow and continued, "Although I haven't seen her since I moved back, or since she became mayor for that matter, I do remember your aunt. I'm not sure she's a fan of my mother's, though. Mom said the week after she moved in, Her Honor raised the fence height in her backyard and instructed the gardener to plant a hedge between the houses."

Caleb snickered.

"Aunt Cynthia is a hard-ass all right," he agreed. "It must drive her insane having a free spirit like your mom next door. Probably afraid people will think she and Cassiopeia are having wild parties in the hot tub after dark."

Pandora laughed, her nerves over the evening starting to fade as he pulled out a chair and got comfortable. She held up the bottle of wine in question, and when he nodded, got him a glass from the counter.

"I guess you've worked really hard to distance yourself from your dad," she said as she poured.

"It wasn't hard. I just had to move out of Black Oak and his sphere of influence."

"Smart," she complimented. Then, honesty forced her to admit, "Tobias comes into the store and the café pretty regularly. Having a parent with an, um, forceful personality myself, I can understand how it'd be challenging to live with such a strong person. But I have to admit, I do like him."

She didn't add the bit of gossip she'd heard earlier that day, that Tobias had hooked up with that nasty piece of work, Lilah Gomez. Telling a man his dad was dating someone younger than him was hardly dinnertime conversation.

"Most people like Tobias," Caleb said with a shrug. "He's got a way with the charm."

"Like father like son?" She smiled, handing him the glass of wine.

"You're kidding, right?" Caleb shook his head, obviously not seeing himself as a charmer. "I was a disappointment on that score. Maya's got a way about her, that's for sure. But Gabriel got the bulk of the charm. Me, I got the short end of that particular stick."

Pandora wanted to tell him just how appealing rough edges could be, but took a sip of her wine instead. Then she gathered her nerve and lifted the platter filled with the promise of sexual nirvana.

"Speaking of sticks and their length," she said with her naughtiest smile, "I have your proof here. If you'd care to give it a try?"

Caleb swore he felt the energy in the room shift. Friendly good humor changed to a sexual thrum in the blink of Pandora's hazel eyes.

Not that he minded, but there had been something nice in that friendliness. He didn't think he'd ever been friends with a woman. Coworker, acquaintance, lover. That was about it.

But, hey. He'd be an idiot to complain about stepping over to the sexy side. And a bigger idiot to regret having her take away something he hadn't even realized he might want to enjoy a little longer.

"Proof, huh?" he challenged as he took an appetizer from the tray and inspected it. "Looks like any other stuffed mushroom. How's this proof?"

"Mushrooms and sausage together are a strong aphrodisiac," she assured him before she bit into one herself.

Caleb had his doubts, but he had just enough of his father's fabled charm to know better than to call his hostess a liar. Especially when she looked so sexy sitting across from him.

So he took a mushroom.

By the end of the meal, Caleb realized two things.

One, he'd never spent this long with a hard-on, and not done anything about it, in his life.

And two, he'd never talked—just talked—to a woman before like this. By unspoken agreement, they'd avoided the biggies like family and career. Instead, they'd shared their favorite Christmas memories, discovered they had the same taste in music and movies, and debated the merits of paperbacks versus ebooks.

It was like an actual date. Caleb had always wondered if that getting-to-know-a-person-on-a-date thing was real or just a myth. But this was, other than the painful pressure against the zipper of his slacks, totally awesome.

"Dessert?" she offered, noting he'd cleaned his plate for

the third time. She'd been a little more delicate in her eating, only having one helping.

Despite his gluttony, Caleb glanced at the rich, chocolaty mounds of fluff with the caramel topping and sprinkling of nuts and his mouth watered.

"Sure," he agreed. Then he realized he'd better clear some stuff up before they got into anything else that made his mouth water.

"But here's the thing," he said once she'd served them both and sat back down at the table. Then she started fiddling with the button, just there at the very center of her cleavage, and he forgot what he'd wanted to say.

Instead, he focused on the silky smoothness of her pale skin. Unlike most redheads, she was freckle free. At least, she was as far as he could see. Instead, her skin was almost translucent. Delicate.

"Caleb?" she said.

He dragged his eyes away from the contrast of the rich black fabric against the tempting swell of her breasts.

"Huh?" he asked, meeting her amused gaze. His lips quirked, knowing he deserved that look.

"The thing?" she prompted.

"The thing…" He frowned, thinking back. "Yeah, here's the thing. This meal was delicious."

Her smile was slow and sweet, those full lips curving in delight as she reached across the tiny table and rubbed her hand over his. Caleb's dick reacted as if she'd licked it.

"Thanks," she said softly. "I'm so glad you enjoyed it."

"I did. And I'm sure I'm going to enjoy this dessert just as much," he assured her, gesturing with the spoon he'd picked up. "But as great as it all was, I'm not getting how you think this proves that aphrodisiacs work."

Pandora gave a slow nod, as if she was agreeing, or at least considering his words. Then instead of picking up her spoon, she swiped her finger through the caramel-drizzled whipped cream.

Caleb tensed.

She lifted her cream-covered finger to her mouth, then rubbed it over her lip, licking the sweet confection away with a slow swipe of her tongue.

Caleb's eyes narrowed. He tried to swallow, but his throat wasn't working right.

Some cream still on her finger, Pandora sucked it into her mouth, her lips closing around the tip just enough so he could still see the pink swirl of her tongue as she licked it away.

Son of a bitch.

He swore he could smell the smoke as his brain short-circuited.

When she reached back into that crystal bowl and scooped up more dessert, this time cream and chocolate both, Caleb held his breath.

But instead of repeating the tasting show, she leaned forward to reach across the table. The move made her dress, unbuttoned so temptingly, shift to show more of the red lacy fabric of her bra. Before he could groan at the sight, though, she offered that fingerful of temptation to him.

"Taste?" she said, her words low and husky.

As hard as it was not to stare at the bounty bound in red lace, his gaze locked on hers. Her eyes were slumberous. Still sweet, he didn't think anything could change that. But sexier. There was a knowledge in them that said she knew exactly what she was doing to him. And that she planned to do a hell of a lot more.

Holding her gaze, he wrapped his fingers around her wrist, bringing her hand to his mouth. The chocolate was rich, with a hint of coffee. Her finger tasted even better. He sucked the sweet confection off her flesh, then ran his tongue along the length of her palm, scraping his teeth against the mound at the base of her thumb.

Pandora gave a little mewl of pleasure.

Caleb grinned.

"So…" she said after clearing her throat.

"So?"

"So that's the thing."

Caleb frowned.

"You said you wanted me. And I obviously am attracted to you," she told him, gently extricating her fingers from his hand.

"Yeah?"

"But let's face it. I'm not your type. I'm what's usually termed a good girl."

"How good are you?"

"Really, *really* good," she promised. "But you don't do good girls. You're a quick and painless, love 'em and leave 'em kind of guy. You keep life, and sex, commitment-free and just a little distant."

Caleb frowned, not sure he liked how well she read him.

"So?"

"So that's my proof," she said.

Before he could point out that it really wasn't proof, she held out her hand. He took it, getting to his feet. She didn't move back, though. So his body brushed against her smaller, more delicate figure.

"Your proof is that we're not each other's type?"

"That," she agreed, turning to lead the way out of the kitchen. Then she looked over her shoulder and said, "And the fact that you're not the kind of guy to sleep with a good girl."

He couldn't deny that truth. In the two days since she'd challenged him and tonight, he'd made some inroads, buddying up with one of the drug dealers unhappy with his slow move up the food chain. He'd come to dinner with the idea of finding out more about her little aphrodisiac sideline. He'd planned to subtly grill her about what she might have seen in the alley between her building and Tobias's.

Despite the excuse for their date, he'd had no intention, none at all, of getting naked with her. But he still wasn't giving credence to some crazy food combination. Nope, the credit for that was all Pandora's.

Before he could tell her that, she stopped in the middle of the living room and turned to face him. She was so close, he could see the beat of her heart against her throat.

He could see the nerves in her eyes, there just beneath the desire. The nerves didn't bother him, though. They were a lot more exciting than acceptance or complacency.

"We spent the last hour and a half talking," she told him. "There was no flirting. No innuendo or teasing or sexual promises, right?"

Caleb frowned as the truth of her words hit him. He'd spent the entire meal horny as hell. Hornier than he'd been with any other woman in his life.

But again, that was due to Pandora. Not the food.

"What's your point?"

And then those delicate fingers skipped down the row of pearly buttons, unfastening her dress as they went. Caleb had faced strung-out drug dealers shoving guns in his gut and kept his cool. But the minute that dress cleared her belly button, he swore the room did a slow spin.

Damn, she was incredible.

She walked toward him, the black dress hanging loose from her shoulders to her belly.

When she reached him, Caleb's hand automatically gripped her hips. She smiled, then leaned even closer so her body pressed tight against his. She reached between them and slid her palm over the hard length of his erection, making his dick jump desperately against the constraining fabric of his slacks.

He groaned in delight.

"And that's the proof that the aphrodisiacs work," Pandora told him just before she pressed her mouth to his.

7

WHEN NERVES MADE HER WANT to turn around and run, Pandora reminded herself that the best things in life were worth fighting for. Even if that meant fighting her own fears.

When her fingers trembled, she just dug them tighter into the deliciously muscled expanse of Caleb's shoulders. He felt so good. Strong and solid and real.

She wasn't going to chicken out, dammit. This was her one and only opportunity for awesome, aphrodisiac-inspired sexual bliss. The experience of a lifetime with a man reputed to be incredible.

So when her knees wobbled, she leaned forward, resting her hips against his for support.

Yeah, baby. There it was.

A whole lot of long, hard, throbbing nirvana.

He wanted her, just as much as she wanted him. Proof was right there, pressing insistently against her belly.

Hello, baby, her body sighed.

"More," she demanded against Caleb's lips.

He gave her the more she asked for, then even more than she'd dreamed. He made her feel like the only woman in his world.

Caleb's mouth slid over hers, taking the kiss from soft, wet heat to intense, raging passion with a slip of his tongue. His hands settled on the curve of her waist, pulling her tighter against that promising ridge pressing against his zipper.

Pandora melted.

She twined her arms around the back of his neck, holding tight as their tongues danced a wild tango. Anticipation coiled tighter in her belly when his fingers slipped up her side, from her waist to the curve of her breast. Her nipples ached with the need to feel his fingers, to know how he'd touch her.

Would he be gentle and sweet? Or wild and demanding?

Wanting desperately to know, she eased back. Not her mouth. Oh, no, she wasn't giving up one second of this delicious kiss. And her hips were fused, as if of their own volition, to his. Although she was pretty sure she could ease back a few inches and still feel the thick heat of his erection pressing in temptation against her stomach.

Instead, she eased her shoulders back. Just a little.

And purred in delight when he proved to be as clever as he was gorgeous, taking the invitation and curving his fingers over the heavy, aching weight of her breast. Her nipple beaded tighter against the erotically scratchy lace of her bra as he circled his hand in a slow, tempting spiral.

Had she ever been this turned on? Heat swirled through her body like a whirlwind. Building, twisting, teasing. Higher and higher, tighter and tighter.

He squeezed. She gasped, moaning and leaning into his hand.

"More," she demanded again.

His hand didn't leave her breast, but the other moved higher up her back. She felt a tiny snap as the hooks gave way. The straps of her bra sagged, slipping down her shoulders.

Before she could decide if this was good or bad, his fingers skimmed under the fabric and flicked her nipple. Like an electric shock, the sensation shot through her body with a zinging awareness. Pandora whimpered, shifting left, then right, as her favorite sexy panties dampened with evidence of her need.

"I like how you follow directions," she said against his lips, her laugh only a little bit nervous.

"Let's see how you do," he returned, leaning back so he could see the bounty he'd released. "Take it off."

"I beg your—"

"Off," he demanded. To emphasize his command, he took those amazing hands off her and stepped backward. Pandora wanted to whimper. She wasn't sure if it was over the loss of his magic fingers, the denial of his body. Or if it was pure embarrassment of having him this focused on her body. It wasn't bad, but it wasn't centerfold quality, either.

Blushing, Pandora twitched the sides of her dress inward. She didn't pull it closed. She didn't want to send a message that playtime was over. But, still, she wasn't sure she wanted to play peekaboo like this.

"C'mon, Pandora. I want to see." His words were husky. His vivid gold eyes were intense and just a little needy.

"Wouldn't you rather taste?" she asked with her most wicked sexy look.

"I'm the kind of guy who likes to cover all the bases," he said with a grin. He sounded relaxed, but she could see the heat in his eyes, the tightness of his body. The oh-my-God huge ridge pressing against his zipper. "So let's start with the visual, then we'll move on to the other senses."

She wanted this, she reminded herself. Wanted to be front and center of attention. And even more, she wanted Caleb. Wanted a night of mindless, wild sexual exploration.

Which meant she had to step up to the plate and play the game. With that reminder ricocheting around her head, Pandora lifted her chin, then took a step backward.

She released the edges of her dress, rounding her shoulders for just a second so her bra straps slipped down under the sleeves, catching on her upper arms. Caleb's eyes were like lasers, sharp and intense as he stared.

She skimmed her fingers up her bare abdomen and cupped her lace-covered breasts. His stare intensified. Pandora's fingers folded over the top of the cups of her bra in preparation for tugging it down. But she couldn't do it.

It was as if her shyness was in battle with the power of Caleb's sexual magnetism, amplified by the aphrodisiacs. She wanted this, like crazy. But it scared her.

Slowly, her eyes still locked on his, she turned. Back to him, her head angled so she could still see him, she pulled the bra straps off her arms, under the fabric of her dress, then let the bra dangle at her side.

"Toss it aside," he ordered.

She tossed it toward the couch, the red lace catching the edge of one magenta pillow and hanging there like a flag of surrender.

"Turn around," he commanded. His voice was husky, his body tense. He looked like the bad boy that rumor claimed him to be. He didn't scare her, though. Instead, his demeanor made her feel…amazing. Sexy and strong.

All because he looked at her as if she was the hottest thing he'd ever seen. The answer to all his sexual fantasies, even.

Holding on to that thought, Pandora turned.

As she faced him again, Caleb kept his eyes on hers for three beats, then dropped his gaze. He arched a brow at her hands clutching the filmy fabric of her dress closed, so she let it go and dropped her arms to her sides. As her breath shuddered in and out, the fabric shifted, sliding over her rigid nipples, adding a whole new layer to the torturous delight going through her body.

He stepped closer. He reached up, his fingers tracing her areola, visible through the veil of black fabric. Her nipples beaded tighter. Heat circled low in her belly, making Pandora press her thighs together to intensify the wet delight.

His gaze shifted, meeting hers.

His eyes were molten gold. Slumberous and sexy.

"Nice," was all he said, though.

Before she could ask him what that was supposed to mean, he leaned forward and took the opposite nipple into his mouth, sucking on it through the fabric. The wet heat of his lips, combined with the subtle abrasion of the material, made her gasp in delight.

Desire melted her body. Her knees felt soggy, so she grabbed on to him to keep her balance.

"You like?" he asked, his teeth scraping over the aching tip before he sucked again.

"I really, really like," she hoarsely agreed.

Her fingers scraped a gentle trail over the wide breadth of his shoulders, then down until she reached those freaking rock-hard biceps. She gave a low growl deep in her throat as she tried to wrap her hands around his arms. Too big, too large, too wide. She hoped that meant other things were big and wide, too.

He swept his hand up the opening of the fabric, his palm hard and warm as it skimmed her body, leaving a trail of tingling awareness behind. He cupped her breast, his long fingers squeezing in rhythm as he sucked.

Her body went into heavenly spasms. Wet heat pooled between her legs, emphasizing the aching pressure building there. So needy she wanted to beg, Pandora wrapped one calf around his leg, pressing tight to try to relieve the ache.

He growled his approval. Then he grabbed her butt with both hands and lifted, making Pandora squeak in shock. Not lifting his mouth from her breast, he swung her around so her back was against the wall, anchored between it and the hardness of his body.

"Oh, yeah," she murmured, letting her head fall back with a thud. It was definitely easier to focus on the pleasure if she didn't have to worry about not falling on her ass.

Finished playing through the fabric, Caleb pushed open her dress and gave a low, husky growl at the sight of her bare breasts. Pandora knew her chest was flushed almost as pink as her nipples, but she didn't care. She loved his reaction. Loved the appreciative heat in his eyes and the way his fingers tightened on her waist as he stared.

"Kiss me," she whispered.

Caleb's eyes met hers and she swallowed the sudden lump in her throat. His gaze was hungry, but there was an appreciation, a sort of soft wonder, in his eyes that made her feel as if she was the most incredible woman in the world.

Then his mouth met hers and she forgot to think at all. His tongue caressed, then slipped gently between her lips. He tasted delicious. Hot and mysterious, with just a hint of chocolate. As he kissed her, his hands slid up to gently cup her cheeks, tilting her head to the side just a little so his mouth could better access hers.

Pandora swore she was melting. Not just sexually, although one more rub of his thigh against hers and she'd explode. But emotionally. The kiss was pure romance. Sweetly sensual, sexually charged and oh, so perfect.

Then he changed the angle. His mouth devoured. His hands skimmed over her shoulders, taking her dress down her arms. He gripped her hips for just a second, pulling her body away from the wall so the fabric could fall free to the floor.

Leaving her naked, except for her tiny little black panties.

She shivered as his fingers, just the tips, trailed a path along her spine. Up to her shoulder blades, where with the gentlest of pressure, he pressed her bare breasts tighter against his chest. Down to the small of her back, right above her butt, where his fingers curved down beneath the strip of elastic and gripped her buns. His fingers grazed her thigh, leaving heated trails of pleasure.

The move brought Pandora closer, so she locked her calf around the back of his knee and hugged tight, trying to relieve some of the pressure building between her thighs, swirling and tightening. Her breath came in gasps now as his fingers slipped around her hip, tracing the elastic of her panties. First at her belly, then around her thigh.

She shifted her knee, pulling back just a little. Inviting his fingers. Hoping he'd take the hint and touch her. She needed him to touch her, to drive her those last crazy steps over the edge.

But he just kept tracing the elastic. Caressing in soft, teasing moves.

He wasn't trying to drive her to passion, he was just driving her insane.

"More, dammit," she said against his mouth.

Then she felt his kiss shift as he grinned. Before she could decide if she was amused or irritated that he'd made her beg, his fingers slipped beneath the silk of her panties and found her.

They traced her swollen folds, teasing, stroking, enticing. Pandora swirled her hips, matching her rhythm to the dance of his fingers.

His mouth left hers to trail kisses, tiny sweet kisses, over her jaw and down the smooth flesh of her throat, laid bare as she tilted her head back against the wall.

His head dipped lower.

Her heart pounded harder.

His fingers slipped, first one, then two, then three, into the hot slick heat of her welcoming flesh.

Her breath came in pants.

His fingers thrust. In, then out. In, then out.

His lips closed over the rigid, pouting tip of her breast, sipping and laving the aching bud in time with his dancing fingers.

Pandora's head spun. Heat coiled, tight and low. Her hips twisted, shifted, undulating in time with the thrust of his fingers. Need screamed through her, demanding release.

Then he flicked his thumb over her slick folds.

And she exploded.

She cried out in delight as the climax pounded through

her, taking her over once, then twice. Her body rang with pleasure. The lights of the Christmas tree flashed before her eyes, echoing the fireworks exploding in her mind.

It wasn't until she floated back to earth a couple of minutes—or years—later, that she realized he'd wrapped his arms around her in a soothing, rocking sort of hug.

Pandora's heart dissolved into a gooey mess.

"See," she murmured against the hard comfort of his shoulder, curving in tighter as he hugged her close. "Told you it'd be great."

"Great?"

"Incredible? Amazing? Mind-blowingly awesome?" she returned, leaning back to smile up at him.

He returned her smile, brushing a damp tendril of hair off her face with gentle fingers.

"Sweetheart, don't get me wrong. This was, and will continue to be, incredible. But in the spirit of honesty, I need to tell you something."

Oh, God. Tell her what? Was she doing it wrong? Passion fleeing Pandora's head like fog in the morning sun, she pulled back to stare in horror. "What?"

Other than his arched brow, his gorgeous face was unreadable.

"You're hot," he assured her. "And this intensity, the chemistry between us, is amazing."

Horror was replaced by confusion. "So…what's wrong?"

"Wrong? Babe, this is way too good to be wrong. No, nothing's wrong. I'm just saying that you had a point here and I don't think you're going to prove it."

"A point?" She'd had a point? Something beyond an orgasm or three?

"You said you were gonna prove that your aphrodisiacs work, remember?" he said with a grin. "I'm still wondering what you're gonna offer up as proof."

Oh. That.

Relief washed over her in a wave, making her want to drop to the couch and sigh in thanks.

"Proof?" she said, her words husky against the soft dusting of hair on his chest. "The proof will be you panting, exploding with an orgasm."

He groaned, his fingers combing through her hair. She could feel his laughter, though, as his chest vibrated against her mouth.

Her lips still exploring his chest, Pandora forced her eyes open to give him an arch look of inquiry.

"Sweetheart, you're hot. I'm wild for you. So the orgasm, that's a given."

She liked that. Wild for her. Pandora shivered in delight, thrilled beyond delight that a guy like Caleb wanted her this much.

"It *is* a given," she agreed. "It definitely is. But you'll be coming before you get your boots off."

His laughter wasn't so silent now.

"That hasn't happened since I was fifteen."

"Kiss that memory goodbye, then," she instructed. "Because thanks to me, and my aphrodisiacs, you'll never be able to say that again."

She didn't know where the words came from. But once they were out, she wasn't scared. Instead, she was empowered. Inspired. Excited.

It was like someone had just broken her from a prison she hadn't realized she'd spent her life in.

And now she was free. Free to enjoy, free to explore. And most of all, free to use Caleb's body for every single kinky sexual fantasy she'd ever had.

CALEB LAUGHED AS PANDORA twirled one finger in the air to indicate they should switch places. She thought she was going to take control of the fun. Not likely. He never, ever gave up control.

But neither did he deny a lady her pleasure.

So in the name of humoring her, he released her leg to let the silky-smooth length of it slide down his thigh. Then, his hands wrapped around her waist, he lifted her and twirled, so they'd changed positions.

"Now what?" he challenged, grinning.

She looked so earnest.

Her hair was a silky cloud around her face, rumpled and glowing in the light of the fire. Hazel eyes, still hazy with pleasure, studied him as though she was figuring out a puzzle. Good luck with that, he thought.

"It's time," she intoned with a smile.

"Go for it," he invited, trying not to laugh.

It wasn't that he didn't think she was gorgeous. Sweet and pretty and so damn sexy. She was all that. But she was hardly a practiced seductress. So he figured this was going to be a hot and sexy time, but he wasn't too worried about control.

Or the state of his boots.

"See, here's the thing, though," she said slowly, her words as soft as the fingers she was tracing down his chest.

"Which thing is that?"

She gave him a chiding look, then shrugged a little, making her breasts bounce and his mouth water.

"The thing is, I'm new to seduction."

Caleb laughed, then grabbed her hands and lifted them to his lips, pressing kisses on her knuckles. "Sweetie, you don't have to do anything you don't want to."

"Oh, but there is so much I do want to do. I'm just letting you know, ahead of time, in case I drive you too crazy, too fast," she said, her smile turning wicked.

His laughter turned a little hoarse as she pulled her hands away and planted them directly on his belt buckle. Talk about getting right to business. Not that he objected, but he'd been kinda looking forward to a little bit of what he'd imagined would be shyly sweet exploration.

She didn't tug his buckle open, though. Instead, she

slipped her fingers inside his jeans and caught hold of his shirt, pulling it free. Her palms flat against his belly, she slid them upward, taking his shirt with them. Following her cue, he lifted his arms, then finished it off himself, tossing it toward the same couch currently holding her bra.

One for one, they were on a roll.

"Mmm," she hummed, staring at his chest as if she was mesmerized. Caleb was already sporting a pretty nice erection, but that look on her face, pure appreciative awareness, made his dick throb.

Her palms still flat, she smoothed them over his shoulders, her fingers warm and teasing as they skimmed his skin. Her nails scraped a hot trail of fire down his arms, pausing to curve over biceps that, yes, he knew it was stupid, but he flexed a little. Her soft sigh of appreciation didn't make him feel stupid, though. It made him feel like a freaking superhero.

Her eyes flicked to his, then back to his chest. But he saw a wicked light in their depths. Like she was up to something. Not wanting to ruin her fun and tell her there wasn't anything he hadn't seen or done, he relaxed and waited.

Then she pressed her mouth, hot and wet, against his nipple. And he damn near exploded.

What the hell? Her hands were skimming, caressing their way over his chest, but it was her mouth that was driving him crazy. Her tongue slipped out, tasting, testing. Tempting. Since she hadn't made a rule against it, Caleb grabbed on to the silky warmth of her waist before sliding one hand up to cup the weight of her breast. Fair was fair, after all.

Apparently she wasn't interested in fair, though.

Pandora shifted, trailing those hot, openmouthed kisses down his chest.

Caleb was going insane. That was the only justification he could find for his inability to hold on to any semblance of control.

For a man who prided himself in his skill, both with women, and over his body, he didn't know what to do here. How to react. It was as if Pandora had woven a magical spell over him. Like she was an addiction, one he couldn't resist.

Her lips, wet and silky, trailed lower down his belly, the rasp of his zipper filling the room as her teeth tugged it down.

Caleb groaned, his fingers clenched in her soft hair. He realized he didn't give a damn.

She could keep the power.

Just as long as she continued driving him crazy.

Then her lips pressed against the tip of his dick.

Caleb growled a combination of shock and pleasure. Taking that as a go-ahead, she tugged his shorts and pants down below his knees, then her fingers trailed a teasing path back up his thighs.

She pulled back, just a little, and looked up at him. With those deceptively innocent hazel eyes locked on his, she leaned forward and wrapped her lips around the throbbing head.

He almost yelped in surprise. Then he closed his eyes, enjoying the delight of her mouth.

She was so good at this. She licked and nibbled him like a freaking lollipop.

Intense pleasure pounded through him, demanding release. Her mouth felt like heaven, the kind that only bad boys got into. Her tongue swirled, then she sucked. Hard.

He damn near exploded.

"No," he shouted instead.

"No," he repeated, gentling it this time and soothing his hands over the tangle his fingers had made in her hair. "Not like this. The first time I come, I want it to be inside you."

Her brow arched and she leaned forward again, but he gripped her hair. "Not inside your mouth, either."

Her smile was a work of art. And not just because she

offered it up from her knees in front of his bare, throbbing erection. He reached out and pulled her to her feet, needing to kiss her almost as much as he needed to come.

"More," he said, borrowing her earlier demand.

"Definitely more," she gasped, wrapping her arms around his neck and kissing him back. Before he could get too serious about it, though, she pulled away.

"Hey!"

"I don't think we want these in the way," she teased, shimmying out of her panties. She hurried over to her purse and grabbed something, showing off the condom with a grin before sauntering back.

Not trusting his body to behave if she touched him again, he held up one hand to indicate she stay where she was. Then he took the condom and slipped it on, reveling in the view as he protected them.

"You're beautiful," he told her, pulling her toward him. "I want you so much."

"How much, exactly?" she teased.

"This much."

Done talking, he grabbed her tight and took her mouth in a deep, devouring kiss. Her moan of delight was all he needed to know she was ready. He grasped her hips, his hands curving into her butt and lifting. Her arms tight around his shoulders, she wrapped her legs around his hips.

In one quick, delightful thrust, Caleb was inside her. She was tight, hot and wet. Delicious. His hands gripping her hips, he thrust, his hips setting a fast rhythm.

"More," she breathed against his throat as she undulated in a tempting dance, pulling him in deeper.

Deeper and deeper. Harder and faster.

Her moans became whimpers. Her breath heated his neck as she dug her fingernails into his shoulders, gripping him so tight her heels dug into the small of his back.

He couldn't think.

All he could do was feel the incredible sensations building. Tightening. Need pounded at him. Her mewling pants were driving him higher.

Then she came. Her gasp was followed by the soft chanting of his name. Over and over and over, she called out to him.

He couldn't restrain himself any longer. As her body spasmed and contracted around him, he exploded in delight.

His mind spinning, aftershocks of the sexual blast still zinging through his body, Caleb let his head fall back against the wall. He unclenched his fingers from the soft cushion of Pandora's butt to let her slide her legs back to the floor. She puddled against him like a purring kitten, nuzzling her head under his chin and giving a moaning sort of sigh that made him feel like king of the sex gods.

"Bed?" he groaned against the warm, smoothness of her throat.

"That door over there," she murmured, her words more a husky purr than anything. Caleb forced his eyes open, looking around for *over there*. There were two doors, one cracked open enough that he could see was a bathroom. Handy. The other was closed. There was a bed waiting on the other side of that door.

The trick was to get to it.

He had a whole lot of warm, wonderful woman wrapped in his arms.

His slacks were around his ankles. Pure class, he thought as he rolled his eyes. His boots were still laced tight, so he couldn't kick his pants off and romantically sweep Pandora into his arms.

Romantically. Holy crap. A hard-core realist, Caleb knew the effects drugs could have on the body. But asparagus and oysters? That all-natural aphrodisiac thing was pure bullshit.

At least, he'd thought it was until now, as he stood with his head still reeling, his jeans jammed down around his socks like a pimply faced adolescent getting it for the first time behind the school gym.

Now? Now he was thinking up ways to be romantic.

Again…holy crap.

Pandora gave a sighing little wiggle, her curves pressing tighter against him, the deliciously pebbled hardness of her nipples scraping against his chest and her flowery-scented hair rubbing under his chin.

A part of him—he swore it was Hunter's voice—was kicking in to lecture mode. He shouldn't be doing this. The plan was to use her store's proximity to keep an eye on his father. Not to use her, in any way, shape or form.

But was it using? his body argued. He was seriously interested in her. She was gorgeous and sexy and fun. And this didn't have to get in the way of his investigation, so what did it matter?

Who gave a damn how he'd got here.

Caleb vowed in that second, as he brushed a soft kiss against the top of her head, that he was going to enjoy the hell out of this night. Whatever was driving it, he was the one having the fabulous ride.

Well, he and Pandora.

And it was time to make sure she got a ride she'd never forget, either.

"Round two," he promised. "This time, I'll show you what I can do with my boots off."

8

"WELL?" KATHY PRODDED in a frantic admonition, leaning across the sales counter so far her butt was almost up in the air. "I can't believe you didn't call me last night to tell me about your dinner. I'm your best friend. Your confidante. Your coconspirator of all things naughty. And I have to drag myself out of bed on a cold Saturday morning and brave the crazy shoppers to nag you into filling in the deets?"

A little freaked at the idea of verbalizing all the images that'd been playing in Technicolor through her head all day, Pandora rolled her eyes. She was trying her best to ignore Kathy's chipper curiosity. Especially since the store *was* filled with holiday shoppers, all with varying degrees of gossip expertise.

Trying to act professional, she struggled to wrap gold foil paper around an octagon-shaped box while the customer tapped her foot impatiently in time with "Jingle Bells" playing through the store's speakers.

"Whose idea was it to offer free gift wrapping?" she muttered as the tape stuck to the wrong part of the foil paper, pulling the glittery gold off when she tried to move it. Wrinkling her nose, she glared at the package, then glanced at the eagle-eyed customer who'd now taken to finger tapping to show her displeasure.

Oops.

"That'd be the same person whose idea it was to try out her hot and horny holiday meal last night and isn't sharing how it went," Kathy said, her voice escalating from whisper to hiss loud enough to garner shopper attention.

Her face on fire, Pandora gave a hiss of her own.

"Shh. I'll share. Later," she promised as she gave in to the finger-tapping pressure and started the wrapping all over. "Now, help me with this ribbon, okay?"

"No." Kathy straightened, keeping her hold-the-ribbon fingers hostage and giving Pandora a stubborn look.

"Pandora, the gossip grapevine is running amok," Laurie, a waitress from the nearby diner, said as she approached the counter with a basketful of holiday shopping. "Lacy Garner claimed Caleb Black was in here flirting up a storm the other day. But Jolene Giamenti was telling everyone and their neighbor that Sheriff Kendall was interested in you. Now I'm dying of curiosity—which of those fine-looking gentlemen are you interested in?"

Pandora's lips curved as she wondered how to answer that. She'd never had two eligible men interested in her, and definitely never had the town gossiping over which one she'd choose. Her ego, starting to show its fragile face again, glowed a little at the idea.

"Which one?" repeated the finger-tapping Mrs. Vincent, giving a nod of approval for the wrapping and indicating that Pandora hurry up with a little wiggle of her fingers. "As if there could be a question. A sweet girl like Pandora is going to date our fine sheriff. Why would she have any interest in a hoodlum like Caleb Black? Of course, all three Black kids were wild. But Caleb, being the oldest, seemed to make a point of being the best troublemaker, too. Why would Pandora date someone like that?"

Why? For fourteen orgasms in one night, maybe? Or the soft sweetness of the kiss he'd brushed over her forehead before he'd left in the wee hours of the morning? Maybe because Caleb had a sense of humor almost as fine as his gorgeous body. Or that he was fun and entertaining and made her feel amazingly sexy and clever.

Pandora shifted from one foot to the other. The movement brushed her thighs together and instantly shot tingling little reminders of her wild night through her body. She shivered. She didn't regret for one second the evening that had led to such pleasure. But still, she needed to keep her professional persona intact. It didn't matter that this was her own sex life and as such, nobody else's nosy business. Just as it hadn't mattered that she was innocent in the debacle with Sean. She'd learned the hard way how easy it was for public opinion to destroy a career.

"Are you going to share, or aren't you?" Kathy prodded, snatching the package and tying the bow herself with a quick, sassy flick of her fingers. "I have a lot to do today. My mother wants to go shopping for matching Christmas sweaters, then I have to take the dog to the photographer to reshoot the holiday card."

"You know if you had cats, those cards would come out a lot better," Pandora pointed out, taking the package back, bagging it and handing it to Mrs. Vincent with a smile. "Cats are great at lying still."

She, Kathy and the two customers all looked toward Bonnie and Paulie, who were curled up together in the window, a picture of furry contentment on the alpaca throw displayed there.

"So what's going on?" Mrs. Vincent prodded, taking her bag but not leaving like a polite customer who minded her own business should. "Are you associating with that riffraff, Caleb Black? I hear he's been a huge stress to his daddy. Not that Tobias Black is a pillar of all that is good and right in the world, what with dating girls his daughter's age, those motorcycle types in and out of his shop and the constant traffic of questionable personalities. But he deserves better than a do-nothing son like that boy."

"Caleb isn't a do-nothing, Mrs. Vincent," Pandora defended, seeing the trap an instant too late.

"Guess that answers our question, then, doesn't it," Mrs. Vincent said with a wicked smile on her benign old-lady face. She and Mrs. Sellers hooked arms and sashayed out of the store, whispering and tossing dire looks back over their shoulders.

Another customer, one who Pandora didn't know personally, gave a judgmental sort of tut-tut, then went back to her shopping.

Panic gripped a tight fist in Pandora's stomach. What had she done? She should have kept things with Caleb quiet. The mess with Sean had been horrible, but the whispers and snide innuendo from everyone who knew them, everyone she'd worked with, that'd almost been worse.

"Pandora, I love what you've done here," a pretty blonde interrupted as she carried a large statue of Eros, the god of love to the counter. She patted his naked ceramic butt before pointing to the tower of boxed aphrodisiac pepper cookies, the day's special. "Can you throw in a box of extraspicy cookies, too? I think they'll be a perfect gift for my Jazzercise instructor."

"She likes cookies?" Kathy asked, apparently not in such a hurry that she didn't have time to be social. She leaned forward on the counter, trying to peek up Eros's flowing strip of fabric to see how he was hanging.

"Sure. But mostly it's because she's got this new boyfriend and wants to make sure this relationship has a chance," the woman said, adding an astrology book, two CDs and a woven celestial shawl to the counter. "I guess she was dating this guy last month who was all about a little chemical enhancement, if you know what I mean. He claimed it'd boost their sex lives and make her look and feel gorgeous."

Starting to ring up the fabulous sale, Pandora exchanged a confused look with Kathy. Before she could ask, though, the woman continued. "She wasn't having anything to do with that fake stuff, though. But now she's paranoid that her new guy thinks she's ugly and that she sucks in bed. So I figured some cookie encouragement, along with a spa gift certificate, might help boost her confidence a little."

"Cookie courage," Pandora intoned with a wise nod.

The three of them joked their way through the rest of the transaction, but as soon as the door bells rang behind the blonde, Pandora frowned at Kathy.

"What do you think she's talking about? Chemical enhancements? Like…" She trailed off, then shrugged. "What do you think she meant?"

Kathy gave her a long, knowing look that clearly said she realized this was a pathetic topic change and she was allowing it for now. But there would be a price to pay. Pandora figured she'd better bring chocolate.

"Well, chemical usually means drugs," Kathy pointed out finally. Pandora nodded. "But the looking-good part? Maybe that means hallucinogens or something? Who knows?"

The two women shared a puzzled look.

"Pandora, did you want to open the café early today?" Fifi asked as she hurried from the back where she'd been prepping the cash register for lunch.

"We don't start serving until eleven," Pandora said, glancing at the clock shaped like a cat wearing a wizard hat. Most of the food was already prepped and ready in the kitchen, but she still needed to put the finishing touches on the asparagus salad and whip a fresh bowl of cream. "That's an hour away."

"I know, but I've had three people ask if we'd consider it. They need to be other places but really want your saffron chicken special."

"It'd be cool to bump up our income with an extra hour of lunch," Pandora mused, glancing at the beaded doorway leading to the café. "But I don't think we can. The store is too busy, I can't afford for one of us off the floor that much longer."

"Maybe we should hire holiday help?" Fifi said, her voice lifting in excitement. "I mean, even if it's only for the holidays. Things are so busy now, we could use another set of hands. I have a friend who'd be great. Russ. You've met him, right? He could come in during café hours. Maybe just until the new year when things slow down again?"

Hire help? Pandora bit her lip. What did she know about choosing employees? Fifi had worked at the store off and on for years, so it hadn't been as if Pandora had hired her so much as rehired her. But someone totally new? With her lousy judgment in people? She shuddered.

"You remember Russ? Kinda geeky guy who's been hanging around the store the last few weeks. He's a nice guy. Sweet and great at math," Fifi prodded. "Want me to give him a call?"

Pandora took a deep breath, looking around again. Her stomach was churning and she wanted to go hide in the office, make a list of pros and cons and debate the idea for a few hours.

But Fifi and Kathy were giving her expectant looks, and she had a store to run.

"Sure," she decided. Then realizing that she needed to be a businesswoman, not a wimp, she added, "I'll talk to him and see if I think he'd fit in well here at Moonspun Dreams."

"Oh, I think he will. He's fascinated by all things mystical and really wants to learn," Fifi said with an excited clap of her hands. "And he knows a lot of people. So I'm sure he'll be talking up the store and how great you're doing here, too."

Great, Pandora thought. Someone else talking about her. Just what she needed.

CALEB STRETCHED OUT on his hotel bed, staring in satisfaction at his stockinged feet. When the hell was the last time he'd taken a nap, let alone lounged around without his boots on?

Always being properly shod was a necessary component of always being ready to run. And he'd spent the past eight years, hell, his entire life, actually, ready to hit the road at a moment's notice.

A job gone wrong. A drugged-out dealer breaking in to kill him. A fight with one of his siblings. One of his dad's cons turning sour. All required footwear.

Wasn't it just a little ironic that the first taste he'd had of the ultimate deliciousness that was Pandora, he'd had his boots on? Or maybe it was some kind of cosmic payback for all his years of running.

He was still grinning a sappy, dork-ass grin when his cell rang.

"Black," he answered.

"Report?"

"Happy holidays, Hunter. How's the shopping coming along? Do you feebies do the secret Santa thing? Or do you buy for the entire task force? If so, don't forget my favorite color is gray."

"Not black?"

"Too obvious."

"Something you never are."

"Exactly."

"Are we finished?"

Caleb considered the white cotton of his stocking-clad toes for a few seconds, then nodded.

"Yep, sure. We're finished. What's up?"

"I'm calling for your status report."

"Is this how you handle your minions? Formal report requests? This businesslike tone that says, 'Dude, I'm in charge!'?"

"Is this how you talk to your superiors? With total disregard for authority? Your smart-ass mouth running on fast-forward?"

Caleb wiggled his toes, then nodded. "Yep. Guess that's why they aren't crying too hard over me retiring, huh?"

"I have trouble believing you actually think you can retire," Hunter said, now sounding more like Caleb's old roommate and beer buddy than an uptight FBI agent. "You're an adrenaline junky. You might be sick of the streets, but you're not going to be able to give up the job. Not totally."

Caleb's toes weren't looking so appealing anymore. Tension, as familiar as his own face, shot through his shoulders as he swung his feet to the floor.

"I could get used to not having people shoot at me. I'm thinking I'd like a life spent not dealing with strung-out hookers and South American drug lords with their zombie army of addicts."

"You'd just let them all go free?"

"I'm not the only guy out there, Hunter. There're plenty of DEA agents who can bring them down."

"As good as you?"

"Of course not."

Neither of them were kidding, Caleb knew. Hunter, because he didn't know how. And himself, because, well, he *was* damn good. But that didn't mean he wasn't finished.

"What'd you call for?" he asked, not willing to keep circling the same useless point he'd already discussed with his boss four times since he'd hit Black Oak for his fake vacation.

"Just what I said. I'm calling for your report."

"No, you're not. You're not a micromanager. If I had something to report, I'd have called you myself. And you know that. So what's the deal?"

The other man's hesitation was a physical thing. If he'd been in the room, Caleb knew he'd see the calculation in his old friend's eyes as he decided the best way to handle the situation. Good ole Hunter, always strategizing.

"Your father has some odd activity going on. A lot of

major part orders, hiring a couple guys with dealing records, parties in the shop after hours."

Stonefaced, Caleb analyzed that info as objectively as
possible. Then he shrugged. "It's the holidays—from what
I've heard, he has a lot of big holiday orders. He probably
needs mechanics to meet them, and isn't that picky about
their backgrounds."

"He's dating some hottie in town. She was in your sister's graduating class."

Wincing, Caleb hunched his shoulders. Just when he
thought his father couldn't embarrass him anymore…

"So my old man is snacking on a Twinkie. So what?"

"You know sex is one of the prime motivators. Have
you checked this woman out?"

"I'm not checking out my father's old lady."

In the first place, the idea was gross. In the second, it
would up the chances that he'd actually have to speak with
his father. In the week he'd been in town, he'd managed to
duck the guy's calls and avoid actually being in the same
breathing space. He was calling it deep undercover. So
deep, he wasn't even coming into contact with the suspect.

"She's the stepdaughter of a known South American
dealer. She's reputed to be estranged from her family, but
the connection can't be ignored."

"Lilah Gomez?"

God, this was like some twisted soap opera. Striding
over to the window, Caleb shoved his hand through his hair.
This day had started out so nice. Incredible sex, a woman
who filled his head with crazy thoughts of tomorrow and,
dammit, relaxing in his stocking feet.

"You know her?"

He wasn't about to admit that after that first day when
he hadn't recognized her, she'd gone on to hit on him three
more times since he'd come to town. He grimaced. Especially since that he didn't know if her thing with his father
was new or not.

"She and my sister were tight growing up. They hung out, had sleepovers, that kind of thing. Then Lilah went over to the wild side, and she and Maya went their separate ways."

Caleb waited, but Hunter didn't say anything about Lilah's current sleepover choices. And that, friends, was why he was still Caleb's best buddy.

"Look, I'm sorry," Hunter said instead.

Staring out the window at the frosty cold coating the bare tree branches, Caleb grunted.

"I'd hoped you'd find someone else. Another suspect or connection."

"Even if my old man's acting like a hound dog, there's still nothing to tie him to this," Caleb argued.

"There's nothing to point the finger in any other direction," Hunter rebutted. "Is there?"

Caleb sighed. "The case is moving slow. I've been connecting my way up the food chain. I'm cozying up to one of the midlevel dealers. He knows names, clearly has the inside track. But he's not sharing. Yet."

"Any hint about who's on top?"

Caleb grimaced. "These guys are cocky, sure they are untouchable. So it's someone with pull. Someone who can influence the law."

He waited, but again, Hunter didn't take the obvious opening. Gotta love the guy.

"I saw one of the couriers last night from a distance. He's familiar. As soon as I figure out where I've seen him before, I'll have the break we need."

"You've seen him on another case?"

Caleb thought back to the brown shaggy hair, all he'd been able to identify from two blocks away. "No, he's local. I'll do the rounds again, figure it out."

"Good job," Hunter said. "In the meantime, I have a remote, wildly impossible thread that if tugged could disintegrate instantly."

"Sounds promising."

He could handle delicate. Hell, if it meant keeping his old man out of jail, he could handle delicate while juggling porcelain and wearing roller skates.

"Intel shows that a new citizen to Black Oak has some connections. A relationship with a pharmacist busted for a prescription scam. She was implicated but skated."

"So why are you grudging after my old man? Why aren't you pounding on her door instead?"

"In the first place, it's not a grudge. Your old man has a record longer than I am tall."

"A record of suspicions. No convictions."

"Minor detail."

"Major legality."

"Whatever," Hunter dismissed. "And in the second place, while there is enough here to warrant a first glance, it's pretty much a waste of a second look. Other than this one relationship, the woman has a spotless rep. No record, no connections, no history to support drug suspicions."

"Once is all it takes." Especially if that once was the hook he needed to prove his old man's innocence. Just because he had issues with his upbringing, a lack of respect for his father's choices and a whole lot of pent-up anger toward the past, that didn't mean he wanted the old man in jail.

"Look, give me the name and I'll look into it," he told Hunter.

Even though the sigh was silent, Caleb knew his friend heaved one. Patience with avoidance had never been the guy's strong suit.

"Fine. Check on a Pandora Easton. I'll email you the deets of her record."

Sucker punched, stars swirled in front of his eyes as he tried to catch his breath. Caleb had been in bed with a pole dancer once, both of them buck naked and sweaty, when she'd pulled a gun on him. To this day, he had no idea where it'd come from.

That's about how he felt at this moment.

"Pandora..."

"Easton," Hunter confirmed. "Twenty-seven, resident of Black Oak and employed at a store there. Her mother, Cassiopeia Easton, has a file. I'll send that, too."

A part of Caleb's brain heard and filed away the details of Hunter's words. The rest of it was in shock.

Pandora? The sweetest woman he'd ever met? The one who'd shown him heaven by the lights of her Christmas tree, blown his control all to hell while giving him the best orgasm of his life? With his damn boots on?

Suddenly, busting his father for running a drug ring held a sort of appeal.

He'd spent hours in that store. Days watching it. He hadn't suspected her for one second. Now this? Unless he'd seriously lost his edge, this was all bullshit. Or was it?

"I've gotta go," he said, cutting off whatever Hunter was saying. He flicked the cell phone closed, shoved it in his pocket and grabbed his jacket. It wasn't until he had the door to his hotel room open he remembered that he didn't have any damn boots on.

There was irony in there somewhere.

Five minutes later, he was on his way. To do what, he wasn't sure. Something with Pandora. He wasn't sure if that something was along the lines of the naked, intense pleasure that he'd been contemplating an hour ago, or if it was because he didn't like being lied to. Zipping his jacket, the leather minimal defense against the cold, Caleb stepped out of the hotel lobby and onto the wide porch steps and almost ran into the body coming up the stairs.

"Excuse me," he muttered, sidestepping and patting his pockets for his bike keys.

"I was coming in to look for you."

Could this damn day get any worse?

Caleb glanced at the keys in his hand, briefly wishing they were his gun. He shoved the keys back in his pocket, eyeing the railing and the drop. Whether it was to jump or to toss someone over, he wasn't sure.

"Dad," he returned, his tone resigned. He kept one eye on the railing, though. Just in case.

He'd been unprepared that first day when he'd seen his father. Since then, he'd spent every minute prepared for this second encounter. Now, he could study the old man with objective eyes. Or at least without the resentment and irritation he'd been sporting.

Tobias Black stood straight and tall, like his sons. His black hair was showing a little gray in the sideburns, but was still as thick and unruly as ever. As a kid, Caleb had seen his father in everything from a three-piece suit with an ascot, to a repairman's coveralls, to surgical scrubs. A chameleon, Tobias had obviously taken to this new role as custom-bike shop owner like a fish to water. Biker boots, similar to Caleb's own, jeans and a leather jacket made up his work uniform.

"I've been waiting for you to come by the house. Or the shop. Either one," Tobias said, shifting to the left and blocking the stairs leading to escape. Caleb smirked, knowing he could take the railing at any time he wanted.

"I've been busy."

"Doing?"

Leaning against one of the porch columns, his arms crossed over his chest, Caleb's smirk widened.

"Tell me, son, why'd you come home? Clearly not to see family, so what's up?"

"I stopped by to see Aunt Cynthia yesterday."

"How is that old bat?"

"She had a lot of great things to say about you."

Tobias's smirk was an exact replica of his son's.

"I'll just bet she did. The woman is still trying to run me out of town. You'd think she'd give up after all this time, but no. That's why she ran for mayor, you know. To make my life hell."

If anyone else had said that, Caleb would have rolled his eyes and called them on their whiny persecution complex. But in this case, he knew Tobias was right. Cynthia Parker had made it her mission to make her late sister's husband's life hell whenever possible. His kids, she tolerated. But Tobias? Not even a little bit.

"I gotta say, even for a harpy, I had higher expectations of her, though," Tobias continued. "She's too busy glad-handing rich donors and getting her picture taken to take care of business, I guess."

Caleb knew the game. If he asked what business, he'd be agreeing to play. Con 101, get the mark to agree. To anything, even if it was only to agree to talk about the weather. And for a master like Tobias, all he needed was that agreement, and he'd win. Always.

So Caleb waited.

Tobias clearly knew what his oldest son was doing.

"I don't suppose you're interested in coming by the bike shop this evening? Big holiday bash, all the vendors, customers, hell, even a few strangers. Probably a few of your old school pals. Good times, food provided by that little sweetheart at Moonspun, booze from Mick's bar."

Caleb saw the trap. Hell, it had a big neon sign flashing a warning at him. But he couldn't stop himself.

"You're tight with Pandora, are you?" he asked.

"Tight? What're you implying? The girl's young enough to be my daughter."

"So's Lilah Gomez."

Tobias's grin widened. Nope, this was his game and he was setting the traps, not stepping in them.

"Girl's gonna be at the party," he said.

"Lilah?" Caleb returned, even though he knew who his father meant.

"Pandora. I heard you had dinner with her the other

night. Hope you're not taking on more than you can handle there."

Caleb's stare was bland. He hadn't discussed his sex life with his father since he was twelve and the old man had shown him the hall closet where the supply of condoms was kept. He was hardly going to start now.

"There's a lot of interesting…stuff coming out of that store," Tobias continued. His blue eyes were intense, the same look Caleb often saw when he looked in the mirror.

"Define *interesting*," Caleb invited. He knew Tobias wouldn't—after all, why waste bait? But he wanted to see where his father was taking this.

"Come by tonight," Tobias invited with a nod. Apparently Caleb had done something right—who the hell knew what—in the old man's eyes. "You might learn a few things."

With that and a jaunty salute, Tobias turned on his heel and sauntered down the stairs.

9

BY SEVEN-THIRTY IN THE evening, Pandora was closing up the store and about ready to scream.

She'd thought she was having a little fun with the most incredible sex of her life. But according to popular thought in the store today, she was actually making a social statement that was quite possibly going to cast her as a pariah in town and ruin her reputation. Having played that role recently, she knew she pretty much hated it.

And, apparently the cherry on top of public opinion was that by choosing Caleb over Sheriff Hottie, she was rejecting all that was good and right in the world for the lure of the bad.

It was enough to make a girl's head explode right off her shoulders. But she knew from experience that obsessing didn't help, so she forced herself to start her closing routine.

It was just as well that Caleb hadn't come by. Or called. Or expressed any interest in a repeat performance. If one night together had the potential to ruin everything she'd built here, what would two nights do? Ruin it twice as much?

And how pathetic was she to stop and consider whether twice as ruined wasn't worth it. Because, dammit, the sex had been incredible. Mind-boggling. So awesome that she got damp just thinking about it.

And she knew he'd been just as blown away.

"Why the hell hasn't he called, then?" she muttered as she wheeled the dolly with its precariously balanced crate into the showroom.

She stopped just short of Paulie, who was splayed over the floor like a cat-skin rug, and wheeled the dolly to the right instead.

"I'm crazy for being upset. I should be grateful he isn't coming around, right? This way I don't have to worry about trying to resist him."

This time she directed her comment to Bonnie, who was sitting on one of the display counters next to a three-foot-high cluster of amethyst, her head tilted to the side as if contemplating Pandora's whining.

Bonnie meowed her support. But Paulie just rolled onto his side, shot one leg into the air and started licking himself. There was nothing like the male perspective.

"Sure, I guess he could take that route," she agreed with the cat as she started wiggling the five-foot-tall statue of Eros from the box, careful not to nick his wings. "But lovin' is never as fun by oneself."

Pandora's lower lip jutted out, but before she could get a real pout on, there was a tap at the door.

She and the cats all turned their heads. Her heart leaped, giddy excitement filling her tummy. Dread filtered in, too. She'd had no idea she was making a public statement last night. But now she was fully informed. Upset, confused and a little intimidated...but still fully informed.

Oh, joy.

Giving Eros's butt a quick pat in the hopes he'd help her choose well, she unwrapped herself from the statue and hurried across the store to unlock the door.

"Caleb," she greeted, her smile a little shaky at the corners. She wiped her hands on the heavy velvet of her skirt and gave her voile blouse a quick tug to make sure the lace was straight at the bodice.

Should she ask him in? Or ask him to leave? Her stomach churned as she tried to decide. Did she go with her instincts and intuition, which said that despite the town's opinion, he was a good man? Or did she accept that her intuition sucked and listen to public opinion?

Thankfully, Caleb took the decision out of her hands by walking right in.

"Hey," he greeted. He didn't kiss her, though. Instead, he gave her a long, searching look, then, hands still shoved in his pockets instead of groping her the way they should be, he stepped into the store.

"What's up?" she asked. She bit her lip. Had he heard the rumors about the two of them? Was he regretting it now, too? "You look a little stressed."

"Nah. I just had a full day, that's all."

Full of what? He wasn't working, was avoiding his family as if they were carriers of the seventh plague and didn't seem like a holiday-partying kind of guy.

Maybe he'd been looking for a job. Or a place to live. Something that'd keep him in Black Oak past the first of the year? Maybe he'd spent the day in bed, recovering in exhaustion from his wild night with her.

And maybe she'd been inhaling too many oyster fumes. Pandora gave herself a quick mental forehead smack, followed by an even quicker get-a-freaking-clue-he's-not-for-you lecture.

"I'm replenishing stock," she told him, returning to unpacking the statue so she could resist the desperate urge to squeeze his ass. Keep it light, keep it polite. Ass grabbing was definitely off-limits. "It was a busy day. The busiest this year, actually."

"That's great that you're rocking the sales," he said. "Have you pinpointed what's making the big difference? Besides your charming personality, of course."

The last was said with a wicked smile and a wink.

"I'm guessing it's either that, or the aphrodisiacs," Pandora said with a smile, unable to maintain her distance when he gave her that look. "I'm not actually sure. I haven't quite figured out how to run the bookkeeping program yet, but I think there's some kind of income-comparison report I can run. As soon as I do, I'll know what to focus more time on."

His eyes narrowed, an odd look crossing his face before he stepped farther into the room. "I'm handy with computers. How about I run the report for you while you unpack?"

"You don't have to do that," she protested, her words a little breathless. "I'm sure you have other things to do."

"Just the party at the motorcycle shop," he dismissed. "And I was hoping you'd go with me, so I'm just chilling until you're through here anyway."

Pandora pressed her lips together. Wasn't that tantamount to publicly stating her intention to take the bad-boy path?

"The party?" she hedged. "I didn't think you were going."

In that second, Pandora wished like never before that her mom were here. As conflicted as she felt, she needed Cassiopeia's clear-sighted vision and maybe a session with the tarot cards to sort through all of this.

Instead, she was stuck with herself. And her own lousy intuition. Tiny pinpricks of panic shivered up and down Pandora's spine as she tried to decide what to do. Her intuition was telling her to go for it with Caleb. Of course, her body's desperate need to taste him at least one more time was probably overriding any teensy bit of actual gift she had.

Obviously catching a whiff of her internal struggle, Caleb waved one hand as if brushing away the invitation.

"Look, I don't blame you if you don't want to go. It's not my idea of a good time," Caleb said with a shrug, moving behind the counter to where she'd left the laptop open. "What program do you use for bookkeeping?"

If they stayed here, she could enjoy his company and not have to face crowds. Or decisions. Oh, God, Pandora thought with a mental eye roll. She was such a wimp.

"You really don't have to do that," she said, feeling guilty over the relief. "I can come in early tomorrow and finish up the stock. We can go to the party now. Or, you know, go do something else."

Subtle, Pandora, she told herself with a mental snicker. Why didn't she ask him to drop his pants and do her instead?

"Nah," he said. "This won't take long and I'd like to help."

Her heart melted a little. So did her knees, so Pandora leaned against the dolly and cleared her throat, not wanting to sound all choked up when she said, "I appreciate it. I feel like I'm…"

She trailed off, scrunching her nose and scraping at the chipped paint on the dolly.

"Feel like…?"

Flustered and wishing she'd kept her mouth shut, Pandora met his gaze with a shrug.

"Pandora?"

"I feel like I've finally found my thing, you know? My niche. I'm having fun getting to know the customers and matching them to the right motivation." She blushed again, giving him an abashed look. "That's how I think of it. Motivation. What products will get them excited, give them the boost or direction they need. Even the aphrodisiacs in the café are all about motivation."

Pushing the dolly toward the back room, Pandora caught his doubtful look.

"They are," she insisted. "The aphrodisiacs aren't like popping a little blue sex pill and getting it up for anyone or anything. They're about amplifying a connection that's already there. About giving a couple the impetus, the energy, to lose their inhibitions and explore everything that's between them."

Caleb leaned against the counter, his fingers tapping the edge of the laptop as he smiled.

"You love it."

Centering her statue, Pandora rubbed Eros's bare shoulder and nodded. "I really do."

"Then let me help you out. I'll just take a peek at your program, see what info I can pull together for you."

Could anyone be sweeter? To hell with the town and the gossip. She was going to listen to her heart. It might not be a special gift like intuition or a honed skill like reading body language. But it was hers and she was going to trust it.

"I APPRECIATE YOU LOOKING at my books," Pandora said, her smile both sweet and sexy at the same time. She crossed the floor, pausing to pet one of the cats, who was sprawled inside a large copper bowl. "I figure I'll take a business class or something after the first of the year. But in the meantime, I really am grateful for the reassurance that the store is really doing well."

Caleb felt like the world's biggest dick. And not in a good way. He spent most of his life lying to people. Using them for information. He'd learned the art of taking advantage of people at his father's knee.

And now?

Now he was standing in front of a woman who made him feel things, believe in things that he'd always scoffed at as feel-good lies before. And he was bullshitting her, poking into her business while pretending to help her out. He was digging into her books trying to find the dirt to convict her of an ugly crime.

No, he corrected himself. He was assuring himself that there was no dirt, so she didn't get unfairly accused.

Big difference, he thought with a mental eye roll.

She reached the counter and hesitated, her smile dimming as she studied his face. A tiny crease marred her forehead and she took a little step back, as if to get a better view of him.

"Seriously. What's the matter? You're really tense and, well, off feeling," she said, studying him through suddenly narrowed eyes.

Caleb was impressed. He'd spent the past eight years working with career cops whose lives depended on their ability to read people. And most of them didn't come close to her aptitude.

"What's wrong?" she asked again, her voice rising to a squeak as she wrung her fingers together. "Is the store losing money and I didn't realize it?"

"No. I mean, I don't know, I haven't started poking into your books yet," he told her. Giving a quick flick of the mouse pad, he gestured. "I need your password to get into the program."

"Ooooh." She reached around, angling the laptop and tapping a few keys, then trailed her hand over the back of his. He felt tingles, freaking tingles, from his fingers to the tip of his dick. It was as if she had some special power or something.

"Have at it," she told him, offering another warm smile before turning back to her naked-angel statue and boxes of stuff. "There are cookies there in that box, too. Help yourself."

He glanced at the box of Decadently Orgasmic Double-Chocolate Delights. Homemade horny treats. Curious, he flipped the lid and tasted one.

Delicious.

As Pandora restocked, tidied and replenished the book-cases and swept the floor, she kept up a steady stream of chatter. Caleb was alternately intrigued, amused and filled with an alien sense of comfort.

All the while, he invaded her privacy in horrible and disgusting ways, poking into all her files, opening her emails and reading her OneNote journal of store plans. He scrolled through the photo album, he checked her recycle bin and he surreptitiously jotted down names and numbers. He also ate her entire box of cookies.

The only loose end he was seeing was Fifi, though. But as far as he knew, she'd been employed at Moonspun off and on for years. He'd dig deeper into her history later, but from what he'd seen in the reports Hunter sent, she had a few financial issues and had been caught with the wrong crowd from time to time. However, she had no record and no real criminal ties.

Done with the laptop, he closed the lid. And gave thanks that Pandora was one of those organized, ethical people who kept their work and private computers completely separate. Because her work computer was clean, and he hadn't had the opportunity—ie: had to force himself—to look through her private files. Poking into her private emails and photos would feel really grimy. As opposed to just slightly nauseating.

"So how's it looking?" she asked as she came out of the storeroom.

It?

His conscience? That was looking like shit.

But he figured she wasn't interested in that. And if he played his cards right, she never had to know that he was so far beneath her in terms of moral values that he should be eating worms.

"The store's doing great. I'm impressed at how low you keep your overhead," he commented, bringing up the only area left that might offer an opening for drug sales through her store. Unrealistic, of course, but once he'd crossed it off the list, he could tell Hunter this was definitely a closed door.

"Overhead?"

"Yeah. You don't have a big employee list. Just you and Fifi, right?"

"Well, yeah. Until tomorrow."

"Beg pardon?"

"Fifi thought we were going a little crazy with how busy it's been. Without knowing exactly how solid we were financially, I wasn't sure about hiring, but she convinced me that her friend Russ would be willing to work just the lunch shift while the café is open, and that he was cool with the fact that the job will end after Christmas." She gave a little shoulder wiggle and added, "Isn't that lucky?"

Caleb sighed. Of course she'd hired someone. She, and Fifi, who had a maxed-out VISA card and rent issues.

"Yep. That's lucky, all right." Bad luck, though. While he hadn't found anything to point fingers, he couldn't in good conscience cross the store off, either. Not until he'd checked out everyone.

"I guess I need to figure out how to add him to the payroll program, don't I?" she asked, biting her lip and giving Caleb the cutest eyelash-batting look that just screamed pretty please.

"I can do that," he offered, feeling like ten times the jerk because she looked so grateful.

"His application is back in the storeroom," she said, hurrying around the counter and stepping over the blanket of black furry cat lying in the doorway.

Since he couldn't have manufactured a better excuse to poke around in her storeroom, no pun intended, Caleb sighed and followed her. The cat lifted his fluffy black head and gave Caleb a long, narrowed look that made him want to hunch his shoulders and apologize.

God, it was time to get out of this business. Now a cat was calling him out on his bullshit.

"This is a storeroom?" Caleb asked, his eyes wide as he stepped into the tiny room. It was maybe eight-by-eight, with shelves lining three walls, boxes stacked in what he assumed were organized piles and a desk shoved in the back.

With a little squeak, Pandora turned to face him. Hand

pressed to her chest, she laughed at herself. "I didn't realize you'd followed me."

He knew he shouldn't be here. He knew it was every kind of wrong to pursue her when she was under investigation. But, dammit, he'd already had a taste and now he was addicted. She was delicious. And he wanted more.

Caleb tried to justify it. He told himself he wasn't officially on the job. He argued that he'd already investigated her enough to know she was clean.

It was all bullshit.

But it was still good enough for him.

"The view wasn't as nice without you out there."

He loved how the color warmed her cheeks, bringing out the red highlights in her hair and making her eyes sparkle even brighter.

"I like it in here," he commented, stepping into the tight space and crowding her against the desk.

"Cassiopeia used this as an office," she said, gesturing over her shoulder to indicate the desk and file cabinet. She sounded a little breathless, though. Good. He liked the idea of taking her breath away. "She, um, she stored most of the stock in the back room. But, you know, I turned it into the café."

Her eyes were huge, so huge he could see the brown rim around the green irises. Her lashes, thick and black, swept down to hide her eyes. But he'd seen the desire in those hazel depths. Which was all the permission he needed.

Caleb took that last step. The one that brought his body within inches of hers. Hot, welcoming and so freaking soft she made his head spin, her curves melded into the hard planes of his chest.

Pandora tilted her head back so her hair swept over his wrists. Her hands slipped over his shoulders and she gave him a saucy wink.

"So you like tight spaces, do you?"

And just like that, his brain short-circuited. Caleb knew

he was on the job here—even if he wasn't exactly "on the job." He knew there was a specific purpose to his being in this office, which was to find proof that would eliminate Pandora from suspicion so he could go back to happily enjoying the delights of her company without guilt. He should be looking for the job application so he could eliminate the new guy as a suspect.

But all he could see was Pandora, her hazel eyes laughing up at him. Her smile, so wide and amused. Her. Just her.

When had she gained so much power over him?

He had to get the hell out of here. Years of living on the edge of his nerves had honed his awareness razor-sharp. He knew when he was in trouble. He knew when he was in danger. And he knew when things had the potential to get freaking scary.

This situation? It was all three.

"Are you hungry?" Pandora asked, running her tongue over the fullness of her lower lip. "Did you want another… cookie?"

He didn't think she meant those delicious chocolate treats he'd eaten earlier. But he didn't care any longer. All he wanted was her. She was worth whatever problems he had to face—on the case, or with his conscience.

"I'm starving," he said. Then he gave in to the desperate need and skimmed his fingers down to gather the material of her skirt. Inch by inch, he pulled it higher, baring the deliciously soft skin of her thighs. "Another round with my boots on?"

"It's going to have to be, since I don't think you're going to have time to take them off," she mused, trailing her hands down to his belt buckle and having her way with it.

Her mouth met his with fervor, her tongue challenging his. She had his jeans unzipped and his dick free before he could do more than groan.

Suddenly desperate, he grasped her waist and lifted her onto the desk. His fingers found her wet, hot core, stroking her through the soft fabric of her panties. Impatient, needing more, he ripped the material away.

Her response was half laugh, half moan. And all delight.

Not sure he could stand much more of her fingers' wicked dance over his straining erection, he grabbed a condom from his pocket and sheathed himself.

His fingers returned to her soft folds, but she wasn't having any of that foreplay crap. Pandora grasped his hips, slid forward on the desk and rotated her hips so her wet heat stroked him.

Losing his mind, Caleb plunged.

It felt incredible. Her body, the power of the passion between them, the need.

Desperate for release, his eyes locked on Pandora's as he pounded into her. She didn't look away. Even as her eyes fogged, as she panted and started keening excited cries of her orgasm, she kept her gaze on his.

It was the most incredible experience of his life. Passionate, raw and emotional.

Terrified and exhilarated at the same time, he gave himself over to the pleasure of her body. His orgasm slammed him hard, exploding out of control. He shouted his pleasure, then, his face buried in the sweet scent of her shoulder, he tried to catch his breath. And restart his brain.

Because while he might not have a clue what he was going to do about the case, he did know one thing for damn sure.

He was in trouble.

And he liked it.

Ten minutes later, Caleb still couldn't think straight. He'd barely had the presence of mind to slip that job application in his pocket while she wasn't looking. He could check into the new employee later, then slip it behind the desk tomorrow. She'd never know.

"Thanks for the, um, help with my books," Pandora said

with a laugh as she gathered her purse, keys and coat in preparation for closing up shop for the night.

He held her long suede coat so she could slide her arms into the sleeves.

"Ready to party?" he said, lifting the silky swing of her hair aside so he could brush a kiss over the back of her neck. God, he couldn't get enough of her. She was like a drug, addicting and delicious. And as far as he could tell, without any debilitating side effects.

"I have to say I feel a little weird going to a party with no undies," she said with a naughty glance over her shoulder. "Even weirder when it's your dad's party."

He wanted to tell her they'd skip it. He'd much rather go back to her place. Or to his hotel room with that big claw-foot tub. He wasn't a foofy bath kind of guy, but he could totally imagine Pandora lounging there, surrounded by steam and frothy bubbles.

But he had a job to do. He'd identified most of the dealers in town by now, so he needed to see if any showed up. And find out who they were hanging out with if they were there.

"We'll just stop in. Thirty minutes, tops," he said. That's all he'd need to gauge the players and gather a few names. "And if we're there too long, all you have to do is whisper in my ear a reminder of your lack of panties, and we'll be out the door in an instant."

Pandora's laugh was low and husky, making him wish like hell that he could toss this whole mess aside and just focus on getting on with his damn life.

As soon as this case was solved, he was through. He had no clue what he'd be doing. He didn't even know where he'd be doing it, although Black Oak offered some serious temptation. Not quite enough to allay the issues it presented, though.

"You sure you don't want to just skip the party and get right to the lack of panties," Pandora said, only sounding as if she was half teasing as she gathered her purse and gave the cats each a cuddle.

"I want to," he said in an embarrassingly fervent tone. Caleb coughed, trying to clear the dorkiness from his throat. "It sounds crazy, but I feel like I have to stop in. I can't figure out what I'm doing until I figure out where things are at with my father. Not just for tonight, but in the big picture, you know."

Pandora paused in the act of pulling catnip-filled toys out a little mesh bag and tossing them around the room for Paulie and Bonnie to entertain themselves through the night. "Big picture?"

"Yeah." Caleb felt like an ass, but still something forced him to say, "I figure it's time we made our peace. Or at least found some neutral ground. See if we can both handle being in the same town for a length of time."

An earless furry bunny dangling from one hand, Pandora pressed the other to her lips for just a second, as if she was trying to hold back a slew of questions. There was just as much worry and hesitation in her eyes as there was curiosity and delight. He wasn't quite sure what to make of that.

"By length of time, do you mean the week left until Christmas?" she asked hesitantly.

While she waited, her eyes all huge and sexy, Bonnie, the black-and-white cat, padded across the floor and started batting the bunny with her paw. When Pandora didn't respond to the command to play, the cat batted harder, sending the toy flying from Pandora's fingers across the room. Both cats bounded after the furry treat.

"I'm…" He trailed off. How did he answer? He didn't want to get her hopes up. He wasn't the kind of guy who made promises. Not even ones he was pretty sure he could keep.

"Don't," she said, interrupting his mental struggle. She crossed over and took his hands. "Please, I didn't mean to make you uncomfortable. I should warn you, though, that the town grapevine is working overtime and you're the main topic. So if you stay, that's only going to get worse."

It wasn't the town he needed to worry about, he realized as he looked into those heavily fringed eyes. It was Pandora. She was more dangerous than an arsenal of AK-47s. At least, she was to his once happily frozen heart.

"Sweetheart, I honestly don't know where I'm going to be, or where I want to be, in two weeks. But I do know I'm exactly where I want to be right this minute."

Pandora's eyes were huge and vulnerable. He'd like to think it was because of his heartfelt declaration. But there was something else there, lurking. Something that made his gut clench. Because beneath the nerves and sweetness there was a fear. Like she was afraid of him sticking for too long. Afraid of what he'd find out.

"Pandora?" he prodded. "Is there something you want to tell me?"

He didn't know if he was hoping more that she would, or that she wouldn't.

"You're exactly where I want you to be, too," she finally murmured. Whether that was true or not, he didn't know. But he was positive it wasn't what she'd been thinking about.

But before he could push, she rose on tiptoe, and, even as nerves simmered in her eyes, brushed a soft kiss over his lips.

It was as if she'd flipped a switch that only she knew existed. His body went on instant hard-on alert, and his mind absolutely shut down. All he wanted was her. All he could taste, could think of, cared about, was her.

More and more of her.

He slanted his mouth to the side, taking their kiss deeper with one swift slide of his tongue.

His fingers still entwined with hers, Caleb let his hands drop, then wrapped both their arms around her waist to pull her tighter, effectively trapping her soft curves against the hard, craving planes of his body.

Why the hell was she wearing this bulky coat? All he wanted, now and for as long as it lasted, was to get her naked.

Lost in the pleasure of her mouth, Caleb didn't hear the key in the door until a loud clatter of the chimes hit a discordant note. Pulling her lips from his, Pandora jumped, blinking the sexual glow out of her eyes as she looked over his shoulder toward whoever had come in.

Her jaw dropped and her face turned bright red even as embarrassment filled her eyes.

"Hello, Mother."

_10_

"WELL, DARLING?" Cassiopeia said as she settled comfortably on Pandora's couch and sipped chamomile tea. "It looks like you have a lot to share. When did you get involved with the likes of Caleb Black? And more important, why didn't you ever mention him in your emails? I'd have stayed away a few extra days if I'd known you had that kind of entertainment on tap."

That entertainment, as Cassiopeia called him, had barely stuck around long enough for introductions before he'd hightailed it out of the store for his father's party.

Now, twenty minutes after Cassiopeia's shocking arrival, she was soothing her travel woes with tea while Pandora resisted the urge to pace.

"I've got so much to tell you. I shared the basics in our emails, but things are really going great at the store," she said, even as a part of her wondered if she hurried her mother along, could she catch Caleb at the party. The other part of her, the one that bwawked like a chicken, was glad her mother's arrival had given her an excuse to keep their relationship quiet for a little longer. Sort of. Nothing was ever hidden from Cassiopeia.

As if reading her mind, her mother gestured with her teacup.

"I'd rather talk about the man," Cassiopeia said with a smile too wicked for someone's mother.

"I'd rather not," Pandora decided. Not while she was so mixed up over the issue. "Let's focus on the store instead, okay? Before we left, I printed out the financial statements. Do you want to see them? I saved the store, Mom."

She felt a little giddy saying that. As if she was tempting fate. But she was so excited she had to share. And hoped, like crazy, that her mom would be proud.

"I mean, it's obviously too early to tell for sure, but I'm betting the café and the aphrodisiacs stay solid, long-term."

"Most likely," Cassiopeia agreed with a shrug that seemed more disinterested than dismissive.

"Don't you care?" Pandora frowned, trying to read her mother. Calm and centered, as always. A little worn-out, which wasn't surprising since it was a long trip from Sedona. But shouldn't there be some relief? Some joy at the prospect of keeping the store a success? Some pride in her only child?

"Darling, of course I care. The café is a brilliant idea and you've done a wonderful job. I knew if left to your own devices, you'd come up with something."

Her mother's smile widened, a self-satisfied look just this side of gloating in her eyes.

"You left to force my hand?" Pandora realized, almost breathless from the shock.

"Well, the store *was* in trouble, of course. And I was having a heck of a time figuring out how to keep things afloat and still meet my commitment in Sedona. But I imagine I could have probably muddled through, canceled the appearance and crossed my fingers until the spring bus tour if I'd had to." Cassiopeia waved a heavily bejeweled hand as if her manipulation didn't matter. "But the point is, I didn't have to. Thanks to your return to Black Oak, and your clever café idea, we're in wonderful shape for the first time in years."

"That was a huge risk to take if you didn't have to," Pandora pointed out, trying to calm her sudden jitters. "I could have ruined the store. What if I'd failed?"

"Then you'd fail," Cassiopeia said with a shrug.

"You'd risk the family legacy to teach me a lesson?"

"The family legacy is talent, dear. It's intuition. It's not a building and a bunch of candles and crystals."

Pandora choked down the urge to scream. She knew what the hell to do with the shop, dammit. But she didn't have any talent. So where did that leave her? She'd thought she'd finally contributed to the family name. That she'd done something worthy of the women who'd come before her.

"Darling, you make it so hard on yourself. Instead of embracing hope, which will help you realize your gift, you spend all your time chasing the Furies, trying to corral misery before it causes hurt," Cassiopeia said, launching into one of her favorite stories. In the Easton family, they didn't believe in choosing a name until they'd discovered the newborn's personality. Pandora had been Baby Girl for eight months until the gods, fate and the tarot cards had revealed her destiny to Cassiopeia. "You need to quit worrying about those miseries, darling. Instead, focus on joy. That's the only way you'll find the right path."

With that, Cassiopeia rose and glided to the kitchen to set her teacup in the sink, returned to kiss the top of her silently fuming daughter's head and left.

An hour later, frustrated tears still trickled down Pandora's cheeks. She didn't even answer when someone knocked tentatively on her door. Eleven o'clock on a Sunday night, it could only be one person. And she was too worked up to deal with her mother twice in one day.

The knock sounded again, a little louder this time.

Who the hell needed to chase misery when it was always right there, tapping her on the shoulder and reminding her that she didn't measure up. That she was a waste of her family name. Ungifted and unworthy.

The urge to run away—again—made her body quiver. But unlike her escape when she'd been eighteen, this time she didn't have anywhere to go. Nor did she still have that cocky faith that she could prove to her mother, her grandmother and everyone else in Black Oak that she could be a success without the family gift.

Pounding replaced the tentative knock.

"Fine," she huffed, jumping to her feet.

Her mother wouldn't give up. She had probably headed home to gather some crystals and cards, determined to help her daughter find that damned path she always harped on.

"What?" Pandora snapped as she threw open the door.

The bitter cold from the icy rain swept over her bare toes as she stared.

"Oh."

It wasn't Cassiopeia on her doorstep.

It was a delicious looking chocolate éclair with what looked like a tub of ice cream and, if she wasn't mistaken, hot-fudge sauce.

Her eyes met Caleb's golden gaze.

"I thought you could use a sugar rush," he said, lifting the dessert a little higher. "It comes with, or without, a second spoon."

She hesitated. Attention was a good thing, but attention while she was having a tantrum? Hardly something she wanted Caleb to remember her for.

"I'm not very good company right now," she demurred, rubbing her hands over the velvet of her skirt and wishing she were wearing sweatpants and a baggy T-shirt. Something innocuous to hide behind. Although, if she was going to do some wishing, she should put all her falling stars and birthday candles toward having washed her tear-stained face instead of answering the door looking like a sad raccoon.

"I'm not looking for entertainment," Caleb said, shrugging before leaning one broad shoulder against the door frame. Catching the arch look she shot him, he grinned. "I'm not looking for that, either."

"Oh, really?"

"Well, I wouldn't say no if you decided to strip naked and paint my name across your body in this fudge sauce before inviting me to lick it off." He waited for Pandora's laugh before continuing, "But that's not what this is about. I'm just here as…as…"

Pandora swallowed hard to get past the lump of emotions suddenly clogging her throat. "As?"

"As a friend."

The only thing that kept the tears from leaking down her face was fear of adding another layer to the raccoon effect. Instead, Pandora sniffed surreptitiously and stepped aside to let him in.

"How'd you know I needed a friend tonight?" she asked as Caleb crossed the room. "Better yet, how'd you know my mother wasn't still here?"

"She stopped by the party." He gave her a quick look, something shuttered in his eyes making her wonder if he'd had his own parental confrontation. "She looked a little stressed herself, so I figured I'd check on you."

So Cassiopeia had decided to skip the crystals and cards and had sent in a sexy ego boost instead. Too dejected to even fake being a good hostess, Pandora dumped two bowls on the table. Caleb, jacket gone and his shirtsleeves rolled up, scooped big fat mounds of vanilla-bean ice cream into them.

Her frustration and hurt feelings shifted, sliding into second place behind her sudden urge to lick hot fudge off his knuckle. Her body warmed, excitement stirring at the sight of Caleb's hands. So strong. So big. So wonderfully good at sending her into a fog of desire where she could forget everything except him and the pleasure he brought.

"What?" he said, noting her stare.

"Just realizing something," she said, color warming her cheeks.

"Again… What?"

"You have magic hands," Pandora admitted despite her embarrassment. "I knew they felt incredible. I've had plenty of proof of their copious talents. But I didn't realize until just now that they are magic."

Caleb's grin was huge as he plopped sloppy globs of whipped cream on top of the fudge-covered ice cream. "Magic, huh?"

"Yep." Pandora pulled one of the bowls toward her, grabbing a spoon with the other hand.

She suddenly felt a million times better.

"Tell me more," he invited, stashing what was left of dessert in the freezer. He joined her at the table, but didn't sit.

"More, hmm?" she said, giving him a slow, teasing smile as she licked hot fudge off her spoon. The rich, bittersweet flavor slid down her throat. "How about we make it a show-and-tell kind of thing?"

His wicked smile didn't change, but his eyes did. They sharpened and heated at the same time. He reached out a hand, pulling her to her feet. Then he scooped up his bowl, handing her the other one, and led the way out of the kitchen.

"We're eating in bed?" she teased as excitement spun and swirled like a snowflake inside her, buffeting through her system and making her breathless with need.

"Too messy," he deemed, continuing through the living room, one hand wrapped around hers to keep her close. He stopped at the bathroom and glanced in, gave a decisive nod, then turned to her with an arched brow. "Do you have a blanket you don't mind getting sticky?"

"Sticky?"

"Babe, even if I paint as carefully as I can, my magic

hands might drip a little bit before I can lick this hot fudge off your naked body."

"That's going to make a mess," she said, not really caring.

"That's what bubble bath is for," he assured her. "I assume you have bubbles."

Bubbles?

Ten minutes ago she'd been wallowing in misery, sure her life sucked hard. And now? Now she had Caleb, with his tub of vanilla ice cream, his gorgeous smile and an intuitive understanding of her that nobody, not even her best friend, had ever had.

He made her feel so many things. Sexual and passionate. Exciting and fun. Brave and strong and interesting.

But most of all, he made her feel safe. Like it was okay to stand in the middle of the room and make a fool of herself. Like he accepted and appreciated her. All of her.

And now he wanted to feed her dessert, then take a bubble bath with her. Yes, it was sexual. But she knew it was more than that. She could see it in his body language. In the set of his shoulders and the concern on his face.

He was doing it to make her feel better.

"I do have bubbles," she said, trying not to giggle at the image of the ultramasculine Caleb Black surrounded by frothy floral-scented bubbles.

And from the terrified nerves jumping through her system at her realization. She was in love with him.

That wasn't the plan. It was crazy. It was a huge mistake. And she didn't care. She wasn't going to let herself. Not right now. It might not be her path, but it was a wonderful place to be. And just for now, she was going to give herself the gift of enjoying it.

"And I'll be happy to share my bubbles with you," she assured him as she grabbed a blanket off the couch and laid it in front of the Christmas tree. "Right after we find out who can get whom stickier."

"You smell like flowers," Fifi observed as Pandora swept into the store the next day. "Is that a new perfume?"

"Bubble bath," she told the blonde, winking. "I'm going to get started on the cookies and desserts for today's lunch crowd, okay? Can you handle the store yourself?"

"Russ is in soon, I'll be fine," Fifi assured her.

Pandora winced. She'd forgotten Russ was starting today. Adding that to her to-do list, she headed back to the café and its tiny kitchen. As she went, though, she heard the whispers start.

Like a wave, the words flowed toward her, softly at first, then crashing in a big splash. *Caleb Black. Dumped the poor sweet sheriff. What could she be thinking? Poor mother, had to come home to fix it.*

Pandora's feet froze on the threshold of the café. A part of her wanted to turn around and face the gossips. To insist they say it to her face so she could refute their words. The rest of her wanted to run into the back room as fast as she could, tugging her hair as she went to relieve the pressure on her brain.

She wasn't going to think about it, she decided as she forced her feet to move. She couldn't. Her mother had told her to choose a path and this was the one she was on. She was in love with Caleb Black. And if that meant dealing with gossip, then she'd deal.

Washing her hands, she let the water trickle over her skin, warming her and easing the tension. Eyes closed, she took some deep breaths and tried to center herself.

Out the kitchen window, a movement caught her eye. Three scruffy-looking guys were arguing in the alley. She frowned, realizing one of them was Russ. What was he doing back there?

Then one of them took a swing at another. She gasped, stepping back and cringing. Before she could go get the phone to call Tobias for help, a fourth guy waded in.

Pandora's heart calmed. Sheriff Kendall. He'd deal with

it. Remembering her mother's warning about chasing miseries, she turned away. She didn't want to see, hear or experience anything else that stirred up tension, so she ignored the rest of the drama and got to work. She had cookies to bake, sandwiches to prep and éclairs to pipe.

An hour later, she was still in her Zen mood as she arranged half the cookies on a large silver platter and the others in to-go boxes.

"Darling, this is wonderful," her mother drawled as she swept into the tiny kitchen, mingling the scent of peanut butter and chocolate with the aroma of Chanel and the nag champa incense she always burned at home. "I love the ambience. And these tables are so adorable. It's so clever, the way you've used the red soy candles in the dish of rose quartz. Love and lust, with just enough liking to keep things from getting sticky, hmm?"

Her Zen shot all to hell, Pandora just shrugged. She knew she was pouting like a brat, but she didn't want to face her mother yet. She'd been happily distracted by Caleb. Incredible sex and the realization that she was falling in love was enough for any girl to handle for one morning, wasn't it?

"Darling, don't be in a snit. You came home for a reason, didn't you?" As soon as Pandora opened her mouth to say that yes, she'd come home because she needed a job, Cassiopeia waved her hand. "And it had nothing to do with that drama you'd fallen into. That was just an excuse. A crossroads, if you'd like. It was time for you to face your destiny, and fate obviously felt you needed a nudge to get you to do so."

"Right. Being under police suspicion, used by the man I was sleeping with and then fired from my job were all the work of fate," Pandora snipped.

"Of course not. Those were all the result of your choices, dear. Not bad or good choices, mind you. Simply ones you made without stopping to listen to your intuition. Fate just used them to move you along."

"Mom, stop," Pandora barked, perilously close to tears again. Was anyone on earth as frustrating as her mother? "I obviously have no intuition. So will you please let it go? I'm never going to be what you'd like. I wish you'd just accept that I'm a failure as an Easton so we can both relax."

Stepping back so fast her rust-and-hunter-green caftan caught on the corner of the counter, Cassiopeia gave a shocked gasp and slapped her hand over her heart. Even though her shoulders were tense with anger and her stomach was tight with stress, Pandora almost giggled. Nobody did the drama show quite like her momma.

"A failure? That's ridiculous," Cassiopeia snapped. She lifted her chin so her red curls swept over her shoulders, and crossed her arms over her chest in the same gesture Pandora herself used when she was upset. "Let's not confuse things here, young lady. You're not angry with me."

"No? Care to bet on that?"

"You're angry with yourself. And with good reason. You can't blame me for your choices, Pandora. Or for your inability to step up and accept responsibility for making them."

Pandora felt as if she'd just been punched in the gut and couldn't find her own breath. Yes, she'd made a mistake. But the mistake was that she'd trusted the wrong person. That she'd fallen in love with the idea of love, and overlooked the warning signs. Blinking tears away, she wanted to yell that she wasn't irresponsible. But her throat was too tight to get the words out.

"Until you trust yourself, you'll never see what's right in front of you," Cassiopeia said with a regal toss of her curls. "You're too busy being scared, running and doubting. And, sadly, placing blame instead of having faith in yourself."

"You have no idea what it's like," Pandora snapped.

Fury was red, hazing her vision and letting truths fly that she'd spent most of her life hiding from. "I grew up in the shadow of your reputation."

"And you have a problem with my reputation?" Behind the haughtily raised brows and arch tone, Pandora heard a hint of hurt. But the words were already tumbling off her tongue and she couldn't quite figure out how to grab them back.

"I couldn't live up to your reputation, Mother. Nobody could. Especially not with everyone in town poking and judging me, and you always prodding me to find something that we both know damn well doesn't exist."

Cassiopeia sagged. As though someone had let the air out of her, her shoulders, face and chin drooped. She gave a huge sigh, then shook her head as if defeated.

"I can't do this again, Pandora. You refuse to hear me. You snub my guidance while hiding behind your insecurities." She swept a hand through her hair, leaving the curls a messy tangle around a face that suddenly looked older than her years. "Perhaps it's my fault. Not, as you seem to think, for being myself. I see nothing wrong with being the best I can and embracing my strengths. But I must have gone wrong somewhere if you're so afraid of life that you have to blame me."

Guilt was so bitter on Pandora's tongue she couldn't get any words past it. Just as well, since she had no idea what the words would be.

"I'm going home," her mother declared. "When you're ready to talk…if you're ready to talk, I'll be there for you."

Pandora didn't know if she wanted to call her back, to try to fix the mess they'd left splattered between them. Or if she wanted a little time and distance, at least until she figured out what she wanted to say.

But, as usual, it wasn't up to her. Her mother swept from the room, taking all the choices with her.

"So what's the deal? You're finally willing to talk? Or are you just stopping by to check out the bikes?"

Hands shoved in the front pockets of his jeans, Caleb grimaced at his father's words. He looked around the showroom of the bike shop, noting the gleaming chrome of the custom hogs and a few Indians and shrugged. "They are pretty sweet-looking bikes."

"Yeah, they are," Tobias agreed. He patted the diamond-tucked leather of one seat and nodded. "Best game in town, too. I get the parts dirt cheap, Lucas puts them together for a song and I sell them at a profit of about one, one-fifty percent."

"Sounds like a legit business to me."

"I told you, son. I've gone straight."

"Why do I find that hard to believe?" He wanted to. He'd spent most of his childhood wishing and hoping to hear his dad say those words. Hell, the last thing he'd told his old man before he'd left for college was that he wasn't coming home until the guy was clean. But when Tobias had called two years back with that same claim, Caleb hadn't bought it.

And now?

"There's plenty of challenge in making this place turn a profit. Between figuring out how to lure in the gullible and get them to open their wallets for a custom bike, special maintenance plans, yearly trade-ins and upgrades, I'm finding plenty to do."

"As challenging as scamming the head of a national bank out of five hundred large? How does customer service stack against selling bridge investments?" Caleb looked around the shop, noting that like everything his father owned, it was pristine, upscale and just a little edgy. "Does monthly inventory give you the same thrill as selling a fake Renoir to a reclusive art buff?"

Tobias's grin, so much like Caleb's own, flashed as he dropped onto a long, glittery red Naugahyde bench that spanned the center of the showroom. "Those were good times, I have to admit. But these are, too. The key to anything in life is to have fun with it, Caleb. If you're enjoying what you do, you'll live a happy, fulfilled life."

One of the pearls of wisdom Tobias had shared many a time with his children over the years. And frustratingly enough, the one that had been ricocheting around Caleb's head for the least year as he'd fought burnout and disenchantment.

"So tell me the truth, son. Why are you really here?"

"To see your shop." Caleb sidestepped. Then he shoved his hands into his pockets and sighed. Or to figure out who he really was, or some stupid touchy-feely thing like that.

Pulling his face in consideration, Tobias gave a slow nod. He got to his feet and walked ov , patting Caleb on the shoulder before stepping around him and heading toward the back room.

Since that's the part of the shop Caleb really wanted to see, he followed.

The room was huge, with a mechanic's bench against one wall, toolboxes and an air compressor along another. He noted an open door leading to a bathroom.

"Here, have a cookie," Tobias invited, gesturing to a tray as he sat down at a small table. "The pretty little gal across the alley made them. Supposed to do wonders for your sex drive."

"I hear yours is doing wonders on its own. Isn't dating a woman your daughter's age something of a cliché?"

Tobias's grin was wide and wicked. He tilted his chair back, balancing on two spindle legs and considered the cookie in his hand as if he'd find the answer in one of the chocolate chips.

"Now, why are you really here? You're ready to quit that misguided cop job?"

Caleb realized that he didn't even feel surprise at Tobias's insight. The man was an expert. At reading people, at twisting situations, at understanding human nature. And as much as Caleb might have wished otherwise over the past thirty years, the old guy was his father.

"I think I'm done," he heard himself admit. Grimacing, he took a cookie. Maybe chewing would give him time to censor his mouth.

"I followed your career, son. You did yourself, and me, proud. Whatever you do next, I'm sure you'll be just as good."

Overcome with an emotion he couldn't quite identify, Caleb looked away. How odd was it that he'd just realized that no matter what his choices, no matter what he'd done in his life, his father had always believed in him.

He didn't know what the hell to do with that.

Before he could figure it out, something outside the small, barred window overlooking the alley caught his eye. Caleb ambled over, looking out just in time to watch two dirtbags exchange a fat wad of cash for several large pill bottles. He'd been right. This was the main drop spot. But why here?

"Do you have storage in the back?" he asked over his shoulder.

Tobias took his time selecting another cookie before he met Caleb's eyes. "Nope. But the pretty little gal does."

Son of a bitch. Pain, fury and disappointment all pounded through Caleb. Son of a freaking bitch.

How could it be Pandora? He felt like scum just thinking of her and drugs in the same thought. But this? They were using her storage unit, her store. Did she have a clue? Whether she did or not, this was going to be a major problem for her.

Caleb dropped his head against the window and closed his eyes, fury and despair ripping through him.

He'd reluctantly come home to clear his father's dubious name. But he didn't want to do it at the expense of the woman he loved.

11

CALEB CLICKED OPEN the file of mug shots Hunter had emailed. Impressed, despite himself, he had to admit the FBI had better toys than he'd had access to with the DEA. Within an hour of calling Hunter with a report of what he'd seen, a laptop had been delivered to his hotel, access codes had been texted to his cell phone and he'd had the files of eight guys who fit the description of both dudes he'd seen selling behind Pandora's store.

Throw in Russ, whose identity didn't match the info on his job application, and Caleb figured he'd nailed down the drug ring's middle-management team.

What he didn't have yet was the person calling the shots.

He took a drink of coffee, letting the flavor mingle with the rest of the bitterness he'd been tasting since he realized that the woman he was crazy for might be a criminal.

He'd been so sure she was clean. Just as he'd been sure Tobias was clean. He'd only dug into her computer files so he could tell Hunter that he'd done a thorough job.

Then he'd read the files Hunter had emailed detailing the illegal activities of her drug-dispensing ex and her part in his little prescription ring. And the note Hunter had attached warning Caleb not to do anything stupid.

What a pal.

Caleb considered pounding his head on the wall a few

times, but figured he couldn't afford the possible loss of more brain cells.

Instead, he was going to ID the two guys, round them up and scare the crap out of them. Sooner or later, someone would spill a name. Or the boss would come looking for them.

Just as he started scrolling through the faces, there was a knock on his door.

He considered ignoring it. He wanted to ID this guy while the face was still fresh in his head. Then, he wanted to hit something—anything—hard, until it broke into a million pieces and left his knuckles bloody and raw.

But whoever was at the door might have another package from Hunter. And Caleb was definitely curious to see what other toys his old friend had to offer.

As a precaution, he closed the file, shut down the program and turned off the laptop. It was a secure machine, requiring two passwords, his own and the one Hunter had provided, to start it or pull it out of the hibernation it'd enter if left idle for more than thirty seconds. But still, it paid to be cautious.

He strode over and pulled the door open.

Well, well.

Not a toy from Hunter, but a toy all the same.

"Pandora," he greeted with a stiff smile.

For a brief second, he missed the old days when he'd opened the door to gun-toting, drugged-out, murdering dealers looking to take him out.

At least he knew what to do with them.

"Hey," she greeted with a shaky smile. Eyes narrowing, Caleb saw the strain on her face. Her makeup was all smudged and drippy, as if she'd been crying.

Yeah, a strung-out dude pointing a loaded .45 at his face would definitely be easier.

But not as important, he admitted to himself, heaving a heavy sigh.

"What's wrong?" he asked.

"Do you mind if I come in?"

Yes.

He stepped aside anyway.

And tortured himself by breathing deep as she walked past, inhaling her spicy fragrance and wishing he could bury his face in the curve of her neck and see if she tasted as good as she smelled.

Stupid.

Totally freaking stupid.

Because he knew damn well she tasted delicious.

"Are you okay?" he asked after a few seconds of indulging himself by staring at her as she wandered the room. She shouldn't be here. But he couldn't kick her out. Whatever her part in this, even if it wasn't purely innocent, he wanted—needed—this time with her.

"I'm…" She stopped by the window, giving him a pained look over her shoulder. "I had a blowup with my mother. Now I guess I'm confused."

"Parents have that effect," he observed. Finally giving in to the fact that running down the hall to avoid confronting her would be blatantly chickenshit, Caleb shut the door. He didn't cross the room, though. Instead, he leaned his hip against the dresser and watched.

"I know you're probably busy. You're not expecting me. But, well, I thought about going by Kathy's, but her family is in town and it'll be really crowded and loud there. And I just wanted to see if, you know, maybe…"

She trailed off, offering a wincing sort of shrug as she wandered the room nervously.

What was he going to do? Kick her out? Grill her when she was already upset? Yes, he knew that both were perfectly solid methods to deal with a potential drug-dealing mastermind. But, dammit, this was Pandora. And she was upset.

So he'd stay and comfort her. After all, he could be a chickenshit here in his room, too.

"What happened?"

"Confrontations and ugly words and painful truths," she confessed, trailing her fingers over the glossy knotty pine of one of the four posts of the large, quilt-covered bed.

"Sounds like a family reunion to me." Although he and his father had skipped over that part of reunioning. Instead, the old man had watched with laser-sharp eyes as Caleb had stepped to the side of the window so as not to be seen while the drug deal went down. Tobias hadn't said a word, though. He'd just arched one brow and given a jaunty salute when it was over and Caleb had said he had to go.

All that cordial silence had creeped him out.

"Not my family," Pandora said with a stiff smile. "Usually my mother is dramatic, I'm quiet and we both pretend everything is peachy keen."

She needed to talk. He could see it on her face, hear it in her tone. The previous night she'd needed sex, a little laughter and a chance to forget about everything else.

Caleb sighed, feeling the weight of the world pressing down on him all of a sudden. The sex was probably off-limits while she was a suspect, and the laughter was beyond him.

Dammit, that left talking.

He sucked at talking.

As Pandora poked a finger between the balcony curtains, closed against the night, he sighed again.

Fine.

"Want to have a seat?" he invited.

Her face brightening, she looked around. The choices were the bed or one of two club chairs next to the small table holding the laptop.

He really didn't want her near, either.

"I would, thanks," she said, taking a second to shrug off her thick white coat, laying it and her purse and scarf over one of the chairs. She hesitated, glancing at the bed, then back at his face. Then she squished into the chair alongside her coat.

Caleb walked over, picked up the laptop and moved it to the dresser, then sat across from her.

"So why's it a big deal that you tossed a few truths at your mother?"

"Because she tossed a few right back at me," she said with a wince.

He grinned for the first time in hours. "Don't you hate it when that happens?"

"I do. I had no idea the truth could be so painful. I think it was easier when she blithely pretended to go along with my claims that I was happy with my life."

"Pretending is never good."

"Sure, that's easy for you to say. You're confident enough to say screw you to everyone who doesn't accept you exactly as you are," she said with a rueful sort of laugh.

Cringing, Caleb's gaze shifted toward the door.

Was he? He didn't even know who he was, so how could he expect anyone to accept him at face value? For his entire adult life, hell, most of his life as a whole, he'd played a part.

"I admire that," she continued. She gave him a shy sort of smile and traced designs on her scarf with her finger. "I wish I were more like you. Only, not, you know. Because I really, really like being a girl with you."

He wasn't an expert on this talking thing, but he knew when someone was trying to sidestep to get out of delving into the deeper emotional stuff. And he shouldn't let her get away with it. She was hurting, and she probably should get it all out, talk and vent and spew and whatever the hell else women did to heal.

Miserably uncomfortable now, Caleb wished he'd paid more attention to Maya when she'd done this kind of thing growing up. That girl had always been talking.

"I guess you have a pretty good handle on your life, hmm?" she said, still sidestepping, though now poking her toes into his business. "You and your dad made up, you're free to come and go as you please. Or, you know, stay if you wanted."

Hey, now. Sidestepping was one thing. Poking into his life? Totally not cool. This was about her problems. Not his.

He leaned forward to tell her just that.

"We didn't make up," he heard himself saying, instead.

"But you went to the party?"

"Yeah."

"And didn't you hang out at his shop earlier?"

Caleb's eyes narrowed. Had she seen him while he was watching the drug deal go down? Was this a setup?

"He stopped by for lunch and mentioned what a great visit the two of you had," she continued, now watching her fingers poke through the scarf's fringe instead of meeting his eyes. "He was sweet. Teased me a little about the two of us, and said he liked me."

A hint of color warming her cheeks, she finally glanced up and gave Caleb a tiny smile. The kind that made him think of shy little girls sitting on Santa's lap, feeling like the most special princess in the world for those two minutes.

"He does like you," Caleb said absently, trying to figure out what Tobias was doing. That the old man was up to something was a no-brainer. But why did it involve Pandora? An inkling, a tiny germ of a hint, started poking at the back of Caleb's brain. He couldn't see it clearly yet, but the same instincts that had saved him from multiple bullets told him it was there.

"He's a good guy," she said quietly. Then she wrinkled her nose and asked, "Am I not supposed to say that? I mean, if you guys didn't make up, you probably don't want to hear someone singing his praises, huh?"

"No," Caleb realized. "I don't mind. I mean, he's easy to like."

"He really is," she agreed, reaching over to brush her hand over his. He turned his fingers to capture hers, making her smile. "So is my mother. If you can get past her larger-than-life perfection."

"Is that a bad thing?" he asked, using a method straight out of Witness Grilling 101. Ask open-ended questions that kept the other person guessing as to what you wanted to hear. They were more likely to go with an unscripted gut response.

"Not totally bad. I mean, she's fun and always makes people laugh. She's got flare and talent and, well, she's just so exuberant and alive. She walks in a room and everyone automatically gravitates to her."

"So why are you so unhappy with her?"

She sighed, staring blankly across the room as she considered that question. He noticed that there was now an actual hole in the knitted scarf from her digging at the yarn.

"Because of all those same reasons." Her smile was a little shaky. "I mean, that's a lot to live up to, you know? She's larger than life. People all around the world know who she is. Then they look at me with this puzzled stare, like they are trying to figure out where she went wrong."

Caleb gave a shake of his head.

"What?" she asked.

"You just described me and my dad."

Her laugh was more a puff of air than amusement. She shook her head. "What are we supposed to do about it?"

He threw his hands in the air. "I don't know. I mean, they do a great job of being who they are."

"I think you do a great job of being who you are, too. So why is not being like them a problem? I don't know about you, but I'm tired of being measured by my mother."

Thin ice. Caleb hesitated before going with his gut. "But I think the only one measuring you by that is, well, you."

There went the sweet look off her face. She pulled back,

her eyes narrowed and her lips tight. She looked as if she was seriously considering smacking him with that scarf.

"Me?" she asked in a tone so arch it was worthy of a queen.

"I guess I have an outsider's perspective," he mused. "I see a town that likes you, one that's actually a little defensive of you, if all the warnings I got not to hurt you are anything to go by. I see an intriguing, attractive woman trying her hand at something new and succeeding. A woman who loves cats, cooks like a dream and always has a smile and a warm word for people. Maybe you're not flamboyant and wild, like your mother. But you're just as interesting, and even more beautiful."

Her smile was bright enough to light the room. Caleb shifted uncomfortably in his chair, wanting to duck out until she stopped beaming at him. This gallant thing was more Gabriel's style than his. But he hadn't been able to stand seeing that dejected look on her face.

"So, I didn't bring any treats," Pandora said out of the blue, nibbling on her lip in a way that made him want to beg for a taste.

"Treats?"

"Yeah. Cookies or chocolate sauce or, well, you know. Aphrodisiacs." She shrugged again, knotting together the frayed pieces of yarn to repair her scarf. "I really didn't intend to come over. I was upset when I left the store and instead of walking home, my feet brought me here. To room seventeen."

Her words ended in a wistful tone he didn't understand. What he did understand was the look in her eyes. Sexy and appreciative. Warm and sweet. God, she was incredible.

Unable to resist, Caleb leaned forward and brushed his lips over hers. She tasted so freaking good. His tongue traced the full pillow of her lower lip, then he nipped lightly.

Her gasp was followed by a low moan of approval. She skimmed the tips of her fingers over his jaw, whisper-soft and so gentle. It was all he could do not to grab her by the waist and carry her over to the bed.

Caleb pulled away and jumped to his feet. Pacing, he shoved one hand through his hair.

What was he doing? She was the prime suspect in an FBI drug case. He should at least settle a few questions before he settled himself between her thighs.

"I can go," she said quietly, her hand dropping away from the buttons of her silk top.

It killed him to see that hurt on her face. To hear the self-protective distance in her tone.

It really all came down to faith.

He'd told Hunter he was sure his old man was innocent. But a part of him, the part that knew that there was a potential criminal in everyone, had wondered.

But Pandora? At the moment, all evidence pointed toward her. With what he'd seen, what he knew and what he'd heard, he'd have felt solid making an arrest.

But his instincts said otherwise. They said she was everything he'd ever wanted in a woman. Sweet and hot and adventurous. And, dammit, innocent.

So while he might be suffering from plenty of burnout and his instincts were raw nerves at this point, he had to listen to them. Because without that, he was nothing.

He'd just have to prove the evidence wrong.

PANDORA WOKE THE NEXT morning with a feeling of absolute contentment. Eyes still closed, she stretched on the lavender-scented sheets and gave a deep sigh of satisfaction.

Yum. What a delicious night.

Shifting to the pillow next to her, she smiled and slowly opened her eyes. Caleb stared back at her, his gold eyes intense and, if she read him right, concerned. Why?

"Hi," she murmured, shifting back a little to get a better look at him. Stiff shoulders, jaw tight. He seemed distant, as if a part of him wasn't even here in bed with her.

Pandora shivered a little, then ran her tongue over her lower lip. What was going on?

But before she could ask, someone knocked on the door.

"Company?" she asked quietly, suddenly realizing she was naked except for the soft rays of morning light. She grabbed the sheet and quilt and pulled them higher.

"Probably Mrs. Mac with another delivery. Or muffins. She thinks I'm going to starve if I don't start each day with a half-dozen blueberry crumbles."

He sounded normal. But he still looked…fake.

"Hang on," he said, shifting out of bed and pulling on jeans, commando-style. He zipped them, but didn't bother with the snap.

Pandora's mouth watered. God, he was gorgeous. Sleek, tanned skin. That wolf tattoo crawling down his shoulder to growl from the gorgeous muscles of his upper arms. She wanted to nibble her way down the small of his back, then bite him. Right there on the butt.

Grinning to herself, she shifted to a more comfy position. Starting the day with muffins and, hopefully, morning sex was a definite positive in her books.

"I could—"

"No," he said, shaking his head as he reached for the doorknob. "Wait there. I'll get rid of her. We need to talk."

She wasn't sure how scooting off to the bathroom for a very necessary morning function, to say nothing of hiding from whoever was on the other side of the door, would stand in the way of talking. But he sounded so weird that she didn't argue.

She watched Caleb peer through the door's peephole. He instantly pulled back and whispered something that sounded like a curse. Shoulders so tense his back looked like something in one of those men's muscle magazines, she heard him suck in a breath, then release it before opening the door.

He only opened it a few inches, though. With his body

shielding her view, she could only surmise that it wasn't Mrs. Mac with muffins.

"Yeah?"

Her brows drew together at Caleb's impatient tone. Then she heard a man's voice. Deep, melodious and compelling.

"Party time," the voice said.

"You have the invitations already?"

Invitations? Party?

"All but the party planner. I'm counting on you for that."

Her frown deepened as she listened to the conversation. What the hell were they talking about?

"Let me in. We have to talk."

"Later."

"Now. Time's become an issue."

Caleb glanced over his shoulder at Pandora. The look in his eyes made her shiver just a little, it was so calculating. She felt bad for the guy on the other side of the door, since she was sure he was the reason for it.

"The hall?"

"Unsecure."

"You're a pain in the ass. You know that, right?" But Caleb stepped back and let the door swing open. "The balcony. Not a word."

Pandora gulped as the second man stepped through the door. Too stunned to be embarrassed, she just stared.

Holy cow.

Pure masculine intensity. He wasn't pretty, his face was too strong for that. But still, the sculpted features, long-lashed blue eyes and full lips did make quite a picture. His black hair swept off his forehead, longer in front and short in back. He stopped just inside the door when he saw her. Those vivid eyes cut over to Caleb and he arched a brow. Pandora tried to read his body language, but he was a blank. She didn't see even a hint of surprise on his part. Like walking into his friend's hotel room and finding a naked woman in bed was the norm.

The man gave Pandora a slight nod, his eyes doing a quick scan of the room, then he stepped over and opened the sliding door to the balcony.

"This might be a while," Caleb said, grabbing his sweatshirt off the footboard before following his friend to the balcony door.

"It's okay. I have to get to the store anyway," she told him with a warm smile. "I'll see you later, right?"

He gave her a long, intense look that made her stomach swoop into her toes. Then he nodded and stepped through, closing the curtain along with the door.

It wasn't until both men were on the other side of the glass with the door firmly closed that she realized Caleb hadn't introduced his friend.

Not that it mattered. She had her man.

And she missed him already.

Grinning at her own goofiness, Pandora tugged the sheet loose from the mattress to wrap it securely around her body, then slid from the bed. She padded over to the sliding glass door that led to the balcony and peered around the curtain.

Yep. Gorgeous and sexy. Both of them.

Giggling a little to herself, she did a mangled skip-step hindered by the sheet on her way to the bathroom.

Time to start her day. She had a feeling it was going to be an excellent one.

"Tacky, Black."

Caleb shrugged, tugging the gray fleece over his head in a useless attempt to ward off the morning chill. California or not, winter mornings were damn cold here in the mountains.

"What broke?" he prompted. He wanted the reason for Hunter's unexpected, and untimely, arrival. He did not want to discuss Pandora, his rotten choices, or what a jerk he was.

"I tugged a few more strings. Ran some numbers, looked at a few different accounts."

As if his toes weren't freezing, Caleb patiently waited.

"I know who the ringleader is," Hunter declared.

Caleb crossed his arms over his chest and arched one brow.

Hunter gave him a long look. Then, his fingers stuffed in the pockets of a very warm-looking overcoat, he nodded.

"You already know."

Even though it wasn't a question, Caleb answered anyway. "I'm pretty sure I do. Did you run the records I asked?"

"Yeah. All the names you provided had arrests that led back to the same person. Why didn't you email me with your suspicions?"

"I figured they might. These guys aren't local to Black Oak, so they had to have connected somewhere. Jail was the easy answer. I figured that'd be a good place for a clever drug dealer to recruit his team." Which was true. But it didn't answer Hunter's question. So Caleb admitted, "I didn't let you know because I don't know if he's working alone or not."

"You're worried about your girlfriend? I couldn't clear her."

Faint though it was, layered there beneath the official tone, Caleb could hear the regret in Hunter's voice. His old friend was hard-line about the law, but he didn't enjoy hurting people. Caleb flexed his shoulders and shook his head.

"It doesn't matter. Whatever you've got, it's bullshit. Because I know Pandora. She's not involved. Not knowingly."

Hunter didn't say a word. He just offered up that enigmatic stare of his. Caleb had lost a lot of poker money to that stare over the years. He wasn't losing Pandora.

"Just wait," he said, wincing, but unable to resist the cliché. "I'll prove it."

12

PANDORA WAS ALMOST skipping when she stepped into Moonspun Dreams an hour later. A night of wild sex with a gorgeous man without any aphrodisiacal aid had done wonders for her attitude.

Well, that and the little pep talk from Caleb the night before had made her realize she needed to come to terms with her issues. After a night of sweet, sexy loving, she figured she was in just the right mood to try to make nice with her mother.

"Hi, Paulie," she said, bending down to rub her fingers over the silky black fur of the cat's purring head. "You having a good morning, too?"

"Hey, Pandora," Fifi greeted, coming out from the back room with an armful of fluffy handwoven blankets. "We can't keep enough of these on the sales floor. I'm blown away at how much demand there is for all this homemade, organic stuff you've brought in."

"I think it's a cyclic thing," Pandora said, straightening up and crossing over to give Bonnie's ears the same loving attention she'd offered Paulie. "Twenty years ago, holistic was all the rage. I'll bet in ten more, it'll be back to New Age glitz."

Something she'd do well to remember.

"Is my mother here?" she asked, heading back to the office to put away her purse.

"Um, no," Fifi said with a grimace.

"Something wrong?"

"I'm not sure. I mean, I know you're running the store now, but I'd thought that, you know, when Cassiopeia was back in town, she'd be involved. At least to do readings or something."

"Well, yeah," Pandora agreed slowly, turning to face her assistant. "Of course she will. That's what she does. We've had dozens of calls while she was gone, and people are going to be lining up to see her now that she's back. So what's the problem?"

"Well, you left right after your mother, so I didn't get to mention it. But I asked Cassiopeia on her way out if she wanted me to start booking readings. She said not until she found a place to do them." Fifi scrunched her nose, looking as if she might cry. "What's going on?"

Pandora shrugged a shoulder that was suddenly as heavy as lead. Like the fragile flame of a candle, her happy, upbeat morning disappeared into a puff of stress.

"What do I tell people?" Fifi prompted. "I've already had a few calls and I don't know what to say. Is she going to come back?"

Pandora almost said that Fifi should tell them to find a new psychic. Lying on the counter with her black-and-white face looking so patient, Bonnie caught her eye, making her wince. Besides being immature and spiteful, doing something like that would sink the store.

"I don't know," Pandora said, biting her bottom lip and trying to figure out how they were going to deal with this. "I guess she's upset about…" Pandora being an ungrateful brat who blamed her momma for her problems instead of pulling up her big-girl panties and facing them herself.

"Something or other. I can call her later, see if we can get this fixed."

As soon as she said the words, the throbbing in her temples faded and her earlier euphoria returned. Yep, all she had to do was take charge and have a good attitude. No more hiding and running.

"I'm glad. I was telling Russ about the readings last night, how totally accurate they are." Fifi's grin made it clear that she'd been sharing a lot more than store gossip with the new guy. "He's a little scared to get one, but maybe after he sees how much people like them, he'll change his mind."

Pandora's gaze cut to her newest employee, who stood out like an awkward third wheel as he tried to help a customer choose between tumbled carnelian or a citrine spear. At least she supposed he was trying to help. It couldn't be easy with his hands hidden behind his back.

"Um, Fifi," she said with a grimace, nodding at Russ. "I know he's only been here a couple of days, but he's got to get past that skittish thing he's got going on."

Fifi scrunched her nose and gave a little sigh. "He's great with some of the customers. Younger ones, you know? He's bringing them in left and right. But with our regulars…" She winced as he held out a handkerchief to take the handful of stones the customer had chosen. "Maybe I told him too many stories about how powerful you and your mom are?"

"Sorry, what?" Pandora asked. The rest of the room faded as she stared at Fifi with wide eyes.

"Well, you know. You're the Easton women. Your gramma was a witch, right? And your mom is a famous psychic. You're so amazing with reading people, and then you made an even bigger splash with the café and all those aphrodisiacs. You always know just what to offer the customers, and how to keep them from getting all silly about it. Everyone talks about it. You're almost as big a legend now as Cassiopeia." Fifi glanced at Russ, who'd rung up the crystal purchase and was now by the books with a young guy who looked as though he should be shopping in the herbal-bath section. "I'm betting Russ is a little freaked, you know? I mean, he's a believer, so it's all kinda intimidating."

Pandora couldn't care less about Russ anymore. She was too stunned by the rest of Fifi's words. She thought Pandora was on the same level as Cassiopeia? Fifi and the customers considered her one of the gifted Easton women?

It was like being enveloped in the biggest, brightest hug in the world. Pandora's heart swelled. Her smile spread from ear to ear and tears sparkled in her eyes.

"You okay?" Fifi asked, her own eyes huge with worry.

With a shaky sigh, she forced herself to focus and pull it together. There was nothing empowering about sniveling like a baby over validation.

"Sure. Yeah," Pandora sniffed. "I'll call Cassiopeia and get this fixed. Go ahead and start taking tentative bookings, letting people know that they might change depending on her schedule."

She glanced at the café and added, "Be sure to make the bookings for after two, when the café is closed. That way she has as much time and space as she needs."

Four hours later, the store was filled with week-before-Christmas shoppers. Both locals and out-of-towners browsed, compared and purchased enough throughout the morning that Pandora was ready to do a happy dance on the sales counter. She'd barely had time to leave her mom a message, let alone worry about how she'd patch things up.

By the end of lunch, her feet hurt, her cheeks were sore from grinning and she was sure they'd just had the best sales day in Moonspun's history.

She'd just pulled up the numbers on the cash register to check, when there was a loud furor at the door.

She glanced up, but couldn't see what was going on because of the throng of bodies. Then she caught a glimpse of red curls.

Showtime.

Cassiopeia took her time crossing the room. She spoke with everyone, stopping to offer hugs and exclamations to friends and strangers alike. With Paulie draped over her shoulder like a purring fur stole, and her flowing hunter-green dress and faux-holly jewelry, she was the epitome of famous-psychic-does-holiday casual.

Pandora leaned against the counter and watched the show. She didn't realize she was grinning until Russ stepped closer and whispered, "Who is she? She's famous, right?"

Her smile faded as she looked at Moonspun's newest employee. Fifi had said she'd known him, like, forever. And hadn't his application indicated he'd lived here for years? How could he have lived in Black Oak for *any* length of time and not know who Cassiopeia was? Heck, everyone in the five neighboring towns knew her by sight.

Before she could ask, though, her mother swept close enough to catch her eye.

"Russ, will you help Fifi cover the store?" Pandora quietly asked him. "My mother and I will be in the back. Please, don't interrupt unless it's an emergency."

His pale brown eyes were huge. The guy was a basket case. He was probably afraid they were going to concoct some magic potion or poke pins in a doll.

It was kinda cute, in a silly sort of way. She just patted his arm, then walked over to her mother. She heard him sputtering behind her as she went.

"Mom, do you have a minute?" she said, interrupting her chat with Mrs. Sellers. "I'd really appreciate it."

"Oh, here I am hogging your time and you must want to see your daughter," Mrs. Sellers said with a sweep of her hand. "You probably have so much to discuss. And you must be so proud of Pandora. She's definitely a chip off the old block. Or in this case, a crystal off the sparkling quartz."

Pandora glanced at her mother's face, expecting to see at least a hint of disdain. Instead, she saw just what Mrs. Sellers indicated. Pride.

Joy, as warm and gooey as her Hot Molten Love chocolate cake, filled her. Had her mother ever looked at her like that before? Or had she always, and Pandora had ignored it since it meant she'd have to move that chip off her shoulder?

"Mom, I'm so glad you're here. People have been asking about you all day." Pandora came around the counter and held out her hand. She put as much love and apology into that move as she could. "They're hoping you'll be available for readings soon."

Her mother's smile trembled a little in the corners and her eyes filled before she blinked thickly coated lashes and tilted her head in thanks.

"I'm glad to be here as well, darling." She rubbed a bejeweled hand over Pandora's shoulder, then spoke to the room at large. "I'm going to be spending some time catching up with my daughter. But I'd love to do readings. Fifi, will you go ahead and set up appointments?"

The perky blonde nodded. Before she'd pulled out a small spiral-bound notebook, there was a line of excited customers in front of her.

"You've brought in a stellar crowd, darling. Shall we go back and celebrate with cake or something sweet?" Cassiopeia said to Pandora, twining her fingers through her daughter's in a show of both pride and solidarity.

Pandora didn't trust her voice, so she offered a smile and a nod instead. Before they got more than two steps, though, the bells chimed on the front door again. Pandora's heart raced when she glanced over and saw it was Caleb. His sexy friend was with him, and the two of them made such a sight. Pure masculine beauty, with a razor-sharp edge.

"Can we talk a little later?" she murmured to her mother.

"I'm glad to see you have your priorities straight," Cassiopeia returned quietly.

Pandora glanced over, trying to see if her mother was being sarcastic. But her vivid green eyes were wide with appreciation. She gave Pandora an arch look and mimicked fanning herself, then tilted her head. "Go say hello, dear."

"Caleb," Pandora greeted, crossing the room. She knew at least twenty sets of eyes were locked on her, but she didn't care. Not anymore. She reached out and took his hand, then, determined to push her own comfort envelope, leaned in and brushed an only slightly shaky kiss over his cheek.

There. That'd show everyone. She was dating that bad, bad Black boy and she didn't care who knew. Or what they thought.

"Hello," she murmured. She was so caught up in her own internal convolutions that it took her a few seconds to notice his lack of a response. Chilled a little, she stepped back to get a good look at his face.

Closed. His eyes were distant and cold. There was something there, in the set of his shoulders, that carried a warning. As if he was about to tell her a loved one had died. But she glanced around, making sure her mother and the two cats were still there, all her loved ones were front and center.

Her gaze cut to Hunter, who looked even more closed and distant. Was Caleb leaving with him? Was that why he was here? To tell her goodbye?

Then he smiled and wrapped his arm around her shoulder. Confused, Pandora stiffened, trying to figure out what was going on. He didn't feel right.

"Sweetheart, I've been telling Hunter how great your cooking is. We stopped by so he could check it out."

She glanced at Hunter, dressed in jeans and a black

sweater that should have been casual but wasn't. Yeah. He looked like a guy stopping by to sample cookies.

"Sure," she said, not having a clue what was happening. But it felt important, and secretive. So she'd wait until she had Caleb alone to ask. "Why don't you both come into the café. We have some pasta salad left, and sandwiches, of course. The cookies are fresh this morning and I have a wooable winterberry cobbler that's fabulous with vanilla-bean ice cream."

She babbled more menu options as she made her way through the curious onlookers, achingly aware of Caleb just a few inches behind her.

Once she and the two much-too-sexy-for-their-own-good men were in the café, though, she dropped the pretense.

"What's going on?" she asked, her gaze cutting from one to the other.

Their faces didn't calm her nerves at all. Instead, her stomach knotted and black spots danced in front of her eyes. Something bad was happening here.

"We have evidence that drugs are being run through your store. We want to use this space, today, to make the bust." The words were fast, clipped and brutal.

"Bust? Drugs?" Pandora's brain was reeling. "What? I don't understand."

Her knees weak, she grabbed on to a chair.

"Ms. Easton, there's a drug ring operating out of Black Oak. Caleb came to town to stop it. His investigation led to your store. We'd like your cooperation in apprehending the people behind the drugs, especially the ringleader."

She gaped. What the hell? Drugs? In her store? No. She'd changed the inventory, she knew every single item being sold here and unless saffron was now illegal, Moon-spun Dreams was clean.

But before she could worry about that, she had to sift through the fury pouring into her system like a tidal wave.

Betrayal raced behind it, adding a layer of pain to her reaction.

"Wait," she demanded, holding up one hand. She arched a brow at Caleb. "You're a cop? You're not unemployed?"

"No. I'm not a cop and I am unemployed." He was, however, as distant as the moon right now. She noted his body language, how he was leaning away from her, rolling on the balls of his feet as if he was going to run at any second.

"Actually, you're on hiatus since your captain hasn't accepted your resignation," Hunter interrupted.

Pandora pressed her fingers to her forehead, hoping the pressure would help her sort it all out.

"I don't understand," she muttered. She took a deep breath and looked at Caleb again. She could see the regret in his eyes, as if he knew he was ripping her heart to shreds and was sorry. But he was going to continue to rip anyway.

"You think I had something to do with this? The drugs?" Her voice shook and she wanted to throw up. It was like déjà vu times a thousand. The humiliation, the pain, the heartache…

"Caleb has cleared you," Hunter said when Caleb stayed silent.

Cleared her. As in, he'd found proof against her guilt. Guilt that he must have believed in at some point.

"You thought I was involved? That's why you asked me all those questions before. Why you kept coming around the store? Why you—" Why he'd made love with her? Would he go that far? They did in the movies, why not in real life?

"I'll step out," Hunter murmured.

The gentle clacking of beads indicated he'd left. But Pandora's eyes were locked on Caleb's.

"You used me?" she whispered, her throat aching as she forced the words out. "You thought I was a criminal? Was everything a lie? Or did I just convince myself that what we'd shared was special?"

"No."

"No?" she repeated, her voice hitting a few of the higher octaves. "That's it? Just no? Care to elaborate a little?"

He frowned, shoving his hands into his pockets. As he did, his jacket shifted so she could see leather straps. He was wearing a gun. The room spun. Afraid she was going to collapse, Pandora reached out to grab a chair again.

"Look, it's like this—"

Before he could tell her what this was like, a rush of cold air swept over them. Then there was a quiet snick as someone shut the door to the alley.

Who the hell was using her back door? Pandora and Caleb looked at each other, her eyes wide with curiosity. His were filled with a cold warning that scared her just a little. His hand shifted to his hip.

She gulped, her heart racing as she tried to figure out when her cute café had turned into a nightmare.

Then she realized who it was and relaxed.

"Sheriff," she greeted, her voice shaking a little. *Way too much going on today,* she thought.

"Pandora. Black," the lawman greeted. He'd looked shocked when he'd first stepped through the door, but now his face smoothed into a smile. "Am I interrupting something?"

"No," she said.

"Yes," Caleb retorted at the same time. "But I'm glad you did. C'mon over. Let's talk."

Kendall's easy grin shifted as he studied Caleb's face. He took a single step backward, glancing toward the alley door. Pandora frowned, nervously gripping her fingers together. There was way too much tension in this room. She glanced at Caleb, trying to figure out why.

Whoa. She'd have stepped back, too. Caleb's smile was just this side of vicious.

"It's good to see you both," the sheriff said after clearing his throat. "I was doing my rounds, checked up the street and the alley and figured I'd come in. I hear Cassiopeia is back in town. Is she here? We've got a lot to catch up on."

His hand on the butt of his service revolver, he gave them a wide berth as he sauntered out of the room.

Pandora slammed her fists on her hips and turned to Caleb to demand an explanation.

"Quiet," Caleb ordered.

So she hissed back, "What the hell is going on?"

"Does he do that often?" Caleb asked, his words low and even.

"Sure, once in a while. Mother gave him a key for security and such."

The grim satisfaction on his face worried her. This was all happening too fast. Caleb being a—whatever he was—questionably employed in some form of law enforcement? Drugs, in her store. The sexy, intriguing man she'd fallen for and shared her body with now acting like something out of a crime novel. Too much!

"Let's go," he said, his large hand wrapping around hers.

"Go?" She dug in her heels. "No, I want to know what's going on. I'm not going anywhere until I do."

"C'mon," he said, gently but firmly moving her toward the beaded doorway with him.

When they reached it, though, he stopped and looked at her. His eyes softened and he gave a barely perceptible sigh. "Just trust me. Please."

With that, and a quick kiss brushed over the top of her head, he pulled her through the beads.

It was like walking onto the set of a crime show, with Hunter playing the part of the sexy agent in charge. He stood behind Russ, one hand on the younger man's back as he faced down Kendall. There were a dozen or more shoppers milling around, whispering and jockeying for the best viewing positions.

"Damn right I'm questioning your jurisdiction," the sheriff snapped. "What the hell do you think you're doing, coming into my town and trying to arrest one of my people?"

"What?" Pandora gasped. She was halfway across the room—whether she was going to Russ's rescue or to smack him, she didn't know—when Caleb grabbed her arm.

Confused and angry, she shot him a glare.

"What'd you find?" Caleb asked, ignoring her, the sheriff and the rest of the crowd to speak directly to Hunter.

"He had the key and the dope in his jacket pocket."

Caleb gave a sigh that probably only Pandora noted. Then he nodded and after giving Pandora a look that said *stay put,* he approached Russ. He stopped a couple feet from the young man.

"So let's hear it," Caleb said. "Who are you working with and what's this store's connection?"

This store? Working with? Oh, God. He really did think she was involved. And now the entire town would, too. Pandora felt woozy as the room spun again. Dope. Drugs. Déjà vu. She was so grateful when her mother hurried over and took her hand.

"You might as well confess. It'll go easier on you," Caleb promised.

Why was he doing this here in the store? Was he trying to ruin her? Pandora gulped as tears filled her eyes again.

Along with the rest of the crowd, she watched Caleb take a step closer. Hunter moved to the front door to block it. Russ shifted away, backing down along the sales counter as if he could escape through the cash register.

He bumped into Bonnie, who was sitting on the counter, watching the show. She gave a low, throaty meow and butted him with her head.

"Git." Russ looked spooked, pushing the cat away.

But Bonnie meowed again, her head tilted to one side.

"What's she doing?" he muttered, a tinge of hysteria in his tone.

"She can read minds," Cassiopeia intoned melodiously.

"Nuh-uh." But Russ inched away from the black-and-white cat like he wasn't so sure.

"You might want to confess before she shares any of your secrets," Cassiopeia continued, sweeping her arm in an arc so the filmy fabric of her caftan flowed, wispy and ghostlike.

Bonnie meowed again.

Russ jumped. His gaze shot from person to person, locking for a long moment on the sheriff before he stepped closer to Caleb.

"I want a guarantee," he said, his voice shaking.

"Let's talk about this in my office," Kendall demanded. The guy looked totally stressed out and pissed, Pandora noted. His face was tense, and if she wasn't mistaken, that was fear in his eyes.

"We'll settle it here," Caleb said quietly. Pandora thought she saw an apology in the quick glance he threw her way, but then he was focused on Russ again. "Now."

"The guarantee?" Russ prodded.

His face impassive, Caleb walked across the room. Everyone held their breath, not sure what he was going to do to the young man. But he passed right by him and stopped next to the cat. Without taking his eyes off Russ, he swept his hand down Bonnie's head.

All eyes cut to Russ. The kid looked as if he was going to puke all over Pandora's imported astrology rug. He tugged at the hem of his T-shirt, his eyes nervously darting from Caleb to the sheriff.

"Who's your boss?" Caleb asked. "Your real boss."

Russ didn't even glance toward Pandora. Instead, he closed his eyes for a second, took a deep breath, then whispered, "Sheriff Kendall."

The chorus of gasps around the room was deafening.

Pandora pressed her hand against her stomach, afraid she might be the one to ruin the rug.

"Did he just accuse…?"

"He can't be saying that the sheriff…"

"Drugs? The sheriff? No…"

"I always knew he was shifty—"

"Enough," Caleb said. He didn't raise his voice or take his eyes off Russ, but the room immediately silenced.

"That's a major accusation."

"It's the truth."

"It's bullshit," Kendall said from the other side of the room. Furious, he looked as if he wanted to pull the gun from his hip and shoot someone. Tension expanded in the room like an overstretched rubber band, ready to snap at any second. Finally, thankfully, he slammed his arms over his chest instead, glaring at one and all.

Pandora met her mother's eyes, though, and tilted her head to indicate his stance. Shoulders rounded, chin low. He was lying. Her mother nodded in agreement.

"Who else?" Caleb asked quietly.

Pandora's heart raced. She glanced at Fifi, who had tears pouring down her face and had already chewed off three fingernails.

"Nobody. I mean, nobody I know."

She noted the set of his chin, the way his fingers were clenched together. She figured he was telling the truth. Her own shoulders relaxed.

"Why here? Why Moonspun Dreams?"

"I don't know. I mean, he, the sheriff, he said it was the most convenient place. That with all the changes going on, the customers being a little weird and all, it'd fly under the radar."

Offended, the "weird" customers muttered among themselves.

"You used the storage out back. How did the store owner not catch on?"

Russ shot Pandora a guilty look, his face miserable and just a little green. "Um, well, I used to come in and hang out. I pretended I wanted to learn about all this stuff. Cards and magic and all that. I flirted a little, convinced Fifi that I could help out. That's it. The ladies, they didn't know anything."

"As far as he knows," the sheriff interjected smoothly. He'd gone from sounding pissed to looking like a lawyer trying to convince his jury. "But I've been watching this place for weeks. Pandora's made a name for herself selling more than just those sandwiches and cookies she's always pushing. Everyone on the street knows to come to her for their pills. Her reputation precedes her. Just check."

Pandora's outraged gasp was drowned out by her mother's furious roar. But neither of them had even inhaled again before Caleb moved. He strode over, and without a word or warning, plowed his fist into Kendall's face with a loud, bloody crack.

His hand grabbing his nose, the sheriff stumbled backward. He glanced, wild-eyed, at the crowd, then ran toward the beaded curtain leading to the café.

He didn't make it, though. As usual, Paulie had plopped himself in the doorway to sleep. Pandora didn't know if the cat sensed the drama, or if all the noise bothered him, but he jumped up on all fours and scurried between the sheriff's feet, sending the man flying into the far wall with another loud crack to his face.

Cheers rang out, but Caleb didn't smile as he strode over and grabbed the guy, hauling him off the floor. He started reciting something, probably the Miranda Rights, but Pandora couldn't hear anything through the buzzing in her head.

She, along with what seemed to be half the town, watched the tall, dark and mysterious Hunter slap handcuffs on her newest employee while Caleb did the same to Sheriff Kendall. Her gut roiled with horror.

"Darling?"

She shook her head at her mother. She couldn't talk about it. Not now. Not here, in front of all the gawking eyes. It had been bad enough last time, when she'd come home to hide from her relationship with a failed criminal and everyone in town had whispered about her stupidity.

Now they were all here to watch, live and up close, as she confirmed it.

"Darling, come on. Let's go home. We'll have a nice pot of tea and some chocolate cake."

"No," Pandora said, sniffing as a single tear rolled down her cheek. She watched Caleb, one hand on the sheriff's back and the other on the gun holstered at his hip, stride out the door. He never looked back. "No. I don't think I ever want chocolate cake again."

_13_

"MORE TEA?" CASSIOPEIA asked, holding up her prized Hummel teapot she used for tea-leaf readings.

Her hands wrapped around her almost-empty cup, Pandora shook her head. "I should get back to the store. Or just go home."

Fifi had been a mess, blubbering and bawling as if she'd been the one arrested. Finally, calling it an executive decision, Cassiopeia had declared that the store be closed for the day.

"You need to go talk to Caleb, is what you need to do."

Pandora cringed, taking a sip instead of answering. The still-warm tea soothed her tear-ravaged throat. Then she stared into her cup, wishing she could find answers in the floating dregs.

"You've proven that you're a strong woman who knows what she wants and can make it happen," her mother continued, her voice both soothing and commanding. "Are you going to just let him go?"

"He lied to me. Worse, he made me look like a fool in front of everyone." Just remembering sent a hot flush of horrified embarrassment rushing through her. The whispers, the stares. It had been terrible.

"Dear, do you really think people care about that? They're so busy talking about Kendall that you're not even going to enter their heads. I'd imagine that's why Caleb played that scene out the way he did."

Pandora tore her eyes off her murky tea leaves to frown at her mother. "What do you mean?"

"He could have asked all those questions at the sheriff's office. Much easier, too, I'd imagine. He did that, made that big scene, just to make sure that people knew the drugs had nothing to do with you. That they had plenty of other things to talk about instead."

Pandora stared, first in shock, then in dawning hope. Her heart raced and she bit her lip. "Do you really think so?"

"What I think is that you need to go ask Caleb."

She was scared to. Pandora dropped her gaze back to her cup and took a shaky breath. She was afraid to hear that this had all been a scam on his part. That he'd used her.

Her mother gently laid her hand over hers and squeezed. "Darling, you have to face this. You can't move forward until you do."

"Is this why your clients all love you so much?" Pandora asked with a teary laugh. "Because you're so good at telling them what they need to do in a way that makes them feel great about themselves?"

"You mean because I'm a nice bully? Of course. Now listen to your mother and go get the answers you need."

Ten minutes later, her face washed and makeup reapplied, Pandora stood at the door of the sheriff's office. Her hand shook as she reached for the handle, so she pulled it back. Maybe she should wait. Come back later. Or better yet, take the week off from the store and wait to see what people really thought about the situation.

Then she realized that none of that mattered. All she cared about was what Caleb thought of her. So she took a deep breath of the cold night air and forced herself to grab the handle. Her knees were just as shaky as her hands, but she stepped through the entry.

Caleb wasn't there. She looked around the sterile, tan room, with its two desks and a few chairs scattered about. The walls and floor were bare, and the place smelled like burned microwave popcorn.

"Wow, Kendall is a sneaky liar *and* a lousy decorator," she muttered.

"Don't forget power abuser and drug pusher."

She jumped, her gaze flying across the room. Framed in the door leading to what she assumed must be the cells was Mr. Tall, Dark and Mysterious.

"Um, hi," she said to Hunter, shuffling nervously from her right foot to her left. "I came to see Caleb…?"

"He's finishing up the interrogation. He'll be out in a few minutes."

She nodded, then looked back at the door. Should she leave? She'd definitely rather, but something about Hunter's stare made it hard to run away.

She glanced back at him, then away again. Twining her trembling fingers together, she stared aimlessly around the ugly space.

"Would you like to sit?" Hunter asked, now leaning against the door frame in what she supposed was a casual pose. Except that he still looked as if he could kill a person with his pinkie.

"Um, no. I'll just… Um, maybe I should come back later?"

"Stay."

Command or request? Did it matter? Pandora bit her lip, then stepped farther into the room so she could set her purse on one of the desks.

"I've heard about your store. Intriguing. I didn't realize your cat was psychic, too, though." His tone was conversational, but his blue eyes danced with laughter.

A giggle escaped, and with it, some of Pandora's tension. Who knew, superhottie had a sense of humor. It was hard to look at him for too long, though. He was so intense.

If she wasn't in love with Caleb, she'd be stuttering and blushing and weaving all sorts of sexual fantasies.

"Bonnie's not psychic. She tilts her head because she had a series of ear infections when she was younger," Pandora replied, finally relaxing enough to lean against the desk. Then she paused, thinking back to both the cats' unnatural behavior toward Russ and Kendall. "I mean, as far as I know, she doesn't actually read minds."

His face impassive but his eyes still laughing, Hunter nodded and walked over to a small refrigerator and took out a bottle of water. He handed it to her with a small smile.

Wow. Maybe he wasn't that scary.

Pandora bit her lip, then unable to help herself, she blurted out, "What does Caleb do for you? He's…what? A cop? DEA agent? Why does everyone think he's an unemployed no-good drifter?"

"Because I am an unemployed, no-good drifter."

Pandora only jumped a little before turning to see Caleb standing in the doorway. Hunter just slanted his gaze toward the other man, then nodded and headed out the front door.

His hand on the knob, he turned back and told Pandora, "It was good to meet you. We'll talk again."

Her heart slamming against her chest, Pandora gave a jerky nod. She waited for the door to close before asking, "What's going on?"

"Russ Turnbaugh and Jeff Kendall are under federal arrest. We've commandeered the sheriff's holding cells until a team arrives to take them in."

"Federal?"

"Hunter's with the FBI."

"And you?"

"I was with the DEA, but I quit a while ago. Right now I'm exactly what I've said. Unemployed and clueless about what I'm going to do next." His words were as guarded as his expression. He looked as if he wasn't sure if she was there to talk or to beat the living hell out of him.

Pandora nodded, then looked away. A part of her wanted to beg him to make sure whatever it was, he did it with her. Another part, burned one too many times, warned her to hold back until she had the truth. All the truth.

"Are you working for the FBI, though?" Her chin high, she crossed her arms over her chest and tried to look in control, instead of on the verge of being a blubbering mess again.

"Hunter was my college roommate." He sounded less cold, more like himself now. She could actually see him starting to defrost. Whether it was because she wasn't hitting him, or he was shedding his interrogation-cop attitude, she wasn't sure. "We're friends. I was doing him a favor."

"I didn't realize the FBI looked into small-town drug problems."

"Not usually." He shrugged. "But there were extenuating circumstances in this case, and the drugs are a new blend. Something they wanted to stop before they gained a foothold."

"And you offered to help out of the goodness of your heart? Because you were bored being all unemployed and clueless?" Pandora winced, not sure where the anger was coming from.

"Don't blow this out of proportion. The bad guys are caught and they won't be using you or your store any longer. You're cleared and everyone knows it."

Cassiopeia was right. He had staged that little scene for her benefit. Pandora's heart pounded, emotions flying about so fast she didn't know if she should be thrilled, grateful or simply furious.

She settled on a combination of all three.

"Oh, no. No blowing things out of proportion. I should be relieved I won't have to go through weeks of grilling questions, false accusations and the loss of my computer and privacy this time." She was yelling by the last word. Apparently she'd glommed on to the fury more than all the other emotions.

Needing to get a handle on herself, Pandora held up both hands, took a deep breath. *Calm, center and collect yourself,* she chanted in her head.

Calm.

Centered.

Another breath, and she was pretty much collected.

"Look—" he said.

"No," she interrupted with a snap, whatever she'd collected scattering again. "I'm not finished. You came on to me. You poked through my computer, you made yourself at home in my house. You slept with me, over and over and over. And the whole time, you were investigating me?"

"I told you, you were cleared. I never suspected you, not really. Hell, you're not even the person I came to town to investigate." His jaw snapped shut. For the first time, Pandora saw Caleb angry. Not the stoic hard-ass thing he did so well, but really, truly angry.

Smoldering heat flared deep in her belly. It was kind of a turn-on.

"Look. You know the truth now. What's the big deal? Can't we just move forward from here?"

Move forward? Where? How? Wasn't this where he mounted his big black hog and rode off into the sunset?

The idea of that, of saying goodbye to him forever, was like a knife in her gut.

"The big deal is that I was falling for you and you were investigating me," she shouted. Horrified, she clapped both hands over her mouth. That was so not the way to dial back the drama.

CALEB FELT LIKE SHIT.

The rush of the bust, with its extra dollop of happy that he'd been able to take a schmuck like Kendall down, was gone. Now he was faced with the reality of what he'd done. With how he'd hurt Pandora.

"I didn't mean to hurt you," he said, knowing the words were totally inadequate, but having no idea what else to say. Pissed, he shoved his hands through his hair. He hated this. Hated not having a clue how to fix things with her.

"You lied to me," she said, her chin wobbling a little. *Oh, God, no. Please, don't let her cry.* Caleb wanted to grab her tight and kiss her until she forgot everything. Especially how he'd hurt her.

But he knew she wouldn't let him until he'd cleared up this mess.

"Not lied," he corrected scrupulously. "Just…withheld information."

"If not me, then who did you come to town to investigate?"

Caleb hesitated. Not only was it an open investigation, which meant the information was still confidential, but this was his father. Sure, the FBI had an entire database dedicated to cons they suspected him of. But most people, especially here in Black Oak, were clueless.

"Look, I'm not at liberty to divulge the details," he started to say. Her eyes chilled and her expression closed up.

"Because, what? You might lose your job? Oh, wait…"

"No. Because Hunter trusts me."

The ice in her eyes melted a little, but she still looked hurt. Then she nodded. "Okay, I get that. It's not fair to ask you to break a confidence."

But it was fair of him to ask her to take him at face value? After everything she'd been through, unless he told her who it really was, she'd never believe it wasn't her. Caleb scrubbed his hands over his eyes, then blew out a breath. "Okay, you have to promise that this stays between us. You can't even tell those psychic cats of yours."

She nodded, a tiny smile playing over her lips.

"The FBI had tips that there is more going on than just the drugs. That someone with a lot of influence was using the town as their own crime ring."

She nodded, then gestured toward the door in the back that led to the jail cells.

"The sheriff, right?"

"Higher."

"The mayor?" she asked, sounding appalled. Then Pandora slapped both hands over her mouth and grimaced. "I'm sorry. I'm so sorry. I forgot she's your aunt. But, I mean, who is higher than the sheriff?"

Caleb gave her a steady look.

It didn't take her long. Her eyes widened and she shook her head in denial.

"Noooo," she breathed.

"Yeah."

"No way. I mean, I don't know what kind of evidence they have, but it's wrong. There's just no way."

"That's what I said."

"So you came home to prove your father's innocence?" she asked. Then her eyes rounded again. "And what? You had to prove mine, as well?"

"It's been an interesting month," he said with a laugh.

"No kidding," she agreed. "You must have been so worried. So scared of what you'd find."

Her brow creased in empathy, she took those two mile-long steps and gave him a hug.

And just like that, everything was okay.

Caleb's shoulders sagged as he returned her hug. He let out the breath he'd been holding and gave a half shrug. She understood. Totally got it. Instead of running disgusted from the room because his father was the kind of guy who triggered a major FBI investigation, she offered comfort and understanding.

He was so freaking in love with her, it was scary.

Tension and a fear he hadn't even realized was eating

at his guts faded as Caleb tightened his arms around her, never wanting to let go.

Needing to taste her, desperate for more, he swept his hands down to the delicate curve of the small of her back, pressing her tight against him. Lifting her head from his shoulder, she arched a brow. Whether she was shocked or impressed by his burgeoning hard-on, he wasn't sure.

He took her mouth in a deep, desperate kiss. Tongue and lips slid together, tasting. She was warm and delicious. Everything he needed. Everything he wanted. Everything he hoped to keep, forever.

Then she kissed him back. Her lips moved against his in welcome, then in passion. Their tongues wrapped together in a familiar dance. Caleb groaned, feeling as if it'd been years since they'd been together instead of twenty-or-so hours.

They needed to get this all settled so he could have her again.

Gently, slowly, he pulled his mouth from hers. He couldn't stop touching her, though. His hands stroked up her back, down to her butt, then made the trip again. A part of him was worried that if he let go, she'd walk out and not come back. He had this one chance with her.

And he'd damn well better not blow it.

"So what now?" she asked, her hands loose around his waist as she stared up at him.

She probably wasn't referring to the investigation.

Time to put up or shut up. Nerves jumped in his stomach, but Caleb was ready for this.

"This is a pretty nice office," he noted dryly, looking around at the barren two-desk setup. "And now it's empty."

"I'm not doing it with you in here," she warned. "There's not enough Foreplay Chocolate Cake in the world to get me to, either."

He snorted a laugh. Grinning, he tucked a strand of hair behind her ear and pressed a kiss to her forehead. Had he ever been as happy as he was with her? Had he ever felt as good about himself as he did when he was with her? Was he ever going to find anyone who made him want to share himself, his life and his heart, the way he wanted to with Pandora?

The answer to all of those was no.

Still grinning, Caleb looked around the office again. Maybe it was time to stop bullshitting around.

"No, I didn't mean sex. At least," he corrected as he pulled her tighter between his thighs, "I didn't mean now or here. I meant…"

Pandora reached up to frame his face in both of her soft hands. Smiling, she arched a brow and asked, "Meant?"

"I meant, the position as sheriff will be open. I've got an in with the mayor, could probably snag an interim appointment until the next election."

Her eyes lit up and her smile was huge. Then she gave a little wince.

"What about Tobias?"

"He's not interested in the position. He runs the town just fine without all the crap that goes with an elected job."

She smirked. "No. I meant, can you live here, in the same town as your father? Does he know you were investigating him? Will you be able to handle being his son *and* the sheriff in his town? That's a pretty big challenge."

A huge one. Because rather than clearing Tobias's name, this bust had only pulled him deeper into things. Kendall had claimed he answered to one person, and one person only. Then he'd invoked the Fifth and refused to say another word. Clearly, the first official job of the new sheriff would be to find out who was trying to turn Black Oak into their own little crime den.

But Caleb wasn't worried about handling the investigation. His old man was a lot of things, but he wasn't involved in this mess.

"Can you live here, Caleb? In the same town as your dad?"

"When I was a kid I guess I thought I had to leave, get as far away from him as I could so I could be myself. And those are just about the most touchy-feely words I ever want to say," he added, making her laugh. "But, really, he was always there. He's a big part of who I am. He's shaped my choices and my strengths. So living in the same town? That just means he's talking to my face instead of being a nagging voice in my head. As for the rest? It'll all work out fine. I have faith that he's innocent in this, and I have faith that the law will prove it."

And wasn't he all freaking grown-up and stuff. Caleb noticed the look in Pandora's eyes. Sweet acceptance mixed with pride and just a tiny bit of lust.

Just as soon as someone showed up to watch the prisoners, he'd get her back to her place to do something about that lust.

"You're really going to stay?"

He hesitated, then put it all on the line.

"Do you want me to?"

Caleb had faced a lot of scary shit in his life, but he'd never been as nervous as he was at this very second.

And, dammit, Pandora wasn't making it any easier. Instead of wrapping her arms around him and declaring her undying love and gratitude that he'd be around, she pulled away.

She removed his hands from her waist, then leaned in to kiss his cheek before stepping back and around to the other side of the desk. What? She thought he'd get violent if she didn't declare her love?

He realized he'd clenched his now-empty fists and had to admit, she just might be right.

"This is hard for me," she said quietly, lacing and unlacing her fingers together. "I don't want to make a mistake."

Caleb's gut churned, but he kept his face clear. He was

a big boy. He'd been shot at, called filthy names and once even been thrown from a helicopter—albeit a low-flying one. He could handle whatever she had to say.

"Don't try to sugarcoat things. Just say what you feel."

"What I feel? I love you," she said, the words coming out in a rush. Caleb grinned, barely holding back a fist pump. But apparently he didn't hide his triumph that well because she shook her head and held up one hand. "But..."

"No, let's skip the buts."

"But," she continued, smiling a little, "I've got a question. Or, more like a confession."

Caleb's triumph fled and his stomach went back to clenching. Shit.

"Are you sure you're not attracted to me because of the aphrodisiacs?" she asked, her words so whisper-soft he barely heard them. "I mean, every time we were together, they were involved."

"What? You're kidding, right?" She stared at him, big eyes filled with worry. "You're not kidding."

He moved to step around the desk, but she shook her head. "No, please. I get confused when you touch me. I need you over there while we talk."

Caleb cringed. Damn. He'd hoped a few kisses would suffice. Now he had to express what he felt with words?

"Pandora, I told you yesterday, you underestimate yourself. I'm crazy about you. I'd be crazy about you if we ate fast food, or if we ate nuts and berries, or if we keep eating all that delicious stuff you make. The food, that's just nutrition. Aphrodisiacs are all in the head, you said so yourself, remember?"

He cringed, knowing he wasn't good with the romantic speeches, but needing her to know how much he cared about her. How special she was.

"You're crazy about me?" she asked, looking at him through her lashes and smiling.

Needing to touch her for this confession, he took a

chance and came around the desk. When she didn't order him back, he reached out for her hands, lifting them to his lips.

"I'm crazy about you," he confirmed. He looked into the hazel depths of her beautiful eyes and pressed little kisses to her knuckles. "I'm wild for you. I want you for you. You make me laugh, you make me feel good inside. You make me believe."

Her gasp was tiny, but he could feel her pulse racing as she bit her lip.

"I love you, Pandora. I really, seriously love you. And I want to give us a chance."

Her smile was brighter than the overhead lights. His heart filled with a joy he'd never imagined.

"I love you, too," she said softly. She shifted her hands so they framed his face, then stood on tiptoe to brush her mouth over his. "I really, seriously love you."

"And together," he promised, "the two of us are going to build a life. Our life, here, in Black Oak. I'm sure it'll have its irritants, given that our parents are always going to be larger than life. But it's going to be amazing, too. Love, laughter and a whole lot of that sexy chocolate cake."

"I have a large slice waiting back at my place," she admitted as she curled her fingers into his hair.

"With whipped cream? And hot-fudge sauce?"

Her smile flashed, as wickedly sweet as her cake.

"Always," she promised him right back.

* * * * *

SEXY SILENT NIGHTS
Cara Summers

Was **Cara Summers** born with the dream of becoming a published romance novelist? No. But now that she is, she still feels her dream has come true. And she owes it all to her mother, who handed her a Mills & Boon® romance novel about fifteen years ago and said, "Try it. You'll love it." Mum was right! Cara loves writing for the Blaze® line because it allows her to create strong, determined women and seriously sexy men who will risk everything to achieve their dreams. When she isn't working on new stories, she teaches in the writing program at Syracuse University and at a community college near her home.

To my nephew Nick and my new niece Kristen. May all your future Christmases together be merry! And especially to my great-nephew Luca—who celebrates his very first Christmas this month.

I love all three of you!

1

CILLA MICHAELS WAS NOT GOING to leave the hotel room without her panties. She'd been a cop for three years, a private security agent for two, and now she headed up G.W. Securities' new office in San Francisco. She was a pro at tracking things down.

On her hands and knees, she inched her way quietly down the length of her side of the bed, using her hand to sweep the space beneath it as she went.

Nothing.

She was not the kind of woman who would abandon anything that had a La Perla label on it. She'd parted with a small fortune for the red lace bikini, and it was part of a set. The matching camisole had already been located near the nightstand. She had a vague recollection of stripping it off and tossing it there herself. While in the throes of uncontrollable passion. Because that's exactly what Jonah Stone had sparked in her.

Ducking her head down, she lifted the dust ruffle and peered beneath. The dim light slipping through the narrow slits in the drapes didn't provide much in the way of illumination.

The rest of her clothes she'd found quite easily near the

door of the hotel suite where Jonah Stone had efficiently
stripped her out of them. The man had fast moves, and just
thinking about what had happened the instant the door had
closed behind them brought back the sensation of those
hard hands on her skin, the impatience, the demand. And
the pleasure.

Heat shimmered through her, pooling in her center and
then radiating outward. He'd taken her the first time right
there. No small talk. No talk at all. But the foreplay had
been top-notch. His hands had pushed into her hair, and
she'd felt each of those hard, slender fingers while he'd assaulted her mouth with lips, teeth and tongue. Each sensation had been so sharp. If she lived to be a hundred, she
would never forget his mouth, his taste.

Then he'd moved those hands over her shoulders, shoving her jacket off and molding her body with such purpose and skill.

He'd smelled so good and felt better—hard and tough
and male. Hadn't she been imagining him just like this
ever since the instant she'd first seen him at that party
yesterday?

When those smoky-gray eyes had collided with hers,
something had clicked inside of her like a switch turning
brains cells off and lust on—full throttle. That was the
only explanation she could come up with for agreeing to
his one-night stand proposition.

His argument had been logical enough—just the kind
you'd expect from an astute businessman. After all, they
were unattached adults, intensely attracted to each other,
and fate in the form of an airport-closing blizzard had
thrown them together. Why not pleasure each other for one
long, sexy night and then go their separate ways?

She might have come up with at least two good reasons
why not. In fact she'd been thinking about them when he'd
suddenly appeared at her table in the lounge of the hotel.

But looking into his eyes had triggered that little click again, and sent logic flying.

That was how she'd ended up against the door of his hotel room, his mouth branding hers. She had only a blurry recollection of how her sweater and slacks had hit the floor. Her focus had been on those hard hands moving up her legs and heating her blood to the boiling point. She'd never before experienced such intense sensations. Never wanted anyone so desperately. He'd opened up a new and wonderful world for her. Sensations flooded through her again as she recalled how he'd slipped fingers beneath the thin lace that still covered her, pushed into her and sent her flying.

Again.

He'd whispered the word so quietly against her mouth. His hands had already slid between them. She caught the rasp of a zipper, the tear of foil. The sounds might have been the most erotic she'd ever heard. Even as he sheathed himself, the need inside her had spiked into craving. She had to have him inside her. She couldn't survive another ten seconds if he wasn't.

Now. Right now.

He'd dug fingers into her hips, lifting her as she'd wrapped arms and legs around him. Then he'd driven into her, and she hadn't cared if she survived at all. His thrusts had battered her against the door again and again. Fast. As if he'd needed this to survive just as much as she had. That was the last rational thought she'd registered before his release triggered an orgasm that had simply shattered her.

Drawing in a deep breath, Cilla pressed a hand against her hammering heart. A little side-trip down memory lane was not going to help her find her panties. All it made her want to do was crawl back into bed with Jonah.

Don't think about that. No more fantasies, either. That's what had landed her in this situation—a one-night stand in a hotel near the Denver airport with Jonah Stone—a man she'd met for the first time only yesterday.

Her new job at G.W. Securities had brought her to a small family gathering at the Fortune Mansion in Denver. The moment she'd arrived at the party, she'd been aware of him. He was a man that any female would look at more than once—tall, dark and ruggedly handsome. He was dressed in a black turtleneck and jeans, which enhanced the broad shoulders, muscled chest and long, lanky legs. His chin was strong, his mouth firm and his cheekbones made her think of a warrior's.

Of course, she'd looked at him more than once or twice. Any woman needed a little eye candy in her life, right? It was when her eyes had finally collided with his that the trouble had started.

She'd heard that click, and she'd totally lost track of where she was, who she was. For seconds, minutes maybe, she hadn't been aware of anyone or anything but him. A stranger she'd seen across a crowded room.

It was the kind of thing she'd only read about in books or heard in song lyrics or seen in a movie. Everything had frozen, including time.

Before yesterday afternoon, Cilla would have sworn that nothing like that could happen in real life. But it had. More astonishing than that, it had happened to her. And of course, she'd been curious.

Who was he?

And how could he have this amazing effect on her?

As a top-notch security agent and investigator, she'd tracked down the answer to her first question within five minutes. His name was Jonah Stone, and he was the best friend of her new boss, Gabe Wilder. That alone would pretty much have classified Mr. Tall, Dark and Handsome as forbidden fruit. The new G.W. Securities office in San Francisco was only six months old, and Gabe had hired her to run it. She *had* to concentrate on her job, on proving herself to Gabe. The last thing she needed was to get involved with his best friend.

But there was another reason to put Jonah Stone on the Forbidden Fruit list. From what Gabe had told her, his friend was a busy and successful entrepreneur, the owner of three successful supper clubs and totally focused on his businesses. That reminded her a bit too much of her father.

But even with the warning flags flying, she'd still tried to satisfy her curiosity about the second question. How could he have that time-stopping, nothing-else-matters effect on her mind and senses? So when he'd approached her, she'd gripped his outstretched hand, felt the hard palm, the firm strength of his fingers, and the oddest feeling of connection. Then she'd met his eyes and her mind had just emptied. And she'd been struck by a vivid image of the two of them, naked and rolling across a wide bed in a dark room.

Both the feeling and the image had faded, and she'd been just fine. But she'd also made her excuses and left the party early. And everything would have been fine if it hadn't been for the damn blizzard.

If the Denver airport hadn't had to close down last night, she and Jonah would have both been back in San Francisco in their separate apartments, and her expensive red panties would have been in her laundry hamper.

But it *had* shut down and she'd decided to switch to an early-morning flight and stay at the airport hotel. She'd been in the bar having a glass of wine and thinking about him when he'd shown up. During the time it had taken him to cross to her table and join her, she'd experienced for the third time in her life what she'd decided to call the nobody-else-but-Jonah effect.

For a moment, neither one of them had spoken. And then he'd made his proposition. And she'd agreed to it. The rest of the night was now history—and the sexiest one she'd ever experienced.

Panties, she reminded herself as she inched her way

around the corner of the bed. *Find them. Get dressed. Leave.* The sooner she got back to San Francisco, the better.

They weren't anywhere along the foot of the bed. They weren't anywhere in the trail of clothes that led to the bed. Chances were good that they were still *in* the bed. But if she got back into that bed, it wouldn't be just for her expensive underwear.

She spotted the red lace the moment she crawled around the end of the bed to Jonah's side. In the light from the digital clock radio on the nightstand, she also saw Jonah. More of him than she wanted to. He was sprawled on his stomach, one arm dangling over the side of the mattress. The sheet covered him only to the waist.

And that strongly muscled back was not what she should be looking at. She dragged her gaze away and glanced down his arm to where his fingers nearly brushed the floor. Threaded through them was her quarry. All she had to do was get those panties and leave.

Very quietly, she crawled forward, scarcely daring to breathe. Gripping just the edge of the lace, she tugged.

Jonah's fingers reflexively clenched the red undies.

Cilla waited, listening hard. His breathing was steady. Only his fingers had moved, so in another moment, they'd relax again. This time she'd just pull harder.

That was one strategy—the smart one. Grab and go.

But her gaze had already betrayed her. It had left the panties behind to run up that arm. Jonah's face was turned toward her and his eyes, those incredible eyes, were closed.

She could easily wake him. There were a lot of ways to persuade a man to give up a piece of lace. Several scenarios ran through her mind.

She snuck a quick look at the clock: 5:15 a.m. The alarm hadn't yet sounded. Technically, it was still night. And if a girl only had one night to spend with a man?

She might as well make the most of it.

Rising, she pulled the sheet down and climbed back onto the bed to straddle Jonah. Then she leaned down to nibble at his ear and whisper, "I have a proposition for you."

2

Yet another sexy silent night, 2:00 a.m.,
three weeks later...

JONAH STONE STOOD AT the window of his apartment, looking out at his own private view of the Golden Gate Bridge.
For almost a month now, he'd stood at the same place, delaying the time before he would inevitably have to climb
up the stairs to his loft and go to bed. Once he did, he'd
dream of her again.

Cilla Michaels.

The dreams that had been haunting him since the one
night they'd spent together at that airport hotel in Denver
were growing more vivid. In each of them, she'd be with
him, right there in his bed. The sensations were always so
intense. He'd smell that elusive scent of hers, feel her heart
beat beneath his lips, taste the salty dampness of her skin
under her breasts, the sweetness at her throat, her inner
thighs, hear the way his name sounded when she gasped
it into the silent night.

Steeped in her, he'd rise above her and look into those
incredibly green eyes as he entered her. Again and again,
he'd thrust into her until he lost all of himself.

Then he'd wake to find himself alone in the bed. And
he'd try to convince himself that was the way he wanted it.

One night. That's what he'd promised himself and her. That's what she'd agreed to. The memory of that night should have faded by now. That's what memories did. But everything about that night was still vividly etched in his mind.

Turning, Jonah glanced at the conference table where he'd left his cell phone. Next to it sat a small green box with a red ribbon. Cilla ran G.W. Securities' new office in San Francisco. So he could use the threatening note that had been tucked inside the box as a professional excuse to call her. Was that why he'd delayed calling his friend Gabe Wilder about it? So that he could call Cilla instead? He'd been tempted to do so more nights now than he could count. More than once he'd punched part of her number into his cell before he'd been able to stop himself.

The little green box with the red bow had been delivered to him that evening just when the cocktail hour at Pleasures had been its busiest. Since his apartment took up the third floor of the building, he frequently filled in for his manager, Virgil, on Monday nights.

He continued to study the box, debating. He'd been in the bar when his steady customer and current business partner, Carl Rockwell, had brought the small gift to him. Before he could thank him, Carl had explained that a man dressed up as Santa had given it to him just outside and asked him to deliver it.

Jonah had felt something the moment he'd taken the box, a tightening in his gut. The hairs on the back of his neck had stirred, too. He'd even turned to look through the windows that lined the wall of the bar to see if whoever had sent the gift might still be watching. There was no sign of a Santa.

Then he'd put the gift behind the bar and out of his mind as a new wave of customers streamed into the club. He hadn't opened it until a short time ago when he'd returned to his apartment. Moving to the table, he took the lid off the box and picked up the folded note he'd found inside.

> 'Tis the season for remembering Christmases past. Pleasures and fortune are fleeting. You destroyed an innocent life in pursuit of yours. You'll pay for that soon. Six nights and counting…

Rereading it had his gut instinct kicking in again. Perhaps it was the wording. And there was something else that kept tugging at the corners of his mind. Some memory that was eluding him. Maybe it was the reference to Christmases past. At twenty-nine he had a lot of them to remember and several that he'd tried hard to forget. Especially that long-ago one when his father had promised to return, but hadn't.

He'd also made his share of enemies. Some of them probably dated back to his early days in foster care. He hadn't always "played well with other children." As a businessman, he was demanding. He hired and fired people. Over the past six years he'd opened three successful supper clubs in the United States and he was in the process of opening another one in San Diego and a possible fifth in Rome.

Pleasures had been his first supper club and the result of a dream that had taken shape during his years in business school. His goal had been to create a place where people could escape into a different world and find temporary respite from the harsher realities of life. And he'd known that he wanted to open the club in San Francisco as a kind of thank-you to the saint the city had been named after, a saint who'd played an important part in his life.

The success of Pleasures had allowed him to open Interludes, a sports-themed bar in San Francisco, and more recently Passions, another supper club in Denver.

He didn't like it at all that the word *pleasures* was used

in the note. But perhaps he was overreacting. It was December 19, a peak time for his businesses, and he wasn't getting much sleep, thanks to Cilla Michaels.

So he wasn't going to alarm Gabe yet. And calling Cilla, who was running Gabe's newly opened office in San Francisco, would be a mistake on so many levels.

He strode back to the window. Not that he could put all the blame on her. He'd known from the first instant he'd seen her at that party in the Fortune Mansion that she was different. That she'd be different for him. Gut instinct again.

His eyes had been drawn to her the moment she'd entered the room. No surprise there. Any man would have given her a second look. Her face had grabbed his attention first with its delicate features and stubborn chin. But he certainly hadn't missed the slender, almost lanky body and those long legs that the charcoal-gray slacks showcased. But it hadn't been just her looks that had pulled at him. She seemed to radiate an energy that tugged at him on a gut level.

Then there were those green eyes. The first time he'd looked into them, he'd felt as if he'd taken a punch right in the solar plexus. And when he'd clasped her hand in his, for a moment, he hadn't wanted to let it go.

The last thing he wanted or needed right now was to pursue a relationship with a woman who could have that effect on him. A woman like that could change your life.

During the past year, he'd seen his two best friends, Gabe Wilder and Nash Fortune, meet the women they'd decided to spend the rest of their lives with. Nash had already married his former high school sweetheart, Bianca Quinn, and Gabe was planning to marry FBI agent Nicola Guthrie on Valentine's Day.

He was happy for his friends, but Jonah liked his life just the way it was. Simple and uncomplicated. The right woman could change that. But on that night nearly a month ago in Denver, had he listened to what his mind was telling him? Had he heeded his gut instinct?

No.

Instead, he'd reverted to the reckless style of his youth when his name had been renowned in the family-court system. He'd followed Cilla Michaels when she'd left the party. He'd even watched her in the airport like a stalker until her flight was canceled. Then he'd followed her to the airport hotel and booked a room. Finally, he'd walked into the lounge, sat down at her table, and propositioned her for a one-night stand.

In the business world, Jonah Stone was never impulsive. He studied his options, planned various strategies. And he was even more careful in his private life and relationships. He'd been nine when his father had decided to desert his family, nine and a half when his mother had stepped in front of a bus rather than go on without the love of her life. He'd vowed never to be that vulnerable to anyone. Happy ever after didn't happen. The most one could hope for was a happy right now.

Instinct told him that Cilla Michaels could have the power to make him hope for the impossible. He turned back to the table and let his gaze rest on the green box with its festive red ribbon. His instinct was telling him something about that box, too, and he might not be overreacting.

Once again, he debated calling Cilla and hiring G.W. Securities. He had no doubt that his friend Gabe would recommend she handle the case. She was here in San Francisco. Gabe was in Denver. And at the party, Gabe had spent some time singing Cilla's praises to him. She'd been involved in a high-profile personal security case in L.A. and she'd saved a client from a crazed stalker. In Gabe's opinion, she had a rare combination of intelligence and excellent instincts.

But if he called her, he'd also have her in his bed again. He pressed his hands against his eyes and rubbed. He didn't have to decide tonight. In the morning, he was flying to Denver to attend the annual Christmas party at the Denver Boys and Girls Club, a place he'd been running for years with Gabe and Nash. They'd opened the club when the St. Francis Center for Boys, the place where they'd all first met, had closed down. He'd discuss the box and the note with Gabe.

Jonah moved toward the spiral staircase to his loft. And there was always the chance that tonight would be the night that Cilla Michaels finally faded from his dreams.

CILLA JOLTED AWAKE AND TRIED to focus. Relief came when she realized she'd fallen asleep on the couch and not in her bed. During the past three weeks, she'd rationed the hours she allowed herself to spend in her bed.

Because the damn thing was cursed.

Each time she fell asleep in it she dreamed of Jonah Stone touching her, tormenting her, taking her.

And each time she woke up to find herself alone, she yearned for him. So avoiding her bed had become almost as important as avoiding Jonah.

Which was why she'd ended up dozing off on her couch during a Christmas movie marathon on the Hallmark Channel. The credits for *Miracle on 34th Street* were rolling down the screen. A quick glance at the time on her digital TV box confirmed that she'd dozed off for nearly twenty minutes.

That pissed her off.

Not only had she missed her favorite part of the movie, the part where Kris Kringle proves he really is Santa Claus, but she'd also missed the cheese and crackers. The plate sitting on the cushion beside her was now empty.

She glared at her cat. Flash, a plumply proportioned calico, lay stretched serenely along the arm of the sofa, a good distance from the scene of the crime.

Pets were not allowed at The Manderly Apartments,

a rule that was explicitly spelled out in the lease and articulated equally clearly by the apartment manager, Mrs. Ortiz, a woman who reminded Cilla eerily of Mrs. Danvers in the old *Rebecca* movie.

But Flash hadn't given Cilla much choice. When she'd moved in a few months ago, the calico had migrated from its former home on the fire escape to the living room via an open window. And stayed.

It had to be for either the food or the conversation since the cat wouldn't allow her to stroke, cuddle or even pick her up most of the time.

"You're supposed to share," Cilla pointed out.

Flash's bland expression clearly said, "You snooze, you lose."

Her phone rang and the caller ID lady chimed, "Call from Wilder, Gabe."

Cilla sprang from the sofa and raced for her desk. Gabe headed up G.W. Securities' home base in Denver. Two months ago he'd given her a new beginning by hiring her to manage his branch office in San Francisco when she'd moved on from a personal security agency in L.A. Gabe wouldn't be calling her at home on her night off if it wasn't important.

Maybe he even had a job for her. Business had been good lately. G.W. Securities offered a variety of services to corporate as well as private clients. Lots of people wanted to give security systems for Christmas, and she enjoyed the challenge of working on their design. But there were times when she missed the action that came with providing personal security.

Mentally crossing her fingers, she grabbed the receiver on the third ring. "Gabe."

"I hope I'm not interrupting anything important."

"Not at all." The cheese and crackers were gone, her favorite movie was over, and working would give her a perfect excuse to avoid her bed.

"I need a favor," Gabe said.

Cilla's heart sank. Not a job after all. "What can I do?"

"I want you to meet someone at the airport and make sure he gets home safely. He's not a client. He doesn't even know I'm making this phone call."

Hearing the worry in his voice, Cilla reached for a pen and paper. "Who is he and what time does his plane touch down?"

On the other end of the line, Gabe expelled a breath. "Thanks, Cilla. It's Jonah Stone and he's due to arrive in San Francisco at 10:15. There was a lengthy delay because of the weather here in Denver. I was hoping the flight would be canceled, but he's on his way."

Jonah Stone.

Just the mention of his name had her heart skipping a beat. His image flashed into her mind—all that glorious dark hair, the handsome face with its sharp cheekbones, clearly defined chin with just that hint of a cleft, and the dark gray eyes… Just thinking about him made her knees weak and she carefully lowered herself into her desk chair.

"Jonah's not going to like that I'm sending you," Gabe said.

Cilla didn't imagine that he would. She'd had a chance to explore every inch of that taut, toned, amazing body. Jonah was a man who could handle himself on a physical level pretty well. That was definitely part of what made him so damned attractive.

More than once since their night in Denver, she'd regretted the fact that he was on her Forbidden Fruit list. More than once, she'd run over the reasons why. She'd done a little research on him. According to Gabe, the man had a real talent for hacking and electronic security, and right out of college, he'd helped Gabe establish G.W. Securities and continued to work there while he'd recruited backers for a supper club in San Francisco. In the past six years, he'd opened two more clubs and others were in the planning stages. A man that successful had to put business first just as her father had.

And still did. Bradley Michaels was handsome, charming and currently working as the CEO of his fourth company. There'd been no time in his life for her mother or her. Not even at Christmas. Christmas had been his time to focus even more on the business and entertaining. After five years of playing second fiddle, her mother had divorced him, and since then Cilla's contact with her father had been limited to phone calls on her birthday and Christmas.

"I'm worried about Jonah," Gabe said.

"Why?"

"Because *he's* worried enough to cancel his plans and fly back to San Francisco early. He received a threatening note today. It was inside a green box tied with red ribbon and hand delivered to him while he was at a Christmas party he and Father Mike Flynn and I were throwing for the Boys and Girls Club we run here in Denver. I have some people still working on the box and the ribbon, but there were no prints, and I've had no luck tracking down the sender. He or she wore a Santa suit and sent it in with one of the kids. An early present for Mr. Stone. I'll send the contents of the note right now in a text."

Cilla grabbed her cell phone. "It's the first one he's received?"

"No. I asked him that right away and he admitted getting one yesterday during the height of the cocktail hour at Pleasures."

"I've got the text." Then she read it aloud.

"'Tis the season for remembering Christmases past. Pleasures and fortune are fleeting. You destroyed an innocent life in pursuit of yours. You'll pay for that soon. Five nights and counting...'"

Today was the twentieth of December. Cilla did the math in her head. "Five nights until Christmas."

"Yeah. The first had the exact same message except that it read, 'Six nights and counting...'"

Holding the phone pressed to her ear, Cilla rose and began to pace. "The first one is delivered to his club here in San Francisco, the next to Denver. The sender wants him to know that someone's keeping close tabs on him."

"We think along the same lines, and so does Jonah."

"Does anything in the wording ring a bell for him?" Cilla asked.

"Not that he can put a finger on. But he has a feeling about the threat. His feelings are usually spot-on, so now I have one, too."

She was beginning to get one herself. Gut instinct should never be ignored. Her mind was already racing ahead. What she had was a reluctant client and the possibility of real danger. A tricky combination, but she could do tricky. In fact, she enjoyed tricky. One reason she'd been delighted when Gabe had approached her was because the jobs in L.A. had become a bit too predictable and boring even before she'd had a disagreement with a client and decided to move on.

"Jonah has an office and living quarters over his club, Pleasures. That's where he's headed."

"Good to know." Going to Pleasures would mean a wardrobe change. The jeans she was wearing would be out of place at the fancy supper club.

"I've known Jonah since we were in our teens. Ask him for help and he'll give you anything he's got. But at heart, he's a bit of a loner. He doesn't like to depend on anyone."

"In other words, he's going to try to ditch me."

"Yeah. He wouldn't let me send anyone with him. He wouldn't even let me tag along."

"Don't worry. I'll stick." The two years she'd spent working personal security for some of Hollywood's youngest and brattiest stars had honed her skills in the sticking department.

The moment she hung up the phone, she raced into her bedroom and threw open her closet door. She didn't have a lot of clothes, but during her time in L.A., she'd acquired some special pieces. She pushed aside hangars and decided on the little black cocktail dress that had visited some of Hollywood's hottest nightspots.

Whirling, she was about to toss it onto her bed, but Flash lay sprawled across the middle. The cat could move like lightning when she really wanted to.

"I have to leave for a while." She tried to keep the excitement out of her voice. "Business. Fancy place."

Pleasures was very upscale. Though she'd never been there, she'd frequently walked by. And each time she'd passed the front doors during the past three weeks, she'd resisted the temptation to go in. If she had, the chances were good that she'd run into him. The plan was to get over Jonah Stone.

So far the plan hadn't worked. And seeing him again…

Jonah was a client, she reminded herself. And she had very strict rules about clients.

She turned her attention to Flash. "Dress needs something, don't you think?" The red peep-toed shoes had cost her half a paycheck, but when she held them up for Flash's inspection, the cat made a sound deep in her throat.

"I agree. These things will dress up anything."

It took her three minutes to change and another ten before she was satisfied with her hair and makeup.

She paused to survey herself in the mirror. She definitely didn't look like a bodyguard. That ought to make it easier for a man like Jonah Stone to accept her as one. At least for the evening.

Then she narrowed her eyes on the image in the mirror and swept her gaze down and up. "Who are you kidding? You're wearing this just as much for him as you are for the job."

Moving closer, she tapped a finger on the mirror. "The man has three strikes against him. Not only is he like your father, he's also your boss's best friend and now he's a client. One night with Jonah Stone is understandable. Enviable. Any more could be disastrous. You are going to handle this."

Turning back to her closet, she grabbed her red leather coat and transferred her gun from her dresser drawer to her pocket. She was almost at the door of her apartment before she felt the eyes boring into her back.

Flash.

"Sorry." Whipping around, she saw that the cat had returned to her station on the sofa. Right next to the empty plate.

"I've got to go, pal." Crossing to the sofa, she crouched down and looked into Flash's eyes. "It shouldn't take long. But it's my chance to impress my new boss." She lifted a hand and then dropped it, reminding herself that Flash didn't like to be touched. "No more food. Remember our little talk about lifestyle choices."

It was one that they'd had several times since she'd taken her new roommate to the vet. Dr. Robillard had prescribed a "modification" in Flash's diet. The pediatrician her mother had taken Cilla to when she was thirteen had used nearly the same words.

"Moderation is the key. It made all the difference for me when I was in my teens. You'll get used to it."

Flash's expression said, "You've got to be kidding."

"Tell you what. I'll leave the Hallmark Channel on. They're having a marathon of Christmas movies. It'll take your mind off food." She snagged the remote, hit the channel. "Look. *A Boyfriend for Christmas*. That sounds like a great one. Santa, presents and romance thrown in."

And now she didn't have to watch it herself. Cilla silently sent up a prayer of thanksgiving to Gabe as she rose and raced for the door.

"Meeow."

Flash's mournful reproach followed Cilla as she headed for the stairs.

3

JONAH STONE HADN'T BEEN HAVING the best of days when he stepped into the airport parking garage. A chilly blast of wind followed him. His flight to San Francisco had been delayed three hours because of a blizzard in Denver, and he'd spent most of his wait time at the airport thinking about another blizzard and another night.

He'd been counting on the time in Denver to give him some respite from thoughts of Cilla. He'd been looking forward to catching up with his best friend, Gabe Wilder. Their other pal Nash hadn't been able to make their annual party because his grandmother had arranged for a private Christmas cruise that would allow Nash and his wife, Bianca, to get to know some recently discovered members of their family.

Though their career paths had drawn them apart since the years they'd spent at Denver's St. Francis Center for Boys, they tried to get together whenever they could, and Christmas usually provided the perfect time. He'd been looking forward to a poker game tonight at Gabe's apartment and shooting some hoops tomorrow.

The note that had been hand delivered that morning had changed his plans. Like the first, it had come in a small green box tied with a red ribbon. The message had been playing in his head in a continuous loop, and each time it repeated, the feeling in his gut grew stronger.

The word *pleasures* had appeared in both notes, so now he was headed back to the club. Pulling his parking stub out of his pocket, he checked the aisle, turned left, and increased his pace.

He nearly stopped dead in his tracks when he saw her. Though he managed not to break stride, he now knew what it must be like to take two barrels of a shotgun right in the belly. She was leaning against the back fender of his car, her mile-long legs crossed in front of her.

Cilla Michaels.

As often as he'd considered calling her, as frequently as he'd imagined her in his mind, nothing had prepared him for the impact that seeing her again would have on him.

It was all he could do to keep his pace from quickening. That night in the hotel lounge, her dark hair had been pulled back into a long neat braid. Tonight, it spilled in dark curls over her shoulders. The open red leather trench coat revealed a very short black dress. The shoes were red with open toes and dangerously high heels. And the legs... well, they were incredible.

But as he reached her, it was the eyes that drew his gaze again, just as they had before. They were a pure and piercing green with a shimmer of gold around the pupils. Fascinating. And looking into them for too long had the same effect he'd experienced the first time. He forgot to breathe.

When he drew air in, he felt the burn in his lungs. No other woman had ever affected his senses, his mind, his breathing, his gut in quite this way.

Nearly a month had passed and he hadn't stopped wanting her. Now, seeing her again, he wanted her even more. He wanted his hands on her. He needed hers on him.

All the more reason to remember that she was dangerous for him. All the more reason to send her away. He had bigger problems on his plate right now. The two notes he'd received needed all of his attention.

"Cilla Michaels," he said. "Gabe sent you."

She nodded. "He contacted me as soon as your plane left Denver. He thinks you need protection, and he warned me you might not like it."

"It's not a matter of liking. Do I look like someone who needs protection?"

"Not in the least." Cilla had had plenty of time to study him as he'd walked toward her, but she was sorely tempted to run her gaze over him again. The black leather jacket and jeans suited his tall, lanky frame and made him look tough and a little dangerous.

"You look to me as if you could handle yourself just fine," she said.

"Good." He opened the passenger door and tossed his duffel on the seat. "Then we're agreed that I don't need your services."

"We're not agreed on that." She waited until he met her eyes, then added, "The least you can do is let me give my sales pitch. It's the job of G.W. Securities to think of things the client might overlook."

He leaned a hip against the car door. "Such as?"

"Would you have thought to check for a bomb under your car?"

He narrowed his gaze. "No."

She smiled. "I did. It's part of the service." She could tell from the look in his eyes that she might have scored a point, but the game wasn't over.

"I know that the first note said, 'six days and counting…'" she continued, "the second said five, but that could be a lie. Sociopaths aren't known for their honesty."

Silence.

"And you're probably thinking it's highly unlikely that someone could have traced your car to this particular parking space, but I got a friend of mine to run down your license plate. Then I simply drove through the garage until I located your car. If I was able to do that, so could someone else. They could easily have booby-trapped it."

"Okay, you've made your point." When he smiled at her, the effect rippled right down to her toes. Then he took the lapel of her jacket and rubbed it between his fingers. Her toes, the little traitors, curled.

"But you've obviously got better things to do tonight. From the looks of it, Gabe's call pulled you away from something or someone special."

She thought of the empty cheese and cracker plate, her disgruntled cat and the movie on the Hallmark Channel's Countdown to Christmas and barely smothered a yawn. Instead, she tried a smile of her own. "Actually, it didn't. I was having a quiet evening at home."

His eyebrow quirked up. "You dress like this for a quiet evening at home?"

"I changed after Gabe called. I thought this was more appropriate for Pleasures. That is where you're headed, isn't it?"

His smile faded. "Gabe is overreacting."

"He said you had a feeling."

"I may be overreacting. It's probably a crank."

"Perhaps." But in the three hours he'd sat in the Denver airport waiting for his plane, he hadn't changed his mind about coming home, Cilla thought. "But you don't think so. You don't like the fact that they used the word *pleasures* in the note."

Surprise flickered for a moment in his eyes. "No, I don't like that."

"Could be coincidence, but…"

"I don't trust coincidence."

"But you do trust your instincts."

He let the silence stretch again, so she pushed her advantage. "Look, I know we have a history. And we made a deal. One night." She waved a hand. "Let's put all of that in a side bar for now. This is strictly a professional offer."

He narrowed his eyes fractionally, and dammit, her toes curled again. For an instant, her mind flashed back to that moment in Denver when they'd first stepped into the hotel room and he'd pushed the door shut and put his hands on her. His eyes had narrowed then, too, and she recalled how they'd glinted in the darkness. Ignoring both the image and her traitorous toes, she ruthlessly focused.

"Gabe's a friend of yours and he's my boss. He asked me to make sure you got to Pleasures safely. As a favor. I'm not even here on G.W. Securities' clock. But I am here as a private security agent. And I'm good at what I do. You can call Gabe and get a recommendation."

He frowned. "I'm not questioning your abilities."

"Then why don't you think of my escorting you to your club as a way to set Gabe's mind at ease?"

"You'll follow me to Pleasures and that's it."

"Not exactly. The service G.W. Securities provides is more than door-to-door. I check out your apartment before you go in. Double-check the security system. And I get a chance to walk you through Pleasures on the way. I've never been there."

He considered for a moment. "Sounds reasonable. I run the risk of sounding like a real prick if I say no."

"Not exactly the way I'd phrase it, but you've got the gist."

"You *are* good at this, aren't you?"

She beamed a smile at him. "I'm the best. How about I follow you to your club?"

HE LIKED TO KEEP HIS ROOM dark. In his opinion, everything was way too bright during the holiday season, as evidenced by the amount of light pouring through the windows. On the screen of his laptop, he could see that Jonah Stone's plane had landed—10:15.

The anger that he'd been keeping tightly leashed for the past three hours eased just a little. He didn't like it at all when he had to adjust his plans. The plane should have landed three hours ago.

But Stone was finally here. It wasn't too late to go forward with the scheme. It would be another forty-five minutes to an hour before Jonah Stone would reach Pleasures.

He took a cell phone from his desk and punched in a number. On the fourth ring, a raspy voice said, "Yeah?"

He relayed the information and gave the order. "Got that?"

"Consider it done."

Turning off the cell, he laid it carefully on the desk. Then he rose, walked to the closet and took out his overcoat, a hat and a long scarf. He trusted the man in charge of the mission, but he would still be on the scene to make sure his orders were carried out.

Five more nights—that's how long it would take to complete his mission. It was all planned out. And during those nights, Jonah Stone would pay for the life he'd taken.

Moving to the nightstand, he glanced down at the picture. It was framed in crystal, and a small flameless candle burned in front of it.

Elizabeth. Poor, innocent Elizabeth. She'd been the only person he'd ever loved. And he'd had to leave her. He had a calling. She'd understood. He'd known that she'd been fragile, but how could he have foreseen that in his absence, she would fall under the spell of a man who'd seduce her and then reject her and kill her?

Five nights from now, on the anniversary of her death, he would exact revenge.

After running one finger down the side of the frame, he put on his coat, the hat and the scarf. Then he walked to the door.

When one set up a plan, part of the pleasure was watching it come flawlessly to fruition.

4

"You've got a classy place here," Cilla remarked as she joined Jonah at the rear of his car. He'd pulled into a private lot half a block down from Pleasures and spoken briefly with the attendant, who'd then waved her through.

"I like it," he said, shifting his gaze to the three-story club on the corner across the street.

And well he should, Cilla decided as she studied it. The location was prime, right in the heart of the city, and the building was old with tall arched windows on two upper floors that recalled a different, more gilded age.

On the second floor, shadowy figures wove their way among tables lit with candles. Through the windows on the street level, she caught a glimpse of a crowded bar. Tiny white Christmas lights twinkled on the awning, a subtle salute to the season.

"I know that I only talked you into letting me escort you here and lock you up tight for the night, but you really should allow G.W. Securities to provide you with round-the-clock protection. At least until we get a handle on what's going on here."

"You talked to Gabe on the drive over."

She shrugged. "He is my boss. He wants to put a couple of men on you even without your agreement. My feeling is that the moment you spot them, you'll shake them. He agreed. So we'd like your permission."

"You've got all you're going to get from me tonight. I have a business meeting tomorrow afternoon, and I don't need a couple of babysitters tagging along. You can tell Gabe that I'll check for car bombs myself in the morning."

She let it rest as they watched a couple exit through the glossy red entrance doors to the club and head up the street in the opposite direction. At this time of night, there were very few pedestrians, and many of the other buildings on the block were dark. So were parked cars. In contrast, Pleasures glowed like a tempting little jewel.

"Shall we go clubbing?" he asked.

"Can't wait."

Jonah extracted his duffel from the front seat and started across the lot. Behind them, the car beeped as he locked it with the remote.

She walked to his left, just half a step in front of him, and when they reached the sidewalk her eyes scanned the street. Directly across from them was a narrow alleyway, but the light from a streetlamp revealed only Dumpsters. To the left was an unmarked van in a loading zone. But it was seemingly empty and already sported a parking ticket on the windshield.

There was nothing at all to cause the itchy feeling at the back of her neck. The door of the club opened, releasing another couple along with the faint sound of bluesy music and laughter. The man and woman turned away from them, crossed to the opposite corner, then disappeared down a side street.

As they stepped off the sidewalk, Cilla slipped an arm through Jonah's, and drew him on an angle toward Pleasures. "I can't tell you how many times I've been tempted to drop in your club for just a drink."

He shot her a sideways glance. "Why haven't you?"

"Usually I'm not dressed for the occasion." That was

true enough, but not the only reason she'd avoided going into the bar. "My apartment's not far from here, so I've walked by on my way home from work. You painted the doors red a few weeks ago."

"My manager Virgil's idea. He wanted to try it out for Christmas."

"Festive. One of these days I'll dress up and treat myself to a glass of champagne at the bar."

"We don't have a dress code."

"But with a club like Pleasures, dressing up is part of the deal—kind of like Cinderella going to the ball. It wouldn't have been the same if she'd worn her work clothes to the castle. Know what I mean?"

"Yes." He looked over at the bright lights of the club. "I know exactly what you mean. Providing the opportunity to dress up and escape the workaday world is part of what each of my venues offers."

The itchy feeling that had been nagging her since they'd stepped out of the parking lot suddenly increased, and Cilla had to exert all her control not to turn around. Instead, she listened hard.

Some kind of movement near the van? Their backs were to it now. Then she heard the footsteps, approaching from behind.

When Jonah tensed beside her and would have turned, she increased the pressure on his arm and pitched her voice low. "We have company, so do exactly as I say. Take me into your arms."

She moved with him, shifting so that her body shielded his, then raised her hands to his face. "Lean closer."

He leaned so close that his lips were nearly brushing hers. She was very aware of the fact that the footsteps were growing louder. But she was aware of other things, too—a flood of sensations. The hardness of his body, the heat of his breath on her mouth, the ribbon of pleasure that unwound right to her toes. Every cell in her body remembered him. Wanted him. For a fleeting moment, one desire—to feel those lips on hers—nearly swamped her.

Ruthlessly refocusing, she whispered, "Be my eyes. How many, what do they look like, and how close are they?"

"Two and they look like Laurel and Hardy." He nipped at her bottom lip, and for just an instant, her mind clouded, then emptied as if someone had pulled a plug. She was aware only of Jonah—the hardness of his thighs against hers, the tightening of his hands at her waist, the heat of his breath as it moved over her lips and between them. Sensations hammered at her, and all she wanted was to melt into him.

"They're about ten feet away. And the fat one, Hardy, has a gun."

"Shit." Adrenaline spiked through her system, clearing her thoughts, stiffening her spine. "I need them closer."

"You're getting your wish, sugar."

"The one with the gun is mine."

"Not going to happen."

She nipped his bottom lip hard. "I know what I'm doing. Here's how it's going to go down. I'll be the helpless female, you the macho man. He won't know what hit him. Trust me."

"Let the girl go," a gravelly voice said.

Arguing time was up, but Jonah dropped his hands. Cilla immediately pivoted toward the men. Eyes widening, she pressed a hand against her breast and focused on her training. "Sweetums, he's got a gun."

"Step aside," the tall, skinny one said to her. "We don't want you."

"Go ahead, sugar," Jonah said. "Run on up to the club. I can handle this."

"Okay. Okay." The words came out on breathless gasps as she took one shaky step, sideways. Without missing a beat, she shot her other leg straight up. Her toe hit Fatso's wrist dead-on and the gun clattered to the pavement. Pivoting slightly, she landed a punch to the man's temple. With a grunt, Fatso fell like a rock.

She glanced up to see Jonah racing after the skinny one. "Dammit!"

Pausing only long enough to kick the gun on the sidewalk out of the way, she ran after them. Her heart shot straight to her throat when the back door of the van near the alley slid open. There was at least one more thug to deal with—the driver. She could see him through the windshield now. Broad shoulders, short gray hair.

Before skinny could nose-dive through the door, Jonah grabbed him by the collar and spun him around. One punch straight to the face took him down. Cilla winced and for the first time registered the sting in her own knuckles.

Then the window on the driver's side lowered and she saw the gun.

"Get down," she shouted to Jonah. He did, hitting the sidewalk and rolling as the shot rang out. Skidding to a stop, she pulled her own gun out of her pocket, gripping it in both hands as she took her stance and fired. Tires squealing, the van lurched away from the curb and up the street. It backfired loudly in the intersection, then roared off. She got the license plate before it disappeared.

Sliding her weapon back in her pocket, she turned to see that Jonah had already sprung to his feet. The relief was so intense that for a moment she couldn't speak. Then she said, "I told you to trust me. I said I could handle it. You could have gotten yourself shot."

So could she, Jonah thought as he walked toward her. He'd rolled over quickly enough to see that she hadn't dropped to the ground as she'd told him to do. Instead, she'd stood there, feet spread, returning the fire of the man in the van like some mythical warrior. He was certain that his heart had skipped two whole beats.

"From my perspective, you did handle it. Very well. I'm not shot, and Laurel and Hardy are out for the count."

He'd taken her arm to draw her with him toward the club. It was only then that he saw they'd attracted an audience. From the looks of it, most of the bar crowd had poured into the street including Virgil, the tall, bronze-skinned man who'd managed Pleasures since Jonah had opened it.

The fat guy he'd nicknamed Hardy was on his hands and knees, shaking his head like a dog. When they reached him, Cilla planted one of her shoes right under his nose where he could see it. "Don't even think of getting up unless you want me to kick you again."

He collapsed onto his stomach.

"Boss," Virgil said. "You all right?"

"Fine. You'd better call the police. Ms. Michaels and I seem to have been the victims of an attempted mugging."

"I already called 9-1-1, and so did several of our customers."

Even as sirens sounded in the distance, Jonah noted that Cilla had crouched down to secure the fat guy's hands behind his back. When she'd finished, there was a spattering of applause from the people who'd gathered. Ignoring it, she retrieved the first man's gun, then secured the man Jonah had knocked out.

Jonah turned to Virgil. "If you wouldn't mind, could you stay here and keep everyone away from the crime scene until the police arrive?"

Jonah saw the questions in his manager's eyes. He also read concern, but all Virgil said was, "Sure thing, but I don't think these guys are going anywhere."

"No." He glanced back as Cilla walked toward him. The sound of sirens grew closer. "I'll try to reassure our guests. You can send the police to me when they arrive."

When Cilla reached him, she put her arm through his and kissed him on the cheek. "You sure know how to show a girl an exciting time." Then she turned to beam a smile at the small crowd of onlookers. "I'm pretty lucky."

There was more murmuring and nods of agreement. One woman said, "I think he's the lucky one. The only other place I've seen a kick like that was when I saw the Rockettes at Radio City Music Hall."

There were more nods and a few laughs as his customers began to move back into the club.

"I'm going to offer everyone a round of free drinks, but you've already diminished the tension level considerably," he murmured as they followed the group.

"You can thank me by trusting me more the next time," she hissed.

Jonah laughed as he drew her into Pleasures.

AN HOUR LATER, JONAH sat in his office watching Cilla pace back and forth in front of his desk, talking on the phone to Gabe. Making her report.

The policemen had questioned them separately, and the one who was in charge, Detective Finelli, seemed to know Cilla. Which reminded Jonah very forcibly that he knew very little about her—only what Gabe had told him at the party. Her name was Priscilla Michaels, but she went by Cilla, and Gabe thought the world of her.

Oh, he'd been tempted to run a thorough background check on her, but satisfying curiosity could lead a man into deep trouble. Finding out more about her could have complicated his decision to keep his distance.

The name Priscilla intrigued him because it didn't fit the woman he'd spent the night with in Denver. Cilla suited her better. It also fit the woman he'd met at the airport and the one who'd turned into his arms out on the street. For an instant when she'd put her hands on his face and pulled his head down to hers, he could have sworn the cement beneath his feet had shifted as if it were beach sand. And all he'd been able to think of was her.

Oh, she was a very dangerous woman. And like it or not, he was learning more about her with each moment that passed. Problem was, the more he discovered, the more curious and fascinated he became. She was good at what she did. She'd not only smoothly maneuvered him earlier into accepting her escort back to Pleasures, but once the police had left, she'd managed to get a call into Gabe before he had.

And the woman who paced in front of him right now was a sharp right turn from the woman who'd met him at the airport earlier or the woman who'd kicked the gun out of that thug's hand. Ever since she'd entered Pleasures, it was as if she'd had a to-do list and she'd been checking off items one by one. Quick, efficient, focused.

It occurred to him that he was dealing with two sides of the same woman. He recalled his first reaction to her given name. But Priscilla fit the woman he was watching now to a T.

She paused in her pacing to fist a hand on her hip and summarize for Gabe what Detective Finelli had assured them before he'd left. The police would do everything they could do—question Fatso and Skinny, put out an all-points bulletin on the van.

"The two men have lawyered up, so they won't be questioned until the morning when their public defenders are assigned," Cilla said to Gabe as she started to pace again. "But my friend Joe Finelli says he'll talk to his captain and get permission for me to observe the interviews."

Her friend Joe Finelli? Jonah recalled what he'd seen of the interaction between the detective and Cilla. Finelli was a good ten years her senior. Had they dated? Been lovers?

And the fact that his mind instantly jumped to those questions reminded him why he'd decided to avoid Cilla Michaels. He didn't want that kind of involvement.

Deliberately he looked past her to the open door of his office. The evening was winding down. By the time the police cars had pulled away, he could see that everything had returned to normal in his club. The bar was still busy, and the jazz band on the basement level would switch to dance music in another half hour.

Virgil would handle closing. What Jonah needed was some quiet time in his apartment to try to figure out what in hell was going on. There was something in the wording of the note that was still pulling at the edge of his mind.

"Joe recommended that he continue with private security," Cilla was saying.

Joe. Her use of the detective's first name triggered a quick surge of impatience. Not jealousy. Because that was ridiculous. And the impatience was with himself.

Because he didn't want to go to his apartment and think about what had happened by himself. He wanted to talk about it with Cilla Michaels. And perhaps with Priscilla, too.

He watched her stride across the width of his office again and wondered if the woman ever stood still. There was such energy radiating off her. She'd been lightning fast outside the club—both physically and mentally. The kick had come out of nowhere. The poor sucker hadn't been expecting it.

And she'd brought those same elements of energy and surprise to her lovemaking, as well. He vividly recalled the speed of those clever hands as they'd moved over his skin exploring, exploiting—until the flood of razor-sharp sensations had left him helpless to do anything but want more.

"Sure I can set up a security detail." Cilla paused at his desk to pull a small notebook and pen out of her purse. "We'll want to give him 24/7 protection, two men each shift."

Jonah took a deep breath and brought his focus back to her. He wasn't helpless. This time it was more than a surge of impatience he felt. Sitting on the sidelines and letting others decide his fate had never been his strong suit.

He'd run away from three foster homes before the judge tired of seeing his face and sent him to Father Mike at the St. Francis Center for Boys.

At the time Father Mike had a reputation in the Denver area for being able to handle "bad" or "problem" boys. Jonah figured he'd been both. And if it hadn't been for the center and the fact that he'd met Nash and Gabe there, he wouldn't be where he was today.

"I'll handle it," Cilla said.

Studying her, Jonah leaned back in his chair. He was used to handling his own affairs or handpicking the people he chose to delegate them to. And whenever he could, he chose people he knew and trusted. Virgil had been like a big brother to him in the first foster home he was sent to. Before he'd opened Pleasures, he'd tracked Virgil down and hired him to manage the club. When he'd opened his sports bar, Interludes, he'd offered the manager's position to Carmen D'Annunzio, a woman who'd volunteered at the St. Francis Center when her boys were in their early teens.

But he hadn't chosen Cilla Michaels. He'd decided not to choose her, hadn't he? She sat on the edge of his desk, her cell phone tucked beneath her ear as she scribbled. "I think we can cover it for now."

We meaning who? He definitely didn't like hearing the plans being made as if he were…what? A client whose life she'd just saved?

Jonah frowned. That was exactly the case, wasn't it? If Cilla Michaels hadn't met him at the airport and pressured him into accepting her escort, he might very well be lying on the sidewalk outside just as Laurel and Hardy had been doing when the police arrived. In fact, he might have a bullet hole in him.

His frown deepened. That scenario didn't jibe with the note that had been delivered to him. If someone wanted to gun him down on the street, why warn him about it first?

And why bother counting down the nights until Christmas? Unless the two incidents weren't connected.

That was something he wanted to talk to her about. Priscilla would have a theory. He was sure of it.

And then there was Cilla.

She strode away from his desk and put her hand on her hip again. The red coat was shoved back, giving him a good view of those remarkable legs. And he remembered exactly how it had felt when they'd been wrapped around him.

It could happen again. Something primal, something that went beyond desire, sparked to life inside of him. In seconds, he could move to the door, lock it and take her against it just as he had in that hotel room in Denver. Seconds and he could have his mouth on hers. God, he wanted that. He wanted to taste her again—that sweet, tart flavor that grew more complex each time he feasted on it. He wanted to touch her again, to push the hem of that dress up those long, silky legs. Seconds. It would take only seconds to sheath himself and push aside whatever lacy barrier was left between them. Then he would fill her. She would surround him.

The image in his mind triggered sensations so vivid that he could almost feel her closing around him as he thrust into her. Seconds, he thought again. Seconds and he could turn the fantasy in his mind into reality. The temptation to do just that was so powerful, Jonah had to grip the arms of the chair tight.

This was why he'd stayed away for nearly a month, he reminded himself. And this was why he should keep his distance now.

"No, we haven't talked about it yet, but I'm sure he'll agree that private security is the way to go," Cilla said. When she shot him a questioning look, Jonah merely returned a bland one.

He wasn't a fool. Until he could figure out what was

going on, he was going to take precautions. A bodyguard wouldn't be a bad idea.

"I can free up David Santos and Mark Gibbons," Cilla said. "They're very good, and I can still handle our other clients."

Jonah refocused his attention on what she was saying.

She slid him a sideways glance. "Great. I'll let him know."

Let him know? Annoyance sizzled through him. Mostly at himself. All evening, he'd let her call the shots. She'd convinced him to let her follow him to Pleasures, then she'd maneuvered him into that little macho man/poor helpless female scenario when the two thugs had approached. And she'd been the one who'd reported everything to Gabe. Now if he'd heard right, she intended to step back and assign two other men to guard him.

That wasn't her decision to make. He was about to stretch out his hand and demand to talk to Gabe when she closed her cell and faced him across the desk.

"We need to talk," she said.

"Indeed we do." Jonah kept his gaze on Cilla for one long moment before he rose and said, "Before you tell me what you and Gabe have decided, let me introduce you to Pleasures."

5

HE WALKED FOR OVER AN HOUR in an attempt to settle his rage. The wind blowing in from the Bay carried a fine, icy mist that stung his cheeks. In spite of the cold and the lateness of the hour, there were still some people walking along the Embarcadero, wandering to and from Fisherman's Wharf.

Normally, he would have avoided the lights and the seasonal decorations, but tonight he would use them as reminders.

Of Elizabeth.

Of his loss.

Of his mission.

But in spite of the litany that he repeated in his mind, every time he thought of what had happened at Pleasures, his fury threatened to rise up like a tidal wave and consume him. At times, the red haze in front of his eyes nearly blinded him.

His plan, his perfect plan had been bungled! Even now, as he replayed the scene in his mind, the panic and anger bubbled up just as it had when he'd been parked down the street from the club.

He'd wanted to jump out of his car and scream.

But he'd controlled the urge. Even when he'd heard the gunshots, he hadn't allowed the panic to take control. His first impulse had been to follow the van and confront his partner. But acting when he was still teetering on the brink of anger would have been a mistake.

Instead, he'd made himself wait until the crowd had gone back into Pleasures, then he'd pulled out of his space and driven down to Fisherman's Wharf.

Just a little bit longer now, and he'd be fine. Something inside of him would settle and his mind would clear.

For two blocks, he concentrated on breathing in and breathing out. No one had seen him earlier. He was sure of that. Everyone had been watching what was going on in front of the club. But he shouldn't have panicked.

That was inexcusable. Panic led to mistakes even when the anger was justified.

He'd explained the plan very carefully to his partner. It was a simple job.

No guns.

Fury erupted again. If they'd shot Jonah...

He bit back the scream that burned in his throat like acid and fisted his hands at his sides. It was *his* job to kill Jonah. His job. And it wasn't time yet.

When the red haze threatened to blur his vision again, he stopped and drew in a deep breath. Then another.

Think. He had to think.

It wasn't entirely his partner's fault that the mission had failed. There was the woman.

She shouldn't have been there. Jonah Stone wasn't dating anyone. She didn't work for him. And she'd spoiled everything.

He began to walk again. He'd find out who she was, and she'd pay dearly for disrupting his plan.

When he finally felt himself settle, he realized that he was standing in front of a restaurant. Through the windows, he saw people laughing and talking at the bar. For a moment, he was tempted to go in and order a drink. Then the door of the restaurant opened and he caught the sound of muted Christmas music.

No. He couldn't go into a place where they were celebrating the season.

So he would return to his room to have that drink, and he would wait for his partner to report.

And he would plan his revenge on the woman.

AS JONAH LED HER AROUND on a brief tour of Pleasures, Cilla could tell he was seriously annoyed. The calm voice and the charming smile didn't fool her.

She could understand what he must be feeling, sympathize with it. But what she admired was the way he kept his emotions tightly leashed. He'd never once interrupted her or tried to take her cell phone from her while she was reporting to Gabe. She doubted she could have been that patient.

He'd taken her on a brief tour of the jazz room in the basement and the private dining rooms on the second floor, but she couldn't recall one detail. Each time his arm brushed against hers or he placed a hand on the small of her back to guide her up or down a staircase, she couldn't help remembering that moment out on the street when he'd leaned closer, his lips nearly brushing hers, and the incredible heat that had exploded through her.

For that one instant, her mind had totally blanked. She'd forgotten her plan, the danger he was in. There'd been only Jonah Stone. And the fierce desire that he alone could provoke had nearly consumed her.

He'd felt at least some of what she was feeling. His hands had tightened their grip on her waist and she'd seen the way those smoke-colored eyes had darkened until they were black as an abyss.

But he hadn't kissed her. He'd maintained control. He'd kept his mind focused on the danger. What woman could resist thinking about what it might take to break that control?

Which was reason numero uno why she had to take herself off the case. Jonah Stone was in trouble. And the best way she could help him was to keep her distance. So she could think—about something besides jumping him.

That last option was totally off the plate since he was now officially a client. In her book, getting involved with a client led to disaster. It was a client in L.A. who'd expected side benefits as part of his security service that had led her to quit and move on.

But Jonah Stone was an entirely different problem. This time she was the one who might be tempted to offer side benefits. Even now she could feel the slow burning flame that she'd felt from the first time he'd gripped her hand at Gabe's party. And she'd experienced how that flame could explode into a flash fire. Her aunt Nancy, who was a Catholic nun, used to talk about avoiding the occasion of sin. Cilla shot Jonah a sideways glance. For her that term summed up Jonah Stone.

And he was still in perfect control. There was no sign of what he had to be feeling. The man had gone through a lot today. Still, when they reached the bar, he smiled and exchanged a warm greeting with an older, handsome and fit-looking man who stepped into their path.

"That was a nasty piece of business out there on the street," the man said.

Cilla remembered that he'd been one of the customers outside earlier. He was about Jonah's height, dark-haired with gray at his temples. He reminded Cilla of a well-aging James Bond. She saw both concern and worry in the steel-colored eyes when they met hers. "Nice work." Then he turned back to Jonah. "What can I do to help?"

"Got it covered," Jonah assured him. "Cilla Michaels, I'd like you to meet Carl Rockwell. Not only is he a regular here at Pleasures, but he was one of my original backers when I opened the club. He believed in me when I was an unknown quantity."

"And I still do," Carl said.

Jonah smiled at him. "He's invested in all my clubs, and now he's a partner in a new place we're opening in San Diego."

Cilla held out a hand and found it firmly grasped.

"Cilla heads up G.W. Securities here in the city," Jonah continued, "and I seem to be her newest client."

"Good." Carl stared directly into Cilla's eyes. "Don't let anyone hurt him, and let me know if you can use some backup."

"He's not kidding," Jonah said. "Before he retired, Carl worked in the security business."

"Virgil can let me know if you need me," Carl said, nodding at the two of them before he returned to the bar.

Jonah led her to an empty booth at the far end of the room. Virgil managed to reach it just as they did.

He beamed a smile at them, then spoke in a low voice. "Does that little sideshow the two of you put on in the street have anything to do with the green box that was delivered here yesterday?"

"Jury's out on that," Jonah murmured. "I received another box in Denver this morning."

"Shit," Virgil breathed. "What can I do?"

"Exactly what you're doing. Run Pleasures."

Cilla studied the two men as Jonah laid a hand on Virgil's arm and reassured him with the same information he'd given to Carl Rockwell. But he didn't tell either man that he was definitely her client. "I seem to be" just didn't make the cut.

She guessed that Virgil had about a decade on Jonah, and from the easy way they talked, she figured their relationship was personal as well as professional. Plus, Virgil was sharp. He'd already tried to connect the dots between the little Christmas gift Jonah had received and the attack.

Virgil turned to her. "If you work for Gabe Wilder, I have to assume you're the best. What you did out on the street was impressive. But keep it up. Don't let anything happen to Jonah." Then he turned and moved back to the bar.

"Well, I've been well and duly threatened," Cilla said as she slid into the back of the booth. "You have some very concerned friends. Does anyone else here know about the green boxes?"

Jonah shook his head. "Just Virgil. I asked him to keep an eye out in case another was delivered here."

From her position at the back of the booth, Cilla had a view of the entire room. The crowd had thinned a bit so it was the first time that she was able to get a good look at the decor. And since a table now separated her from Jonah, she could give her surroundings more attention than she had on her tour.

The rich combination of dark mahogany and gleaming brass on the bar itself was repeated in the furniture and in the wood panels and sconces that lined the walls. The booths were red leather and the candle flickered in an old-fashioned hurricane lamp.

"What do you think?" Jonah asked.

"Sumptuous. It reminds me of another era where life moved more slowly, before airplanes, when people had the time to travel on a luxury liner to Europe. I got the same impression earlier when I looked up at the second-story windows. It makes me think of the times F. Scott Fitzgerald or Henry James captured in their novels."

He nodded. "That's exactly what we're going for here. Although we don't expect every one of our customers to name the era or to have read those particular authors."

"You have, I bet," Cilla guessed. "What was your major in college?"

"Marketing and Finance, but I minored in English Lit. How about you?"

"Psychology, but I like to read. And I minored in Criminal Justice to pave my way into the police academy."

"You were a cop?" he asked. Then he said, "Here in San Francisco. That's how you know Detective Finelli."

"Right."

"Why'd you leave?"

"Greener pastures. Plus I had a five-year plan. Get some experience in providing personal security and then open up my own office."

Jonah's eyes narrowed. "And running Gabe's satellite office in San Francisco is part of your five-year plan?"

"It is now."

Cilla was prevented from giving him more details when Virgil once more appeared at the side of the table. "What can I get for you?"

Jonah met her eyes. "You mentioned champagne earlier. Does that still sound good?"

"Perfect."

He nodded to Virgil. "We'll have number thirty-five."

For one moment, Cilla let herself wish that the circumstances were different, that she was just sitting at a booth in the bar with an exceptionally handsome man, having a drink. If only there weren't those threatening notes and her decision that Jonah Stone was off-limits, she could have nothing more on her mind than spending another long sexy night with him.

When Virgil moved away, she reluctantly forced her mind back to reality. "I'm not sure what we're celebrating. I need to tell you what Gabe advises."

"I got the gist of it—24/7 protection. But I make my own decisions."

She frowned at him. "He warned me you have an independent streak, but you're not stupid. You have to be willing to hire private security—at least until we figure out what's going on here."

"I'm willing to hire private security."

"But…?" She leaned forward. "I hear a *but* in there. G.W. Securities is the best. And Gabe is your friend. Mark Gibbons and David Santos are the two most experienced agents I have working here in San Francisco. Gabe's even thinking of sending a couple of men in from the Denver office."

"He can stop thinking about that right now."

"I don't…"

Virgil's appearance had her letting the sentence trail off. While he performed all the rituals surrounding the opening of a champagne bottle and filled two flutes, she marshaled her thoughts. Logic would be the path to take.

The instant Jonah signaled his approval of the wine and Virgil walked away, she said, "You need the best. There's more going on here than is immediately apparent."

"What do you mean?"

"The notes you received yesterday and this morning don't jibe with what went down tonight. Whoever sent them is trying for a cat and mouse game. They've set up a ticking-clock scenario—'so many nights and counting…' They want you to worry, anticipate." She waved a hand. "You canceled your plans in Denver and flew back here. What do you want to bet that you'll get another note soon that will have you flying back to Denver?"

His brows quirked upward. "I hadn't thought of that."

She tapped a finger on the table. "That's why you need some pros—to think that way."

Jonah studied her. There was determination in her eyes. Priscilla's eyes, he decided. Logical, focused and a lighter shade of green. Would she taste different if he kissed her now? He was going to find out, he promised himself. But for the moment, he said, "Go on."

"The ticking clock agenda doesn't fit with the guys the police just hauled away. They're grab and go. Instant gratification. They just don't make a match with that note and the Christmasy way it was wrapped up."

"I agree. But it's hard to believe that I have two different people who are out to spoil my holiday."

"True. But we need to consider the possibility. And that's exactly why you have to see the wisdom of hiring G.W. Securities. We have the manpower to check it out."

"I wouldn't hire anyone but G.W. Securities." Then he smiled and lifted his glass. "But if I'm taking on a personal bodyguard, 24/7, you're the one I'm hiring. Not Mark Gibbons or David Santos or anyone Gabe wants to send down from Denver. I want the best of the best."

He tapped his glass to hers. "And didn't you already assure me that's you?"

6

WHILE HER MIND RACED, Cilla took a sip of her champagne. Then for a moment, she allowed herself to be totally distracted by the taste. "This is really good."

"It's the best."

Looking down, she inspected the tiny bubbles. "Don't tell me number thirty-five is that really, really expensive stuff that retails for a few hundred bucks a bottle."

Jonah winced. "The winemakers who bottle Cristal would shudder to hear it described that way."

"Well, I don't think I've ever tasted anything better."

"That's their goal, and they charge a lot when they achieve it."

Looking up, Cilla couldn't prevent the smile and felt a little flutter right below her belly when he returned it. "You didn't have to order something like this. I don't have what they refer to as an educated palate."

"I disagree. You knew right away that it was special. And you did say you've been thinking for some time of dressing up and coming into Pleasures for a drink. Just think of the Cristal as part of your side trip into a different world."

Cinderella-land, she reminded herself. With a very dangerous gatekeeper. Who was now a client. Her current job was to convince Jonah Stone that she could do a better job for him if she kept her distance.

But the more time she spent with him, the more she thought of what she could have—what they both could have—if she closed that distance. And looking into his eyes didn't help one bit because he was thinking the same thing. For an instant, everything around her faded, the noise, the decor, and there was only Jonah.

He was the only one.

No. A sliver of fear shot up her spine. He couldn't be. She wouldn't let him. Her mother had believed that each and every time she'd walked down the aisle. Ruthlessly, Cilla tore her gaze from his and took one more sip out of the glass. It truly was better than any champagne she'd ever tasted. And something she would never be able to afford again. That little reality check gave her back her focus.

Then she met Jonah's eyes. "If you want me to work on this case personally, you have to let me do it my way. The best way that I can protect you is to keep my distance."

"Explain."

This was always the tough part in handling a client—knowing which buttons to push. "You're a businessman. What does your schedule look like tomorrow?"

Jonah pulled out his phone, tapped it a few times and said, "What's your cell phone number?"

When she gave it to him, he said, "I'm sending it to you right now."

"Give me the highlights."

"Since I was still supposed to be in Denver, my morning is free. But now that I'm back in town, I'll drop by Interludes, my sports club, around lunchtime. They're hosting a Christmas party for the boys and girls clubs here in the city. Later, I have a meeting here at the St. Francis Hotel with Carl Rockwell and Stanley Rubin. Stanley is my other partner in the San Diego club we're opening. He's in town to visit family, and there's a problem he wants to discuss.

I'll end my day here at Pleasures. We're busy with parties this time of year."

"How about the rest of the week?"

"There's a charity event at Pleasures the night after tomorrow. I'll be attending."

She frowned. "That isn't a good idea."

"Not negotiable. I'm hosting the event. Bring in some of the cavalry, if you want."

"I *will* want. And something like that is all the more reason for me to assign someone else to you."

When he opened his mouth, she held up a hand. "Let me finish. As a businessman, you know the importance of looking at the whole picture. That's what I'll be doing, and in that position, I'll be free to run down any leads that might turn up, knowing that you're fully protected."

"I don't see why you can't manage that while you're with me. That way you can keep me constantly updated on the big picture. I'm going to insist on that."

She tilted her head to one side and studied him. The glint of humor in his eyes told her that he was being difficult on purpose. And he was enjoying it. Truth told, so was she. She liked matching wits with him. But with Jonah, she had to do more than match. She had to win. So she folded her hands in front of her and met his gaze head-on. "You need someone at your side who can be objective and won't be distracted. Because of our history and the fact that I'm seriously attracted to you, I'm not the best person for that job."

He took a sip of champagne and set the glass down. "How seriously?"

She tapped a finger on the table. "See? That's not the question you should be asking."

"I'll ask another one as soon as you answer—how *seriously* are you attracted to me?"

"Seriously enough that for a moment when you were holding me in your arms out on the street, my mind went blank. There were two guys approaching, one of them was armed, and all I could think of was that I wanted you to kiss me and that I wanted to kiss you right back. That's a serious problem."

"A mutual one. Maybe we should just get it out of our systems."

The humorous glint in his eyes turned reckless and dark. The color made her think of the black smoke that explodes with a spray of sparks from the flames of a bonfire. Hot and dangerous. For the first time in her life, she thought she knew why a moth might be stupid enough to fly into a flame.

She had to fight past the dryness in her throat. "Kissing you again is not going to solve anything."

He moved quickly then, sliding out of his side of the booth and into hers. Without touching her, he studied her for a moment. "You're not afraid."

"No." That was a lie. She was, just a little. Annoyance added to the mix of everything else she was feeling. He was so close now that she could smell him above the scents in the restaurant. Soap and water and something that was very male. Everything inside her began to melt.

He took a strand of her hair and twisted it around his finger. "You're not my type."

She frowned. "Ditto. You're at the top of my Forbidden Fruit list."

"Isn't forbidden fruit even better the second time around? Maybe that's why I've been wanting to taste you again ever since I saw you leaning against my car at the airport."

When his gaze dropped to her mouth, Cilla could feel her lips actually burn. Good glory, she could only pray they still worked. "Look," she managed. "Let me work this case the way I want to and we won't have this problem. You won't have to worry about wanting to kiss Mark or David. I guarantee it."

He laughed, a rich, deep sound that helped her to ease back just a little.

"You're probably right about that." He fastened those razor-sharp eyes on hers. "You strike me as a practical, focused woman. What we shared in that hotel room might have been a fluke."

Her brows shot up. "A fluke with a hell of a lot of chemistry that made us both do things…"

"Delightful things."

"Things that were unwise."

"If I had a dollar for every unwise thing I've ever done…" His lips curved.

And she shouldn't be watching those lips. She took a deep breath and tried to focus. "The chemistry between us hasn't died down, and you're insisting we work together 24/7?"

"Exactly." He lowered his head just a little. "And I think we ought to find out exactly what we're up against so we can handle it."

She wanted to handle it all right. She wanted to handle *him*. Naked. And dammit, he'd boxed her in. She could smell him, nearly taste him, and she couldn't shove past him without touching him.

And if she touched him? Oh, hell…

"Handle this," she said as she clasped the sides of his head and drew his mouth to hers.

At last. At last. At last.

Those were the words that steamed through Jonah's mind and thrummed in his veins. The memories that had haunted his dreams for the past weeks vanished in the reality of the moment. How could he have forgotten how soft her lips were? Her flavor was even more exciting than he'd recalled. And the sweetness—surely that was new. It reminded him of ice cream that ran down a cone in the summer heat so that you couldn't lick it fast enough.

When she opened for him, he used tongue and teeth to

take them both deeper. He couldn't have said who moved first. All he knew was that her strong, slender body was molded to his in a perfect fit. He couldn't seem to get enough of it as he ran his hands down her sides, then up again to cup her breasts.

The low sound of desperation she made in her throat had his blood racing like a river just before it tumbled over the falls. He knew what it was like to throw caution to the winds, but he'd never wanted so badly to do just that.

He wanted to touch her. No, he needed to touch her, to strip her out of that dress and explore the skin beneath, inch by inch by inch. More than that, he wanted to have her now, right here.

Not possible, he warned himself. He wasn't so far gone that he'd lost track of his surroundings. Not yet. But he couldn't seem to control his hands, couldn't seem to give up her taste.

Even when glass shattered nearby, he had to exert some effort to pull away. And it took even more discipline to drop his hands and ease back from her.

Her eyes were still clouded. And her mouth…

He only had to look at it for the intensity of his desire to spike again. No other woman had ever taken him as far as she had. And he wanted to experience—no, he needed to experience—just how much further they could take each other. He met her eyes. "Come with me now."

"No." But she didn't retreat from him. "I didn't kiss you and you didn't kiss me as a prelude to seduction. We did it to clarify the problem. And I'd say mission accomplished. Now you have to agree that I should work this case from a distance. That way we can both think."

"Distance won't solve the problem of what we're thinking about. And thinking about making love again while we're apart might prove even more of a distraction."

Cilla waited three beats, then sighed. "Compromise time."

He smiled at her. "I'm ready to negotiate, as long as you're my personal bodyguard until we figure out what's going on."

"And stop it."

His expression sobered. "Yes."

"We need some ground rules. I don't sleep with clients—as much as I might want to. Or as much as the client might want me to. During the last job I worked in L.A., the client believed our security service should provide some side benefits."

He caught her hand. "I'm sorry."

"I don't want you to be sorry. I want you to understand. Whatever it is we've got going between us has to take a backseat until we figure out who's sending those notes."

"We can put what we're feeling in the backseat. That doesn't mean it will stay there."

She saw the humor in his eyes again, and it didn't help that she had quite a vivid image of the two of them in the backseat of a car, their limbs tangled. It helped even less that she knew he was thinking the same thing, and she had no one to blame but herself for the expression.

"Look. We're both adults. We stayed away from each other for nearly a month. From now until we get your note sender, our relationship has to be strictly professional—security agent and client."

"It's a reasonable ground rule. I'll agree with one modification. I won't be sidelined. I want to be kept informed of everything you know, and I want to be part of running down leads. I don't like threats, and if I'm not working with you, I'll be working on my own. Until this is over, we're partners."

"Gabe won't like it."

"Gabe will have to live with it. Will you?"

"As long as we agree that when it comes to any kind of imminent threat, I take the lead."

"Unless I have a better idea."

"We won't always have time for negotiations," she warned.

"True. But I followed your lead earlier this evening. And there is a chance that I might on occasion have a better idea."

Since it was the best deal she was going to get, she nodded. "Okay. But I'm going to take the lead on this one. I'm going to have someone from G.W. Securities outside watching when I leave tonight."

"Agreed."

She took out her cell and checked the schedule he'd sent her. "And if we're going to be working on this together, I get to go where you go—everywhere you go, including business meetings."

He grinned at her. "You're going to cause quite a stir in the men's room."

"Not funny. You need to decide how you're going to explain me to your partners, Stanley Rubin and Carl Rockwell, when I show up with you at the St. Francis Hotel tomorrow. Unless you want them to know about your problem."

The reminder didn't wipe the grin from his face, but it did make his eyes darken. And it only took him a few beats to come up with a solution.

"Carl Rockwell already knows you're from G.W. Securities, and I'll tell Stanley I'm taking precautions because of the attempted mugging." He refilled their glasses, then handed her one before he raised his in a toast. "Now let's drink to *our* partnership."

LESS THAN EIGHT HOURS later, Cilla stood with Jonah looking through a two-way glass as Detective Joe Finelli questioned the man she'd kicked with her red shoe. They'd already watched his interview with the skinny guy, Lorenzo Rossi. Chubby's name was Mickey Pastori, known to his friends as Mickey P., and the shiner he was sporting paid tribute to the punch she'd given him. The public defender assigned to his case looked tired—as if she'd been rousted out of bed at a very early hour.

Cilla could sympathize with that since she'd gotten the call from Detective Finelli at 7:00 a.m. Both Rossi and Pastori had consulted with their Public Defenders and claimed they wanted to cooperate. She'd debated notifying Jonah, but a deal was a deal. He'd been very explicit about wanting to be in on everything.

So he was here right now in an observation room listening to Joe Finelli tell Mickey P. to take it from the top one more time.

She flicked a glance at Jonah's reflection in the glass that looked into the interrogation room. His attention seemed totally focused on Mickey P. She wished it were that easy for her to concentrate on the interrogation. But she was so aware of him standing only inches away from her. Each time she took a breath, she inhaled his scent. And if he made a move to touch her…

No. The problem was that after a night on her couch—a night in which Jonah Stone had invaded her dreams every time she'd managed to slip into sleep—she was the one who wanted to touch him.

"I don't know nuthin'," Mickey P. whined.

"I still need to hear it from the top again," Finelli said.

Cilla shifted her gaze back to the interrogation room. She'd worked with partners before, and she'd find a way to work with Jonah Stone. Or around him. And she wasn't going to let her thoughts stray to being wrapped around him, or underneath him.

Stop it. Ruthlessly, she shoved the images out of her mind. He was following her ground rules. So far, he'd even let her take the lead. Last night, he'd allowed her to check out his apartment, including the security, and this morning he'd waited for her knock on his door before he'd opened it and stepped out. He'd offered no objection when she'd insisted that they use her car to get to the police station. In short, he was being Mr. Perfect Client.

She looked over at his reflection again. This time he met her eyes in the glass. And any idea of Jonah as a client, perfect or not, vanished. There was such heat in his gaze that she was amazed it didn't burn a hole right through the glass. And everything else suddenly faded just as it had the first time he'd looked at her.

"This is not working." He took her arm and turned her before she could think. Before she could breathe.

"I need a kiss," he said as he framed her face with his hands. "Give me one."

Heat flooded her system and her mind began to empty. The man had fast moves. She should have remembered that. "But…ground rules."

"You'll have to agree, I've followed them so far."

"Yes." She had to move. But the brain cells that controlled motion had evidently been the first ones to shut off. His were still working. He'd gripped her shoulders and somehow moved her against the wall.

"I should get points for being good so far. And if I'm going to listen to one more word of Mickey P.'s whining excuses, I need a reward."

Then his mouth was on hers. The kiss was hard, demanding, everything she'd been imagining since the last time. She couldn't think, no longer remembered that she should. Suddenly, she could move again. Her arms wrapped around him and she pressed closer. She had to get closer.

Yes, Jonah thought as he molded her against the wall. The desire to kiss her had been building since she'd picked him up at his apartment. No—since she'd left the night before. And as they'd stood in the tiny observation room watching Joe Finelli question the two thugs, desire had intensified until he needed the kiss the way a starving man needed food, or a man dying of thirst needed water. He didn't understand it. He wasn't sure he wanted to.

What he wanted was Cilla. Only Cilla. He ran his hands down her quickly, wishing he had more time, taking what he could get. But when he heard Finelli's voice again from the interrogation room, he pulled back. If he didn't, he was afraid he wouldn't be able to.

Still, he couldn't completely let her go. For one more moment, he held her close and rested his forehead against hers. "Thanks," he managed. "Now I'll go back to being good again."

For how long? If she'd been sure her voice was working, Cilla would have asked the question out loud. But there was a part of her that didn't want him to be good. As Jonah moved away, she concentrated on making sure her legs carried her back to the glass window.

Inside the room, Mickey P. said, "Lorenzo is the one you should be talking to. I just agreed to go along because of the money. Easy-peasy. That's the way Lorenzo described the job. Five hundred in advance and another five when the job was done."

As he whined on, his story didn't change. The driver of the van had hired them. Mickey P. didn't even know who the guy was except that he called himself Tank. They were to wait for Jonah Stone to arrive at his club and rough him up a bit.

"No one was supposed to be with him," Mickey P. complained to Finelli.

"Several witnesses saw your pal, the driver, take a shot at Mr. Stone," Finelli said.

"I don't know nuthin' 'bout that," Mickey P. insisted. "Shooting Stone was not part of the deal."

"Then why did you bring a gun and threaten Mr. Stone with it?"

"If he'd been alone, I wouldn't have had to use the gun. We were just going to scare him, take him into the alley and punch him a few times. But we had to get the woman out of the way. Then she kicked me."

"Spoilsport," Jonah murmured beside her.

"All part of the service." She didn't look at him. She didn't dare. And she wasn't going to look at his reflection, either.

"Think Mickey P.'s telling the truth?"

Cilla considered that. Lorenzo Rossi had claimed just as much ignorance as Mickey P. He only knew the driver of the van as Tank. A tall, broad-shouldered guy with a gray buzz cut had walked into a bar where he and Mickey usually hung out and hired them for a dream job. All they had to do was rough up Jonah and the payoff was one grand. Both Mickey P. and Lorenzo had rap sheets, but they were small-time.

"What's your gut instinct?" Jonah prompted.

In the room in front of her, Mickey P. groaned about a headache.

"I think they're both essentially telling the truth. Joe will keep after them for a while, and Lorenzo may eventually remember more about this Tank person. But something about their story rings true."

She looked at him then. "What does your gut tell you?"

"Same thing," he said without hesitation. "Neither one of them are Einsteins. They went for the easy money. Neither of them counted on you, and neither has the ability to think on their feet."

"That would jibe with my take on it," Detective Finelli said.

They both turned to him as he entered the room. "Except I wouldn't mention either of them in the same sentence with Einstein. I've got a couple of men calling other precincts to see if anyone's heard of this Tank. I'm thinking he's pretty small-time, too. And the license plates on the van are a dead end. They were reported stolen yesterday afternoon."

"So the large man with the short gray hair who goes by 'Tank' could be behind the notes or he could be work-

ing for someone else," Cilla said. "And since Skinny and
Fatso are a few bologna sandwiches short of a picnic, we're
probably not any closer to finding out who that person is,
or if Tank's behind everything."

Finelli shot a grin at Jonah. "She's real good at sum-
marizing the bad news. How about you? You've had all
night to think about it. You got any thoughts about who
sent the notes?"

Jonah had given it some thought. He'd had no choice
since Cilla had assigned him to make a list of anyone he
might remember who could have a grudge against him
going back to the days when he'd been in foster care. But
his mind had frequently slipped back to Cilla. In fact he
wasn't sure whether it was the note or the woman standing beside him that had stolen more of his sleep. He felt a
little better now that he'd kissed her, but he wasn't at all
sure how long he could wait to do it again.

"I've made a list for Cilla of people who might have it
in for me, but I don't think the note sender is on it. None
of them feel right. We'll just have to keep working on it.
What's next?"

Finelli inclined his head toward the glass. "I'll keep
working on them. And we'll keep looking for the van. If
you want to hang around, I can offer you both some very
bad coffee." He grinned at Cilla. "But if I remember correctly, that's one of the reasons you quit being a cop and
went private."

"One of many," Cilla said. "I'm going to take Jonah
to G.W. Securities so we can discuss what we know and
strategize. The coffee's excellent there." Then she gave
Finelli a hug. "Thanks for letting us watch. I'd appreciate
it if you'd keep me posted."

"Ditto," Finelli said. Then he nodded at Jonah. "You're
working with the best."

Jonah didn't need convincing. As they threaded their
way through the desks in the bull pen, he noted that a cou-

ple of the uniforms waved at her. That didn't surprise him. As soon as she'd left his apartment the night before, he'd given in to the temptation to check into her background—something he'd avoided doing for nearly a month. She'd put in three years on the SFPD and she seemed to be well liked here.

He'd also checked into the agency she'd worked for in L.A. It was small and specialized in providing discreet personal security for celebrity clients. He'd also located the story Gabe had told him about the client whose life she'd saved. But there'd been nothing about the one who'd expected side benefits.

"So, besides the lure of greener pastures, better coffee and your five-year plan, why did you go the Charlie's Angels' route and move to L.A.?"

She laughed then. "Don't I wish I'd become one of Charlie's Angels. They always looked like they were having such fun. They got interesting cases, they got to go undercover and they always had Charlie and Bosley watching their backs. Maybe I had that in mind, but the real world is very different. Mostly I got to babysit the spoiled teen idol crowd."

He took her arm and waited until she met his eyes. "Was it one of the teens who wanted side benefits?"

"Yeah. But he didn't get them, and that case is history. Plus, I got a better offer from Gabe."

Her tone was offhand, but the increased tension in her body told him that was just the surface story. He was willing to bet there was a deeper one. He'd have it when the time was right.

The desk sergeant hailed them as they passed her desk. "Ms. Michaels. A delivery service just left this for Mr. Stone. I saw his name next to yours on the sign-in sheet."

There was a coldness in Jonah's gut as he looked at the small green box tied with a red bow.

"What delivery service?" Cilla asked.

"Some private one," the sergeant said. "He asked me to sign a clipboard."

"What did he look like?" Cilla pressed.

"Tall, broad-shouldered, short gray hair. I'd say he was in his late fifties."

"Thanks, Sergeant."

"Sounds like our man Tank." Cilla hurried Jonah quickly into the street and scanned it. Because of the early hour, the pedestrian traffic was thin. "Dammit. There's no sign of him. No sign of that van."

Jonah waited until they were near Cilla's car before he opened the box. Then he lifted out the note and held it so they could read it together.

Four nights and counting… Have you remembered yet why you're going to have to pay? You have some time left. But even in this most joyous of seasons, peaceful interludes are short.

Cilla took out her cell. "I'll let Joe know."

7

SHE WAS RIGHT ABOUT THE coffee, Jonah had to admit. It was very good. She'd poured a generous mug for each of them before she'd excused herself and left him standing in front of her desk.

G.W. Securities occupied the top floor of a modern-looking building. Cilla's corner office offered a spectacular view of the Golden Gate Bridge and was spacious enough to hold a gleaming conference table as well as a cozy sitting area with a leather sofa and two chairs.

Her desk was meticulously clean and bare of any photos or mementos. The office clearly belonged to Priscilla. But on the only solid wall hung a painting where red, yellow and purple pansies exploded in bursts of color. That was Cilla. In the bright colors, he saw a visual representation of the energy that always simmered inside of her.

Initially, it had surprised him that she was an ex-cop. But the part of her that he was coming to think of as Priscilla would have made an excellent cop with her focus and her attention to detail. Before they'd left the police station, she'd checked her car for a bomb. And she'd kept her eye out to see if anyone followed them the short distance to her office. So had he, and he hadn't spotted anyone.

But he also hadn't spotted a tail on the way to the police station. And the Tank person must have followed them.

Otherwise, how would he have known to deliver the note there? He didn't like the idea of that, and he had a pretty good idea that she didn't, either.

Through the other three glass walls, he noted some of the staff and agents settling in at their desks. He sipped coffee as he watched her turn the green box with the red ribbon over to Mark Gibbons. She'd introduced him when they'd arrived. Jonah recalled that he was one of the two men she'd wanted to assign to him, but it was only when he'd seen Mark that he'd recognized him as an agent who'd worked for Gabe in the Denver office. Gabe had hired him about six years ago when Jonah had left G.W. Securities to open Pleasures.

Tall with a swimmer's build, Gibbons had thinning hair and a neat goatee that was just beginning to show signs of gray. Cilla was assigning him the task of hand delivering the box and note to a lab G.W. Securities used here in San Francisco.

On the short drive over from the police station, she'd filled Jonah in on her plans to do that much. She'd also put in a call to David Santos, the other agent she'd mentioned. She was going to put him in charge of tracking down the people Jonah had written on his possible enemies list. Locating them would be the first step. If they were alive and well and otherwise occupied, they could be crossed off.

All of which would take time, probably more than his ticking four-night clock would allow them. They hadn't talked about the latest note. Not yet. He was fine with that. Her silence during the drive had given him time to think.

In his mind, he pictured each of the notes. There was something in the messages that he was still missing. Six nights, then five and now four. It was December 21 and kids everywhere had started their countdown to Christmas a long time ago. Why had the writer of the notes waited to begin with day six?

He pushed down hard on both frustration and temper.

That was something he'd started training himself to do ever since he'd first met Father Mike and begun what had become a new life. His first day at the center had been early December—sixteen years ago. White lights had twinkled on the trees in the prayer garden that bordered the basketball court. In the center of the tiny garden was a statue that he'd later learned was St. Francis. And it was where the social worker had taken him to meet Father Mike on that first day.

He'd never met a priest before. What he'd expected was someone wearing black who'd lecture him and give him the worn-out lie that good deeds would be rewarded and evil ones punished. In the four years he'd spent in foster care he'd heard that one often enough. Father Mike had been wearing a T-shirt, shorts and sneakers, and instead of a lecture, he'd offered Jonah a game of one-on-one on the basketball court. Within the next fifteen minutes, they'd been joined and then challenged by two other kids—Gabe Wilder and Nash Fortune. The other guys had been good, but he and Father Mike had won.

A smile tugged at the corner of his mouth as he recalled the competition as well as the brownies and milk that had followed. There'd been no lecture, not that day or any other day. The St. Francis Center for Boys had never been about lectures. Now he understood that it had been about giving young boys a place to channel their fear and anger and frustration and, most of all, to have fun and formulate dreams.

His gaze sharpened and his mind returned to Cilla as she began to move back toward her office. Even through the glass wall and the distance that separated them, his senses were attuned to her. He watched her take a circuitous route, pausing on the way twice to speak to people. In addition to protecting him, she still had an office to run, and she looked very much at home checking with her colleagues.

He continued to study her as she took a call on her cell.

She wore her hair in a neat braid, but the bright blue blazer spoke of the passion he knew lay beneath the surface. A passion that had drawn him from the first.

He'd had time to think about it during the night, to try to analyze what she was doing to him. It wasn't just desire that she was able to trigger in him. The feeling he got when he looked at her was more complicated, similar to that flash of intuition he experienced when he was drawn to a new business venture. A feeling of rightness.

That was what he'd felt when he'd first seen her, and again during the long night they'd spent together in Denver. He'd never gotten that feeling about a woman before. He'd never wanted to. It was too close to the way his mother had described her first meeting with his father.

As a child, he'd loved to hear the story, especially during his dad's long absences when he'd been away working on secret missions for the government. As his mother told it, they'd met at a fancy party. She'd been a waitress working for the caterers and he'd been a guest. They'd seen each other across a crowded room, and that had been it. Within days, they'd run away to be married. A real Cinderella story—except there hadn't been a happy ever after. Thanks to his father.

He wasn't at all comfortable with the idea that he might have experienced the same feeling his mother had described the night he'd first seen Cilla.

So the smartest thing to do would be to play by her rules and keep their relationship strictly professional.

Then he saw a tall, lanky man stride past the reception area and make a beeline toward Cilla. His long dark hair curled over his ears and reached the collar of his shirt. In the faded jeans and worn leather jacket, he looked as if he'd be more at home on a ranch than in the sleek, modern office.

A vague sense of recognition tugged at Jonah. He rarely forgot a face, and he'd seen the man before. Where? The smile that spread over Cilla's face as she spotted him and the easy way the man returned it left a coppery taste in Jonah's mouth and something twisted in his stomach. He'd taken a step toward the door before he stopped himself.

Jealousy. He'd felt it before, but never about a woman. And no woman had ever triggered this kind of possessiveness before. The kind that made him want to forget all about rules or playing it smart.

She entered the room with the cowboy only a step behind her. "David Santos, this is Jonah Stone."

The other man she'd been going to assign to him, Jonah recalled. Stepping forward, he gripped Santos's outstretched hand. "I've seen you before. Where?"

Santos smiled. "You may have caught a glimpse of me at one of your clubs, Interludes. Been there a couple of times, and I'll be back. Great place."

"Come anytime." Jonah found himself returning the smile. "Cilla tells me you have the unenviable job of tracking down all my possible enemies. Good luck with that."

"Slight change of plans," Cilla said. "David's going to distribute that task to our staff and from now on he'll follow us around from a distance and provide backup as needed. Gabe thinks it's a good idea."

"I agree." As Jonah looked from Santos to Cilla, he didn't miss the slight easing of tension in her shoulders.

Santos nodded at him. "I'll get started on the traces."

The moment he left the office, Jonah said, "You're reassigning Santos to give us backup because you think someone followed us to the police station."

"How else would they know to deliver the green box there?" A trace of a frown appeared on her forehead. "But I didn't see or sense the tail."

"Neither did I, and I watched." It was his turn to frown. "You're thinking that you didn't sense the tail because I was distracting you."

"That crossed my mind. You made me forget where I was in the police station."

He smiled at her. "I've been good since then. And I haven't seen any indication that you're distracted enough to keep you from doing the job."

"The thing is—I didn't *feel* like we were being followed." She raised a hand to rub the back of her neck. "Usually, I get an itchy feeling. If you're interfering with my instincts, you'd be better—"

He stepped forward as he cut her off. "I was watching, too. What if neither of us sensed or spotted the tail because there wasn't one?"

She frowned. "Then how did your gift giver know to deliver the package to the police precinct?"

"How else would *you* trace the movements of a car?"

"Shit." She fisted her hands on her hips and paced to one of the glass walls and back again. "Some kind of tracking device. And it wouldn't have to be in the places where I checked for a bomb." Whirling, she moved quickly to the door. "Come with me."

She stopped to let Santos know they'd be right back. Then Jonah had to lengthen his stride to keep up with her as she led the way out of the office to the elevator. In two minutes flat, they were at the level where she'd parked. Thirty seconds after that, they stood at the rear of her red sports car. It was now boxed in snugly by two large sedans that had managed to take more than their allotted space between the yellow lines.

"I'll take the driver's side," he said.

She didn't argue. Instead, she squatted down and ran her hand underneath the rear bumper. Nothing. Inching her way forward, she examined the right rear fender. Nothing again. It was the right front fender where her fingers struck pay dirt. "Got it."

She ran her fingers over the object. "It's tiny, maybe three inches long, maybe two wide."

Circling around the back of the car, Jonah joined her and reached under the fender to check it out. "You want me to remove it?"

"No way." She gripped his wrist with her fingers and withdrew his hand with her own. "If we leave it, we may be able to find a use for it."

"Like leading him on a wild-goose chase. I like it."

Turning her head, she smiled at him and found that he was much closer than she'd thought. Their knees were brushing, and his mouth was only a few inches from hers. Awareness shimmered through her.

The quick curve of that mouth and the amusement in his eyes triggered something inside her. Not the heat that she'd felt before, but something warmer and sweeter that spread like a slow-moving river. Fascinated, she wondered how a simple shared smile could be more intimate than the kisses they'd shared. Or the long night they'd spent together in Denver.

She could move back. Oh, she should move back. Because if she wasn't mistaken his mouth had edged just a little bit closer. Her fingers still gripped his wrist, and she felt his pulse jump just as hers was doing.

"I like the way your mind works, Cilla."

"Same goes."

Her pulse jumped again when he freed his wrist and took her hand, linked his fingers with hers. "I want to kiss you again."

"Same goes there, too. But we can't." Still, she didn't move. She was no longer sure she could. She was experiencing that same disconnect between brain and body that she'd felt in the police station. His mouth was closer now, only a breath away. "Rules."

His lips brushed hers. "I've always thought they were meant for bending."

His mouth was on hers. Not hard and demanding as she'd expected, but soft, testing, tasting. There was no pressure, only invitation, and every cell in her body urged her to accept. When he changed the angle, and gently nipped at her bottom lip, she trembled.

He'd never tempted her this way before. No one had. All the lectures she'd given herself during the night and the ride over from the police station were wiped away as her senses sharpened one by one.

There was so much to feel. A chill in the air that contrasted sharply with the warmth of his skin, the heat of his mouth. She smelled the lingering fumes of exhaust, but also caught his scent, soap and something that was unique to him. She heard the rumble of traffic on the street below, the growl of a car's engine on the level above them. And she could hear her own sigh escape as she moved closer and slipped her tongue between his teeth.

His taste seeped into her then, his flavor just as hot and pungent as she remembered. How had she lived through all those long lonely nights without having it again? She kept her eyes open, though she badly wanted to close them, to yield completely to the moment and to him. But she had to see who he was, to understand what there was about this one man that could make her forget everything but him.

It was so wrong to let him do this to her. So dangerous. But she couldn't gather the will to stop. As he deepened the kiss, slowly, persuasively, everything became involved in that mouth-to-mouth contact. She felt not only her body yield but her mind and her heart, as well. The warmth that had spread through her shifted seamlessly into an ache that started to build and sharpen. She laid her free hand on his cheek and tightened the fingers still gripping his hand.

The sound, explosive as a gunshot, had her pushing him down on the cement floor of the garage, covering as much of his body as she could with her own.

"Stay," she ordered in a whisper when he gripped her shoulders. Even as she dug beneath her jacket for her gun, she felt his moment of hesitation.

"My call," she snapped. "Look under the car to your right. Tell me what you see."

Even as he turned his head, she did the same and scanned the area to his left. There was no one approaching on foot in her limited sight line. But she caught the sound of the engine before Jonah said, "Car turning in from the level above."

There was little space to maneuver between the parked cars so she had to wiggle her way far enough up his body in order to grip the gun with both hands.

The vehicle shot past in a blur. A black van with a big man behind the wheel. She would have moved then, but Jonah's arm clamped hard around her waist. Tires squealed as the van took the turn to the lower level, and another loud crack echoed off the walls of the garage.

"Let me go," Cilla said. "It's Tank and our backfiring van. I'd swear to it."

"You're not going to catch him," Jonah said, his breath tickling her cheek. "And last night he had a gun he wasn't afraid to use."

Tires squealed again, and there was the sound of a muffled crash, then a noisy engine speeding up.

"See?" He released her. "It sounds like he didn't even have time to pay his parking ticket."

"Stay put for a minute." Cilla got to her knees, but she didn't reholster her gun until she'd risen to her feet and scanned the parking area. Nothing moved. The only sound came from traffic on the street below.

She glanced back down at him. He looked very relaxed lying there on the cement floor. And there was a part of her that wanted very badly to join him. Another part of her wanted to imagine in great detail what they might have been doing if the backfiring van hadn't interrupted them.

Firmly, she latched onto the part of her that had a job to do. "This might have been worse." She didn't like to think about that. She hadn't taken into consideration that someone could have been waiting in the garage for them. She certainly hadn't been thinking about work when Jonah had kissed her. "There are very important reasons not to bend the rules. From now on, we're going to follow them."

He grinned up at her. "Don't I even get some points for following orders and letting you take the lead?"

"That's one of the rules."

He held up a hand. "How about helping me up."

She shot him her sweetest smile. "Not when you're still thinking about helping me down."

"Can't blame a guy for trying." Jonah rolled and had one palm pressed to the ground and one knee under him when he suddenly lowered his head and peered more intently beneath her car. "What have we here?"

"What is it?"

When he met her eyes this time, the amusement had faded from his. "I'm no expert, but my guess is that there's a bomb on your rear axle."

8

HALF AN HOUR LATER, JONAH followed Cilla into a coffee shop two blocks down from her office building. Janine's. Cilla had suggested the place to him when the officer heading up the bomb squad informed her it would be another half hour or so before he could clear the garage and her office building for reentry.

Janine's was small, not part of a chain, with red-checkered tablecloths and miniature poinsettia plants on each table. The music was instrumental and muted, featuring a saxophone crooning "Silent Night." The air was rich with the scents of bacon, coffee and cinnamon.

A pretty waitress in her late-twenties approached them. "Your usual table, Ms. Michaels?"

"That would be great, Janine."

Not merely a waitress, Jonah mused, but young to be the owner.

"There's a lot of excitement down the block," Janine said. "Fire engines, police cars."

"Bomb scare in the garage of my building," Cilla told her. "Someone phoned it in. It's all being taken care of, but they had to evacuate everyone temporarily. It's just a precaution."

"Well, jeez," Janine said, then added, "My grandmother says Christmas always brings out the crazies."

"How is your grandmother?" Cilla asked.

"Great. She's totally annoyed that she can't come in here seven days a week. But she manages two or three. She doesn't trust my mom and me to make the cinnamon buns right."

They followed her to a table at the back where they could both sit with a view of the door and the street.

At Cilla's instructions, David Santos had followed them and chosen a table closer to the door. Gibbons, who'd returned to the building just as the first police cruisers had arrived, was going to check the security discs just as soon as the building was cleared.

Cilla had a point about sticking to the ground rules. Jonah was more than willing to concede that as he ordered coffee from Janine. It was the main reason he'd let her slip totally into the role of security agent since he'd spotted that bomb.

If that car hadn't backfired and jerked him back into reality, he'd have done more than bend the rules in the parking garage. They'd have made love right there only a few inches away from the bomb. While she'd been placing phone calls to her office and the police, he'd used the time to leash in the fury and the fear that had gripped him tight in the belly when he'd seen the wires hanging from the underside of her car.

She'd been a cop, he'd reminded himself. And the Priscilla part of her believed in following procedures. So she'd have checked the car before she'd driven anywhere in it. She'd have found the bomb. That conviction was strengthened by the methodical way she'd contacted Finelli and Gabe before they'd even left the garage.

"You're angry," she said.

"Damn straight. That bastard planted a bomb under your car. But I know temper is never the answer."

She met his eyes. "I agree. What we need to do is focus all of our attention on discovering who is behind the notes."

The chilly, almost lecturing tone of her voice had him wanting to smile. "In other words, I'm the client and you're the pro."

"Yes."

Tilting his head, he studied her. She'd been pulling back from him ever since he'd spotted the bomb. He was beginning to suspect there wasn't going to be any backing away for either of them. But he could be patient when he wanted to be.

"Fine. We still can't be sure if this Tank person is working alone or if he's been hired by someone else. Sometimes the best way to figure out the who is to discover the why."

She pulled a legal pad and a pencil out of the bag Santos had brought her when he'd joined them in the garage. "I think better when I'm writing—or at least scribbling."

"You mind sharing? I'm a bit of a doodler myself."

She ripped off some sheets and fished out another pencil. Then she grabbed her cell, flicked the screen a few times with her finger. "According to the text you sent me with your schedule, we're not due at Interludes for another hour. And you have a meeting with your partners, Carl Rockwell and Stanley Rubin, at the St. Francis Hotel at four-thirty."

"That's correct."

"From now on we'll use taxis," she said. "While we have some time, I'd like to ask you some questions that I was going to ask in the office earlier. They're the same ones I'd ask any client that came to me with a problem like yours."

Jonah decided he'd been playing the role of "good client" too long. "I'd like to start by discussing this." On one of the sheets she'd given him, he wrote *td*. Then he held it so she could read the letters.

"'Td'?"

"I'm wondering when that little tracking device was put on your car?"

She pursed her lips and thought for a moment. "My

guess is that it was last night when I was with you at Pleasures."

"So our friend Tank must have revisited the scene of the crime after his getaway and planted it then. Gutsy bastard."

"Yes. The van was parked across the street from the parking lot. He would have seen us drive in. He'd know my car."

"He couldn't have been happy with the way you interfered. So he puts a tracking device on your car, and now he probably knows who you are."

"And your point is?"

There was an edge to her tone, and he liked it a lot better than the chilly, lecturing one. "We're not merely security expert and client. We're partners, and you may need someone to watch your back as much as I do."

"David Santos is watching both of our backs." She leaned closer, the edge in her voice sharpening even as she lowered it. "As soon as Mark brings us what he's found on the garage's security discs, he'll join the team. So I think you should remember that you are the client and let me do my job."

Janine appeared with their coffees and a plate of cinnamon buns. "They're on the house." She was shaking her head as she walked off. "Bomb scares four days before Christmas."

As soon as she was out of earshot, Jonah said, "Your eyes get darker when you're angry but not as dark as when I'm kissing—"

"Stop!" She hissed the word as she poked a finger into his shoulder. "Stop that right now or you'll be proving that I was right all along and David and Mark should be sitting here, not me. We should not have been doing…what we were doing in that garage."

"Maybe not." He took a strand of her hair, tested the silkiness between his fingers. "I'm not sure we can prevent…what we were doing…from happening again."

"Backseat rule," she reminded him. "Let me do my job."

"Okay." He leaned away from her. "I'll go back to playing good client for a while on one condition."

She shot up a brow. "What?"

"You're staying at my place tonight."

"Why should I do that?"

"The tracking device and bomb were put on *your* car. This guy has gotten you in his sights. If we stay together, we can make better use of G.W. Securities' resources. Hopefully, we can prevent more people on your staff from becoming targets."

He pulled out his cell phone. "Until this is over, we're together, 24/7. I can make that argument to Gabe right now if you'd like."

Cilla frowned at him while her mind raced for an alternative argument. But dammit, he was right. Gabe would not only agree with him but wonder why she didn't. "I can see why you're good at negotiating deals."

He smiled at her. "I'm good at other things, too." He gripped her chin in his hand and gave her a brief kiss. At least, he'd intended it to be brief. But that intention flew out the window when her lips softened and opened for him, and her taste lured him into taking more. Each time he kissed her, there seemed to be more flavors to explore—layers of sweetness and spice that changed as the heat grew.

He'd expected her to pull back. But she had yet to do that. And the thought, the challenge of it had him adjusting the slant of the kiss and plunging them both deeper. The flavors changed again. Now what he tasted was a mix of surrender and greed, and he was no longer sure that he had the power to pull back. He sank fast, further and further until something inside of him gave way.

He was vaguely aware of a smattering of applause, a couple of whistles. But that wasn't what gave him the strength to draw away. It was the realization that this woman might be able to take everything from him. Everything.

Jonah leaned back in his chair and reminded himself to breathe. His head was still spinning but he managed to keep his hand steady when he reached for one of the buns.

He took a bite, watching her and waiting for her eyes to clear before he pointed at the plate Janine had brought. "We're going to need another order of these. Suddenly, I'm starved."

Cilla spoke in a very low voice. "You were supposed to play good client."

"I tried."

"Try harder." She lifted her pencil. "This is a question I would ask any client during a first session so don't give me any grief. How exactly would you describe what's happening to you? I want it in your own words."

He sipped his coffee again. She had to have been as affected by that kiss as he was, and he admired the way she could snap right back into Priscilla mode. But it had been Cilla he'd kissed. Cilla who was as vulnerable to him as he was to her.

"I'm not asking for a novel here or a dissertation," she said, "just a short description, twenty-five words or less."

The thread of sarcasm in her tone had him smiling. "Someone has sent me three mildly threatening notes all wrapped up as Christmas presents. And they hired some rather incompetent thugs to mug me."

"Why 'mildly' threatening?"

He paused long enough to bite into another bun, chew and swallow. "Because the notes aren't specific, I suppose. Reminding me that life and fortune are fleeting doesn't amount to a death threat. Life and fortune *are* fleeting. Everything can be lost in a heartbeat."

"But they also want you to pay."

"For what? Even that's vague. Maybe the notes are leading up to some kind of ransom demand."

She tapped her pencil on the pad. "For money?"

"Yes."

"And the attempted mugging, the bomb planted under my car are geared to scare you and motivate you to pay." She considered for a moment. "None of the people on the list you gave me rings a bell yet?"

"Not a one."

Cilla studied him closely. "Any ex-lovers who might hold a grudge?"

He smiled again. And just that sudden curve of his lips softened her bones. She could no longer feel the pencil she held in her hand.

"No complaints so far," he said.

There wouldn't be. Cilla certainly didn't have any. And she didn't seem to have any resistance to him. Not in the garage earlier and not when he'd kissed her a few minutes ago. It didn't matter where they were when he kissed her, she wanted. Nothing, no one else existed but him. It was that simple. That terrifying.

A man who could kiss the way he did could probably ease his way out of a relationship as easily as he indulged in one. With no hard feelings on anyone's part. Wasn't that exactly the deal he'd offered her in that hotel bar? The thought brought the feeling back to her fingers.

"And the use of words like *pleasures* and *interludes,* names of your clubs—does that seem mildly threatening also?"

He frowned. "Yes. And more specific in a way."

She glanced up and met his eyes again. "Your businesses mean a lot to you."

"Yes."

Although it was the answer she expected to hear, Cilla felt a tightening around her heart. To a man like Jonah Stone, the businesses he'd created would take precedence over everything. That had always been the case with her father.

Then she refocused. "You're more worried about the threat to your clubs than you are about the possible threat to you."

There was a beat before he said, "Yes."

"Who would know that about you?"

He thought for a moment. "My close friends, anyone who works for me. Perhaps even anyone I've done business with."

"A manager like Virgil would certainly be aware of this. How about the manager of Interludes?"

"Carmen D'Annunzio. Yes, she would. She volunteered at the St. Francis Center my last year there when opening Pleasures was on my mind 24/7. Her two sons were regulars. I thought of her a few years later when I opened Interludes and she agreed to move here to San Francisco."

"I'll want to talk to Virgil and Carmen. They could have valuable insights." After jotting down the names, she glanced at him again. "It would be better if I could speak with them alone."

"We'll be at both places today. I can give you some time with them."

"What about your family?"

"I don't have one."

The sudden coolness in his tone was a perfect match to what she saw in his eyes. He wanted her to back off.

She kept her voice calm, her tone reasonable. "Everyone has a family, even if we'd rather trade them in for different models. Gabe wouldn't have to ask the question because he probably already knows. But I don't, and you insisted that I work the case. What happened to your family?"

He said nothing for a moment. "I'll tell you about my family if you'll tell me about yours."

She bit back a sigh. "I'm not asking you to satisfy idle curiosity. Finding out about your family is part of my job."

He nodded. "A job you're good at, so you must have to negotiate with difficult clients. I don't like to talk about my family. So if I have to dig them up, what can it hurt to humor me a little?"

She raised her brows. "This is your idea of playing good client?"

He lifted his mug, his eyes laughing at her over the rim. "You didn't stipulate perfect. And I haven't really shown you bad yet."

She couldn't prevent the laugh. And when he joined her, she was charmed by the sound. "Okay. But you first."

He cupped his hands around his mug. "My parents were Susan and Darrell Stone. They met at a party my mother was waitressing at. He was a guest. It was love at first sight. Darrell Stone had some kind of secret government job that kept him away from home more than he was there."

As Jonah spoke, his tone was neutral. So were his eyes. Cilla felt her heart twist all the same.

"When I was a kid, the happiest days of my life were the ones he spent with us. He used to tell stories of the adventures he had, some in countries I'd never heard of. The year I was nine, he'd called my mom and promised to be home for Christmas. We waited and waited to open the presents and have dinner. But he never came, never sent word. Because of his work, my mother never had any way to contact him. Shortly after Christmas, the checks he always sent us stopped coming, and my mother went back to work waitressing. I watched her grow sadder and sadder. She kept telling me that he would come home soon, but I think it was to convince herself."

Jonah set down his mug, and Cilla reached out to take his hand in hers. The image of Jonah as a nine-year-old boy was so vivid in her mind.

"Six months after Christmas, a beautiful June day, my mom was struck and killed by a bus. Later, when I was older, I read the reports of the accident. Witnesses said she stepped in front of the bus. I don't think she could live without him."

"I am so sorry about your mother." Both parents had abandoned him and she couldn't begin to imagine what that might feel like. "Didn't anyone try to find your father?"

"Sure. A social worker told me they were doing their best to trace him, but no branch of the government employed a Darrell Stone who matched my father's description or age. So I went into foster care."

"Did *you* ever try to trace him? Gabe tells me you're the best hacker he's ever met."

"No. When I was young, I hadn't developed that skill yet." He shrugged. "By the time I did, I had no interest in finding my father. He'd been dead to me for a long time."

Cilla met his eyes steadily. "We'll have to try to locate him, see if he's still alive."

She waited a beat, and when he said nothing she continued, "We're already tracking down names of families and kids you met in foster care. Gabe is getting the names of people you came in contact with when you worked at the St. Francis Center."

"It's a long list, but you've already met one of the kids I knew in foster care. Virgil."

She glanced up at that.

"The first foster home I was in, he stood up for me. When I knew I was going to open Pleasures, I tracked him down. He was working in a bar over in Sausalito, and I hired him to manage my club."

"You hire Virgil from your first foster home, then you hire Carmen from the St. Francis Center. You don't abandon your friends, Jonah Stone."

"I make good business decisions. Now it's your turn."

She set her pencil down. "My parents are Penny and Bradley Michaels. My mother has Boston blue blood in her veins, and my father met her when he was getting his MBA at Harvard. They divorced when I was five because my mother wanted more attention and he was focused totally on his work. He's had a stellar career and become a

CEO at four Fortune 500 companies. He's currently trying to get a fifth one on the list. My mother's mission in life is to find Prince Charming. She's sure that husband number four, Bobby Laidlaw, is the one."

He studied her for a moment. She was giving him the same *Reader's Digest* version he'd given her. It only made him more curious. "How in hell did you end up becoming a cop?"

She smiled at him. "Textbook case of rebellion. My career still annoys my father. He calls me twice a year—on my birthday and at Christmas—and he always offers me a job with his current company."

"That's not the only reason you do the work you do."

"Maybe not. How did you end up creating places like Pleasures and Interludes?"

"I like creating worlds that offer people a chance to escape from the ordinary."

Her gaze didn't waver. "That's not the only reason. But—" she picked up her pencil "—we have other things to discuss."

Adjusting the pad so they both could read it, she wrote: *Christmases past, Interludes, Pleasures, fortune, fleeting* and *you're going to pay, six, five, four* and *counting*.

She tapped her pencil on *Christmases past*. "My hunch is we're going to find the answer here."

"I agree, but I'm coming up empty."

She moved her pencil to *six*. "That number has to mean something. What was going on at Christmas six years ago?"

He hadn't thought of that angle and he had to concentrate for a moment before it came to him. "I was still in Denver working for Gabe at G.W. Securities while I was getting together a business plan and attracting backers. Any spare time I had during the holiday season, I always helped out at the St. Francis Center."

"That would have been 2005. Can you think of anything more specific?"

Jonah frowned as the year suddenly rang a bell. "Yeah, now that you mention it. That was the year I spent Christmas here in San Francisco. This was where I wanted to open my first club because of St. Francis. I figured he'd always brought me good luck before, so I thought it was a good idea to begin in a city that was named after him. Nash's grandmother, Maggie Fortune, had gotten together a group of backers, and I asked her to come with me to look at some properties I had lined up."

"Was Carl Rockwell around? You said he was one of your original backers."

"No. I hadn't met any of them yet. It was just Nash's grandmother and me. Nash was overseas and I had some idea of getting her away from the Fortune Mansion over the holidays. We came up with the name of the club on that trip."

He smiled. "We spent every day for a week, save Christmas Day, looking at real estate. And we found the building where Pleasures now stands."

"So that year, you were particularly focused on business."

"You could say that."

Cilla turned the pad around and began writing. "Gabe can check with Father Mike and contact Mrs. Fortune to see what they can remember about that December. In the meantime, we can't ignore other possibilities."

"But this is a good one. I can feel it." He placed a hand on hers. "You're good, Cilla Michaels."

"I need to get better." With her pencil, she tapped on the paper where he'd written *td.* "We need a better handle on who this Tank guy is. Part of what he's doing is carefully planned. The notes, the boxes and ribbon, even some of the places he chooses for delivery—it all needs to be precisely orchestrated."

She tapped her pencil again. "But there's a part of him that's less careful and more open to going with impulse. There's no way that he could have known we'd be at the police station this morning until we actually got there."

"You're right," Jonah mused. "And why would someone who has been so meticulous with this countdown-to-Christmas scenario hire a couple of low IQ thugs like Mickey P. and Lorenzo?"

"Or why drive a van that backfires? And last night at Pleasures, why lower the window and shoot his gun? Why not just drive away?"

"Temper? Maybe we're dealing with someone who isn't as stable as he thinks he is," Jonah said.

When her cell phone rang, she took the call. "Finelli, what have you got?" As she listened, she summarized the information for Jonah. "The bomb hadn't been fully wired yet. The bomb squad thinks we may have interrupted whoever was working on it." Then she went silent, listening hard.

When she finally disconnected Finelli's call, she looked straight at Jonah. "Someone on the bomb squad recognized the type of explosive. He'd served in the military and seen similar ones used in Iraq. Whoever built it was good, probably ex-military, and it would have had to be set off by a detonator. When Joe learned that, he had someone search the garage and they found the detonator in the stairwell on the floor where my car was parked."

Jonah thought for a moment. "The tracking device allowed Tank to locate your car and he was planting the bomb when we interrupted him. He slips away, and when he sees us checking the car, he panics and runs."

"And he tosses the detonator into a stairwell as he rounds the curve?" Cilla shook her head. "Why not take it with him?"

"Because his job was to plant the bomb. It was someone

else's job to detonate it. I'm thinking Tank was working with someone who was standing in that stairwell waiting."

"A strong possibility." Then she shook her head again. "But there are still four nights and counting. Why would he blow you up today?"

Jonah reached for her hand and gripped it hard. "Not me. *You.* And with a detonator, he could have blown you up anytime."

"I would have found the bomb."

"That's what I've been telling myself. But if he was standing in that stairwell waiting, he could have detonated it while you were checking for the bomb." Fear snaked through him as he imagined what might have happened in the garage if they hadn't interrupted the driver of the van. Maybe he'd been wrong to insist that she personally handle his case. "Cilla…" he began.

"If you're thinking of firing me, forget it." Turning her hand, she linked her fingers with his. "You're the one who wanted a partner, and now you're stuck."

He was, Jonah realized as he gazed into those green eyes. He'd been stuck from the first. The thought tied an uneasy knot in his stomach. But the damage had been done. He wasn't going to be able to prevent himself from kissing her again, from having her again. And as he watched her eyes darken, he knew that she was coming to the same realization.

Cilla was the one who broke eye contact when Mark Gibbons arrived at their table and pulled out a chair. He placed four prints in front of Jonah. "Here's what we were able to get off the security discs."

The images were grainy, but the buzz-cut gray hair was clear. The man wore sunglasses, he had a square chin, and Jonah guessed him to be in his mid- to late fifties. He took his time, studying the prints one by one. Finally, he looked up and met Cilla's eyes. "I have no idea who this man is."

WHEN HE COULD THINK WITH SOME clarity again, the red mist was still a haze in front of his eyes. Blinking rapidly, he willed it away and focused on his surroundings. He was seated in his car, his fingers gripping the steering wheel.

The fire engine blocking off traffic at the corner told him that only a short time had passed. There were people standing on the street, huddled together for warmth in the chill winds. He'd heard the approaching sirens when he'd still been inside the garage. Bits and pieces of what had happened flashed into his mind in a series of quick-moving still photos.

He'd been standing in the stairwell watching through a narrow opening in the door when the plan he'd devised had been bungled again. His partner had promised no more failed missions, but he'd abandoned his assignment before he'd completed it. Then he'd panicked and driven off.

Again.

Just thinking about the backfiring van careening through the garage had his fury building again.

Stupid. Stupid. Stupid. Releasing his hold on the steering wheel, he beat his fists against it. Then reaching deep for control, he made himself breathe. And settle.

His partner was only partly to blame. That woman had interfered again. The bomb hadn't been fully engaged when she'd strode out of the elevator and headed toward her car. If it hadn't been for the clicking of her boots, his partner might have been discovered.

But he'd slithered out from under the car and crawled quietly along the wall in front of the other parked vehicles.

She'd come out too soon. Struggling again to control the anger, he gripped the steering wheel. If it hadn't been for her, he could have enjoyed the scenario he'd mapped out in his mind.

Closing his eyes, he replayed it. He would have been in the stairwell watching as she'd stepped out of the elevator. And he would have detonated the bomb then. It held a small blast, one that would have severely damaged her car and perhaps the adjacent vehicles. But it wouldn't have killed either Stone or the woman—not unless they were in the car.

It hadn't been his intent to kill Stone yet. Just as it hadn't been his intent to have him seriously hurt in the alley last night. But he would have had the pleasure of seeing Stone's face when the explosion occurred.

He would have seen fear on it this time. The man hadn't looked scared at all when he'd opened the green box in front of the police station this morning. He should be feeling the impact by now.

But Stone's face hadn't changed expression.

It was the woman's fault again. She was protecting him, making him feel safe by kicking guns out of people's hands, checking the cars.

It would have given him great satisfaction to see her face when her car exploded into smithereens.

He drew in another breath and let it out. He felt himself begin to calm. He still had time. Four more nights. Before this was over, he'd see fear on Jonah Stone's face.

There were all kinds of ways to create fear.

A smile curved his lips as the plan took form in his mind. It was the season for surprises.

9

INTERLUDES WAS NOT WHAT Cilla had expected. Her first surprise was the sign on the door that read Closed Until 4:00 p.m. on December 21 for a Private Party. The second surprise was the wall of noise that slapped into them the instant they stepped into the place.

The party was in full swing. And nearly everyone there was a kid. Out of habit, she moved slightly in front of Jonah. "I feel like I just stepped into munchkin land."

"Christmas party," Jonah explained.

"I can see that." The huge Christmas tree at the far end of the dining room with its multicolored blinking lights was a big clue. And blasting through the din of noise, "Jingle Bell Rock" poured through the sound system. She let her gaze take a quick sweep of the venue.

Two rooms opened off the large entrance area where they stood. Her image of a sports club had always contained lots of huge-screen TVs hanging from the ceiling, crowds drinking beer from big mugs and noise. Shouts, cheering, people doing happy dances and a lot of arm pumping.

Interludes provided all that. There were shouts of "Hey, Jonah," when she and Jonah moved farther in. And the dining area to the left had the big flat-screened TVs all right. It also boasted a movie screen that nearly filled one wall.

The pint-size customers were drinking beer from big mugs. But since none of them looked to be over twelve, she guessed it was root beer, and most seemed more interested in a buffet spread that offered a seemingly endless variety of pizzas than they were in watching TV.

When she was able to drag her gaze away to meet Jonah's, he pitched his voice so she could hear it above the clamor. "Christmas party for all of the boys and girls clubs in the area. We throw them at other times of the year, but this is the big one."

It was big all right, she thought. At a rough estimate, she figured there were nearly a hundred children easy—just in the dining room. She looked around her. Small people in various shapes and sizes also filled the long room to her right. Only here, pool instead of food was the attraction. With its gleaming mahogany paneling and carved ceilings, the space reminded her of the game room of an expensive and exclusive men's club. Green shaded lamps hung over each of the more than a dozen pool tables. And here and there, adults helped the kids chalk cues and generally supervised the fun.

A woman stepped away from the nearest table and strode toward them. Cilla guessed her to be in her mid-forties. She wore a bright emerald colored silk shirt over slim black leggings, and her long, ash-blond hair was layered.

"Jonah, I was afraid you wouldn't make it." The rich voice with its genuine warmth and slightly Southern lilt had Cilla thinking briefly of the TV celebrity chef Paula Deen.

"Carmen, I'd like you to meet Cilla Michaels. She runs Gabe Wilder's office here in San Francisco." He turned to Cilla. "Carmen D'Annunzio runs Interludes even on a day like today when chaos is king."

Carmen laughed, and the sound was as rich and warm as her voice. "Long live chaos and Christmas. They make a perfect couple." Then she turned to Cilla and took one of her hands. "Welcome to Interludes."

"Jonah, come and play." A skinny boy with riotously curling dark hair shot over from one of the tables. "You promised that at this party you'd clear the tables again."

"Rack the balls," Jonah said, stripping off his jacket as he followed the boy.

One of the other boys raced into the bar and whistled for silence. When the din lowered a few decibels, he said, "Jonah's going to hit all the balls into the pockets. C'mon."

Carmen put two fingers into her mouth and did her own whistle to prevent the stampede. Raising both hands, she said, "Hold on. I'll get it on the TV screens."

"C'mon," she said to Cilla as she moved quickly to a console in a corner of the dining room and punched a few buttons. Suddenly all the screens showed Jonah bending over the pool table. Cilla stared fascinated at the large movie screen as he made his first shot. Three balls disappeared into pockets.

"He's good," she murmured.

"Never seen anyone better," Carmen said. "We've been open four years now, and he puts on this show a couple of times a year. Closes down the place for the afternoon and lets the kids party. How about a root beer? I've also got lemonade and more traditional colas. I'm only serving the soft stuff this afternoon."

"I'd love a root beer." Cilla climbed onto a stool at a raised table while Carmen filled two glasses and joined her.

The din in the room had quieted a bit as the kids grabbed more food and settled into seats to watch the show. Jonah's next shot ricocheted off two others balls and sent them into different pockets.

Cilla positioned her seat so that she had a good view of the pool room. She watched as David Santos slipped through the front door. Mark Gibbons was with him. She signaled Santos into the room with Jonah and Mark slipped behind the hostess desk. They'd arrived in three separate taxis she'd had Mark call before they'd left Janine's.

Catching Carmen watching her, she said, "Two of my men."

"I know David Santos. He's a regular customer here."

Cilla glanced back up at the nearest TV screen. Jonah was walking around the table considering his next shot. He looked so relaxed that his only care in the world might have been to sink another ball. It was as if he'd shed the first part of the day including the bomb scare as easily as he'd shed his jacket.

If he had, she envied him. More, she needed to emulate him. Thinking about the might-have-beens would only distract her from thinking about the what-might-bes. Using taxis for transportation could work for a while. But the bastard who wanted to hurt Jonah would have a backup plan, too.

She turned her gaze to Carmen. "I need a quiet place to make a quick phone call."

Carmen pointed to a door at the far end of the room. "My office."

Cilla left the door open as she punched a number into her cell. From her position, she could see Jonah on the screens. A more direct view of him was blocked by the kids who'd moved closer to his pool table.

"Hello, my favorite cop."

"Not a cop anymore, T.D." Five years ago, T.D. short for Top Dog, had been her first snitch when she'd been a beat cop. He'd given her two of her first collars, and she'd arranged for him to get a legitimate job as a limo driver. Last time she'd talked to him he was well on his way to an associate's degree at a local community college, and then he'd married his boss's daughter.

A laugh boomed into her ear. "And I'm not your snitch. Instead, I'm driving around San Francisco in a honey of a limo."

"I want to hire you later today. Can you do it?"

"For you, sugar, I'll rearrange my schedule. When and where?"

"I need a pickup at least four or five blocks away from the St. Francis Hotel between 5:30 and 6:30. My client has a late-afternoon meeting there. Someone may try to tail us from the hotel, so I'll shake them and then come to you."

"You got it. When you're ready, give me a call and I'll give you my specific location. Bye, sugar."

After disconnecting, Cilla punched in Gabe's number. When he picked up immediately, she filled him in on the day's events and the fact that both she and Jonah had a feeling about the Christmas of 2005. "Was Mark Gibbons working for you then?" she asked.

"He started that fall. You want me to check him out."

It wasn't a question. Still, she waited a beat. "I do. Do you think I'm being paranoid?"

"No. One of the reasons I hired you, Cilla, is because we think alike. I'm already checking Gibbons and Santos out. Santos is from Denver and he was in the Marines until two years ago. He worked with explosives, and some of his records are classified. But I can't find a connection between either of them and Jonah. Yet. Anyone else you want me to check into?"

"Yes. The backers that Mrs. Fortune put together for Pleasures. The deal was coming together that year."

"So it was. I hadn't thought of that angle."

"One of his current partners, Carl Rockwell, was also one of the backers for Pleasures."

"Got it. Call me if you want anything else. And, Cilla?"

"Yes?"

"Don't let him get hurt."

A deafening roar of applause and cheers had Cilla glancing up at the big screen again. She'd missed the shot, but the children were jumping up and down around Jonah's table.

When she returned to her seat at the bar, the kids had quieted, their eyes glued on Jonah.

His back was to her, larger than life on the screen. Though she knew she should, she didn't look away. Instead, she let her system absorb the way his black wool turtleneck fit over the broad shoulders like a second skin. The burning sensation in her hands reminded her of how hard those shoulder muscles had felt beneath her palms. Her pulse skipped as she let her gaze drift down the lean back to the narrow waist, the tight, hard butt and those long legs. Her throat went dry as dust.

It had been nearly a month since that body had been hers to touch, to explore at whim. And she hadn't been able to stop thinking about touching him again. Not during those long lonely nights and certainly not since he'd walked toward her in the airport garage yesterday. The kisses they'd exchanged had only deepened her hunger.

She had to touch him again. Slowly, thoroughly. She needed to feel his naked skin heat, then tremble. She wanted to once more hear her name on his lips. Desire burned in her belly and simmered in her blood. She wasn't even looking directly at him, just at his image on a screen, and yet the pull, the attack on her senses, were as intense as if she had been standing directly behind him in the room.

And if she *had* been standing behind him? Would she have been able to resist putting her hands on him? She drew in a breath and felt the burn in her lungs. She thought of all those nights she'd spent without him. Long silent nights filled with nothing but sexy fantasies of touching Jonah, tasting him, feeling him thrusting inside of her again. And again.

She didn't want the fantasy anymore. She wanted the real thing. Longing spread through every pore of her being, and she had to grip the edge of the table hard to keep herself from going to him. No man had ever triggered this kind of response in her, this kind of greed. She might talk a good game about ground rules, but it wasn't to Jonah that she had to pitch her argument. It was to herself.

When she reached for her root beer, she was stunned to realize that her hand was trembling. She fisted it on the tabletop and looked back at the screen.

"A lot of eye candy there," Carmen murmured. "The girls all have a crush on him, the boys all want to *be* him."

Cilla blinked, then dragged her eyes away from the image of Jonah. *Job,* she reminded herself. "What about the grown-ups who are here? How do they feel about Jonah?"

"Probably a mix of admiration and envy."

"Do you know all of them?"

"Met a few of them for the first time today. They're parents or volunteers and workers at the various clubs."

"Any of them come alone?"

"No. They all came with groups of kids."

Cilla glanced back at the pool room and saw that Santos had chosen a space within a few feet of Jonah.

"Virgil told me what happened at Pleasures last night," Carmen said. "He was nearly mugged. But that's not all of it, is it? There's more."

For a moment, Cilla didn't speak. Jonah trusted Carmen and Virgil, but she couldn't discount the fact that someone close to him, probably someone from his past, had a hand in the threats.

But her gut told her that Carmen wasn't that person. And Jonah's gut was telling him the same thing. Going with those feelings, she outlined what had happened.

"Well, shit." Carmen set her root beer down with enough force that it sloshed over the rim of the glass. "This is his favorite time of year. And to me, he embodies the true spirit of Christmas. Jonah loves throwing the parties. Not just this one. The shindig he has going on at Pleasures tomorrow night—all the movers and shakers in the city will be there. Over the years, he's built it into *the* event of the season, and the money he collects goes to the boys and girls clubs." She swept a hand around. "Eventually to these kids."

"Do you have any idea who might be sending the notes?"

"No." She met Cilla's eyes. "Tell me what I can do to help."

"You can start by answering some questions."

"Go ahead."

"Jonah told me that you used to volunteer at the St. Francis Center for Boys in Denver. How well did you know him?"

"I knew him mostly through my sons. He's wonderful with kids. When my husband died ten years ago, my boys were ten and twelve. They were a handful even then. The only job I could get was bartending. I hired someone to come in at night, but I needed a place for my boys to go after school and on weekends. The St. Francis Center was perfect."

Cilla couldn't help but think how closely Carmen's story echoed Jonah's and his mother's experience. Except that Jonah had lost his mother as well as his father. Both of his parents had abandoned him. But Jonah didn't abandon people. "Were you surprised when he asked you to move here and manage Interludes?"

"I was stunned." Carmen met her eyes, and Cilla saw a glint of tears. "It meant I had to uproot the kids, but they were older, close to making me an empty nester. And Jonah made everything so easy for me. It's the best decision I ever made."

The skinny kid with the mop of curls came racing up to Carmen at the bar. "Jonah needs fuel."

Carmen's brows shot up. "Well, load a plate up for him. We can't have the boss going hungry."

"Yes, ma'am." The boy shot off to the buffet.

"This is a very different place than Pleasures," Cilla commented.

"Well, you're seeing us on a special day. But if I were to use some of that fancy business school mumbo jumbo that my oldest son, Jack, uses, I'd say that the mission statements of the two clubs are the same. Basically, Jonah's goal is to create places for people to shed their cares and worries for a short time. Places that they can enter into for a while and just play. And people have different price points and different images of their escape spaces."

"Fantasy worlds," Cilla murmured.

"You could call them that. But for a short time, they're reality. It's not a whole lot different from what Father Mike did when he started the St. Francis Center. He created a safe space for kids to play and learn and grow, a place that sheltered them and helped them deal better with the reality outside."

"It's like what a home should do," Cilla commented.

"Yeah," Carmen agreed. "When everything's ideal. But that can be a hard thing to pull off. I know."

Cilla thought of her own home—her father working, her mother unhappy. She might not have liked it; her mother certainly hadn't. But it had been there. Her parents, as imperfect as they might be, were still there.

She glanced up at the big screen again and saw that Jonah had set his pool stick aside to eat the pizza the skinny boy had brought him. As she watched, the kid burst into laughter and Jonah joined him. She felt her heart take a tumble. He looked so right standing there.

He claimed that he'd created these clubs to provide customers with an escape, but she wondered if he hadn't really built them as a way of establishing a home for himself.

And she was letting him distract her again. Turning to Carmen, she said, "You were volunteering at the St. Francis Center six years ago, right? That would have been Christmastime, 2005."

"Sure. My boys were still in high school—sixteen and fourteen. Tough ages. I was there when I could be. Why?"

"I want you to think about that year at Christmastime. Jonah wasn't in Denver. He was here in San Francisco checking out possible places for Pleasures."

She frowned, thinking. "What happens at my age is that the years begin to blur."

"That year, 2005, might be important. Think about it." She passed a card to Carmen. "And let me know."

Carmen met her eyes. "I'll do more than think about it, I'll ask my sons. The younger one will have pictures. Father Mike got him his first camera, put him in charge of making a pictorial history of the center. Ben fell in love with photography. That's his major in college, and he kept pictures that he took at the center. What are we looking for?"

Cilla shook her head. "I wish I knew. The notes he's receiving are telling him he has to pay for something. And they mention Christmases past."

"The Dickens's *Christmas Carol* thing," Carmen murmured.

"If you can remember anyone he offended that year. Any feathers that got ruffled around the center. Maybe somebody took it wrong that he went off to San Francisco on business." Cilla remembered the Christmases that her father had been away on business and how much she'd resented it.

"I'll have Ben find the photos," Carmen said.

A cheer went up from the kids in the bar. Cilla glanced up at the screen to see that Jonah's pool table was clear of balls except for the cue ball. "He is really good."

"Yeah." Carmen put a hand over hers. "Jonah's like a kid brother to me. Virgil feels the same way. And he says that Jonah's more than a case to you."

"Yes." No use denying it. A man with Virgil's eagle eye hadn't missed their kiss in the bar last night. And she'd spent most of her time here staring at Jonah on the big screen like a teenager.

Carmen's gaze turned assessing and some of the warmth faded. "You're not his type."

She lifted her chin. "I don't want to be his type. I didn't want him to be more than a case to me."

The warmth returned to Carmen's eyes and her lips curved into a smile. "Sometimes it happens that way. Just don't let him get hurt."

Carmen was the third person who'd said those words to her in just that tone. Jonah seemed to have quite a loyal following, and that didn't surprise her. He wasn't the career-minded businessman she'd first thought him to be.

Over Carmen's shoulder, she watched him striding toward her, one arm around the skinny kid, the other around a chubby redheaded girl with freckles. When she met his eyes, absorbed the smile, something moved through her. Even though her toes curled, it wasn't merely the pull she always felt. Or the fire in her belly she was almost getting used to. What she felt was that warmer, softer feeling she'd experienced when he'd kissed her so tenderly in the garage. As it spread, she all but heard a click inside her as something unlocked.

She pressed a hand to her stomach as fear bubbled up brightly. How had it come to this? How had she fallen in love with him?

And those weren't questions she could afford to think about now. She had to focus on keeping him safe. Her gut told her that the clock was ticking on that one.

IT WAS NEARLY FOUR BEFORE Jonah hung his pool stick on the rack and watched the last of the kids reluctantly exit through the front door of Interludes. There was a part of him that looked forward to this party every year. But he was also aware there was a part of him that had wanted very much for the party to end.

And that was because of Cilla.

Usually, he could completely lose himself in a game of

pool. Playing allowed him to clear his mind for a while. Today, there hadn't been one moment when he'd been able to totally focus on the position of the balls or to imagine the possible angles for a shot.

Because she'd been watching him. Sometimes, he would look up and catch her doing just that. Other times he was pretty sure he'd felt her watching him on the TV screens.

How in the hell was that possible? He ran a hand through his hair.

He studied her now as she paced in the dining room, the phone pressed to her ear. She was in Priscilla mode, jotting down notes, figuring the angles.

But there was that moment earlier when he'd walked into the dining room and his eyes had met hers—she'd been Cilla then. Something in her look had slammed into him like a Mack truck, triggering so many emotions, so many needs.

He'd been outrageously tempted to just go to her, grab her off that stool, and carry her off somewhere. Only the fact that he'd been surrounded by kids and someone was trying to kill her had stopped him. Caveman tactics had never been his style, but as he watched her pace, he was beginning to see their value.

It had been hours since he'd touched her, kissed her. It might as well have been years. And it was going to be far too long until he could get her back to Pleasures and into his bed.

A quick glance at his watch told him that they were due at the St. Francis Hotel in half an hour. And he'd never been more tempted in his life to blow off a business meeting. Carl would understand. But Stanley Rubin had called the meeting as a favor. Jonah couldn't let him down.

One thing he was sure of, the two quick kisses he'd stolen during the endless day hadn't been enough. But they'd certainly tapped out his self-control. He'd better keep his distance and play by her ground rules until they were safely in his apartment.

Pushing himself away from the pool table, he strode into the entrance hall.

"I'll lock the door," Mark Gibbons said.

Jonah turned to the man, who hadn't left his post at the hostess desk all afternoon. Carmen had brought him a plate of food at one point, but he'd remained where he could check out anyone who came through the door.

"Boss wants to have a brief meeting before we leave for your business appointment at the hotel," Gibbons said.

Turning, Jonah saw that Cilla now sat at a table with Santos, out of the way of the waitstaff that was whisking away the debris of the party.

Jonah turned to Gibbons. "I have a couple of questions for you. Why did you leave the Denver office?"

"Gabe asked me to come here temporarily." Gibbons studied him for a moment. "If you're wondering if I wanted her job, if I'm carrying some kind of grudge because Gabe put her in charge of the office instead of me, I'm not. And I didn't plant a bomb under her car."

"Why didn't you want the job?"

"Because I've got a girlfriend back in Denver who is not happy about the situation. I go back there on my weekends off. She comes here on the others. If I took a permanent job here, she'd send me packing."

"So Gabe asked you to play what—big brother-slash-mentor until Cilla is comfortable?"

"Gabe is less concerned about her than the rest of the staff. Santos is new, both to the business and to G.W. He's great with the electronic security. He got some training in the military and then he worked for a casino in Vegas. I've been training him in the personal security side. Cilla's only new to G.W., but she's smart, she has good contacts here in the police department. Plus, her political instincts are good. Her instincts are good, period. She's got a mind that's always figuring the angles."

"Do you know why she left her personal security job in L.A.?"

"Sure. She told all of us at our first staff meeting. One of the teen idols she'd been assigned to got a little high and made some advances. She defended herself and as a result the production on his movie was delayed. The producers made a stink."

"But you dug a little deeper than that," Jonah guessed.

"Sure." His expression turned grim. "According to my sources, the guy tried to rape her. She knocked two of his teeth out and gave him a black eye. No charges were filed, but pretty boy couldn't film for nearly a week and the firm she worked for was being pressured to fire her. She quit first."

As Jonah studied Cilla, anger mixed with admiration. "She's one tough cookie."

"I'd say so." Mark patted him on the shoulder. "And in one more minute she's going to come over here and read us the riot act because we're delaying her strategy meeting. I'd like to keep my teeth."

"Me, too." Jonah walked with Mark to join her.

10

A HALF HOUR LATER, CILLA stepped out of a taxi in front of the St. Francis Hotel. After a quick scan of the area, she signaled Jonah to follow her. The late-afternoon sun was low in the sky and the air was cold and crisp.

The plan had been to take three taxis again—she and Jonah in the first, David Santos in a second and Mark Gibbons in the third. Out of the corner of her eye, she noted David's taxi had stopped across the street. He was already mixing into passengers disembarking from a cable car.

Pedestrians loaded down with packages milled along the sidewalk in front of the hotel. She steered Jonah through them. She hadn't spotted a tail, but if someone had followed them, they'd have to deal with the parking issue. She and Jonah wouldn't.

They were halfway up the steps when Mark strode past them and into the hotel. The lobby was aglow with Christmas. Tired shoppers with packages stacked on the floor had filled the bar to overflowing. Above the laughter and conversation, she caught the sounds of a string quartet playing "White Christmas."

They moved toward the elevators where Mark was already waiting for a car. Everything was going smoothly. The ride over had been short. And Jonah had played the role of good client perfectly. He hadn't touched her. She'd been so sure that he would kiss her. An afternoon of watching him on the big screen and not being able to touch him had been nearly as frustrating as the three-and-a-half weeks she'd spent avoiding her bed because he wasn't in it.

By the time she'd decided that she should play bad security agent, the taxi had stopped in front of the St. Francis.

On the bright side, she'd been able to fill him in on what she'd discussed with Carmen. He'd filled her in on the Rubins.

One of the elevator doors opened. Quickly, she moved into the car with Jonah, then shifted so that she stood in front of him as she scanned the lobby. Mark followed a crowd of shoppers into the same car. She spotted David Santos leaning against one of the walls, reading a newspaper as the elevator doors closed. His job was to keep watch in the lobby. If there was any sign of the driver of the backfiring van, he would notify them.

Everything was going smoothly, like clockwork. And it wasn't disappointment she was feeling because Jonah had finally decided to stick to her ground rules. She should be worrying about why she had an itchy sensation at the back of her neck. There was no reason for it—unless it was connected to the sexual frustration she was feeling.

Focus, she told herself. As the elevator crept slowly upward, she reviewed the information Jonah had given her on Stanley Rubin, who'd amassed a fortune building condos and upscale apartment complexes in San Diego.

Just as he'd promised, Jonah had notified Stan that he was bringing a personal security agent with him because of the attempted mugging last night. According to Jonah, Stan's reaction had been concern and then approval that Jonah was taking precautions.

Joining Stan and Carl at the meeting would be Rubin's wife, Glenda, and his young associate, Dean Norris. When she'd asked Jonah who had initiated the meeting, he'd said, "Stan. We're due to start renovating the property for our new club right after the first of the year. Norris has some new design ideas that Stan wants Carl and me to see. My understanding is that they conflict with the vision I originally presented them for the club. Both he and Glenda are coming to the party at Pleasures tomorrow evening. And since Stan loves to mix business with pleasure—his words—he asked for a meeting."

"And what about this Dean Norris?" she'd asked. "What do you know about him?"

"Norris joined Rubin Enterprises a year ago when he left the army. Stan believes he's got a bright future with the company."

When they finally reached the top floor, Mark stepped out of the elevator ahead of them and led the way down the hall. He'd keep watch on the door to the Rubins' suite until they left.

But as they approached the suite, Cilla felt the itchy feeling at the back of her neck intensify. Turning, she glanced back down the hallway.

Empty except for a woman in a cap and down jacket inserting her key into a lock.

"You can relax." Jonah spoke softly as they reached the door. "Gabe vetted Stan thoroughly. I don't go into business with anyone I have questions about. You're going to like him."

Like him or not, Cilla glanced down the hall in the other direction as they waited. But she spotted no one other than Mark, and he was turning a corner to check out the rest of the floor. For a moment the hall was empty.

But the itchy feeling remained. Maybe it *was* due to sexual frustration. When Jonah raised his hand to knock, she grabbed his wrist.

"What's wrong?" He gave the hallway a quick scan.

"You didn't kiss me in the taxi."

She saw surprise in the look he gave her, but it didn't come close to matching her own surprise at what she'd said.

Then she saw the heat and the hint of recklessness flash into his eyes, and her bones began to melt.

"I've just spent a whole afternoon wanting you and not being able to so much as touch you. If I'd kissed you in the taxi, I wouldn't have stopped with a kiss." He picked up a piece of her hair and twisted it around his finger. "Have you ever made love in the backseat of a taxi?"

"No." But she had a quick flash of what it might be like with Jonah, and she couldn't feel her legs anymore. Leaning against the door of the Rubins' suite didn't help one bit. Because then all she could think of was the door in that hotel room and what he'd done to her. What she very much wanted him to do again.

"I decided that I wanted a little more space and some privacy the next time we make love." He released her hair to run a finger slowly over her lips. "The next time I kiss you, I'm not going to stop until I'm inside you making you come."

Everything inside of her clenched at the image. For a moment, she thought she might come right then.

Jonah tore his gaze away from her and knocked on the door. Glenda Rubin answered the summons almost immediately. If she hadn't, Jonah wasn't quite sure he could have kept from taking Cilla right there in the hallway.

And if he had? Well, he'd spoken nothing less than the truth about the reason he'd kept his hands to himself in the taxi. But saying the words out loud had badly weakened his self-control. And it hadn't been in good shape on the ride over. Each time the cab took a corner and her shoulder brushed against his, he'd nearly been a goner.

A hallway provided more space and at least the possibility of greater privacy than the backseat of a taxi with hundreds of pedestrians out Christmas shopping. But he wanted more than that the next time he touched Cilla.

And he intended to touch her soon.

Glenda enveloped him in a hug. "Merry Christmas.

Carl's already here and Dean is on his way." She grasped Cilla's hand when Jonah made the introductions. "Welcome."

The suite she led them into was large and airy. Windows along one wall offered a stunning view of the Golden Gate Bridge, where the late-afternoon sun was moving closer to the horizon.

Carl Rockwell and Stan Rubin already stood near the conference table. The sight of them helped Cilla snap back into security agent mode. But she was very careful not to look at Jonah.

Stan was a tall man with white hair and a neatly trimmed beard and mustache. His eyes were blue, his smile warm, and if he'd been portly instead of slim, Cilla decided that he would have reminded her of Santa Claus. Carl Rockwell looked as fit and dapper as he had when she'd met him in the bar at Pleasures.

Cilla liked Glenda, too. The woman was nearly as tall as her husband. She wore her blond hair pulled back in a classic chignon and looked quietly elegant in a champagne-colored sweater and slacks.

The Rubins looked to be in their late fifties, just about the same age as Carl. All three expressed genuine concern about the attempted mugging. Carl had evidently given them a blow-by-blow description already. Glenda took Jonah's hand in both of hers. "How troubling. This should be a season filled with joy."

"You're smart to hire protection," Stan said.

"And G.W. Securities is where you started out, isn't it?" Carl asked. "I admire loyalty."

Jonah glanced at Cilla. "And I like hiring the best."

Stan smiled. "Always the smart move. Dean will be joining us in a minute, but before he does, Glenda and I have been thinking of investing in this winery in Napa, and I'd like your opinion about this Cabernet I picked up. You, too, Carl."

As the men moved toward the conference table, Glenda took her arm. "I asked room service to send up some canapés. Would you mind helping me with them?"

Cilla followed Glenda to a small kitchenette and watched her remove a bottle of white wine from the refrigerator. She could use a little break from being elbow to elbow with Jonah.

At the other end of the large suite, still in plain sight, she could see Stan Rubin uncork a bottle of red wine and fill three glasses. But she couldn't hear what the men were saying. The young man who joined them wore dark-framed glasses. He had a slender build with straight dark hair that fell over his forehead. He carried a laptop computer.

Dean Norris, she surmised. He had a military bearing and precise movements, which matched the brief résumé Jonah had given her. He had to have joined the army at a young age because she judged him to still be in his mid-twenties.

"I'm sorry about sweeping you away like this," Glenda said. "It's so women-in-the-kitchen, men-doing-the-important-business." She wrinkled her nose. "But because I love Stan and know him, I've schooled myself to think of it in other terms. Stan spent a few years in the Air Force. You should have seen him in uniform. I tell myself that he wants me to play the role of wingman. Are you familiar with the term?"

"Sure. As a bodyguard, that's my role with Jonah."

"And he's right there where you can see him," Glenda pointed out as she uncorked the bottle.

"But Stan wants a private meeting with Dean, Carl and Jonah," Cilla said.

"Exactly." Glenda poured wine into two glasses. "Stan favors the reds, but I love the whites. I know they're not as fashionable. But this one is really good. Would you like a taste? I know you're on duty."

"I can probably handle a taste."

Glenda beamed a smile at her. "I knew I liked you. Sometimes it happens that way. You just feel it." She glanced over at the men as she handed Cilla a glass. "The meeting is about Dean. Stan believes he has a lot of promise and he wants to encourage him."

Cilla said nothing as Glenda pulled out some trays from the small refrigerator. "Dean has some design ideas that would change the theme of the club we're opening in San Diego. Stan doesn't agree with them, but he wants Dean to run them by Jonah and Carl so that he'll feel his ideas are being given serious consideration."

"And Stan gets some backup for rejecting them."

"Exactly."

"What kind of theme change does Dean want to make?"

"Have you been to any of Jonah's clubs?" Glenda asked.

"I've been to Pleasures and I just spent over two hours at Interludes. Pleasures takes you back in time to a gilded age. I'm not sure I got the full theme of Interludes because there were about two hundred kids romping through the rooms."

Glenda laughed. "You were at the Christmas party he throws every year for various youth organizations. Stan and I visited the Easter Party he gave for them last spring before we decided to propose this new club."

"Did you watch him shoot pool with the kids?"

"Yes. The way the kids looked at him—that was the clincher for me. I knew we should do business with him. Stan bought in when Jonah showed them how to clear the table. His work with young people is what inspired Stan to take on Dean Norris as a special assistant on this project. Dean was the one who suggested Stan look into the idea of opening a club in the first place. He even suggested he contact Jonah. He's such a hard worker and he wants so badly to impress Jonah."

Cilla glanced across the length of the suite and saw that Dean had set up his laptop on the conference table. A screen had been lowered on the wall, and the young man was hooking his computer up to a projector.

"How did you meet Dean?"

"About a year ago, he showed up at Stan's office one day and asked for work. He said he wanted to learn the business from the bottom up. He'd take any job. It was exactly the right approach to take with Stan. He's a self-made man. He wasn't born with blue blood or a silver spoon in his mouth, and he made it to where he is on his own. Jonah, too. That's one of the things Stan likes about Jonah."

"And Stan saw that same possibility in Dean."

"Yes."

For the first time, Cilla saw the hint of a frown in Glenda's eyes. "You're worried about this meeting."

"Dean doesn't always take criticism or rejection easily, and since he feels it was his idea, this club in San Diego is very special to him. He's very enthused about his designs. You'll be able to see them on the screen."

Cilla watched the sketches flash onto the large panel. The drawings reminded her a bit of what she'd seen at Pleasures, the feeling of an elegant world in the past.

"What do you think?" Glenda asked as she took a sip of her own wine.

"They remind me of Pleasures."

Glenda let out a soft sigh. "That's what Stan thinks, too. Jonah's designs for this club are much more modern, more edgy. They're calling it Inclinations, and the idea will be to attract young people."

When the screen went dark, Stan hit a wall switch to enhance the light and handed Dean a glass of wine. Glenda picked up her tray and moved across the room. With her own glass in hand, Cilla followed.

"Your designs are impressive, Dean," Jonah was saying. "Hold on to them. They might work very well in a club I'm thinking of opening farther up the coast in Seattle."

"I'd appreciate that, sir."

"Jonah."

Dean nodded. "After my years in the service, it's hard to break the habit." He turned to Carl. "What did you think, sir?"

Carl smiled at him. "I have to agree with Jonah. Your designs show real promise, but I think we have to go with Jonah's concept for the San Diego club."

Stan placed a hand on Dean's shoulder. "It's got to be a disappointment, but I have to agree with Jonah and Carl. Sticking with our original concept is the way to go."

"It's your call, sir. I appreciate your giving me the chance to show you my ideas."

"Time for refreshments." Glenda moved around the conference table and offered the canapés. Stan topped off Carl's and Jonah's glasses and turned the conversation to the wine.

When the doorbell of the suite rang, Glenda set the food down and frowned. "That can't be my sister Barbara. I told her six."

Stan glanced at his watch and sighed. "Barbara is always early. And if she and Hank have been in San Francisco shopping with that clan of theirs, I'm figuring they both are in need of a large glass of this red."

Cilla felt her cell vibrate. Moving closer to the balcony doors, she saw that it was a text from Mark Gibbons. "Thirteen people in front of the suite. Eight adults, three young boys, two teenagers."

As she thumbed in an acknowledgment, the sound of voices and laughter floated in from the foyer. Above it, she heard Stan say, "I know you have plans, Carl, but, Jonah, you and Cilla are welcome to stay for dinner if you want. Barbara and Hank's three grandchildren are what I kindly refer to as a 'handful.' That's why we ordered room service instead of taking them out to a restaurant."

"Thanks," Jonah said. "But I'll want to check in at Pleasures."

"Figured. Big night tomorrow. Glenda and I are looking forward to it. We'll see you there, Carl?"

"Wouldn't miss it."

A burst of laughter shifted Cilla's attention to the foyer area, where Glenda was receiving hugs from three small boys.

"We haven't been formally introduced."

Cilla turned to see that Dean Norris had joined her at the balcony windows. He had a smile on his face, the first one she'd seen since he'd entered the suite earlier. And there was none of the stiffness she'd heard in his tone when he'd been fielding the bad news from Jonah and the others.

"I'm Dean Norris and I work for Stan."

She took his outstretched hand. "Cilla Michaels. I work for Jonah."

"He's a very lucky man. I envy him. Stan mentioned that someone tried to mug him outside his club last night. That's got to be hard, especially during the Christmas season. But the upside is that he gets to have a beautiful bodyguard."

Cilla was saved from having to make a reply when three little boys, the ones who'd been hugging Glenda, exploded into the room and shot straight toward the balcony doors.

"Watch out." Dean took her arm and drew her away from the stampede just in time to avoid a collision.

"Look, the sun's a ginormous red ball and it's setting," one of them shouted.

"It's going to hit the Golden Gate Bridge on the way down and 'splode!" the second boy said.

"Nah," the third one argued. "It'll just sink into the water."

"You're wrong, too," the first one insisted. "The sun isn't sinking. The earth is rotating. Simple third-grade science."

Cilla heard Stan mutter to Jonah. "A handful. The one with the stellar science knowledge is my namesake, Stan."

Carl set his glass down and patted the older Stan on the shoulder. "Enjoy them. I'll see you both tomorrow at Pleasures. Take care, Jonah."

"Enjoy them," Dean spoke in an impatient undertone to Cilla. "Someone ought to control them. I only wish I had Stone's or Rockwell's excuse for leaving."

As other guests filtered in, Cilla kept her gaze on Dean. Seconds ago, he'd been affable, almost charming. Now tension radiated from every pore in his body. "Can't you just say that you want to work on your designs and sneak off to your room?"

Anger flashed into his eyes. "I'll have to say that I'm working on some new ones since the ones I brought today were a total failure. Stone's a tough man to compete with, especially since he's got the money to make sure his designs win."

"But Glenda says that you were the one who urged Stan to open a club. If it's successful, he's going to give you the credit for that."

"And if it fails, I'm sure I'll get the credit for that also. Stone will still come out on top. That's what he's always done. It's…frustrating."

The words had come out in a rush and it wasn't just anger she heard now, but passion. "You believe that your designs are truly better than Jonah's?"

"I know they are. I just need a chance to prove it."

"Then take Jonah up on his offer. Talk to him about the club he's thinking of opening in Seattle."

Dean's eyes narrowed. "He just said that to make me feel better."

She reached out and laid a hand on his arm. "No. He's not a man who lies to people he does business with."

Whatever Dean might have responded was prevented by

Glenda's approach. She had her arm linked with a woman who might have been her twin.

"Cilla, I want to introduce you to my sister Barbara and her husband, Hank."

She'd barely acknowledged the introductions before her cell rang. "Pardon me," she murmured to Glenda, then stepped away to take the call.

"Santos," the voice said. "I just spotted our guy Tank in the hotel."

"You're sure?" Cilla asked.

"Not at first. He was wearing a baseball cap, and I might have missed him if he hadn't raised his voice to the bell captain. I circled around to get a better look at him, and the instant he spotted me, he took off. By the time I got out to the street, he'd vanished. And there's more."

Cilla felt the back of her neck begin to itch again. "What?"

"I'm talking to the bell captain right now. He says the guy tipped him to deliver a gift bag to Room 820."

"That's Stanley Rubin's suite."

"Bingo. I tipped the captain again and told him I'd deliver the bag. It contains a little green box tied with a red ribbon."

"Stay there, but let Gibbons know what's going on. I'll come to get the bag. Call me if you spot Tank again." Then she turned to signal Jonah.

THE INSTANT CILLA FILLED him in on the delivery of a new gift bag, Jonah took her arm and steered her toward the door of the suite. As he nodded and smiled to Stan and Glenda's relatives, questions swirled in his mind, each one increasing his sense of urgency. Why had another green box been delivered? The bastard had already sent him one today. Did that mean he was moving up the timetable? And how had the man known Stan's room number? Hotels were pretty careful not to give out that information.

Anger sparked to life inside him, and he leashed it down hard. It wouldn't do him any good. Hadn't he learned that lesson years ago from Father Mike? He could almost hear the priest's voice in his ear telling him that anger never solved anything. You had to push it aside or it could blind you to everything life held in store.

But he wanted Cilla out of the hotel and back at Pleasures. She would be safe there. And he wanted to spend time with her. Not just to make love with her—although he wanted that, too. But they needed to talk. Maybe together, they could make some sense of what was happening and put an end to it.

Finally, only Glenda and a room service cart stood between them and the door of the suite. She pushed the cart out of the way and gave Cilla a hug. "I'm so glad to have met you." Then she took Jonah's hand and gave it a squeeze. "Thanks so much for letting Dean down easy. Stan and I won't forget it."

Jonah smiled at her. "Tell him I meant what I told him. I think his idea might work for a place I'm thinking about in Seattle."

Glenda leaned in and kissed his cheek. "You're a charming man, Jonah Stone. We'll see you both tomorrow night."

She opened the door, then said, "Wait." Turning, she took a gift bag from a small table and handed it to Jonah. "I left this here so I wouldn't forget it. But I nearly did."

"A gift?" Jonah asked. "You shouldn't have."

"I didn't. The man who delivered the room service cart gave it to me. He said that someone handed it to him while he was loading carts into the elevator and asked him to deliver it. A surprise for Mr. Stone. I left it here because I didn't want it to get lost in the circus going on in the other room."

Even before he glanced into the bag, Jonah knew what

he'd see, and there it was. Another little green box with a red ribbon. The third one of the day. Anger boiled up. He wanted to throw it against the wall, and he might have given in to the temptation, the momentary pleasure, if Cilla hadn't clamped a firm hand on his arm.

11

As Cilla PULLED HIM INTO the corridor, Jonah still struggled to get a grip on his temper. It had been years since he'd totally lost it, not since that long-ago night when he'd been with Father Mike praying to the statue of St. Francis in the little prayer garden near the center and screaming curses at his father.

Cilla beamed a smile at Glenda and said, "We'll see you tomorrow night."

Her hand remained an iron clamp on his arm as she pulled him down the hall. A few doors down a family of three stepped out of their room and headed toward the elevators where several people, including Mark Gibbons, already stood waiting.

"Wonderful party," she said in the same tone that she'd used with Glenda. Bright, cheerful, as if neither of them had a care in the world.

Then she eased the gift bag out of his hand and slipped it over her arm. "It was so kind of them to give us a present."

Jonah looked at her then. She'd taken out her cell phone and was thumbing in a text message. Was it possible that she hadn't seen the green box inside the gift bag?

That thought shot straight out of his mind when she met his eyes. Hers were flat and coplike. She'd seen it all right.

She glanced down at her phone. He followed the direction of her gaze and read the text she'd written.

Play along with me. I feel like someone is watching us. I had the same feeling when we first arrived. I want you out of here before we open the boxes.

"But I'm so glad we're going home," she said in a voice that wasn't flat at all. It held promises.

Out of the corner of his eye, he saw two of the people waiting for the elevators glance their way.

Ignoring them, Cilla rose to her toes, clasped her hands on each side of his face and drew his mouth down to hers. She brushed her lips over his. "I have plans for when we get home."

While her breath feathered along his cheek and her scent twisted into him, Jonah decided there were ways to channel anger other than throwing things. "Let's give them something to watch." He jerked her closer and covered her mouth with his.

Cilla should have been prepared for the kiss. After all, she'd started it with the playacting. She'd sensed the fury in him and she'd wanted to deflect it.

Mission accomplished.

When he nipped her bottom lip and tightened his grip on her waist, heat streaked to her toes.

Confession time.

She hadn't just wanted to deflect his temper. She'd wanted this. The fire streaking along her nerve endings, the glorious spiral of pleasure.

This was the kiss she'd wanted in the taxi, the one that she'd been hungering for the whole time she was watching him on that big screen at Interludes. There was no teasing, no gentle exploration, just raw demand. And all she wanted to do was meet it.

When his hands tightened again at her waist, she slid

her own into his hair and moved in until her body was fully pressed against his. Then he lifted her off her feet.

All she could do was feel—the hard length of his thigh, the sharp angle of his hip, the quick beat of his heart. All she could hear was the hammering of her own heart—so loud that she wondered why people didn't run out of their rooms to quiet the racket.

Touch me. She wanted to shout it and hoped she hadn't. She should pull back. There was still a sane part of her mind that registered whispers and the giggle of a child. She was vaguely aware of the whoosh of elevator doors opening, people moving away, doors sliding shut again. But when he started to draw back, she gripped him even harder and took his mouth with hers.

Doors whooshed again, and she registered the sound of a gasp, then a deep chuckle.

"C'mon, Amanda, let's give the nice couple some privacy."

She drew back then and found that she was looking right into Jonah's eyes. What she saw—the heat, the recklessness—nearly had her damning the consequences and going back for more.

Someone coughed. "If you want, boss, I can get the two of you a room. We did a favor for one of the managers here a couple months ago."

Mark Gibbons. She'd forgotten he was there. He was standing right behind Jonah, holding the doors of the elevator open. He'd seen everything. Embarrassment gave her the strength to release Jonah and get her feet fully on the ground. Not that she could feel them. But they did their job and propelled her into the elevator.

Jonah and Mark followed.

Punching the button for the lobby, she prayed that her voice would work. "We won't need a room. That was—" Several words flashed into her mind. A mistake? A show for anyone watching? The closest she'd ever come to having sex in a public place?

All of the above?

"Absolutely delightful," Jonah said, squeezing her hand.

She managed to shoot a glare at him before she said, "Can you stop the elevator before anyone else gets on?"

"Sure." He reached out and pushed a button. The car shuddered a little as it stopped.

Cilla turned to Gibbons. "With three of us watching, someone got this little gift bag into the Rubins' suite." She opened the bag so that Gibbons could see the green box. "I want to spread out our manpower. Someone gave it to the room service waiter and told him it was a surprise for Mr. Stone. I want you to find out what that waiter can remember and get a description."

"Maybe after our friend Tank delivered one box to the bell captain, he snuck back into the hotel through a service entrance and Santos missed him," Mark commented.

"That's what we want to verify, and a description would help."

Jonah leaned back against the door of the elevator and watched Cilla slip into Priscilla mode. Because the walls of the car had mirrors, he could see more than one of her as she fisted her hand on her hip and used the limited space to pace. He knew that she'd been just as affected by that kiss as he had. Her cheeks were still flushed, her voice just a little bit breathless. God, he had to admire the way she was able to snap right back into ace security agent.

"I want Santos to go back to the office and do some research on what was going on here in San Francisco at Christmastime six years ago," Cilla said. "Gabe has someone in his office digging into missing persons, mysterious deaths, etcetera in Denver, but maybe the motivation for the revenge is here and not in Denver. I'll contact Finelli and ask him to check into missing persons and unsolved and solved murders in December 2005."

Gibbons glanced down at the gift bag. "You going to wait for Santos to give you the other box and open them together?"

"I'm going to wait until we're clear of this place before we open either one. Once we get to the lobby, Jonah and I are going out the side entrance. I'll make sure we're not being followed before I hail a cab." She lifted the bag. "We'll take this and the other one to the office. Join us there when you're through."

"Why don't we meet at Pleasures instead?" Jonah asked. "We can all grab a bite to eat." He met Gibbons's eyes. "And I can assure you that the security at my club is excellent. Better than a nearly empty office building."

"Good point."

Jonah reached out and punched the button. A few seconds later, the doors opened and a family of five poured in. Once they alighted from the elevator in the lobby, Cilla waited only long enough for David Santos to hand her the other gift bag before pulling Jonah with her toward the side exit and out into the street. Darkness had settled over the city, but the pedestrian traffic was still heavy, and Cilla set a fast pace. She was angry. He could feel it radiating off her in waves, but she was not letting her emotions interfere with her job.

First she used her cell to call someone named T.D. Whoever it was made her laugh. The rich sound of it left that coppery taste in his mouth again. Next she called Finelli and told him what she needed. All the while, the path she cut through the heavy pedestrian traffic had them hugging the buildings, and at each intersection, she took a quick scan of the crowd behind them.

But she was ignoring the taxis.

"I know you're angry, partner. But don't you think it's time you filled me in on your plan? What are we doing?"

"Exactly what I said. I'm getting you away from the St. Francis without a tail."

"We're a good five blocks away from the hotel, and you haven't flagged a taxi yet."

"Sorry." She took a deep breath and let it out, and for the first time slowed their pace a bit. "You're right, I am angry. I got angry the instant Glenda handed you the gift bag and I saw another green box."

Remembering his own instant flash of blinding fury, he took her hand and squeezed it.

"If I hadn't been angry, I never would have…we never would have…"

"Kissed? But you complained that I didn't kiss you in the taxi."

"We shouldn't have kissed like *that*." At the corner, she swept her gaze to their rear, then strode into the street. "People were watching us. Mark was watching us."

"Well, I'm open to experimenting with other methods. Other techniques. Anytime."

She tried for a quelling look, but she had to swallow a sudden urge to laugh. "That's not what I'm talking about."

He smiled at her. "I'll have to persuade you, then."

She narrowed her eyes. "I thought you were interested in my plan."

"I'm interested in that, too."

This time the laugh escaped and some of her tension eased. "I made arrangements earlier for different transportation from the hotel."

"Different?"

"A friend of mine, T. D. Walters, is a partner in a private limo service."

He pulled her into the entranceway of a shop. "And just who is T.D.?"

She cocked her head to the side and studied him. "If it wasn't such a ridiculous idea, I'd say you were jealous."

"That is a ridiculous idea." But it didn't make it less true, Jonah decided.

"T.D. is a friend of mine." This time she spaced the

words as if she were speaking to someone who didn't understand English. "When I worked for the SFPD, he was my first snitch. T.D. stands for Top Dog. I like him a lot, but he's not my type."

"I'm not your type, either."

She smiled at him. "Then the two of you should become best buds." After taking a quick scan of the street, she led the way onto the sidewalk again.

"I called T.D. when we were at Interludes because I wanted to have a backup plan. Getting into a taxi in front of the St. Francis at this time of day makes it much too easy for someone to follow us." She waved a hand toward the bumper-to-bumper traffic on the street. "And this kind of congestion makes it all but impossible to lose a tail."

"But you didn't tell Gibbons or Santos about your limo plan."

"No. I wasn't sure I was going to use it. But I had a feeling we were being watched from the time we got to the hotel. Tank is still on the loose out there. And I'm more convinced than ever that he's working with someone."

She lifted the gift bags. "It doesn't take a Sherlock or a Watson to figure out where you're going to be today and that you'll eventually end up at Pleasures. Which has me wondering why the guy is choosing such public places to deliver the notes."

"A police station and the St. Francis when it would have been easier to drop them off at Interludes or even at Pleasures. My guess is he wants to show off how clever he is."

"And how vulnerable you are," she said. "He wants you to know he can find you anywhere."

"So when two boxes turn up at the St. Francis, the limo goes from being backup to Plan A," Jonah mused. "You want to show him he isn't as clever as he thinks he is."

"What I want to do is stop him."

He heard the anger flare in her voice again. Glancing at her, he watched her tamp it down and shrug it off. "And call me paranoid, but I don't want to give him a chance to watch while you open these. I think he likes to watch. That's another reason to choose public spaces to deliver the boxes."

Jonah thought of the detonator the police had found in the stairwell of the garage and of how many eyes would have been on them if he'd opened the boxes in the lobby or in the long taxi line in front of the hotel.

"We won't have to worry about watchers in the backseat of T.D.'s limo," he said.

"Exactly."

A stinging mist had begun to fall. More than a few pedestrians had pulled out umbrellas. When they stopped for a red light at the corner, he said, "You didn't want me to open the box and read the note in the elevator in front of Gibbons, either. Do you suspect that he or Santos might be involved in what's going on?"

"No." The look she shot him was one of surprise, but then she sighed. "I hate the fact that I even considered it. Or that I talked to Gabe about it. But he was already on it."

"I'm not surprised. I've considered them also. I can tell you that I don't think Gibbons is mixed up in this—even though he was working for G.W. Securities six years ago."

"Gabe says Santos was in the Marines six years ago and he worked with explosives. But there doesn't seem to be any connection to you."

"Has Gabe found any trace of my father?"

She sent him a sideways glance. "He thinks I ought to put you on that because you have superior skills at hacking."

"I can't imagine that someone who vanished from my life over twenty years ago would be interested enough to come back now. If he's even alive. When we get to the point that we're grasping at straws, I may give it a whirl."

"We could be approaching that point. Whoever is sending these little gifts is stepping up his game. It's still four nights before Christmas and he's given you three green boxes today."

He'd already given some thought to that himself. "He doesn't have to send just one note a day." He squeezed her hand. "We're going to figure this out."

"Okay. Okay. T.D. should be waiting for us up the block."

Top Dog Walters was just where he'd said he'd be, standing by the side of the limo when they turned into the alley. He was a large, powerfully built man with black hair that he wore pulled sleekly back into a ponytail. In the light thrown by the headlights, Cilla couldn't help but admire the neatly pressed chauffeur's uniform. It was a far cry from the ripped T-shirt and threadbare jeans she'd first seen him wearing during her days as a street cop.

There was more bling, too. He'd always favored a few earrings, but she was sure she spotted a new gold chain around his neck. The gold ring on his finger she'd seen before. In fact she'd watched his bride place it on his hand two years ago.

By the time she and Jonah reached him, he had the back door open. Then without further ado, he wrapped his arms around her and gave her a huge hug. "Sugar, it's been too long."

Releasing Cilla, he extended his hand to Jonah. "I'm T.D. Walters, by the way. And she saved my life."

Jonah shook the offered hand. "Jonah Stone. She may be in the process of saving mine."

"I didn't save T.D.'s life. I merely saw his potential and introduced him to a friend who saw even more potential." Cilla poked a finger into T.D.'s chest. "And it didn't hurt your upward mobility that you married the boss's daughter. How's the new baby?"

"Beautiful, but she doesn't sleep much."

"I've heard that about a lot of babies." She gestured for Jonah to get into the limo first, then followed him.

When T.D. had climbed behind the wheel, she said, "This is lovely, T.D. And it still has that new leather smell."

Turning in his seat, he beamed her a smile. "It's our top-of-the-line model. You can see out, but no one can see in. There's hot coffee in a thermos, wine, champagne, and there are some snacks in the cooler. Help yourself. I'll drive around. When you decide on a destination, let me know through the intercom." Then he pressed a button and the privacy screen lowered.

When the engine hummed to life and the limo started to move slowly forward, Cilla allowed herself one moment to lean back against the seat.

"Perfect plan, partner." Jonah reached over the two gift bags that lay on the seat between them and took her hand. "This is much better than the backseat of a taxi and we don't even have to break our ground rules."

"We don't?" Lord knew she wanted to, and what she saw in his eyes had her wondering why she'd ever established them in the first place.

"We agreed that making love again had to remain in the backseat until we solved the case." He gestured with his free hand. "This qualifies as a backseat, so I think we're good. But you'll probably want to open these boxes first."

It was more than heat she saw in his eyes. There was humor and intelligence and an understanding that she'd never hoped to see. Never realized she wanted to see.

Releasing her hand, Jonah opened the box closest to him and read the note aloud, "'It's still four nights and counting. Have you remembered yet why you have to die?'"

Fear knotted in her stomach as she met his eyes again. "I'd say that was more than mildly threatening."

"As you said, he's stepping up his game." He lifted the second bag and was about to take out the green box when he suddenly frowned. "There's a tag on the bag. I didn't notice it earlier." Opening it, he held it for her to see. "It has your name on it."

Cilla thought back to the few minutes in the foyer when Glenda turned away to pick up the gift bag. She'd been totally focused on getting Jonah out of there. "Glenda said it was a surprise for Mr. Stone."

Jonah already had the box on his lap and was untying the ribbon. Inside was the same piece of folded, cream-colored paper that had been in the other four boxes. He flipped it open, then took her hand and held it as they read it together.

One night and counting… You've interfered with my mission for the last time. It's too bad that you won't live to see what I have in store for Jonah Stone.

12

"THIS CHANGES EVERYTHING," Jonah said.

"No." But for a second she couldn't unglue her eyes from the note.

One night and counting...

She forced herself to think and was pleased that her hand didn't tremble as she carefully took the note, refolded it and placed it back in the green box. "It just means he's modified his plan."

"Modified?" Jonah took the box from her hands and put it on the leather banquette that ran along the side of the limo. Then he took her shoulders and turned her to face him. "That note is a death threat. That bastard is going to try to take you out."

She met his eyes. The fear she saw beneath the fury helped her settle and focus. "*Try* is the operative word. He's not going to succeed."

He gave her a little shake. "He sure as hell isn't. He isn't even going to get to try." He pulled out his phone. "I'm calling Gabe. He can send someone else out here. You're going to disappear until this is over."

She brought the edge of her hand down hard on his wrist. The instant the cell phone dropped to the floor, she kicked it out of reach.

"Stuff that idea, partner. And if you go after the phone, I may have to really hurt you."

There was still anger in his eyes when he turned to face her, but she had his attention. And he was rubbing his wrist. "I want you out of this."

"And I've always wanted Santa Claus to be real. That's why I love the movie *Miracle on 34th Street*. You'll have to learn to live with the fact that I'm staying in." She poked a finger into his chest. "And you have only yourself to blame."

He frowned. "I know I'm to blame. I insisted you work on this, and now the guy wants to get rid of you so he can make a run at me."

She opened her mouth, then shut it. "I'm beginning to think that's not all of it."

"No, now he wants *you.*"

"Not just that, either. He has this long-term plan to make you count down the six nights before Christmas. To make you wait and wonder and suffer before he makes his run. At the same time, he's giving the best security agency on this side of the country six days—now four—to track him down."

"What are you saying?"

She waved a hand. "He also wants this. He wants us to react, panic. Spin our wheels. If we decide to bring some-one else in to bodyguard you, maybe bring in more pro-tection for me, we're not totally focused on finding him."

"Dammit." Jonah sighed. "You could be right."

"Yeah. Look what happened after we discovered the bomb. No, he didn't succeed in blowing my car up, but the distraction still worked. I pulled Mark and David in to help protect you. They're the two best men I have and I kept them with us babysitting all day."

Jonah glanced at the green box. "If we'd opened that before we left the St. Francis, I wouldn't have let you send Gibbons and Santos off."

She followed the direction of his gaze. "Thank God for my attack of paranoia. But that note is still deflecting us. Everything he's done so far has split our attention. Hiring Mickey P. and Lorenzo to rough you up in the alley makes more sense now. He wanted you to bodyguard up."

"He didn't want them to get arrested."

"No. But then he delivers the second note to the police station and arranges for Tank to install the car bomb. All that directs our attention away from finding him. Whoever this guy is, he bounces back and he's not at a loss for ideas. He'll have other things up his sleeve."

Jonah took her hand, linked his fingers with hers. "We'll handle them, and we'll figure out who he is. Tonight, I'll try my hand at tracing my father."

She squeezed his fingers as something tightened around her heart. "It may be a wild-goose chase."

"Maybe it's time we went on a few." He met her eyes. "I'm not sending you away."

"Waste of time. I'm not going anywhere."

"I'm not forgetting that the number on your note was *one*. I don't intend to lose my partner."

"Remember that the next time you try to dump me, ace."

He laughed, then leaned in closer. "I also remember that we agreed to take a break after we opened the gift."

She placed a hand on his chest. "And I know exactly what you had in mind, but the clock is ticking here."

"Oh, I can be fast. Let me show you."

The thought of it sent a hot thrill right to her core. But his mouth was slow and soft as he brushed it over hers, and she couldn't prevent the sound that escaped.

"There's a practical side of you that thinks we should go back to Pleasures so that I can get started on tracing my father. I'm attracted to that part of you." He kissed the corner of her mouth. "I think of her as Priscilla. She wants to pull out her cell and check in with Gibbons and Santos." He kissed the other corner of her mouth.

Each time his mouth made contact, every pore in her body yearned.

"Then she'll want to touch base with Finelli." His teeth scraped along her jawline. "Then update Gabe. Have I left anything off Priscilla's list?"

She wasn't sure because every time his lips brushed hers, more of her thoughts faded.

"But I'm also attracted to the other side of you, the Cilla part. She isn't afraid to throw that to-do list away and risk everything for the moment. It was Cilla I found in the hotel bar in Denver. You're both of those women. I want you. Let me show you how much."

He whispered the words against her lips, the same words he'd said that night after he'd closed the hotel door.

"It's not that simple anymore." But her hand fisted his shirt.

"Then let's see where complicated takes us."

His mouth covered hers. Not softly this time. But she didn't want soft. There was nothing seductive about the way he was kissing her now. But she didn't want seduction.

She just wanted him.

"Touch me." She got the words out this time. Or he read her mind. For one wild moment, his hands seemed to be everywhere, inciting, arousing. In one fluid movement he had her out of her jacket and he pulled the sweater over her head. It might be cold outside, but she was suddenly plunged into hot, drenching summer. And she wanted to simply drown in it. He shifted her, then slid to his knees between hers to deal with her boots and slacks.

Shrugging out of his jacket, he brought his mouth back to hers, hot and greedy. She tasted hunger and desperation, but she wasn't sure whether it came from him or her.

And it wasn't enough. Not nearly enough.

She jerked his turtleneck free of his jeans and together they dragged it over his head. But before she could get her hands on him the way she'd imagined doing at Interludes, he gripped her hips and pulled her to the floor. Finally, his hands were on her bare skin, demanding, exploring, finding new pleasure points, rediscovering old ones. Wave after wave of pleasure washed through her until she knew only him—the taste, the feel, the smell of him.

Her heart had never beat this fast. Not even in that hotel room. And it still wasn't enough. She rolled, pushing him back into the soft carpet so that she could press kisses, quick and hungry, over his face, his neck, his chest. Everywhere.

Then he shifted, bringing his mouth to hers, and they rolled again.

More was all she could think.

More.

After a month of remembering, fantasizing, Jonah couldn't stifle his hunger. Nor could he seem to satisfy it. He simply had to touch and mold every inch of her with his hands, his mouth. Each separate sensation hammered through his blood and burned through his brain.

Her skin was softer than he'd remembered. It seemed to flow and then burn beneath his fingers. Her slender body enchanted him. Would he ever get enough of those long lean lines, the taut and ready strength, the delicate give of curves? They'd haunted his dreams for so many long silent nights.

Shifting, he pinned her against the side of the banquette and ran his hand up those slim thighs. She still wore her panties. He toyed with the edge. Lace. And he recalled the lace she'd worn on that long-ago night.

"Look at me, Cilla."

She did. They were eye to eye, and he could see himself in the cloudy green depths. He skimmed a finger beneath the lace. "I'm going to make you come, and then I'll make you come again. Tell me that's what you want."

She twined her arms around his neck. "Yes. That's what I want. I want you."

He slid a finger into her and then studied her face, watched the pleasure build in her eyes as his pulse beat in wild drumbeats. When he felt her crest, when he was sure she thought only of him, knew only the pleasure he was giving her, he shifted and rose to his knees to shove down his jeans and deal with the condom.

"Cilla."

She opened her eyes and that's all he could see—just the dark glint of them—as he lowered himself over her.

"Again," she whispered.

He entered her. As she closed around him hot and tight, the thought seared into his mind—she was everything. Everything he wanted. Then even that thought shattered as his control snapped.

The moment he began to move, Cilla gasped his name. The pleasure he'd already given her flashed to frenzy as he pounded into her with fast, powerful thrusts. Lost, unbearably thrilled, she matched him beat for beat. As new sensations tore through her, she raked her nails down his back and dug them into his hips, urging him on. This time, the orgasm built fast and ripped through her, filled her, and then seemed to empty her out.

She wasn't sure how long they lay there on the floor of the limo while her mind swam back to reality. But gradually she could absorb details—the hum of the motor, the muffled sounds of traffic. But she was also aware of the rapid beating of his heart against hers, his hair brushing her cheek.

And one of them had to break the silence. Bring reality fully into focus. "Did we just make love or war?"

She felt the curve of his mouth against her cheek. "I don't care what we call it. I want to do it again."

"Yeah." And as she felt him harden inside of her, she was outrageously tempted.

Then her cell phone rang. He rolled off her and took it

out of her jacket. She frowned when she saw the caller ID and put it to her ear. "It's my apartment manager."

"Ms. Michaels?" The voice held annoyance.

Sitting up, Cilla held the phone so Jonah could hear. "Mrs. Ortiz, what is it?"

"Mr. Linderman called me to complain about the noise in your apartment. First, there was a loud crash, and now your music system is playing at full blast. I'm knocking on your door right now. Could you please turn it down?"

"I'm not in my apartment right now."

"Then who is making all that noise?"

"Good question," Jonah murmured as he gathered her clothes.

"I'm on my way." First, she hit the intercom button to give T.D. her address. "Fast as you can legally make it."

"I'll engage the rockets," T.D. said with a laugh.

"Our note sender may have broken into your apartment," Jonah said.

Mind racing, Cilla pulled on her sweater and slacks. "And then turned up my sound system to call attention to himself? More likely Flash did it."

"Flash?"

She grabbed her boots. "My cat. I call her that because when she wants to, she moves like lightning. She's not strictly speaking an alley cat, but close. When I moved in, she was living on the fire escape outside my apartment. I saw her through my living room window the day I moved in and made the mistake of feeding her. Next time I opened the window to the fire escape, she shot in. And stayed."

"And Flash knows how to operate your sound system?"

"She's learned exactly what button to push on the remote. She usually does it to get my attention when I'm working."

She joined him on the seat and did what she could to finger comb her hair. "I would have had to swing by the apartment anyway to pick up some clothes—for tomorrow and that fancy, schmancy thing of yours tomorrow night. And I'll fill Flash's dishes and lock up the remote. She'll be pissed, but at least Mr. Linderman and Mrs. Ortiz won't be."

Jonah laughed, slipping his arm around her and pulling her in for a quick hug. "Welcome back, Priscilla."

T.D. OPENED THE LIMOUSINE door, "Welcome to The Manderly Apartments." Cilla got out first and scanned the street.

"Clear," she said. Then she turned to T.D. "I know we weren't followed, but keep an eye out, will you? I've got you on speed dial, but call me on my cell if anyone comes into the building—even if it looks like they have a key."

"I got your back, sugar," T.D. said.

Jonah climbed out and took his own scan of the street. The night sky was clear enough to allow a quarter moon to wink through. Streetlights offered enough illumination for Jonah to realize that the neighborhood seemed familiar to him. The eclectic mix of architecture ranged from a church built along contemporary lines to an art deco building housing a bank and other shops.

But it wasn't until he swept his gaze over The Manderly Arms with its gothic architecture that the memory fully clicked. He'd taken morning runs right past the place. He even knew where the fire escape was—on the back corner of the building.

"Creepy place," he said as they walked toward the entrance. "Reminds me of that New York City apartment building in *Rosemary's Baby*."

"Wrong movie. Wait until you meet Mrs. Ortiz. She's a dead ringer for Mrs. Danvers in *Rebecca*."

He opened the front door, but he preceded her into the building, then stepped aside so that she could unlock the second door.

"How long have you lived here?" he asked.

"Since I moved back to San Francisco."

All those long nights when he'd stood at his window thinking of her, wanting her, she'd been only walking distance away. If he'd known, would he have climbed that fire escape?

Wasted time, he thought. And what if neither of them had much left to waste?

The lobby was a round, airy space with a circular staircase that rose to the second floor. A plump woman with steel-gray hair pulled back into a tight ballerina bun waited at the foot of it. She wore a black dress with a stiffly starched white apron over it. Her arms were folded, her expression disapproving.

"The music has stopped," she said. "But I want you to know that it was loud enough to hear all the way down here. It was playing 'We Need a Little Christmas.'"

"I'm so sorry. I don't know how it happened." Cilla waved a hand in the air as she moved past the woman and started up the stairs. "Probably a short in the electrical circuit. I'll unplug it until I can have it fixed."

As they rounded the first landing, Jonah saw Mrs. Ortiz was still frowning, and she was pointing one finger accusingly.

"I tried my master key," she called after them. "It doesn't work. You changed the lock. So I need a copy of your key," she said. "If I'd had one, I could have turned the music off myself."

"I'll get you one," Cilla called back. "Promise."

The loud *humph* followed them up the stairs.

Jonah spoke in a low voice. "You changed the lock on your apartment?"

"Pets aren't allowed."

His brows shot up. "You could move. There are pet-friendly places in San Francisco."

"I could move, but would Flash? Since she's never even let me pick her up, that could be a problem."

At the top of the stairs, she led the way down a hallway so dimly lit that he could see slits of light spilling out from beneath closed doors. Only the murmur of TV shows marred the silence. At the last door, she stopped and pulled out her key. It was half an inch from the lock when she turned to him and held a finger to her lips.

She didn't have to tell him that she'd gotten one of her feelings, because he'd gotten it, too. Cold air pushed into the hall from beneath the door. Gesturing him to one side, she turned the key in the lock, then stepped to the other side and took out her gun.

She met his eyes, mouthed the word *Stay,* and then used her foot to open the door. He swept his gaze over the room as she fanned it with her gun. It was empty, but one of the panes on the window had been smashed, and a chubby-looking cat sat on the fire escape looking in.

Cilla, holding her gun in both hands, moved into the room. The feeling he'd had in the hall grew stronger, a hard clenching in his gut.

"Cilla?"

"Stay back until I check the kitchen and bedroom."

No way. He stepped through the doorway and caught a blur of movement before something slammed against his head and lights starred behind his eyes. He had a dizzying impression of the floor speeding toward him before there was nothing but black.

13

CILLA WHIRLED AT THE SOUND and saw that a large muscle-bound man had a gun pointed at Jonah's head.

His eyes were cold and very steady on hers. "Set your gun down easy, or I'll put a bullet in his brain."

"No problem." Very slowly, she lowered her weapon and squatted to set it on the floor as she took his measure. Early fifties, she thought. Gray hair cropped short. Both details matched the grainy images on the security tapes. His boots were scuffed, his jeans and the leather bomber jacket well-worn, but she bet the body beneath the clothes was well-toned. And there was a silencer on his gun.

At the edge of her vision, she saw blood blossom on the side of Jonah's head, but she pushed down on the flood of emotions that threatened and kept her voice very cool. "You're the man who drove the van last night at Pleasures and planted a bomb under my car."

"You're the woman who interfered with my mission."

There was temper in his tone. She might be able to use that. But he still had his gun pointed at Jonah's head. She had to get his attention and the weapon focused on her. So she laughed. "And your mission was?"

"That's for me to know."

"Where'd you hire those two goons you brought along? At 'Thugs R Us'?"

"Shut up," he said, swinging the barrel of the gun toward her. "I've already taken enough crap about that."

More temper, but this time it wasn't entirely aimed at her. She shifted to the balls of her feet, gauging the distance between them. She had to get closer if she was going to disarm him. "I imagine your boss was really pissed."

The man frowned. "He's not my boss. We're partners."

"A partner who sends you out on missions and lets you take all the risks?" She edged a step closer.

"Stop right there. I didn't come here to chat. You and I are going to take a little ride."

Even better, she thought as she took a step toward the door. If she could get him down to T.D.

"Not that way. You think I don't know you got a couple of agents out there waiting? I saw them following you earlier today. But I knew you'd have to come back here eventually."

Keep him talking, she decided. "And today's goal is to get me? Was that your decision or your partner's?"

"Mutual. Someone interferes with my mission, they pay."

"So you decided to enjoy some Christmas music while you waited?"

"Damn cat! I would have killed her but she was too fast."

He gestured with the gun. "We're going out the fire escape and right into my van. You first."

Turning, she walked toward the window and opened it. The faster she got him away from Jonah, the better. Then she'd make her move. As she climbed out, she caught a glimpse of Flash on the level above them. Dropping her gaze, she gauged the distance to the cement floor of the alley. Too far to drop.

Then Tank was right there with her on the fire escape. "We're going down to the alley nice and slow. Try any of your tricks, like kicking the gun out of my hand, and I'll toss you off this thing."

She didn't doubt he'd try. Her mind racing, Cilla gripped the railing and started down the first flight of stairs. They creaked and swayed a little beneath her weight. The farther she could get him away from her apartment, the better. But she didn't like the idea of waiting to make a move until they reached the alley. Her chances of distracting him and taking him on the fire escape might be better.

On the second landing, she purposely missed a step and stumbled, lurching hard against the railing.

He snaked one arm around her neck, dragged her against him and squeezed hard. "You ever been shot in the gut?" He jabbed the gun into her waist. "I've seen men bleed out that way in Iraq. I can place a bullet where the pain will be excruciating."

Then he tightened the arm he had around her throat. Her vision grayed, but she managed to slip her hand into her pocket and press a number that would speed dial T.D. He'd take care of Jonah. But if she didn't find a way to delay the guy, he'd have her in the van and away from the building before T.D. could do a thing to help her.

When Tank finally released her so she could pull in a breath, she gripped the railing hard and let her knees sag.

"Let's go," he said.

"I need…a minute…here." She sagged harder against the railing and dragged in a ragged breath. Ego and temper. Those were his weak spots. She had to use them. Fast.

JONAH LIFTED HIS HEAD and opened his eyes. Pain spiked at his temple and the room spun once before he could focus on the details. The one that struck him first was the plump cat perched on the back of the couch.

Flash. That's what Cilla had called her. She hadn't been in the room when they'd arrived, and the window behind her hadn't been open. Just the pane had been broken.

Panic joined the pain as he got to his feet. "Cilla?"

No response.

How long had he been out? Long enough for whoever had hit him to get Cilla.

Flash shot out through the window and landed gracefully on the railing. When he reached the sill, he leaned out and followed the direction of the cat's gaze.

For a moment, his heart stopped. Two landings below, Cilla leaned against the railing and a man the size of a small Mack truck stood a few feet away. He had a gun aimed at her.

He wanted to call out, get the man's attention on him, but he knew Cilla well enough now to be certain that she'd use the distraction to attack. And while he'd seen some of her moves and knew she had skill and strength, the man was huge, the space was small and they were still two stories off the ground.

A sound had him whirling to see T.D. standing in the open doorway of the apartment.

Jonah put a finger to his lips, then motioned him to the window and pointed. He didn't have to say much to fill in T.D. The man with the gun aimed at Cilla spoke volumes.

"Distraction," T.D. whispered.

"First, I want to get out there and move closer," Jonah whispered back. "Once I'm close enough, crank on the sound system again."

T.D. nodded, and Jonah very carefully ducked low and moved one leg out onto the fire escape.

"I CAN SEE YOU'RE A LOT smarter than your two employees," Cilla said, spacing her words and keeping her voice raspy. "But your partner is the one with the real brainpower."

"What are you saying?"

"You're here. And he's not."

"So? This is what I'm good at."

"And he's good at staying out of sight. He's the one who takes care of sending the little green boxes, right?"

"Yeah. He's good at strategy and planning. I'm good at the actual combat."

"And it's always the combat people who put their lives on the line. Your partner doesn't even deliver the boxes in person. He's a ghost, but you've been spotted. The camera at the garage where you planted the bomb this morning got a good shot of your face, an even better one of your license plate. I'm surprised the police haven't picked you up yet."

His grin was quick and crooked, the swagger in his tone clear. "Because I'm too smart for them. I changed the license plates."

"How about your name? I sure hope you've got a second ID up your sleeve."

Something in his eyes told her she'd hit the nail on the head.

"But no one knows who your so-called partner is." She sent him a pitying smile. "He's smoke."

"I know who he is."

She could see she had him thinking now. Just then she caught a blur of movement above and saw Jonah climb out onto the fire escape.

And Tank still had the gun.

Ready or not, she had to make her move now. No space to use her foot.

He started at the sudden blare of music. She fisted the hand she'd kept on the railing and rammed it hard against his gun hand.

The exploding bullet made her ears ring, but the gun sailed away, and he took a quick step back. Ducking her head, she sprang forward and bulldozed into him with enough force to send him back against the wall of the building. The impact had pain singing from her shoulder and down her arm.

He didn't even grunt. Instead, he yelled, "Bitch!"

Even as she jumped back onto the balls of her feet, footsteps thundered on the stairs above them. Before she could aim a kick at his groin, he rushed her, grabbing her shoulders and lifting her off her feet.

Then she was suddenly dangling feetfirst over the railing, and the only thing preventing her from falling like a rock were the ham-size hands gripping her shoulders.

For a split second, they were face-to-face, eye-to-eye. His gleamed with fury. She didn't struggle, letting her arms hang loose.

"Told you I'd toss you over." He bit out the words, then pulled his hands away.

She grabbed for the railing and caught it with one hand. The wrong hand, she decided as the pain started singing again in her shoulder. But she held on and wrapped the fingers of her other hand around an iron post.

When she glanced up, she saw he had his fist raised, ready to hammer it down hard on her hand. Mentally, she prepared for the fall. Hit, tuck and roll.

Then there was a blur of movement. Flash landed on his shoulder and went for his face.

The man's scream pierced the night as his hands flew upward and he whirled. Off balance, he lurched against the railing, then pitched over and dropped.

When Jonah heard the sound of the body hitting the cement, his heart leaped to his throat and stayed. Not Cilla, he told himself. She was still clinging to the railing. He rounded the last landing and took the steps three at a time, jumping over the cat on the last one. Then he gripped her wrist with both hands. "Got you."

"Let me help." T.D. leaned over the railing and grabbed her other wrist.

Jonah's heart was still pounding in his throat as together they hauled Cilla up until she could get her leg securely over the railing. Then he pulled her into his arms and simply held on. Until his legs began to tremble. Lowering himself to one of the stairs, he shifted her onto his lap.

"I'll check on the scumbag." T.D. started down the next flight of steps.

Overhead, "Angels We Have Heard on High" blasted into the cold night air while feelings poured through him—he couldn't even begin to name them all. He hadn't allowed himself to feel them for years. Not since that night he'd stood in the small prayer garden with Father Mike and railed at the statue to bring his father back so that he could kill him.

Everything, he thought. He'd nearly lost everything that mattered to him. Again.

When Cilla stirred in his arms, he managed to take one steady breath.

She tipped back her head and met his eyes. "Are you all right? I saw the blood on your head, but I couldn't afford to keep him in the apartment. His temper was too volatile."

"You think?" He framed her face with his hands and allowed himself to take one desperate kiss. *Mine,* he thought. And this time the word hummed in his blood until it settled in his heart.

He drew back just far enough to lay his forehead on hers. "You scared me, Cilla."

"Back at you."

Maybe, in a hundred years or so, he'd get the image of her hanging over the edge of the railing out of his mind. A few hundred more and he might rid himself of that feeling that he wasn't going to be on time. Right now, all he could do was hold on.

"There are definitely two of them in on this," Cilla said. "Tank isn't an employee. He claims to be a partner. We need to get a name from him."

"This guy needs an ambulance," T.D. called up.

Rising, Jonah set Cilla on her feet, keeping one arm around her as they moved to the railing.

Tank was lying faceup on the cement and T.D. was pulling out his cell phone. "He's breathing, but he hit his head in the fall and he's bleeding like a pig."

Overhead the music segued into "We Need a Little Christmas." Flash leaped up to the railing next to Jonah.

Jonah ran a hand over the cat. "You do good work, Flash."

Above them, the music went suddenly silent. Mrs. Ortiz poked her head out the window of Cilla's apartment. Flash jumped down and settled in between Jonah's and Cilla's legs.

"I've warned you about that music, Ms. Michaels. I'm going to have to call the landlord."

Cilla hissed, "She's in my apartment—she'll see the cat food, the toys. I'm so busted."

"A tank with a gun doesn't bother you, but your landlady does." Then he turned to call up the stairs. "There was an intruder in the apartment. Ms. Michaels is calling the police."

"Right. Finelli." Cilla pulled out her cell.

"The police?" Mrs. Ortiz sounded shocked.

Stooping down, Jonah lifted up Flash and settled her into the crook of his arm.

"The intruder had a gun and he would have gotten away if it hadn't been for the intervention of this cat," he called up. "Must live in the alley back here."

Cilla shifted her gaze from him to the cat and muttered, "She never lets me pick her up."

"An intruder, you say?" Now the landlady sounded horrified. "This is a safe neighborhood."

"I'm sure you'll want to inform the landlord," Jonah said.

"Yes. Of course. I'll do that right away. And the police are coming?"

"They're on their way," Cilla assured her.

When Mrs. Ortiz's head disappeared, Jonah murmured, "Distraction works wonders."

Down in the alley, T.D. muffled a laugh. "The two of you go on up," he said. "I'll babysit the trash until the police get here."

14

IT WAS NEARLY NINE O'CLOCK before Cilla and Jonah entered his apartment above Pleasures. They might have been delayed even longer, but once Finelli had taken their statements, he'd allowed her some time to pack what she needed. Then he'd personally escorted them to T.D.'s limo and ordered them to go into lockdown at Jonah's place. He'd call them there with any updates or new questions.

The EMTs who'd arrived with the ambulance hadn't been able to report much on the injured man's condition except that he was unconscious and might have fractured his skull. Finelli had tracked down a name from the set of Colorado license plates that he'd found inside the van. It matched the registration of the van, which belonged to a Paul Michael Anderson. Finelli had also sent two uniforms to the hospital with Anderson.

So they had a name now, but not much else. And ever since they'd arrived at his apartment, she and Jonah had been on their cells or on a wide-screen conference call with Gabe.

She had to award Jonah's apartment kudos for pacing room. No walls marred the long expanse of honey-colored parquet floors. Lovely arched windows ran the length of one wall and offered a cushioned window seat and a distant view of the bay. You had to love a place where you could sit and just stare out at the water and think. Flash had settled in one of the window seats for a while after they'd arrived. But when Jonah had moved to his desk to work, she'd decided to curl up at his feet.

Cilla swept her gaze over the space again. When she'd been here the first time, her mind had been on business. But even then she'd noticed the economical way the apartment was designed. At the far end a marble counter blocked off a galley-size kitchen. The balconied loft space above held two bedrooms and two baths.

In the center of the apartment, a comfortable-looking U-shaped couch sat in front of a brick fireplace and a large flat-screened TV. Closer to the entrance was the office space Jonah was using now with its state-of-the-art equipment. Across from it was a steel-and-glass conference table that could also be used for dining.

She sank down on a chair at the conference table. The room-service waiter had claimed it was a woman who'd given him the gift bag to deliver, but he'd been short on details. Mark Gibbons was checking out Paul Michael Anderson, and David Santos's summation of December 2005 in San Francisco was that babies had been born, old people had died, but there didn't seem to be anything that could be related to the St. Francis Center for Boys, or Jonah. So far, Gabe hadn't found any more than that in Denver. His fiancée, Nicola Guthrie, was checking into FBI records.

In short, they were still spinning their wheels, and the clock was ticking.

During their conference call with Gabe, it had been Jonah who'd asked what his friend had been able to find out about his father, and Gabe had offered to send what he had, but he'd warned them that it was a series of dead ends.

Basically, Darrell Stone had ceased to exist shortly after he'd last visited Jonah and his mother in Denver. Gabe had been able to trace him to Texas and then to Phoenix. But after that, there was no credit card trail, no evidence of anyone using that social security number ever again. And there was no death certificate, either. Nothing.

Jonah had decided to try to trace his father prior to the last time he'd visited his family, and he'd been at it for quite a while. Flash still lay curled at his feet.

As she leaned toward him, he glanced up. "I don't think I'm going to find my father."

"Do you think he must be dead?"

"There's no death certificate under that name. I've located a birth certificate for Darrell Jonah Stone, and I have death certificates for his parents, who died when he was eighteen. But I haven't been able to find much else. Gabe was able to dig up information on his credit card transactions after he left that last time twenty years ago, so I dug a little deeper, but I can't find records of his using that card anywhere but in the Denver area."

"So what did he use during the times when he was away from you and your mom?" Cilla asked.

"Good question. But I found something even more interesting. His Colorado driver's license and his car registrations only date back thirty years. I can't find any previous registration or license under that name from any other state. Even more interesting is the fact that his social security number was also issued thirty years ago. According to the birth certificate, Darrell Stone would be fifty-eight now."

As she turned the information over in her mind, she got up and began to pace in the small space between Jonah's desk and the conference table. "Thirty years ago. That's about the time when he would have met your mother at that party and it was love at first sight."

"That's right."

She turned and met his eyes. "What do you make of it?"

He leaned back in his chair and folded his hands behind his head. "One theory I'm entertaining is he created enough of an identity for himself to be able to get a marriage license and live in Denver as Darrell Stone, but during the times he was away, he lived as someone else."

"Why would he do that?"

"That's the big question. He said he worked for the government."

Cilla studied him for a moment. She knew that Jonah had recently worked with Gabe and their friend Nash Fortune to find and reunite a family living in the Witness Protection Program. She had been providing security for part of that family when she'd met Jonah at the Fortune Mansion in Denver that first day. "You're not thinking witness protection."

He shook his head. "No. If you're in the Witness Protection Program, you have to stay put or they kick you out. It's possible he was a bigamist. Maybe he had a family here and another one somewhere else. There are men like that."

"But they usually don't stop juggling the families and living multiple lives until someone discovers the bigamy. And they usually get outed and prosecuted. So why didn't you hear about it? Or why didn't he come back and try to explain?"

"There's always the chance that he was telling the truth. He did work top-security jobs for the government and for some reason he wanted to keep his marriage and his family a secret. But even that theory doesn't answer why he didn't come back."

Something tightened around her heart, and she walked to him and took his hand in hers. "I'm sorry that I opened up this whole can of worms for you."

"I'm not sorry. I thought I'd stopped being angry at my father years ago, but I think I just buried it. And not trying to find him was a good way to keep that anger buried. But now I'm curious."

"If he was using two identities, it could be that there's a death certificate, just not under Darrell Stone."

"I know." He smiled.

She saw the light in his eyes and felt a little tingle along her nerve endings. "But you don't think he's dead, do you?"

"No."

She pulled a chair from the conference table and sat down across from his desk. "Talk to me."

"It's just a feeling that's been growing since you prodded me into looking for him. Lord knows, I've wanted him to be dead." He put his hands on his face, rubbed his eyes. "You know, I once prayed that I would find my father, but it was so I could kill him."

"How old were you?"

"I was thirteen and I'd bounced through a couple of foster homes, run away a couple of times. A judge who'd gotten tired of seeing me in her court sentenced me to a year of going to the St. Francis Center every day after school and on Saturdays. She threatened—no, promised me that if I didn't give my foster home and the center at least a year, she'd send me away to a juvenile detention facility. I saw in her eyes that she meant it.

"But I was still so angry. There was this statue of St. Francis in a little prayer garden. It was close to Christmas during the first year I was going to the center. I liked Father Mike and I was getting to know Nash and Gabe. But Father Mike could sense my anger. On Christmas Eve, he took me to the statue of St. Francis. He told me that I should say the prayer in my heart, to ask for something that I really wanted. So I did. I shouted the prayer out loud. I prayed to St. Francis to bring my father back to me so that I could kill him. All I could think of was that Christmas when we'd waited and waited for him. And I wanted him to be dead for leaving my mother and me."

Cilla covered his hand with hers, and when he turned his to link their fingers, she held on. "Understandable. There were times when I entertained fantasies of making my father suffer because he was always too busy at Christmas and he made my mother so unhappy."

"The problem is that the statue of St. Francis I prayed to has special prayer-granting powers. My friends Gabe and Nash—their prayers have all been answered. The church where the statue now resides has become a Mecca for tourists."

"So…you not only think he's alive, you think you're going to find him."

"Something like that. I hope to God I'm not going to end up killing him."

"For what it's worth, I don't think he's mixed up in what's going on now."

When the phone on his desk rang, Jonah reached for it. "Yes, Virgil? Sure, bring Carmen and Ben up." He turned to Cilla. "Virgil says that Carmen might have the answer to a question you were asking her earlier today."

Cilla got that clutch in her gut the instant that Carmen stepped off the elevator. Ben, a tall young man with dark hair and his mother's smile, followed her. He had a laptop tucked beneath his arm. Bringing up the rear of the small parade was Virgil pushing a cart.

"I brought refreshments," he announced, and then began to unload trays of sandwiches and drinks on the glass table.

Carmen spoke to Jonah first. "I've got Dickie and Pete covering the closing of the club. But when Ben called and told me he remembered something from six years ago at the St. Francis Center, I thought you'd want to know right away."

Jonah moved from behind his desk to take her hands. "You did the right thing. Cilla and I feel like we've been bumping into brick walls all day." He turned to Ben. "Why don't you show us what you've got?"

"Photos mostly. I was pretty snap-happy in those days. Father Mike asked me to record most of the events at the St. Francis Center. He got me the camera and provided the film. When I looked through the pictures I started to remember."

A flush spread over Ben's face as he spoke. "There was this young woman who volunteered at the center. She was eighteen or nineteen. I was fourteen and a little immature."

"Smitten is what you were—puppy love," Carmen said as she placed a hand on her son's arm. "The first time it hits you, you fall hard. And Ben had it bad. When he brought his laptop into Interludes and showed me some of the pictures, I started to remember, too."

"And you thought Ben's crush might connect to what's happening now," Cilla prodded.

Ben glanced at his mother. "The thing is, as big a crush as I had on this girl, she had an even bigger one on Jonah. She was a volunteer. She helped out in the office and sometimes she worked with the younger boys. But whenever Jonah was there, she practically stalked him. I didn't stand a chance. She was following him while I was sort of doing the same thing with her—but with my camera."

He held out a photo to Jonah. "I brought my laptop, but when I came across this one, I blew it up and printed it out. Mom told me about the presents you've been receiving, and I thought you'd want to see this."

Cilla moved to Jonah's side as she studied the picture. In it a young blonde woman stood in front of a Christmas tree. The camera had caught her in profile, offering a gift to Jonah—a green box tied with red ribbon.

Cilla felt it then. Not a tingle, but something pushing at the edge of her memory.

"Do you remember her?" Ben asked.

"Vaguely," Jonah said. "Let's see if we can connect the laptop to the TV and we can view the pictures on the big screen." He led Ben over to the U-shaped couches in front of the TV.

Carmen turned to Cilla. "I may be making a mountain out of a molehill, but you said to tell you anything that seemed out of the ordinary about that Christmas season six years ago."

"I did."

"You think what's going on now goes back that far?" Virgil asked.

"It's a theory," Cilla said.

"I was here in the San Francisco area back then," he said. "Jonah opened Pleasures the summer of 2006, and he hired me away from a sweet little place in Sausalito where I'd been tending bar for a couple of years."

"I was here, too. Fresh out of the police academy, my first year on the streets." Cilla felt something again—just a little tug. "Jonah was here in San Francisco, too. He was looking for this building. Can you stay for a while, Virgil, and look at Ben's pictures?"

"Sure." Virgil crossed to Jonah's desk phone. "I'll just let my assistant manager know where to call me."

A few minutes later, they were all seated on the couches in front of the flat-screen TV over the fireplace. Ben tapped keys on his laptop and a series of photos began to appear.

"Mom told me to start with December," Ben explained.

There were candid shots of a Christmas party in progress—kids of various ages opening presents, eating cake. Jonah was in a couple of them handing out presents. And she was pretty sure she spotted her boss, Gabe Wilder, dressed up as Santa and wearing a beard.

There were posed shots, one with a large group standing around the Christmas tree, another with the priest she knew as Father Mike standing with a smaller group around a statue of St. Francis. They were all wearing coats and hats and waving at the camera.

"The Christmas party was early that year, and the weather was mild," Ben said. The next series of shots were all taken on the basketball court. Once again, Cilla was able to recognize Jonah and Gabe. They seemed to be refereeing games for the boys and girls who went to the center.

But there was another person who was beginning to look familiar, too, a tall, slender young woman. The same woman Ben had captured handing the present to Jonah. She wasn't young enough to be one of the kids. And not pretty exactly. You might not have been able to pick her out in a crowd except for the long blond, Alice-in-Wonderland hair.

Cilla felt the tug again.

"I do remember that girl," Jonah said. "Her name was Elizabeth something."

"Baxter. Elizabeth Baxter," Ben said. "I didn't have the courage to even say a word to her. Not that she would have paid any attention to me. She only had eyes for you, Jonah."

Jonah frowned. "Nice girl. Quiet. I was so busy then, working part-time at G.W. Securities, still volunteering at the center, and trying to line up places that Mrs. Fortune and I could see in San Francisco." He paused, his frown deepening. "I'd forgotten all about her. But earlier that fall, someone had started leaving notes in my mail slot at the center. All of them signed by a secret admirer."

"What kind of notes?" Cilla asked.

"Silly stuff. Poems, sometimes with pictures of flowers on them. I just ignored them. I figured they were harmless enough."

Ben clicked on his keyboard and brought up a shot of the young blonde woman putting an envelope in a mail slot. "Here I am, super stalker in action."

Jonah rose to his feet, moved closer to the TV screen. "Then there were gifts—little things—a paperweight with my initials, a framed photo of Gabe and me shooting some hoop. I still didn't think anything of it. I was too busy."

When Ben brought up the picture of Elizabeth handing Jonah the green box, Cilla moved to his side. "What was in the box?"

"A ring. And a note telling me that she'd fallen in love with me. That we were destined to be together."

"What did you do?" Cilla asked.

"Father Mike had had to leave the party early to say a vigil mass at the Capuchin monastery. But I felt that I had to do something immediately, so I asked Gabe to stay. He and I met with her together after the party, and I gave her back the ring. I talked to her. Or tried to. I told her that what she was going through was normal. We all get a crush on somebody. It's part of growing up."

"That's the same speech that Mom gave me," Ben said.

"Not that it worked," Carmen said. "Puppy love is tough."

"Well, with Elizabeth, what I said seemed to work. She said something about some people being destined to be together, and that when we died and came back in another lifetime, we would find each other. I don't know what I'd expected, but when she left, she was smiling. And Gabe thought I'd handled it pretty well."

Pausing, Jonah ran a hand through his hair. "I never thought any more about it. That night I left for San Francisco to scout out places for Mrs. Fortune to look at. Finding the right building and making Pleasures a reality kept me away from the center for a while. When I finally did go back, she wasn't there anymore."

"She stopped coming to the St. Francis Center before Christmas," Ben said. "She told everyone that she was moving away. The day she made the announcement, I took several shots. To remember her by." He brought up more photos on the screen.

Cilla's stomach knotted as she moved closer to the TV. She tapped a finger on one of the images. "Can you enlarge this one, Ben?"

"Sure."

As soon as he did, the memory that had been nagging at her slipped into place and her stomach sank.

"She cut her hair," Cilla said.

"Yeah," Ben said. "Everyone was kind of shocked. But she said she was about to begin a new life and she was leaving everything about her old life behind. She was so looking forward to starting fresh."

"I'm pretty sure I remember her, too," Cilla said. "I didn't recognize her when she had the long hair because it was short like this when I first saw her. If I'm right, she did leave her old life behind. And she did it right here in San Francisco."

She paused to study the picture on the screen again. But it was almost a perfect match to the one she'd carried in her head for years. Moving closer, Jonah linked his fingers with hers.

"She was one of the first cases I was assigned to during my rookie year on the force," Cilla went on. The details flooded into her mind. "Joe Finelli was my partner then. It was Christmas Eve and we'd pulled the night shift. We got the call around late Christmas Eve. A drowning. We weren't sure where she went in, but her body was discovered floating beneath one of the piers. A Jane Doe. No ID. No one in the area was ever reported missing."

"I remember reading about it," Virgil said. "A couple of days after Christmas, an artist's sketch ran in the local papers. On TV, too."

"We never got an ID," Cilla said. "All she had on her was a note. It had been sealed in waterproof laminate. It read, 'I'm leaving for a whole new life. This time I'll be with my true love.'"

"Good Lord," Jonah murmured. "She committed suicide because she believed it was the only way she could be with me? How could that possibly be?"

"If she was into that reincarnation stuff, she might have believed that dying was the fastest way to get to the next life where you and she could be together," Ben said.

Carmen put an arm around her son. "Or it could be that she was a total nutcase. All the loonies are not in the loony bin."

Cilla kept her fingers linked with Jonah's when she turned to Ben. "Did Elizabeth ever mention any relatives?"

"Not to me directly," Ben said. "I never did get up the

nerve to talk to her. But when she worked with the younger kids, she used to tell stories about her twin brother and her uncle. They were both in the military."

"If she was telling the truth, we should be able to trace them." Jonah moved to his computer.

"I'll update everyone else," Cilla said, pulling out her cell.

Virgil gestured to Carmen and Ben. "You guys are coming with me. The chef has a dessert he's creating tonight for the staff to test."

AT 3:00 A.M., HE SAT IN HIS car and watched as the lights at Pleasures blinked off one by one. Except for those on the third floor.

They were still on. The two of them were still working, trying to find out who he was.

His fingers tightened on the steering wheel as he pushed down hard on the anger. Thanks to the bungling of his partner, they had to be one step closer to identifying him. When the red mist appeared in front of his eyes, he blinked it away.

He'd nearly given in to his anger when he'd seen what had happened in the alley outside Cilla Michaels's apartment. From his vantage point at the mouth of the short alley, the plan he'd devised had seemed to be going according to schedule.

Cilla was leading the way down the fire escape. And the limo driver who'd dropped them off was pacing at the front of the building, checking his messages on his phone.

Then his partner had changed the plan. Suddenly, Cilla was dangling feetfirst over the railing. He was supposed to kidnap her and kill her someplace else. So they would have to look for her and spin their wheels.

And Jonah Stone would know what it was like to lose someone he loved.

But the plan might still have worked. The drop from

the second story could have killed her. It would certainly have injured her and caused Stone both suffering and distraction.

But she hadn't been the one who'd dropped to the cement in the alley.

She hadn't been the one who'd been taken away unmoving in an ambulance.

The red mist had blurred his vision several times as he'd followed the ambulance to its destination. An emergency room. So his partner was alive. But the police would have his fingerprints. They'd be able to trace his identity.

That would take time. And it would take even more time for them to put things together and find him. If they ever did.

As one of the lights blinked off on the third floor of the club, his hands tightened on the steering wheel again. They were going to go to bed now. And they'd make love. This man who should have loved Elizabeth would make love with the woman who was trying to spoil everything.

And they shouldn't be sleeping. This was time they were supposed to spend chasing their tails. And it wasn't his partner's fault. No, it was the woman's fault. He'd had the perfect plan. But she wasn't supposed to be in it.

Time, he reminded himself as he rested his forehead against the steering wheel. It was still on his side. And he was good at measuring people and finding their vulnerabilities. A new plan began to form in his mind. He could still take her out of the picture. Still make Stone experience what it was like to lose the person you loved most in the world.

He could still avenge Elizabeth's death.

Tomorrow night at Pleasures.

15

THE APARTMENT WAS SILENT except for the hum of his computer. Jonah studied the two screens on his desk. They were scrolling and sifting through data. As soon as Carmen and her son had left, Finelli had called to report the bad news that the name Paul Michael Anderson was an alias with a driver's license, a car registration and a social security number that only dated back one year. Cilla had contacted Gabe to report on their progress and divide up the work. Gabe was digging into Elizabeth Baxter, and he wouldn't be reporting in until he was sure he had everything.

Jonah had opted for the more complicated assignment, tracking down who Paul Michael Anderson really was. Following his best hunch, he was running the photo on Anderson's driver's license through military databases, hoping for the real name to pop.

Which would take time.

A glance at the bottom of his computer screen said 3:00 a.m. Time to call it a night. Flash had deserted him for one of the window seats over an hour ago. He turned in his chair, intending to tell Cilla it was time for a break, and he saw that she'd already fallen asleep on the couch. Rising, he moved closer.

Moonlight fell in rectangular patches across the floor. Other than that the room was dark, save for the dim glow from a table lamp and the computer screens. She lay curled up like a child, her hand beneath her cheek. Her face looked fragile, her wrists delicate. He'd never thought of her as either, he realized.

It had been her aura of strength and of competence that had drawn him from that first meeting of eyes. But he'd never watched her sleep before. Not even in the dreams that had haunted him for so many long silent nights. But when he'd dreamed of her, when he'd tossed and turned hoping to find her in his bed, sleeping had never been part of his fantasy.

No, what he'd wanted more than anything was a repeat of that long, sexy night they'd spent in that hotel room in Denver. Wanted it with a desire that had begun to boil in his blood. Looking at her now, he couldn't bring to mind why he'd waited so long to go to her and take what he'd wanted. What he still wanted.

Only now, he wanted more. And he knew that the wanting wasn't going to stop. The qualities he was seeing in her as she slept, the vulnerability that she kept so carefully hidden were pulling at him and arousing him even more than the fearlessness that he found so admirable.

When he reached the couch, he dropped to his knees and pushed a dark curl of her hair off her forehead.

She stirred, just as he wanted her to. And when she opened her eyes, he watched the cloudiness of sleep fade into recognition and desire.

I want you. Neither of them had to say the words aloud. Keeping his eyes on hers, he took her hands and drew her up with him as he rose to his feet. They undressed each other in silence, not touching except for the brush of a fingertip—on his chest, at her waist. Over his shoulder, down her arm.

Cilla had been dreaming of him before he'd awakened her, wanting him with the same intensity that she'd been experiencing for so many nights. When he'd touched her to push her hair back, she'd thought for a moment that she was lost once again in the dream that she'd had for so long. Her mind had already been filled with him, her body heated in anticipation. But this time she wasn't dreaming of his touch. He was real.

Moonlight slanted through the narrow windows. She loved how the mix of light and shadow heightened the desire and the pleasure she saw in his eyes. And when he skimmed his gaze over her, her heart began to thud.

In silence still, he stepped out of his slacks and she out of hers. Then she moved into his arms and pressed herself against him. "Jonah." His name was a quiet sigh as she cupped his face with her hands and brought his mouth to hers.

But he didn't kiss her, not in the way he'd done in her dreams. Not in the way he'd ever done before. He kept the pressure soft, taking her hands from his face and linking his fingers with hers as they sank to their knees.

His mouth was so warm, his lips so gentle, coaxing and teasing, only taking more when she sighed his name again. No one had ever kissed her like this—as if he had all the time in the world and intended to take it. Only Jonah, she thought as ribbons of pleasure unwound through her system. And when he released her hands and began to touch her, there was such tenderness in his fingers that it might have been starlight only moving over her skin.

Even as she began to float, emotions welled up in her. Her eyes stung, her throat burned, and the liquid yearning he was building in her sprang as much from her heart as from her body.

Home, she thought, and the silent sound of the word in her head trembled through her. She didn't want him to be a dream anymore. The dream would never be enough. Ever.

Jonah used his hands gently to touch, explore, exploit. He knew her now. During all those sexy silent nights when he'd relived every moment in his imagination, he'd had the time to review and file away what pleased her most. What made her catch her breath, what made her sigh. And each time she did, he offered more. Took more.

His heart ached to tell her what he was feeling. But he wasn't sure she was ready to hear the words. Or whether he was ready to say them aloud.

But at least he could show her.

Lowering her to the floor, he used his mouth on her. Each time she trembled, his heart pounded harder and his blood burned hotter. Still, he forced himself to keep the pace slow. Torturing himself as well as her, he took the time to savor the flavors of her skin, the saltiness of her neck, the honeyed sweetness of her breast. He lingered there for as long as he could. But his hunger was building for more. Her taste grew darker at her waist, darker and richer still as he moved lower. And when he nudged her thighs apart and found her core, he feasted.

She erupted. When her body quaked and reared, he tightened his hold on her hips, and when she settled, he began to build the pleasure again—slowly, steadily. When she was close to a climax again, when he could feel every muscle in her body tightening, reaching, he moved up and over her.

"Cilla?" he whispered.

When she opened her eyes, he looked into them and saw everything he was looking for. And he filled her.

She groped for his hands, linked her fingers with his. "Everything."

The sound of the breathless word filled the air, and still Jonah fought for control. Her eyes stayed open and on his as each thrust brought them both closer.

And when he was flying off the edge, reeling, his mouth moved to hers and whispered her name as they fell together.

CILLA FOUND HERSELF SINGING in the shower. Twice. The first time was before Jonah had joined her. After the night they'd spent together, she hadn't thought it possible to want him again so desperately. But she had.

And now she was singing again.

So what?

She might be falling in love with a man who had three strikes against him. She pressed a panicked hand against her heart. She was not going to think about that now. She didn't have time.

Gabe had called from the airport. He'd flown in with Father Mike Flynn and they were on their way to Pleasures. Finelli had called next. He was bringing over the cold-case file on Elizabeth Baxter. Cilla didn't have time to sing anymore.

When Jonah opened the bathroom door, she pulled the shower curtain in front of her and pointed a finger. "Stay right where you are." The fact that he was fully dressed didn't fool her. He'd been fully dressed in different jeans and T-shirt when he'd joined her the first time. "Gabe and Father Mike are going to be here any second."

He grinned at her. "They're here now. And I could convince you to make the time." He brought out the mug of coffee he was holding behind his back. "Instead, I brought you this. Finelli's here, too."

He strode toward the shower and grabbed a quick kiss before he handed her the mug. "Hurry. We need your insights on this."

She had two problems, Cilla thought as she watched him walk toward the door. And she didn't have any insights at all on how to solve the one she was looking at.

THE MEN WERE ALL GATHERED around the flat-screen TV when Cilla joined them. Finelli had brought donuts as well as the file on Elizabeth Baxter. She saw four photos on display. One was the close-up of Elizabeth that Ben had enlarged the night before. Another was one of Elizabeth with her long hair, handing Jonah the green box tied with red ribbon. A third was the photo of Elizabeth that had been taken by the coroner. The fourth was a young man with close-cropped blond hair and the same high forehead and blue eyes that Elizabeth had. It was the photo of Robert Baxter that Gabe had taken from his military file.

"How sure are we that it's the same girl?" Finelli asked, gesturing with his donut at the pictures of Elizabeth.

"Elizabeth Baxter was an army brat," Gabe said. "She and her twin brother, Robert, lost their parents when they were five and the uncle, Paul Baxter, became their guardian. Paul was a career man in the army so they moved around a lot. Spent their high school years in a private boarding school near Colorado Springs. I've got some men on it. They're visiting the school this morning. We may be able to track down dental records through them and identify your Jane Doe."

Finelli waved at the TV screen. "Until we can be sure, I say we go with the theory that our Jane Doe is Elizabeth Baxter. What else do we know?"

"I believe the man who fell off Cilla's fire escape is Sergeant Paul Baxter." Jonah clicked a key on the computer and another image joined those on the screen. "I ran the photo we had from the security discs through military databases during the night and the match was waiting this morning."

"I traced Paul Baxter through more conventional methods," Gabe said. "But I agree with Jonah's ID."

"He sure looks like the guy we've been calling Tank," Finelli said. "We can check his fingerprints to confirm that. His doctors have him in an induced coma because of the head injury he suffered during the fall. They say there is some scarring in the brain because of previous injuries, and it may be days before I can question him."

"That fits with what I learned," Gabe said. "Paul Baxter was trained in explosives, and in Iraq, he worked on a special ops team. He received a medical discharge a year ago when he suffered head injuries in a land-mine explosion."

"That also fits with what he told me yesterday," Cilla said. "He said he was the tactical man and that his partner was the strategic planner. What do we know about the twin brother, Robert?"

"He was honorably discharged from the army a year ago," Gabe said. "That's all I found. Jonah is using his special talents to dig out more details on his military career as we speak."

"You can get into those kinds of records?" Finelli asked. Jonah smiled.

"You don't want to know the details," Gabe said. "And I have even more interesting news. I've run a quick check, but so far, I can't find any trace of Robert Baxter once he shipped back from Iraq and got his walking papers from the army. No record of taxes filed, no record of employment using that social security number. No death certificate."

"He may have changed his ID," Cilla said. "The uncle changed his, so he may have helped Robert."

"That would be my guess," Gabe agreed. "The bad news is we don't have any idea what name he's operating under now."

"And he's been smart enough to keep in the background and let his uncle do the dirty work. The twin certainly has to be a person of interest, and we have to find him."

"I agree," Finelli said.

Cilla turned to Father Mike. "How long was Elizabeth at the center?"

"Six months," the priest said. "Gabe asked me to check the records. I remember meeting with her and she said that she had just moved to Denver. In the fall, she was going to enroll at the community college. She said that she wasn't Catholic but she enjoyed working with children."

"Robert Baxter was deployed to Iraq at about the same

time Elizabeth moved to Denver," Gabe said. "I've got men who are going to check out the community college today and perhaps even track down where she was living in Denver."

"Do we know anything else?" Finelli asked.

Cilla moved closer to the screen and tapped on the green box with the red ribbon. "We can theorize. Twins are close. I'm guessing Elizabeth must have kept Robert fully informed of everything that was going on in her life, including the Christmas present she gave Jonah that year."

"Letters," Father Mike said. "I didn't know her all that well, but she was always carrying a notebook and she would write frequently in it."

"If the first time they were separated was when they left that boarding school, she probably let him know that she was falling in love with Jonah," Cilla said. "Who knows how she told that story in her letters? And what if she told her twin Jonah rejected her, and she'd decided that the best way to eventually be with her true love was to commit suicide? What would that do to you if you received those letters on the other side of the globe and you had no way to get back to her?"

Finelli frowned at the TV screen. "I can buy into your theory so far. But if he's been out a year, why wait to get his revenge?"

"Planning," Jonah said. "And he obviously wants more than to just push me into my next life. He wants some payback first. He's already targeted Cilla—not merely because she's interfered with some of his plans, but also because he's sensed she's important to me. I think he's going to try to target Pleasures also."

"Because it was Pleasures that took you away from Denver," Cilla said. "That has to be why she followed you here to San Francisco and committed suicide here."

"If you're right," Finelli said, "I suggest you shut down

the place until Christmas is over, or until we catch this whack job. Or at least figure out if your theory is correct."

"No," Cilla said.

Everyone turned to her then, but it was Jonah's eyes she met and held. "Shutting down Pleasures could be exactly what he wants. It's December 23, and tonight you're throwing a huge party at Pleasures. I think he'd love to see you cancel it. Number one, you'd annoy the people who've traveled here especially to attend. Number two, you'd lose all those checks that the guests were going to write for the boys and girls clubs here in San Francisco. The club takes a hit. Your favorite charity takes a hit. It's another way of making you suffer before he takes a final run at you on the twenty-fourth."

"I think you're right," Jonah said. "Not only that, I'll bet you when I don't cancel, he finds a way to join the party. He hasn't made a mistake yet. Maybe we can lure him into making one tonight."

"It's going to be a hell of a job to handle the security," Gabe said.

Jonah grinned at him. "You don't think G.W. Securities is up to the job?"

Gabe didn't return the grin, but Cilla could tell he was thinking. "You've already got the security cameras in place. We can use this apartment as our headquarters, and we'll wire you and Cilla." The smile formed slowly. "And I've got a couple of new gadgets we can use."

Jonah turned to Finelli. "We can also use the San Francisco Police Department."

Finelli sighed in defeat. "This could turn into a real Christmas nightmare."

_16_

THE PARTY AT PLEASURES was a Christmas fantasy come true. From her position at the top of the staircase, Cilla was able to see the expressions on the faces of the guests entering the club. None of them was aware they were using the occasion to trap a would-be killer.

She could also see Jonah standing at the foot of the stairs, greeting everyone as they came in. He looked totally relaxed, smiling and shaking hands as though the Christmas event was the only thing on his mind. Gabe stood next to him so he was safe for now. But her stomach was in knots because she had a feeling that the person behind the notes was indeed going to make an appearance at the party.

And soon. Cilla let her gaze sweep the place again. On the second floor, the tables had been shoved against the wall. Crystal chandeliers glittered overhead. Women in jewel-colored gowns danced with their partners on a gleaming parquet floor while a band played slow tunes in the background.

On the lower floor, drinks were being offered to the arriving guests in the bar, and in the dining room, long tables held an array of food. Silver-and-white trees twinkled in the corners.

Gibbons and Santos were in Jonah's apartment monitoring the surveillance cameras. The wire she was wearing had a remote switch tucked beneath the strap of her dress so that she could turn it off or on. And tucked into a small flower on the same strap was a little video camera that would send close-up pictures of anyone who talked with her.

For the past hour, there'd been no reason to activate either the camera or her mic. Guests had been arriving in a steady stream. She even recognized some of them, including the nightly news anchorwoman who had been dominating Jonah's time for the past ten minutes.

Next year, Cilla was going to make sure Jonah threw a Christmas party that she could enjoy. Sans anchorwoman.

Next year.

As the two words ran through her mind again, Cilla felt her stomach plummet. Somehow in the past few days, a one-night stand she'd been determined to walk away from had morphed into *next year*. Maybe longer? Her stomach pitched again.

She pressed her hand against it and focused on the next group of people coming in the front door.

"Do you need something to eat?"

"I'm fine." Cilla turned to face the pretty brunette who stood beside her. Nicola Guthrie, a special agent with the FBI office in Denver, was also Gabe's fiancée, and Gabe had arranged for her to fly in for the party and assigned her to watch Cilla for the evening. "Just nerves."

Nicola glanced down the staircase to where Jonah stood in the receiving line with Gabe. "Gabe won't let anything happen to Jonah. Nash would be here, too, if his grandmother hadn't arranged that cruise with their new family members."

"Jonah is safe for tonight," Cilla agreed. But it wasn't Christmas Eve yet, and if they weren't able to stop whoever was behind the threat tonight… All day long as they'd waited for Gabe's men to report in on the Baxter twins, she'd been plagued by a growing certainty that time was running out.

And they still had very little to go on. The only thing they now knew for certain was that the body that had washed up six years ago beneath the piers was indeed Elizabeth Baxter.

Gabe's men had been able to contact her advisor and one of her professors at the community college where she'd attended classes. The professor had confirmed her interest in Eastern religions and reincarnation.

All they had on her twin, Robert, was that his teachers at the private boarding school considered him brilliant but subject to drastic mood swings. And they all remarked on how close the twins were, inseparable almost. One of Robert's teachers had encouraged the young man to apply to West Point, but he was too impatient to follow in his uncle's footsteps and serve his country in combat. The guidance counselor described him as borderline genius but with anger issues that at times resulted in drastic changes in personality. The counselor had also remarked on the closeness of the twins.

What Jonah had been able to unearth from Robert's military files didn't shed much further light. Several times he'd been reprimanded for insubordination, but his commanding officer had also reported frequently on his bravery and his aptitude for strategic planning. Although his advice had been unsolicited at first, the unit had learned to rely on his insights before going on a mission. It would have helped to be able to speak to his commanding officer, but the man had died in Iraq.

"There's so much we don't know," Cilla said. "If our current theory is correct and Elizabeth's twin is behind this, he could wait us out. Maybe he isn't even here. Or he could be here just enjoying the party, and relishing what he has planned for tomorrow. Or if we've rattled him too much, he could make a move on Jonah that we don't stop."

Nicola took her hand and squeezed it. "You'll stop it. Gabe and Jonah and I will help you stop it. We've got every available agent from G.W. Securities here. Your friend Finelli brought quite a few cops, and they have good eyes."

Nicola was right, Cilla told herself. The security was as tight as they could make it. Several of Gabe's agents were circulating on the first floor, and Finelli was all suited up in a white waiter's jacket in the bar.

"Who is that man talking to Jonah right now?" Nicola asked.

Cilla glanced down the stairs. "That's Carl Rockwell. He was one of the original investors in Pleasures and he's one of Jonah's partners in a new club they plan to open in San Diego. Why?"

"For a second, when he smiled at Jonah, he reminded me of someone. But I can't place him."

"I asked Gabe to check him out because his association with Jonah began when he invested in Pleasures. But that was after Christmas." She turned to Nicola. "And you can see I'm grasping at straws. I'm not sure I'm even thinking clearly anymore."

"Jonah is more than a case to you."

Cilla hesitated, then said, "He shouldn't be. I didn't want him to be."

"You've fallen in love with him."

Cilla's stomach dropped as hard and fast as a rock, and panic spewed up to fill the space left behind. "No. Maybe. We haven't known each other long enough. I like him, of course. But I keep telling myself we're just having a… thing. It's just a chemistry thing."

And she was babbling.

"Uh-huh."

"He's… We're…all wrong." But the more she spoke, the greater the panic became.

"That's a sure sign," Nicola said. "That 'all wrong'

thing. When I ran into Gabe a few months ago, I thought he was an art thief just like his father. I wanted to arrest him."

"But you didn't."

Nicola grinned at her. "It was a chemistry thing. I decided to jump him instead, and it turned out to be a much better choice. We're getting married in February on Valentine's Day."

Married.

No, she thought. There was no fairy-tale ending for her. She didn't believe in them. That had always been the dream her mother had chased so unsuccessfully. She opened her mouth to say so, and then shut it as Father Mike Flynn started up the stairs toward them. When he reached them, Nicola leaned in to kiss his cheek. "Father Mike, will you keep Cilla company for a minute? I'm going to run down and get us a plate of food."

As soon as Nicola was out of earshot, Cilla said, "I hope you're saying a lot of prayers."

He reached out and took her hand in both of his. "I'm sure you've said quite a few yourself."

"Yes, but sometimes God doesn't answer them the way you'd like him to. My aunt Nancy, who was a nun, always said that sometimes, God just says no. But I understand the statue of St. Francis has some pull. You wouldn't happen to have a direct line to it, would you?"

Father Mike smiled. "I mentioned the situation to him before Gabe picked me up this morning."

Glancing down, Cilla saw Stan and Glenda Rubin enter the club. They had an entourage with them that included Dean Norris as well as Glenda's sister and brother-in-law. When he reached Jonah in the reception line, Stan pulled him into a hug and Jonah returned it. The gesture had her thinking of Jonah's father again.

She turned to Father Mike. "Did Jonah mention to you that he's trying to track down his father?"

Surprise flickered over the priest's face. "No."

"It wasn't his idea. I nagged him into it. When you're working on a case like this, you have to pull on every thread, and you have to look at everyone who might have a motivation. Family always pops to the top of the list."

"Of course," Father Mike said.

"Knowing what we do now, I think it's highly unlikely that his father is involved. Jonah hasn't been able to find any trace of him, not even a death certificate. But he believes that the life Darrell Stone lived in Denver may have been based on an identity he created solely for the purpose of living with his family—for whatever reason. I think he'll keep looking."

"I've never known Jonah to give up once he sets his mind to something." Father Mike gave her hands one final squeeze before he released them. "I can see you care a great deal about him. What I can tell you is that the first part of Jonah's prayer to St. Francis on that long-ago Christmas Eve will be answered."

He turned then and surveyed the partygoers below them. "If Jonah's father hadn't failed to return to his family, Jonah might not be doing the kind of work that he's doing for boys and girls in Denver and here. When the St. Francis Center for Boys had to close down, he was the one who convinced Gabe and Nash to open a new one to include both boys and girls. They put their own money into it."

Another group of guests entered the club.

Glancing down, Father Mike clasped her wrist. "Who is that young man shaking Jonah's hand right now?"

Cilla tensed as her gaze shot to Jonah. "That's Dean Norris. He's a protégé of Stan Rubin, the older man talking to Gabe. Stan is Jonah's new partner for the club he's opening in San Diego. Why do you ask?"

"Maybe nothing. He took his glasses off to wipe them when he arrived. And for a moment, I thought…"

"What?" Cilla pressed. Below her, Dean took a glass of champagne from a passing waiter. Glenda laughed.

With a sigh, Father Mike shook his head. "My eyes are playing tricks on me. Looking at those images of Elizabeth Baxter and her brother on the TV screen for so long this morning brought back memories of when she worked at the center. For just a moment, I thought that young man down there resembled her. But I can see now that he doesn't. I must be getting old."

At that moment, Dean brushed his hair off his forehead, then glanced up at her and waved.

The feeling tingled up her spine.

For just an instant, she thought she caught a hint of resemblance, too. Not to the image that had been in the old case file, but to one of the photos Ben had shot. Then Dean smiled and the impression faded.

But the feeling didn't. It only grew as he turned to say something to Stan and then started up the stairs toward her. Jonah was already talking to the next arrivals, so there wasn't any time to tell him what she was feeling.

"Father Mike," she spoke in a low voice, "I'm going to get Dean to give you his champagne glass. There'll be fingerprints on it, so guard it with your life until you can get it to Nicola."

"Will do," Father Mike murmured.

"Cilla," Dean said as he reached her. "I was hoping we'd have a chance to chat. I want to apologize for using you to vent yesterday. I was letting my disappointment take control. I tend to do that a bit too often."

"No problem. I'd like you to meet Father Mike Flynn. I was just telling him that you're working with Stan and Jonah on the new club they're opening in San Diego."

Dean held out his free hand. "Father Mike."

The priest grasped it.

While the two men exchanged greetings, she studied Dean. The hair color and eye color were wrong, but when he stood in profile as he did now, her feeling grew even stronger. Elizabeth would be twenty-four now, and that matched her guestimate of how old Dean was. Plus, he'd just been discharged from the military when he'd approached Stan for a job.

But she needed evidence. "Dean, I feel it's such a shame to waste this music. Will you let Father Mike hold your champagne while you dance with me?"

He turned back to her. "I'd love to."

She took his arm and urged him onto the dance floor. If he was Robert Baxter, then the best thing she could do was keep him away from Jonah. And the glass might give them the evidence they needed.

She slipped her finger beneath the flower on her shoulder strap and flicked the switch on the little camera and mic.

They were in the center of the dance floor before Dean turned her into his arms. "I wanted to thank you for what you said to me yesterday. When I know I'm right about something, and others just don't see it, I get impatient."

She looked up and met his eyes. "You get angry."

His grin was a bit sheepish. "I do have a temper. And a bit of an ego problem, I admit. But talking with you made me realize that I *will* see my designs become a reality someday. I just have to be patient."

And the man dancing with her *was* patient. He was the same young man who'd come over to introduce himself in the Rubins' suite. Before he'd become impatient with the children.

"Stan told me that once our San Diego club gets on its feet, he's going to join Carl Rockwell and Jonah to finance that club in Seattle. Then my designs could come to fruition."

As he guided her into a turn, Cilla studied his face. There was none of the tension, none of the barely controlled anger radiating off him that she'd noted when he'd talked about his designs before. It was almost as if this young man and the angry one she'd seen yesterday were two different people.

What if they were? As Dean guided her around the dance floor, her feeling grew stronger. Two people. She turned the idea over in her mind. If Robert Baxter was suffering from some personality disorder, it might explain his guidance counselor's description of him as brilliant at times and childish at others. It might also explain the different reports in his military file. And hadn't she and Jonah believed from the beginning that they were dealing with two people? One an impulsive risk taker, the other a planner? Not Robert and his uncle, but perhaps two Roberts?

Her experience with multiple personalities was limited to old movies—*Sybil* starring Sally Field, and *The Three Faces of Eve* starring Joanne Woodward. But she knew the trick would be to get the other Robert, the angry Robert, to come out.

The music segued into another song.

"One more dance?" she asked. "I know I can't monopolize your whole evening."

"I'd love another dance."

She noted that they were at the far end of the dance floor now, about as far away from Jonah as she could hope for. She'd turned her camera and mic on. As he guided her into a waltz, she tilted her head back and met his eyes. "You must have had a tough time in the military."

The smile wavered. The hand at her waist and the one holding hers both tightened.

"What do you mean? And how did you even know I was in the military?"

"Glenda mentioned your military background to me when you were presenting your ideas for Jonah's approval. And I just meant that having a hair-trigger temper must have been a problem for you when you were in the service."

"It wasn't." The smile was completely gone now, and his tone was defensive. "I was written up for bravery several times. Anger in the army can be channeled toward the enemy. Plus, my commanding officer often complimented me on my ideas on mission strategy."

There was tension radiating off him now, so Cilla decided to go for broke. She sent up a quick prayer that her mic and camera were working and that at least one of her men in Jonah's apartment was paying attention.

"What if I told you that I know who you really are?" she asked.

He missed a step but quickly recovered. "I'm Dean Norris."

"No." She smiled, kept her tone reasonable, friendly. "You're Robert Baxter and your twin sister, Elizabeth, committed suicide here in San Francisco six years ago on Christmas Eve. You want to avenge her death."

"I don't know what you're talking about."

But he did. She saw the flicker of fear in his eyes and the flash of fury before he could mask either. She decided to push again.

"Yes, you do. I worked on Elizabeth's case when she died. I've been looking into it again. You and your sister were close. When you left her to go into the army, she must have been very lonely. She wrote you letters, but I bet you didn't have time to answer all of them. You have to feel some responsibility that she turned to Eastern religions and some cockeyed theory of reincarnation."

He squeezed her wrist so hard that Cilla was surprised she didn't hear bones snap.

"It wasn't cockeyed if Elizabeth believed in it. And I wasn't the person who caused her to commit suicide." The words were a hiss. The breath he drew in was ragged as he blinked his eyes. "She died to be with Jonah Stone."

Cilla felt the hard poke just above her waist.

"You're making me change my plans again and you'll pay. I have a gun in my pocket. You'll do as I say or I'll shoot the people around us."

The look in his eyes told her that he wasn't kidding. She'd gotten just what she'd wanted. The angry childish Robert had come out to play.

He smiled. "And then I'll shoot you. It's not my favorite plan, but Jonah will come, and I'll kill him a day early."

Terror buzzed in her head, but she ignored it. She had to get him away from the crowd. "What do you want me to do?"

"We'll just walk toward the staircase. Jonah is still greeting guests at the bottom."

She swallowed hard and thought. "No. You're not thinking, because you're angry." Her mistake for bringing out the childish Robert. Now she needed the brilliant Robert. "Gabe Wilder, his best friend, is with him. Detective Finelli is in the dining room. They won't let you take him."

He hesitated.

"There's a staircase to the kitchen just a few feet from here. You can take a breath. Think." She had to get him away from the guests, away from Jonah. "If you take me to the staircase, Jonah will come to you."

"Yes. Good." He drew in a breath and let it out. "Go."

THE LINE OF ARRIVALS was finally thinning. Jonah continued to smile and chat, but the feeling was growing that something was going to happen. Soon.

And he was missing something. He'd looked every guest in the eye, shaken every hand. If one of them was Robert Baxter, he hadn't been able to either see it or sense it.

He let his gaze sweep the dining room, then the bar. But all he could see was people enjoying themselves at a party. Stan Rubin caught his eye and lifted a glass. He wanted to talk after the holidays about financing another club in the Seattle area. It would be an opportunity for Dean Norris to try his hand at design. Glenda was laughing at something her sister was saying.

But Dean Norris wasn't with them. Something akin to

panic worked its way up his spine. He glanced around the bar again. No sign of Norris there or in the dining room.

His gut tensed. Norris had the wrong coloring, the wrong hair, but he was the right age, and he'd been in the military. Why hadn't he thought of that before? Sweat pearled on his forehead as he turned to Gabe. "Where's Cilla?"

"Same place she was when you asked a few minutes ago. Top of the stairs with Nicola and Father Mike."

Jonah whirled around and saw Nicola talking to Father Mike. No sign of Cilla. Fear hit him like a punch to the gut. "She's not there. Dean Norris has her."

He no sooner had the words out when Gabe put a hand to his ear. "Gibbons and Santos confirm that. She has her mic and camera on. They're in the back staircase."

Jonah was halfway up the stairs before Gabe grabbed his arm and stopped him. Gabe held out a small earpiece. "Listen. She knows what she's doing. If you rush into that stairwell, he'll panic and shoot her."

While Jonah put the piece on, Gabe used a small mic to talk to his men.

17

As they stepped through the doors to the service staircase, Cilla said a little prayer that they wouldn't run into any of the waiters. One of the Roberts had an iron grip on her upper arm and she could feel the barrel of the gun pressing into her side.

The kitchen would be crowded. Before she let him lead her into it, she wanted to make sure she had the more rational Robert with her. So she stopped short on the steps.

"Keep going." He jabbed the gun into her back.

"Take a minute," she said. "Think it through. Killing Jonah can't be all you wanted out of this."

She had to stall, give Gabe a chance to get their men in place. "You didn't join Stanley Rubins's company and wait a year just to get revenge on Jonah. You must have wanted more."

For three beats he didn't say anything. He wasn't moving, either. But his grip on her upper arm didn't loosen.

"What was your original plan?" she asked.

"I wanted to become what Jonah is and take everything that he's built for himself. When he's dead, I'll convince Stanley to buy his places. One day I'll run them. I'll have it all and Jonah Stone will finally be with Elizabeth."

"You could still have it all. Think about designing that new club in Seattle. Maybe you can still figure out a way to get everything you want. I'm the only person who's standing in your way. You don't have to kill anyone else. You don't have to expose yourself."

She paused, hoping that Gabe would figure out what she was going to do.

"There's an exit door in the kitchen that leads to the alley," she said.

"Yes. We'll go into the kitchen and out through the back exit."

She started to move even before he prodded her with the gun. The kitchen when they entered it was crowded and noisy. Pans clattered, steam hissed, a chef called out orders in some kind of chef talk. She took as much time as she could to weave her way through the waiters and cook staff.

She caught a glimpse of Finelli, a loaded tray in his hands. But there was no sign of Jonah or Gabe. Hopefully, they'd be in the alley already.

She reached for the door handle and fumbled with it. He released her upper arm just long enough to pull the heavy door open. And she had just enough time to get her gun out of her wristlet purse before they stepped outside. She held it down, flat at her side.

The night air was cold, the mist like icy fingers on her bare skin. The sky was dark, the illumination from a streetlight dim, and there was no sign of life as they moved quickly along the back of the building. In the distance the sounds of traffic were not loud enough to drown out their footsteps.

They were nearly at the mouth of the alley, close to a couple of large Dumpsters, when he pulled her to a stop. "I'm going to have to shoot you now so I can get back to the party. If my uncle had completed his mission successfully, I would have taken more time with you."

"You've had quite enough time with her," Jonah said from behind them.

Cilla jerked free of Robert's grip, dropped to the ground

and rolled. Several gunshots sounded. One of the bullets came close enough to singe her ear. By the time she got her own gun trained on Robert, he was on his knees gripping his now weaponless hand. It was bleeding. Jonah, Gabe, Finelli and Nicola had him surrounded, their guns drawn.

Beyond them, she saw others pour through the kitchen door into the alley—Virgil was in the lead with Father Mike and Carl Rockwell behind him.

"We got him covered," Gabe said to Jonah. "Why don't you help the lady up?"

Jonah picked her up and held her hard against him. She'd barely gotten her arms around him when he drew back far enough to look into her eyes. He'd nearly lost her. Again.

Grabbing her shoulders, he gave her a hard shake. "Dammit, Cilla, we had a deal. We were partners, and you decided to take on that lunatic by yourself."

She raised her chin. "You were my client. I did my job."

"I heard what you said to him. You invited him to kill you." He gave her another shake.

"He didn't. I wouldn't have let him. You didn't let him."

He dragged her back against him and this time covered her mouth with his. As her taste poured through him, some of the fear inside of him eased.

Someone whistled, others applauded. This time when Jonah drew back, he saw that Finelli was loading Robert Baxter into a patrol car that had pulled into the mouth of the alley.

Gabe moved toward them. "She's right, you know. She did her job. Not only do we have Robert Baxter in custody, but very few people at your party even know what went down. She's the best."

Jonah turned and looked at her. Gabe was right. And she'd been right. She was the best. "We need to talk. Right now I have to tell Glenda and Stan what happened out here."

Then he turned and walked back into Pleasures.

FOR THE NEXT TWO HOURS, Cilla found herself fighting off boredom. Jonah hadn't let her stray far from his side except for the short time he'd spent in his office talking to Glenda and Stan Rubin. Even then, he'd told her to stay put outside his office and he'd asked Gabe to keep her there within sight. And since then, if he wasn't directly at her side, Gabe or Nicola or Father Mike was.

Both Gabe and Nicola flanked her now as Jonah announced the results of the silent raffle that had been going on all evening. Cilla had to stifle a yawn. Now that the excitement was over, she was finding that a Christmas charity event, even at Pleasures, was about as exciting as a silent-movie marathon.

And it wasn't just boredom she was feeling. It was nerves. So far Jonah hadn't spoken even one word directly to her.

Not since he'd looked at her in the alley and said, "We need to talk."

"He's still pissed at me," she said to Gabe.

"He nearly lost you. It'll take some time for him to come to terms with that."

"I just did my job."

"Exactly," Nicola said. "And he knows that."

"I'm not sure what to do next."

"I may have an idea for you there," Gabe said. "I found something interesting when I ran the background checks you asked for on the original backers for Pleasures. Then we focused in on the Baxters and I put it aside."

Cilla felt that tingling feeling again. "What did you find?"

"Carl Rockwell worked for various government agencies up until his retirement six years ago. But everything he did is classified. I would have pushed further if I hadn't had to focus on the Baxters. Jonah will be able to find more."

Cilla turned to look at Carl, who was talking to Father

Mike. "And he's been backing Jonah's investments ever since he retired from secret government work."

Gabe nodded. "That's what I thought was interesting. You might want to mention it to Jonah."

She looked at Gabe and Nicola. "The two of you stay right here. I'm going to mention it to Carl."

Striding across the room, she made excuses to Father Mike and then drew Carl with her to Jonah's office. Once they were inside, she closed the door and gestured him into a chair. Then she came right to the point. "Why did you leave Jonah and his mother twenty years ago and never come back?"

Carl focused his eyes on her. "Well, you don't beat around the bush, do you?"

No denial. Cilla sat on the edge of Jonah's desk and regarded him steadily. "No. Maybe you should stop beating around the bush and answer my question."

Carl raised his hands to his face and rubbed his fingers against his eyes in a gesture so like Jonah that her heart tightened.

"I've just been having this same conversation with Father Mike."

"Why didn't you come back?" Cilla pressed. "That's the question Jonah's going to ask you."

He glanced up, met her eyes. "I couldn't. The op I was working on went on longer than it was supposed to. Then it went south. I was injured badly. When I woke up, I found myself in a hospital. Years had passed. I'd spent nearly four of them in a coma, and at some point I'd had to have some reconstruction done on my face."

"Why didn't you come back then?"

"I did. I found out where he was and I read the accident reports on my wife's death. I went to Father Mike first, and I was supposed to meet him that evening in the little prayer garden next to the St. Francis Center. I was just outside when Jonah screamed a prayer that he wanted to kill me."

Cilla pictured it in her mind, the man standing in the shadows, the angry boy screaming that he wanted his father back so he could kill him.

"I'd failed both my wife and my son. The life of adventure I'd been leading had been more important to me than they were."

"So you walked away again," she said.

There was pain in his expression. "I went back to the life I was good at. The life that I hadn't been able to give up even when I fell in love, even when I had my son. I wasn't supposed to be married. I created the identity of Darrell Stone because I didn't want the government to know that I had a family. I didn't deserve Jonah. And look what he's made of his life."

Cilla studied the man in front of her. The truth was he'd finally come back into Jonah's life and supported him. And it hadn't taken much trouble on Gabe's part to find information on Carl Rockwell that would raise questions for anyone looking for a connection.

"Well, are you going to walk away again or are you going to tell him?"

"How can he forgive me when I can't forgive myself?"

"You've known him pretty well for six years. If you want the answers to your questions, I'd say Christmas is the best time to get them. The decision is yours."

When Carl said nothing, she pushed it further. "I can tell you one thing. He's looking for you, and knowing Jonah, he'll find you. There's a lot to be said for making a preemptive strike."

HOURS LATER, WHEN PLEASURES was finally dark, Jonah led Cilla up the stairs to his apartment, and with each step, he felt the nerves in his stomach tighten. The evening had gone by in a blur, which had kept those minutes while Cilla had been at the mercy of that lunatic from replaying in his mind. But his duties as host had also prevented him from getting things settled with Cilla.

Stan and Glenda were going to be all right. The shock of what he'd had to tell them about Dean Norris/Robert Baxter had taken its toll. They'd started to think of him as the son they'd never had. But they were going to hire an attorney for him, and Glenda had hugged Jonah before they'd left, thanking him for the idea.

When he opened the door of his apartment, for one moment he entertained the idea of just closing it, pushing her up against it and taking her just as he'd done in that hotel room in Denver. Maybe it would ease the tension inside of him.

But it wouldn't solve the problem of what he was going to say to her. And why didn't he know what to say? He always knew exactly what to say to get what he wanted.

Dammit. No woman had ever succeeded in tying his tongue into knots before.

He just needed a few more minutes, he told himself as he pushed the door shut and strode down the length of the room.

Jonah was still pissed. Maybe Cilla could understand it, but he had to understand her. Flash jumped off her favorite window seat and followed him into the kitchen area. Two against one was not fair. And recalling what she'd said to Carl Rockwell about a preemptive strike, she strode after him.

"You said we needed to talk."

"We do," he said as he pulled a bottle of champagne out of the refrigerator.

She climbed onto a stool and faced him across the counter that separated the kitchen area from the rest of the space. "I'd do it all over again."

"What?"

"Push Robert Baxter into admitting what he'd done, and then getting him out of Pleasures."

"I know you'd do that again. That's who you are." He drew two glasses out of a cabinet, then began to uncork the bottle.

A little bubble of panic formed in Cilla's stomach. She couldn't get a handle on what he was thinking. Why couldn't she do that?

He poured champagne into the glasses and handed her one.

"We're celebrating?"

"I certainly hope so." He lifted his glass and tapped it against hers. "To the conclusion of a job well-done."

"Done?"

"You're no longer my bodyguard. I'm no longer your client or your partner."

A mix of fear and anger shot through her. Was he going to drop her flat after all she'd done, after everything he'd made her feel?

Over her dead body.

She set her glass down with a loud click and leaned forward. "I have a proposition for you."

"You do?"

"The job may be done, but I want to continue the partnership. I want to move in here."

As the words stopped his ability to breathe, something inside Jonah eased. This was Cilla talking. He took a sip of his champagne and studied her, simply enjoying the sight of her sitting at the counter in his kitchen. In the long nights they'd been apart, he hadn't pictured her here.

She frowned at him. "Well? What do you say?"

"Why do you want to move in here?"

"You allow cats and Flash has grown attached to you." He sipped his champagne. "Any other reasons?"

"I'll be closer to the office."

His brows rose and he nearly laughed. "A whole three blocks closer. How about the real reason, Cilla?"

She narrowed her eyes on him and frowned. "Okay.

Here it is. I don't want to spend any more nights without you."

He looked at her and saw everything he'd ever wanted. And he was going to hold on to it. To her. Setting his glass down, he held out his hand. When she took it, he gripped hard. "Just one modification. Once you move in here, you're stuck. You stay. I don't want to spend any more nights without you, either."

Smiling, she crawled up and over the counter to wrap herself around him. "When it comes to sticking, I'm the best."

"I'm counting on it," Jonah said as he lowered his mouth to hers.

Epilogue

New Year's Eve...almost midnight

"IT'S NEARLY TIME." JONAH filled the last champagne flute on the tray, then set the bottle down on his kitchen counter.

"This will be the first time I've ever toasted in the New Year with Cristal," Cilla said.

Behind them, guests chattered, and the large TV screen played a delayed broadcast of the partyers in Times Square awaiting the descent of the glittering ball.

Jonah met her eyes as he handed her one of the flutes. "It's a special night, one I want you to remember."

She smiled at him slowly. "I have no trouble at all remembering each and every night I spend with you." There'd been eleven of them so far, and she didn't intend to stop counting.

Virgil joined them at the counter. "Let me do that." Taking the tray, he strode away to serve the rest of the small group in Jonah's apartment.

A much larger party, a bash in fact, was going on below them in Pleasures, but Jonah had invited a few people up to his place to toast the New Year. Gabe, Nicola and Father Mike had returned to Denver on Christmas Eve, but the rest of the people in the room had all played some role in what had happened the night that Robert Baxter was shot and taken into custody in the alley.

Virgil offered flutes of champagne first to the Rubins. They'd extended their stay at the St. Francis Hotel so they could make arrangements for Robert Baxter's defense. Carmen had brought her two sons, and T.D. had brought his pretty wife. Carl Rockwell laughed at something T.D.'s wife was saying.

Carl hadn't waited until Christmas day. He'd visited Jonah's apartment on Christmas Eve. Just in the nick of time as it turned out, because Jonah had been working on his computer most of the afternoon. Cilla figured another day and Carl might have missed his chance to make a preemptive strike. She'd left them alone so she didn't know all they'd talked about that day, but when Carl left, Jonah hugged him and Carl had held on.

"I'm glad Carl's here," she said.

"Me, too. He's my partner, and we've been good friends for a while. Lots of fathers and sons aren't friends. Gabe and Nash don't have their fathers anymore. Carl and I can't get back the years we missed, but we have a future to share."

"Five minutes until the ball drops," Ben called out.

Jonah took her hand as she started toward the TV. "I have something to ask you before we join them."

When she turned back to him, she saw that he had a small box in his hand. When he opened it, all she could do was stare.

It held a ring, and it was so beautiful it made her blink. Something fluttered right under her heart. Panic.

"I know we have an agreement—no more nights apart," Jonah said. "And I know it's a big step, but I want to make what we have definite. Permanent."

The panic fluttered again. And she couldn't quite get a full breath. She thought of her mother and how many times she'd walked down the aisle. Nothing was permanent. Maybe if she could just stop looking at the ring, the panic would stop. She'd be able to breathe. Think.

But when she turned, she found herself facing a group of people and several of them had warned her not to hurt Jonah. It was Carl's look that held hers for a long moment. He raised his glass to her. And she remembered what Jonah had said. *We can't get back the years we missed. But we have a future to share.*

"Cilla?"

Turning back, she looked into his eyes and saw what she wanted. A future to share with Jonah Stone.

Certainty replaced the panic. "Well, are you going to ask me?"

"That's my Cilla." Grinning, Jonah lifted her off her feet and swung her around. "Marry me?"

"I will."

Putting her back down, Jonah slipped the ring on her finger.

"Happy New Year!" Everyone in the room raised their glasses and cheered.

* * * * *